"No writer working today so effortlessly packs such intelligence, humanity, and wit into good old-fashioned storytelling as Ransom Stephens. His latest, The 99% Solution, is his best yet. Breezily paced and yet full of suspense, this topical, whimsical, heartfelt novel kept me merrily turning pages deep into the night. Buy it, read it. You'll thank me."

–David Corbett, award-winning author of *The Mercy of the Night*

"I loved this. It's lively science fiction from a guy who knows his science, knows his fiction, and by God knows how to tell a story. In fact I got so caught up in the story, I didn't notice until later that Ransom's book was raising deep thoughts and intriguing questions in my mind."

–Tamim Ansary, author of *Destiny Disrupted*

"Tossing us into the maelstrom at the birth of the Occupy Wall Street movement, Ransom Stephens has created a brilliant science fiction thriller that thoughtfully depicts the class warfare of our era."

–Alex Dolan, author of *The Euthanist*

Other books by Ransom Stephens

Novels:

The Sensory Deception
The God Patent

Popular Science:

The Left Brain Speaks The Right Brain Laughs: A Look at the Neuroscience of Innovation & Creativity in Art, Science, and Life

THE 99% SOLUTION

A NOVEL

By Ransom Stephens

STRANGE FUSE

an imprint of Short Fuse Publishing,
a division of Fuse Literary, Inc., www.fuseliterary.com

ISBN: 978-1937791759

Science Fiction > Humorous
Science Fiction > Time Travel
Science Fiction > Alternate History (prevented)
Mystery, Thriller, & Suspense > Technothrillers
Mystery, Thriller, & Suspense > Historical
Mystery, Thriller, & Suspense > Psychological Thrillers
Mystery, Thriller, & Suspense > Suspense
Literature & Fiction > Humor & Entertainment > Satire
Literature & Fiction > Political

For Karen

Whether we gauge time by the revolution of a planet,
the period of a swinging pendulum,
or the duration of a heartbeat,
the time between two ticks is never exactly the same.
Our story, indeed everyone's story, is about
the uncertainty of destiny and the oscillations of fate.

1. Wall Street

2011-Sept-23 10:37am
Pivot point peak probability: 88 minutes

Something is going to happen on Wall Street that will alter the course of history and it's going to happen soon. I take another look at my phone to check the calculation. You see, while anything is possible some things are more probable than others; Volodya, Fiona, Winter, and I are in the business of calculating these probabilities. We don't know exactly what will happen, which is embarrassing. We know where it will happen to within a few blocks, which isn't bad. And we know that it will happen in 62 to 109 minutes from now, an uncertainty of 47 minutes that can hardly make a good impression, but don't fret, we'll have a more accurate computation soon.

A strong autumn breeze tugs at my clothes as Winter pulls me through New York City's skyscraper-lined streets. The four of us stop at the corner of Broadway and Cedar.

Volodya, whose name rhymes with melodious but whose voice does not, says, "I will survey Occupy from perspective of authorities." His voice has a sharp Russian edge to it that his blue eyes do nothing to soften. "There will be a problem."

"Right," Fiona says, her accent resounds with the big-hearted, vowel-amplifying sound of Australia. "That makes me an Occupier, then."

Volodya steps away with an efficient stride, a gliding motion that betrays the smooth tread of a sprinter. With his hands in the pockets of his tight-fitting black jacket, his narrow shoulders folded inward, and his face tucked away from the wind, he gives the impression of a man concentrating on his destination, and he is, but his countenance also indicates a lack of interest in his surroundings which is well practiced but hardly the case.

Fiona chuckles. "Imagine that, he expects a problem." She knocks her forehead against mine and says, "He's got more than a bit of the Eeyore to him." She's wearing jeans and a button-down shirt and leans on a cane. Fiona lost a leg from the hip many years ago. She wears her prosthesis more to reduce the attention of strangers than for its mechanical engineering prowess. She prefers her cane, a titanium short-staff that includes three clichés: a half pint reservoir at the handle usually filled with scotch and, at its base, a ten inch dagger-like blade that can be released by a stiletto mechanism located beneath the third cliché, a duck-head handle.

She untucks her blouse, unfastens the two lower buttons, and ties the tail in a knot just above her naval. Then she releases the shirt's top two buttons. If she had cleavage, it would show. Instead, she reveals a tattoo of a smiling crescent moon with a sexy, witchy-looking woman sitting on the moon's pointy chin. She runs a hand through her hair. It's short and brown and this motion spikes it. Prior to this adjustment, her narrow face and soft, square jaw looked quite scholarly. She looks like a proper rebel now.

I ask, "Aren't you chilly?"

She looks me over. I'm wearing my favorite suit, gray wool herringbone that's been to the cleaners so often that it's soft as velvet. She says, "Simon dear, try to pretend that you don't know me."

She slides down her cane to Winter's level and scratches him behind his ears. He jumps up and they exchange a kiss. He's a beagle with a black and orange coat, white belly and paws, and brown ears. With the aid of her cane, she rises to full height, says, "I'm off to the revolution!" and away she goes.

Winter tows me around the Occupy gathering in a way that belies his "service dog" vest—an annoying affectation that he has to wear in this species-ist country or risk banishment from polite company.

Nearly 32% of the crowd have their phones out. I'm holding my smart phone, too, though mine is smarter than most. I check the application that's running on the fleet of computing servers located at our lab in Vienna. The program engages our cell phones' cameras, microphones, and GPS positioning as well as the vast mine of information contained in the networked computing devices across the world, all to perform a complex calculation.

Let me elaborate as best I can without invoking hundreds of pages of mathematics and thousands of lines of software and please allow me to apologize in advance for the avalanching spray of inadequate and occasionally contradicting metaphors. A single past is carved from the weave of possible futures the way that a trickle of melting ice on its way from mountaintop to sea carves first a creek, then a river, and finally a canyon. When we ponder what fate has in store, it is the fork in the river, the knot in the tree, indeed, the pivot point in time that sets our course.

We build our predictions, our timeweaves, from the cumulative influences of billions of events—whats and whys—that lead us to when and where pivot points will occur. But since most pivot points are directed by many pebbles rather than a few boulders, we're not so good at discerning their hows and whos. Our goal is to determine the probabilities for each possible destination, at which we are quite proficient, and to find those variations in the timeweave that decide history's course, which is a mighty struggle.

Over the last 782 days we've calculated an increasing likelihood for two such pivot points. The first has an inordinately high probability of occurring within seven blocks and between, now, 53 and 100 minutes of the very point in space and time where I now stand: 10:46 am EDT, on the 23rd of September, 2011 in Zucotti Park, New York City.

Depending on the direction in which this first pivot point reorients history, the likelihood of a pivot point of far greater historical significance occurring within 6 months exceeds 90%. This latter knot in the tree of human history would alter the course of humanity for centuries. We may have to do some pruning.

With the app churning through the world's data to determine the precise time and place of the initial pivot point, I shake my phone as though this action can improve the calculation's precision—rather like whacking a toaster to improve the shade of emerging bread. I loathe imprecision and poorly toasted bread.

2011-Sept-23 10:49 am New York City
Initial pivot point peak probability: 76 minutes
Conditional pivot point: sooner than 6 months

Just as I slide my phone into my coat pocket, it emits the chorus of *Somewhere Over the Rainbow*, the ringtone I reserve for Gwinnie, the partially-requited love of my life.

I manage to restrain Winter long enough to reacquire the phone, though now I find myself with one hand to my ear and the other outstretched at the end of his leash.

I say, "Gwinnie!"

"Are you in New York City?"

"We landed an hour ago." Volodya, Winter, and I flew in from our lab in Vienna and Fiona from her bookstore/bar in San Francisco.

Gwinnie says, "I'm worried about Lucy."

Lucy could've been my daughter, but in this life, at least on this timeline, she is the daughter of my friend Gwinnie, who should've been my wife if I would've had more courage. I regret to admit that I am haunted by the could'ves, should'ves, and would'ves of life.

Gwinnie's voice increases in volume as she gets going. "Lucy isn't answering her phone or replying to texts."

"Please don't worry. Lucy is fine."

"How do you know?"

"The likelihood that Lucy is in Zuccotti Park enjoying the Occupy Wall Street festivities exceeds ninety-nine percent." I'm aware that Gwinnie finds my cavalier response annoying, but I'd rather annoy people with my best estimate than please them with a conservative approximation.

She says, "I haven't talked to Lucy in ten days" and starts to cry. I can't think when Gwinnie cries.

I fumble about my brain for appropriate words. Then my phone vibrates, indicating that the timeweave has updated. Sufficiently distracted that I manage to speak through her weeping, I say "It's okay, Gwinnie. I'll ask Lucy to call you, email, text, tweet, tag you on Facebook, Skype. I'll suggest she send you a postcard."

She blows her nose, an elegant two-tissue blow. In my desire to absorb all the Gwinnie I can, I find myself envious of her tissues. The thought provides a mix of desire and repulsion that gives me the wherewithal to pull the phone from my ear. It hasn't merely updated; the calculation is complete. The display shows a map with two arrows, one where I now stand and another three blocks from here. Above the map, a clock counts down. We have roughly 71 minutes and 13 seconds, make that 71:12, 71:11—you know what I mean—until this annoyingly unknown event occurs that will alter the somewhat chaotic, not altogether well-behaved, but on the scale of the last century, comparatively peaceful and prosperous historical epoch.

I put the phone back to my ear. Gwinnie's still nattering.

"—and no, I don't want a frikkin' postcard!" She hangs up.

I know better than to call back and beg her forgiveness. My dear Gwinnie is a woman of passion who steadfastly resists the temptation to grant apologies willy-nilly.

Winter draws me along a sidewalk lined with cardboard signs that recommend outrage for a variety of causes including disparagement of the wealthy, support for labor, conservation of resources, humane care for animals, regard for climate change, disregard for carnivorous eating habits, and, more than any other, derision of the financial industry. Some contain full length essays, some are parodies, others have slick one-liners, but Winter won't afford me the chance to catch up on my reading.

Zuccotti park has acquired the ambiance of a music festival, that tension one feels between opening and headlining performances. Youths mill about in colorful clothes, though 22 dress in black as though at a Johnny Cash tribute. They laugh and argue, imbibe beer and coffee, emit scents from patchouli to fancy perfume, waft tobacco and ganja smoke, all on a base of excitement emphasized by the coarse smells of human sweat and sexuality. Police pace the edges, talking both among themselves and with the Occupiers. From this vantage, I see 1156 people but estimate the total at 1480 and growing at an accelerating rate. The structure of the crowd exhibits the fluctuating clumps typical of random processes with sticky centers. My attention is again drawn to the tiny fraction of Johnny Cash fans. Those in black are not clumping; they're evenly distributed about the crowd.

I hold up my phone, snap a picture, and initiate an app to process the photo. The app calculates a less than one percent probability that random processes could so evenly distribute people dressed in a single color. I also notice that those in black carry similar backpacks and have black scarves tied at their necks. Fascinating.

Winter navigates us among tents and cliques and drum circles. Following his nose, we land in the queue of a food cart.

"Coffee, please, four sugars, two not-milk packets."

I don't know why the proprietor looks at me twice, but Winter distracts him and the man says, "How 'bout a canine dog?"

The apparent redundancy of this statement is clarified when he places a frankfurter on a paper plate. I hand Winter the wiener and he seems to derive unparalleled enjoyment from this particular meal, which in no way distinguishes it from any other.

Though the coffee will relieve some of my six hour jet lag, the sight of a bench exacerbates my desire to relax. I settle between a young man with an expanse of thick hair captured by a knit cap of yellow, green, and black and a weathered, musty smelling fellow about my age whose head lolls against the armrest.

Just in front and to my right, a young woman engages a police officer. They are a study in American multiethnic mono-culture. The woman stands precisely five feet tall and the officer surpasses her by 18 inches; the woman's pale skin is decorated with orange freckles that match her shoulder-length, carrot-red hair and the man has flawless mahogany colored skin, a shaved head, and a manicured black goatee accented by a hint of gray. The woman stares up at him, flailing her arms like a Sicilian on the telephone.

A wave of pride passes through my heart, for this passionate, erudite, young woman is Lucy.

She says, "Your job is to keep the peace."

"My job is to protect and serve," the officer replies. He attempts to disconnect from her gaze by surveying the crowd beyond her, but when she speaks, her voice compels him to look straight down at her. While he is in fact looking down, the literal direction is inconsistent with the metaphorical reality of who leads the conversation.

"Where were you when those crooks up the road were destroying the economy? Where will you be when they steal your pension or foreclose on your neighbors?"

Lucy's injustice detector has always operated with hair-trigger sensitivity. Empathy wells up in my heart for this man. I have lost every debate with Lucy and have yet to see anyone emerge from such an argument in any form but defeated and confused. Indeed, while learning to swim she blamed the water for insufficient buoyancy. The hapless water evaporated elemental feelings of remorse.

"Ma'am, I'll arrest a man in a suit just as fast as a woman in a, umm, in one of, um …"

"You mean a skirt, don't you?"

And the trap is laid.

"You are wearing one."

"It's either skirts or suits to you, isn't it?"

"No, I, no, umm, ma'am—"

"Will you protect me?"

Winter's tail sweeps the pavement in anticipation of Lucy's victory.

"The New York City Police Department is committed to protection of every citizen."

"Officer, the question is, if you are forced to make a choice, will you protect people or wealth?"

He has now managed to look away from her and that seems to enable him to repeat his stock answer. "The New York City Police Department is committed to protection of every citizen."

But she draws him right back to her web. "What if it's your mother?"

Instead of answering, he pretends to watch the crowd, but in the movement of his eyebrows, just slightly piqued, he confesses defeat.

"Of course you'd protect your mother!" Lucy takes his gloved hand, compelling him to look at her.

Resignation, nearly despair, settles across his face. "Do we have to bring my mother into this?"

Lucy makes a point of searching out his nametag. "Officer Tyvon Justin, you've been trained to handle crowds. We both know that Occupy will commit a few petty misdemeanors. I just want you to keep one thing in mind." She takes a breath and Officer Justin attempts to break away, both his hand from her grip and his eyes from her gaze. Lucy yields neither. "The institutions you'll be protecting may not have broken the letter of any laws, but they have violated the very spirit of civilization. We are the citizens in need of protection."

"Yes ma'am," he says. "Now, please excuse me." He pries his eyes and hands away from hers and steps toward a passing pair of fellow officers.

In a warning tone, but with a triumphant grin, Lucy says, "Officer Justin …"

With two comrades nearby, he reassumes his stature. Adjusting his gloves, he asks, "What's your name, ma'am?"

"Lucy Montgomery."

He takes another step from her.

"Officer Justin?"

"What is it now, ma'am?"

"Come here, your collar is turned up." She reaches as high as she can and fixes the offending collar. "Officer Justin, please don't forget the reasons that you became a police officer. Please?"

I love this child.

He pushes his hat back and says, "Ms. Montgomery, it's been a pleasure, please excuse me."

As he joins his comrades in their patrol of the park perimeter, Lucy's eyes follow him and as they follow him, they pass over Winter and me. She does a double take.

Winter's tail starts whacking the bench.

"Uncle Simon?"

"Lucy!"

Oh those two syllables.

2011-Sept-23 11:13am New York City
Initial pivot point peak probability: 51 minutes

Lucy is an ideal optimization of her parent's genetics: her mother's coloring, petite size, and ability to exact a situation in seconds, but with her father's high cheekbones and aquiline nose, penetrating stare, and a feminine version of his captivating voice. For an instant I believe that she has benefited by the twists of time. Her father is a far finer physical specimen than I am.

"Did my mom send you?"

"We were coming here anyway."

"You came from Vienna to check up on me?"

"I have an appointment this afternoon with a customer."

She kneels down and Winter gives her forehead a thorough

licking.

I rise from the bench and she hugs me; such a dear, our Lucy. I ask her to call her mother.

"Right now?"

"Could you text her?"

"I'm busy."

"Tag her on Facebook?"

She turns and leads us into the Occupy camp. I take a covert photo and send it to Gwinnie, hoping that it will assuage her fears and cast me in a positive light.

As we pass a large white canopy, three other young adults join us. She introduces them as friends who accompanied her from San Francisco: a woman named Penelope who has long thick brown hair, skin utterly devoid of impairment, a nose upturned by less than 4 degrees, and a rich, generous forehead, and two young men. Bill and Rob have tattoos, broad shoulders, and narrow waists but diminished foreheads; they both wear dark hooded sweatshirts and baseball caps, and have an affinity for the term, "yo," as in "What up, yo?" Bill seems wittier than Rob and Rob better organized. Bill has short tightly curled hair and Bill has dreadlocks yet I find them difficult to distinguish. Both defer to Lucy's implied authority and appear distracted by Penelope's dimensions.

The four of them express excitement about the march on Wall Street that will begin within the hour. Rob focuses on logistics, yo, providing advice on safety and how to behave should they be arrested—sometimes "yo" seems synonymous with "you," as in, "Yo, be proud when you get busted, yo"—and Bill blends in suggestions for advice they might provide the 1% should they penetrate the New York Stock Exchange. His recommendations don't seem in any way helpful to the goals of those in the top percentile of financial wealth.

I take a stealthy glance at my phone, the initial pivot point will occur in 38 minutes. That the pivot point and march on Wall

Street are in synch comes as little surprise. That our technology offers no indication of who will play the loud earth-moving roles and who will play the quiet, but no less important, chaotic-butterfly roles frustrates me to distraction.

The six of us work our way to the geometric center of the park. The four of them express their excitement through a discussion that twists from politics to philosophy and back again. I find myself enchanted by the sounds of their voices and the intensity of their passion, yo.

I'm interrupted from my reverie by Fiona's voice in my earbug. You see, Fiona, Volodya, and I wear tiny Bluetooth earbugs that put us in constant auditory contact. They're off-the-shelf parts, almost all of our hardware is, but we've modified the software so that our earbugs automatically connect through encrypted cell phone connections. She says, "Brilliant, you found Lucy. Don't forget why we're here."

While I have sufficient self-discipline to avoid scanning the crowd for Fiona, I do answer her out loud: "Of course, yo."

Lucy and her friends shift their attention to me. I add, "Would it be acceptable for me to meet the movement's leaders?"

Penelope says, "You want us to take you to our leader?"

Before I can answer, and before I realize she's joking, Lucy says, "Occupy is a do-ocracy, there are no leaders. It's organized and we have committees and anyone can be a facilitator, but no one has more power than anyone else."

"Oh!" I say, "I've always been fascinated by anarchy but have never understood it." Looking across the crowd, I add, "Except for pirates."

The young men stop in a way that indicates I've offended them.

I add, "Pirates are uniquely classless."

Penelope says, "But enough about their wardrobe."

"Almost unique in history," I continue, "pirates shared their winnings. Those who swabbed the decks received no less than half as much booty as the nominal captain. Those captains who attempted to hoard winnings experienced rapid and conclusive mutiny."

"Well, Uncle Simon," Lucy says holding her arms out as though to embrace the encampment and its now roughly 2130 Occupiers, "here's our mutiny, because the 1% has no right to all the booty."

Following Lucy's gesture, I take in the crowd once more and start to laugh. "Classless wardrobe! I get it now."

Passing into a dense region, people make way for Lucy as though she is Occupy royalty. She acknowledges many of them with high fives, fist-bumps, and comments like "Are you ready?" I wonder if her acts of leadership contradict her claim and reconsider pirates; they did, after all, have nominal captains.

We approach four people closer to my age than Lucy's, two women and two men, one of whom wears black. Where Lucy attracts attention, these four seem to be ignored by the crowd, though with a level of deference, as though they are important but invisible, somewhat like chaperones.

One of the senior women, this one perhaps the eldest in the crowd, hands a thick stack of paper to Rob. He hands a sheet to Lucy first. It includes a map and a list of dos and don'ts for holding a proper riot. The other woman converses with the men. Their conversation stops when Lucy introduces me.

"This is my uncle, Dr. Simon Wentworth," Lucy speaks with the authoritative timbre that I can't help but associate with her father. Though she's facing the man wearing black, he continues to stand with his back to me. Lucy says, "Gus, I really want you to meet—" But before she finishes, he walks away as though busy with another task.

Lucy turns to the older woman. "Uncle Simon, this is Jane Vinson." And then introduces me to a man about my age, Mikk Lesa, and a woman a decade my junior, Naomi Gross. I recognize Mr. Lesa as the Canadian publisher who suggested this gathering in a blog post 104 days ago. The youngest of the four, Ms. Gross, is a Canadian author specializing in the flaws of consumer-based capitalism. Lucy concludes her introductions by indicating the man dressed in black now 17 meters from us. "And that's Gus Reser."

The name of this man raises the sort of internal flag that you've experienced upon leaving your home with bread plunged in the toaster; a vague indicator that you've overlooked something but no indication of what. The human brain is annoyingly more efficient at arousing than resolving suspicion.

Mr. Lesa touches Lucy's elbow and then backs into the crowd, leaving Lucy alone in the figurative spotlight. She says, "Excuse me, Uncle Simon, I need to facilitate." She steps up on a bench. Bill releases a shrill whistle that generates a wave of hushing sounds through the crowd.

"We are here to stand up for the 99%," Lucy says. Her voice easily penetrates the crowd. Were her father present and were he not a prick, he would, or at least should, experience terrific pride. I assume the role in his stead.

She pauses for the time it takes a cheer to incubate and then speaks over it. "The 1% will protect the 1% by buying government—when corporations legally bribe government officials can it be considered democracy?"

The crowd offers responses to each question so coherent that I wonder if the handouts Bill and Rob are distributing provide the proper answers, like a political singalong.

"When corporations are too big to fail they become too big to compete. When every cost lands on the back of the 99% and every benefit in the hands of the 1%—can it be considered capitalism?"

Lucy's speech covers the injustice of poverty, the hope of youth, and the power of numbers. In one form or another, this speech has been repeated thousands of times over the 15,000 or so years of civilization.

Fiona appears next to me. She puts an arm across my shoulder as though to congratulate me for this progeny who is not mine. No, my mistake, she's trying to draw my attention to a photo on her phone of the man Lucy attempted to introduce as Gus Reser. Captured from some distance, the image lacks sufficient resolution for our software to identify him, though the sense that I'm overlooking something returns. I take out my phone and tap an icon of Tigger, the character from *Winnie-the-Pooh and the Blustery Day*. Fiona's screen appears on my phone just as it does on hers. I type in "Gus Reser" as a candidate name to help the software identify the man, but nothing comes up.

Lucy raises a fist. "As the government bail out the banks with our money, who suffers?"

The crowd replies, "We suffer!"

A tasteless joke involving Jewish mothers crosses my mind.

"The criminals aren't going to jail unless we put them there!"

Bill and Rob leap onto the bench at her side waving signs. Bill's says, "Privatized profits + socialized risk," and Rob's says, "= tyranny."

With the cadence of a chant, Lucy concludes her speech: "Right now, we're the center of historic change."

I check the app and see that "right now" is not the accurate when, though it will in 21 minutes and 5 seconds.

2011-Sept-23 11:45 am New York City
Initial pivot point peak probability: 19 minutes

The still growing crowd of 2978 Occupiers assemble on Broadway. The wail of approaching sirens builds a dissonant undertone to the drumbeat percussion and chanting protester rhythm. The march begins.

A young man yells: "Banks got bailed out." The crowd responds: "and we got sold out." As we proceed to Wall Street, the chant switches to "people united—never defeated!" An hour ago the blue-uniformed men and women strolled through the Park as a stabilizing component of the crowd, surveying the perimeter and chatting with the protesters, but the closer we get to the Stock Exchange, the more they present the countenance of challengers in black helmets with full face guards and truncheons out and ready.

With the wind at our backs, Fiona, Winter, and I take in the colors, sounds, and smells. As we step around a newspaper kiosk, a vertiginous nausea akin to the feeling one gets just prior to fainting comes over me. Overlapping shadows and stuttering images conspire with echoing sounds to pull the contents of my stomach up my esophagus. I find myself kneeling in the gutter among the wind-driven debris. I see shadows shift. It's my shadow, but it doesn't seem to follow me. I experience that feeling one has upon waking in a foreign hotel room unsure of where I am. People step in and out of themselves, sights flicker, even scents acquire a sort of nasal reverb.

I've yet to find a journal article on my affliction, though an incompetent psychiatrist once attempted to persuade me that the phenomenon is closer to schizophrenia than the sensory detection of intersecting realities. He even had the gall to ask if I experienced parallel universes—an absurd question, given that the defining quality of all things parallel is their lack of intersection and it is specifically the intersections of different realities that I experience. I've since discounted the entire field of psychiatry.

Passersby jitter between images and soundtracks. Men in baseball caps and women in jeans flicker into men in bowler hats and dungarees. The Occupy Wall Street protest signs written in felt-tip marker on cardboard waver into paint on wood. Now they say: "Property is theft," "Revenge! Revenge! Workingmen to Arms!" and "When innocents are jailed we are all jailed." I look up and around and am horrified to see that the police have changed, too. Now they wear private security uniforms, Pinkertons and Pullmans. In the flux of realities, the crush of histories, the uniforms shimmer, baseball caps seem to push through a thin green barrier, like the edge of a pane of glass, only to fade into a hopeless future. A man with a bushy mustache in a floppy-brimmed hat throws something into the ranks of authority. An explosion catapults a dozen officers into turbulent fear and pain, limbs and screams, and rage that grows into a vortex.

I search for a seam. Gunfire answers the explosion as if it were a question. Another green-blue edge crawls up from the dirt that had once been concrete separating me from the chest down. I fall across the edge into a horrified calm. A horse drawn carriage, all velvet and gilding, stops at the crowd's edge. A man rushes out of the riot. His knife reflects strobes of color as he slashes the horses. They rear up and a man in a two-foot top hat tumbles from the carriage. As the rioter pounds the knife into his chest, he screams: "You spend in an hour what would keep my family for a year."

I jerk this way and that, caught in a past that I cannot affect. A wave of confusion buries me, a kaleidoscope of light, sound, and sensation. I fall as though from a bridge into a timeweave river. I lean this way and that, navigating the currents of fate, searching, grasping for a timeline that brings a hint of contentment in this river of dissatisfaction. I find my balance in an orientation that leans against tentative hope in a current of insecurity. Winter barks at me and the sound, no longer echoing, presents an island of presence. I concentrate on the street beneath my hands and knees, willing its transformation from dirt to pavement. The vertigo-driven nausea recedes beneath the concrete reality of 2011 New York City.

But this is either not where I came from or I am not who I was before—a fine distinction between the directions of a causal chain. What I do know is that I have never been here before, though humanity has. This weave of reality is a reflection of another, the same signal with different noise, the same pendulum but a different swing, the same heart but a different beat.

* * *

Fiona leans over Simon. His knees are in the gutter and his elbows on the curb. He holds his Beagle tight in his arms. He wavers from side to side and forward to back without a trace of rhythm. He lunges and falls. Winter jumps out of his arms but stays at his side.

Fiona's been watching Simon navigate reality's rapids for decades. Sometimes she doubts that he detects time differently than the rest of us. Volodya finds the notion that multiple timelines could be observed by human senses absurd. Fiona thinks he protests it a bit too much because, when their technology comes up short, Simon's insights bridge the gap in their data trail.

Winter looks up at Fiona as though to convey that they'll be a few more minutes.

Well-meaning protesters offer to help and Fiona assures them that Simon has merely tripped and will rise momentarily. These episodes don't happen often enough for her to be as confident as she sounds. He convulses as though in a seizure that reminds Fiona of the old myths of epileptic seers.

She checks her phone, the app timer shows 12:45. If Simon doesn't recover within two minutes, she'll ask Volodya to come and help. She wonders how much time has passed in Simon's mind since he got caught between realities.

Winter barks and wags his tail. Simon sits up. The two of them shake off the experience. Starting at their heads, the shaking continues like a wave down their torsos. Simon then takes Fiona's hand. He looks pale, but it's hard to tell if his skin looks more or less gray than usual.

* * *

Fiona helps me to my feet and examines my face for answers as if I'm some sort of timeline-choosing savant. She straightens my coat and I reengage in this particular here and now. I breathe deep and slowly until my mind settles into it's usual hum. And, like that, it's behind me, like waking from a nightmare, memories of those realities dissipate. They already have the sheen of stories

I once read in a book, similar to but nothing truly like my own experiences. It's a coping mechanism, of course—I'm quite talented at the practice of denial.

When I shake, most of the horror flies off of me, like water from Winter's coat. I look up and around. Barricades have been erected across Wall Street about fifty feet from the Greek temple-like Stock Exchange building. Helmeted police stand shoulder to shoulder behind the barricade. The line they form reminds me of the row of pawns at the outset of a chess match. Behind them, as though rooks, knights, and royalty, officers in white shirts wearing traditional pointy police caps and with badges affixed to their breasts mill about; some carry bullhorns, others hold large aerosol cans of what I presume is pepper spray, and a few carry shotguns, hopefully loaded with non-lethal rubber bullets.

A police van arrives from the opposite block. More officers emerge from the van in thick navy blue jackets with gas masks dangling from their necks. An empty bus marked with the NYPD logo takes position at the far end of the building.

Farther behind the barricade, Wall Street is empty save for the occasional well dressed business person treading beneath the two giant American flags that drape above the doors of the New York Stock Exchange facility. A few of the business types step toward the crowd. The police easily persuade them to continue their business. I wonder if the police realize that the appearance of protecting those doing business while confronting those doing the protesting lends credence to the crowd's worst suspicions.

The march stops at these barricades and a new chant emerges, Lucy calls out: "Tell me what a police state looks like!" which brings the choreographed response "This is what a police state looks like!"

I can't help but comment: "I don't think police states look quite like this." I look around and add, "This resembles a tolerant democracy," but Fiona, Winter, and Volodya by way of his earbug, are the only ones likely to hear.

Lucy, Penelope, and the two young men who follow them work their way to the front of the crowd and stop at a seam between two sections of barricade.

I reach down to pick up Winter. He rarely appreciates being carried, but this time he settles in my arms with his muzzle resting on my shoulder oriented at Fiona. We shift laterally toward the sidewalk opposite the Stock Exchange. Still within twenty meters of the barricade but now clear of any points of contention, Fiona leans against me. Her prosthesis must be chafing her hip. She points across the crowd. Two groups have formed at the Stock Exchange entrance. A well-dressed group, who I presume are traders, watch the crowd with amusement, some waving. To their right, Volodya stands between two subgroups of people wearing suits of far lower quality. He scans the crowd and I can tell that he's looking for the three of us. I say, "Directly across from you." He cocks his head toward a pair of men and Fiona and I hear him whisper "NSA." Then he crosses his arms and, in the process, indicates a woman and three men in thick conversation and whispers "FBI."

Behind Volodya, a man dressed in what must be the latest fashion, a bright green blazer and khaki trousers, emerges from the building. He exchanges a few words with the well-dressed crowd, eliciting laughter. Then he steps to the NSA representatives, shakes hands with them, and does the same with the three people from the FBI. The man rests his arm on Volodya's shoulder. For an instant I fear for his safety. Winter is the only creature I am aware of who can safely exercise free reign over Volodya's physical presence. The man leans in and says something to Volodya that I can't pick up on my earbug. The stylish gentleman laughs, though elicits no more than a sour smile from Volodya.

A police officer in a white shirt uses a bullhorn to suggest that the crowd disperse. The request confuses me. What would be the point of gathering if the crowd were prepared to leave at the will of a single authority figure?

I'm struck by a further observation: it is as though people in wool oppose people in cotton: suits vs jeans, heels vs sandals, ties vs T-shirts, sport jackets vs hoodies. And with that observation, I recognize something more specific: navy blue with helmets vs jet black with masks. Yes, the 22 people dressed in black have either wrapped scarves across or applied Guy Fawkes masks to their faces.

I jostle Winter enough to access my pocket and retrieve my phone. The timer now shows 8:16—yes, our calculation claims an uncertainty of less than one second. I feel at once impressed by our work and suspicious of a bug.

The stylish man in the bright green jacket approaches the barricade. As he works his way through the police line, he shakes hands, pats shoulders, and even exchanges a few fist-bumps. In his wake, the officers' posture alters from poised for battle to relaxed and jovial. I almost expect an officer to pat the man on his posterior.

The man in the green jacket now stands directly across the barricade from the spot indicated on my cell phone. He points a finger at the Occupiers across the barricade. We can't hear the exchange, but it begins with smiles and laughter.

Fiona elbows me. She raises her cane, pointing to someone standing against the barricade on the opposite side of the flamboyant fellow. "Isn't that Lucy?"

I step up on my toes. Even with Lucy's diminutive height, her red hair makes her easy to spot. She stands within a meter of the spatial point where a historical event will take place in 6:52 and she's too far away for me to protect.

The night Lucy was born, Dick brought her out to the waiting room to meet her grandparents. I stood behind them. Dick pretended not to see me and I did nothing to contradict him. I'd somehow believed that Gwinnie herself would present her newborn child; some things are less obvious to me than they should be. The grandparents made appreciative baby sounds and then followed Dick and Lucy into Gwinnie's room. I stayed behind, but Gwinnie's mother smiled back at me, pointed at Lucy and mouthed the words "Isn't she beautiful?" I nodded and she mouthed, "I'll tell Gwinnie you're here." I shook my head and mouthed, "No, let her be." I left the hospital without seeing Gwinnie. A couple of weeks later Gwinnie thanked me for being there. I guess her mom told her.

Aware of my sudden anxiety, Winter crawls from my arms to Fiona's which eases my ability to work my phone's user interface.

The crowd's density continues to increase, compressing people against the barricade.

Forty-one seconds ago, the man in the green jacket was leaning back, shoulders wide, gesticulating with open hands. Now he's leaning forward, one hand clenched in a fist, the other pointing at a protester across the barricade who stands within two meters of Lucy.

A police officer steps in front of the green suited fellow who has not quite completed his end of the conversation. The protester with whom he had been speaking, a man wearing a knitted gray cap with the emblem of the New York Giants NFL franchise, drops the sign he'd been holding.

The Giants fan leans over the barricade yelling. I can make out his voice above the drums, the sirens, the bullhorns, and the chants, but not his words. The man in the green jacket yells back, suggesting that the other fellow seek employment at a fast food franchise cooking potatoes.

A tall man whose blonde hair contrasts with his black clothing and the bandana covering his face rushes through the crowd from behind, shoves the Giants fan, and then retreats.

The Giants fan falls across the barricade and lands precisely at the spatial position of the pivot point, which will occur in 5:37. A police officer drops his shield and tries to catch the man, obviously attempting to break his fall. On the opposite side, protesters grab the man's legs and try to pull him back. Lucy leans over the barricade and grabs his belt.

They spend three seconds at a standstill, but in those three seconds, more police converge to this point and more protesters wedge themselves along the opposite side.

The police tug him over the barricade and, as they do, the officer who had tried to break the man's fall tumbles to the ground. Three people, including Lucy, are pulled over the barricade with the man. The police push the four protesters down and, in the tumble of limbs, the fallen officer is unable to stand.

Using a bullhorn, an officer on the sidewalk bellows, "Officer down."

More police converge on the pivot point wielding truncheons. The protesters scream. I try to decipher Lucy's voice among those screams but can't.

One of the white-shirted peace officers steps into the gap between the protesters and the fallen police officer, he raises a large aerosol can and paints the protesters in pepper spray. Now I can hear Lucy speaking at the height of her voice. While a tiny woman, she certainly musters quite a decibel count.

A group of protesters rush the barricades and one of the black-clad individuals hurls a bottle.

Lucy, now standing, is still lecturing. Her clothing is stained in pepper spray but she's not suffering its effects.

Fiona says, "I absolutely must see this," and pushes forward. I follow and Winter crawls over her shoulder into my arms. He lets loose a long howl directly in my ear in perfect harmony though one octave below the siren of an arriving ambulance.

As she works her way through the crowd, Fiona smoothes her hair into position, buttons her shirt and tucks it in. Complete with her cane, she now resembles a trader more than a protester. In my comfy suit, I pass for a businessman, which strikes me as a paradox. My well-worn herringbone uniform, complete with elbow patches, should identify me as an intellectual and anyone who's cracked a history text must be aware that intellectuals inevitably take the side of the obvious People over that of the unseen Man. Still, when the police see us approach, they invite us to step around the barricade away from the Occupiers.

I set Winter down and the three of us pretend that we're approaching the Stock Exchange but pause twenty steps from Lucy, on the other side of the gaggle of police engaged in the riot.

The officer who had fallen is now towering over Lucy. He puts a hand underneath his helmet as though stroking his chin. It's Officer Justin! The very policeman she'd been speaking with when I first saw her.

The timer is down to 3:46.

Officer Justin steps away from Lucy, back to his comrades and the growing turmoil along the barricade. More police advance. The Giants fan, Lucy, and the two others who were pulled over the barricade have their hands tied behind their backs with plastic cable ties and are being guided away. All but Lucy caught some of the pepper spray in their eyes.

The lull ends with a series of crashing bottles. A large stone lands in the windshield of a police cruiser, shattering the window. Three people in Guy Fawkes masks launch over the barricade and a torrent of others follow like water flowing over a dam. Eight police officers, including Officer Justin, advance, reconstructing the dam with their clubs. New sounds join the cacophony: arrhythmic thumping of clubs on bodies and the consequent groans.

Any protesters who had been standing near that location must now choose between being trampled and crossing the barricade. More police rush in, more clubs come down, and more protesters fall to the ground.

Winter tucks his muzzle under my chin.

The timer is down to 2:07.

Police on the periphery pull protesters aside and wrap their wrists in cable ties. Blood rushes down the faces of protesters. One of the white-shirted officers holds a clipboard and, despite the turmoil, asks the protesters for the proper spelling of their names. One of the black-clad fellows, his mask nowhere in sight and his nose a mess of blood, spells his name: d-e-r f-u-h-r-e-r, the cleverness of which escapes the police officer.

Back at the barricade, a woman shrieks. Two batons come down simultaneously and the shriek becomes a scream, an extended, high-pitched wail of sheer agony. Winter empathizes with his own low-throated moan.

Fiona says, "It's Penelope—they're beating Penelope!"

The timer reads 0:44.

Lucy pulls away from the police officer who had been guiding her to the bus. Perhaps resulting from a faulty cable tie, she has worked her wrists free. She sprints into the fray.

Then something happens that Fiona would later describe as "power, real power, an absolutely brilliant use of power."

Upon reaching the fray, Lucy stops. Clubs rise and fall inches from her. She cranks up that voice of hers and says, "Protect and serve!"

The timer reads 0:26.

A coincidence occurs that Volodya and I will spend hours analyzing: the constant blare of sirens ceases and the chanting pauses. Lucy's voice is clear to everyone, punctuated only by the background beat of a few drums.

The officer takes the yellow Taser from his belt.

Lucy shouts, "We are the citizens you should be protecting. It's your duty and you know it." She repeats the last phrase word by word: "It is your *duty*." a pause "And you know it."

The officer points the Taser at her.

She says, "Remember this moment. Remember the day that you electrocuted an unarmed, innocent woman."

Lucy faces the officer with the Taser. A small, unarmed, red-haired woman, her hands raised in the universal signal of surrender, facing a giant of a man in a black helmet with complete face shield wearing a bullet-proof vest and holding a bright yellow weapon leveled at the woman's heart.

Several realizations form in my mind. First, it is Officer Justin. Second, I'm certain that he will not pull the trigger. And third, our pivot-point prediction algorithms are remarkably accurate.

Time does not stop. Time never stops, but people do. The instant, the comparative quiet, continues for a full 12 seconds. Lucy says, "Officer Justin, please protect me."

Officer Justin drops the Taser. It dangles from his belt by its yellow chord. He holds his gloved hand out to her and she reaches for it. Within three hours, this image will become the most shared photograph in the history of humanity.

My phone vibrates in my hand and emits the sound of a beagle's howl indicating that the timer has reached 0:00.

A club comes down from behind her, glancing across the back of her head, making impact with her left shoulder. Lucy falls, her right arm outstretched, hand still held by Officer Justin. She doesn't make a sound. He pulls her forward. The policeman raises his club again but Justin pulls her out of range.

Lucy uses the momentum provided by Justin and keeps right on going. She sprints past him, parallel to the barricade, to the sidewalk where Fiona, Winter, and I had observed most of the riot.

More sirens approach. Chanting resumes: "Save the people, Tase the bankers." But one facet of Lucy's speech endures. The protesters do not resume crossing the barricade and the police do not resume beating the protesters.

Lucy reaches the curb, turns into the crowd, and winds her way through.

Fiona, Winter, and I, now with Volodya, run to the sidewalk where we hope to see Lucy emerge on Broadway, but she doesn't. I scan the crowd but can't find her.

Volodya points at a motorcycle speeding down Broadway and, sure enough, a wisp of red hair sticks out of the rider's helmet, trailing in the wind.

As we walk away, we each check our phones. A preliminary update indicates that Lucy's action has set humanity on course for what could be quite an adjustment. The when and where is still vague, the who is less vague, but the how is indecipherable. I admit to being haunted by the nightmare of baseball caps becoming bowler hats.

2011-Sept-23 12:10pm New York City

On the opposite side of the protest from Simon, Fiona, and Volodya, stands an old man wearing black clothes. Guenther Rader has fought for the people for longer than he cares to recount. A sensation comes over him that feels foreign. It causes him to take stock and then he recognizes it: glory.

Of all the places to find hope against capitalist tyranny, he'd have never thought to look here on the steps of the temple of greed. He releases a full, contented sigh.

The vision of that young woman standing up to authority fixes in his mind as surely as it is being formatted on websites, transmitted by television programs, and printed in newspapers around the world. He repeats the girl's name under his breath: Lucy Montgomery.

An hour ago, Occupy looked more like a party for American bourgeoisie children than a political uprising. And then that girl—he repeats her name again, Lucy Montgomery—accomplished something he hasn't seen since the Berlin Wall came down: Lucy Montgomery made a pig do the right thing. And then she rode into the sunset on a motorcycle. The symbolism would disgust him, but right now, in the shadows of corporate greed, he feels the wind of destiny at his back.

A woman with dark hair and soft features runs up to him. He leans down and speaks into her ear in Italian, "It would be useful to know about the man Klaus pushed over the barrier." She says something that he can't hear over the rabble. He says, "Yes, the man in the Giant's cap. You might like to find him, follow him, learn about him." Rader believes that his protégés follow his advice out of respect for his wisdom, not out of fear and guilt-ridden recognition of false-authority.

He watches her jog back into the crowd. Her name is Alina and she is his favorite. A walking contradiction, she looks lean and pliable, but she's the only one of his council who understands the value of violence.

Another of his council approaches, the young Russian. Rader suggests he track the woman who the pigs beat up. It's a good assignment for a pacifist and she could be a useful tool.

Rader has participated in and instigated hundreds of protests over the last forty years. Forty years of fleeting hope and resounding disappointment. He feels a presence behind him, turns and smiles at another young man in black: Adriaan, the Dutch hacker. Rader recommends that he do whatever is necessary to assure that every image of Lucy Montgomery trends to the top of the internet. Adriaan replies that it has already been done.

Rader pulls the young man into a hug.

Despite the decades of failed attempts, Rader believes in the will of the people. The one belief he holds that has never been shaken is that people free of false authority will always do the right thing. He need look no farther than the cop who chose not to fire that Taser at Lucy Montgomery. For just that instant, the man let his true nature emerge. Of course he'll pay for it. The machine will destroy him for that revolutionary act.

From his position among the Occupy ranks, Rader watches that cop's punishment begin. With his head hanging, the tall black man submits to the authority of a short, fat, white pig in a dress shirt. Rader whispers a promise to the cop: "You will be rewarded for your decency."

Another of his black-clad comrades approaches. The lanky man from Dresden with long blonde hair, Klaus Schmidt. Rader reaches out and pulls him close. After pushing the Occupier over the barricade, Klaus removed his black bandana.

"You saw that woman?" Rader speaks directly in Klaus's ear.

"I did."

"You know her name?"

"*Ja.*"

Rader tightens his grip on Klaus's shoulders. "Do not speak German here."

"Yes, her name is Lucy Montgomery."

"It might be helpful to find her and follow her. We can help her."

Klaus steps away.

Rader adds, "You've done well today." He then turns to look back at Broadway and re-lives the vision of Lucy riding into the sunset.

2. The Woodley-Carlyle Group

2011-23-Sept New York City
Historic pivot point peak probability: 53 days

Winter and I join the river of well-dressed men and women of expensive tastes and exotic scents that flow along the sidewalk. Volodya drops back with the authorities and Fiona heads to the Occupy camp at Zuccotti Park.

I'm nearly 78 seconds late for and seven blocks away from my meeting!

The address is posted in thick brushed-nickel numbers on gray marble veneer. The revolving doors mix prescribed doses of air inside and out. They oscillate, too; round and round at the speed of commerce.

The two security officers standing behind a chest-high oak desk look down at Winter but don't comment. We're first in the elevator, pushed to the back by people returning from lunch. The wall opposite the doors consists of more brushed nickel and gray marble veneer. The other two walls are mirrored from floor to ceiling. I ask for the 99th floor and a woman near the console says that proceeding above the 90th floor requires a card-key. I hand her one and she slides it in for me.

Winter and I are alone for the last nine floors.

The elevator can illustrate my experience with weaving realities. Standing in the center with mirrors to both my left and right, I'm looking in a mirror that looks in a mirror that looks in a mirror—an infinite sequence of reflections. Time is like that for me. Where most people see the one reflection of their lives in time, I perceive a weave of images, shadows, and intersections of probable futures during my episodes. Each is a unique timeline. The metaphor collapses at this point. Where the mirror images are separated in space, tied together in what they reflect, timelines weave together, intersecting and interfering. That is, similar timelines can merge and increase the probability that history will assemble into their future, but if they differ in just a few key aspects, they can also cancel each other out and remove any likelihood of those futures occurring. These dynamics make it possible to shift from one reality to another.

Combining my peculiar ability with our timeline weaving technology constitutes a formidable toolset. We use these tools, we hope, to guide humanity on a course of decency and compassion if not humility. Our company TLA, which stands for either Three Letter Acronym or Time Line Associates, depending on whether Fiona or Volodya does our taxes, must also support our endeavors, which is what brings me here.

The elevator doors open and we step into a rarified world, not the world of the one-percenters that Occupy vilifies; this is the one-thousandth of a percent. This is where tolerant oligarchy and plutocracy give permission for, and sometimes the illusion of, democracy.

The dark red carpet has the resilience of a mattress. Chrome lettering embedded in glass doors presents "The Woodley-Carlyle Group"—a company that owns hundreds of other companies in dozens of countries that provide military and industrial support to US forces and allies.

The Woodley-Carlyle Group is the 21st century version of an empire and I am here to visit with the emperor himself. I am very fond of this man. He once saved my life, not my physical being but something more important: my will.

Winter puts his nose against the gap between the doors. It will leave a nose print, which pleases both of us. I press a button that's also embedded in the glass. With no indication of wiring, the button must be powered by battery and transmit by WiFi, a chrome island in thick green-edged glass.

A woman at a desk ten steps on the other side of the door looks up.

"Simon Wentworth for Gordon Woodley?" The voice surrounds me. There are no obvious speakers, but the ceiling is recessed.

I say, "I am Simon Wentworth" and the woman at the desk nods and the doors swing slowly open.

She looks to the side at a monitor. I can't see the screen, but I can figure out the security system. A set of cameras has scanned my face and matched it to a photographic record. I don't have to sign in or wear a visitor security tag. Cameras will track my movement. The system gives a pleasant illusion of familiarity and trust. I wonder if they'll bother to monitor Winter. I also wonder if he should be offended if they don't.

I say, "Thank you," and walk along a corridor. A sea of cubicles rolls out to my left, each one personalized by photographs and level of tidiness. The opposite end of the room is a floor-to-ceiling wall of windows overlooking the city. I feel vertigo from here. A woman says, "What an adorable pup!" Winter straightens his shoulders and perks his ears.

Gordon's office is a glass enclosure set in the corner of the building. The blinds are closed, as is the door. I knock. I've known Gordon for twenty-seven years. Ours is both a fraternal and mentoring relationship: he's the mentor.

Gordon opens the door. I know that his perfect-fitting coal suit with red and blue striped tie is a uniform, but I'm accustomed to seeing him in shorts and sandals. His appearance conveys no more than 60 years and he could pass for 50, but he is 82. He greets me with a smile and kneels down to pet Winter. "It's good to see you, nice to finally get together outside of The Grove." The Grove to which he refers is a redwood forest north of San Francisco in my hometown, Monte Rio, where 1500 powerful men, The Bohemian Club, spend two weeks each summer. I'm an honorary member since I worked there as a boy and am now a scientist with a long list of publications, though hardly a Nobel reputation.

He stands and guides me to a round table composed of still more glass and brushed-nickel surrounded by leather chairs. He sits with his back to the windows and their view of Manhattan Island. He crosses his legs. I sit next to him, oriented away from that view. I drop the leash and Winter circles the carpet in front of the door three times before lying down.

Gordon checks his watch. "I've only got fifteen minutes before my next meeting."

"I understand." I see the torn and empty Tyvek tamper-resistant envelope in which our report was delivered on the far end of his desk over a small, walnut-enclosed paper shredder. "We've made several projections."

"Just give me the summary. Things are changing here." He waves to the shredder and adds, "I can't afford a written record."

Information provides a strategic advantage that most of our customers keep to themselves, but I'm a bit taken back. Gordon has always been the sort of gentleman who shares his assets with the people he trusts.

Like our customers, we require secrecy. Our company, TLA, appears to the world as an international research and consulting agency.

If the identities of our customers were public knowledge, we'd go out of business. For example, if Halliburton knew that we worked for Greenpeace, they'd never hire us; likewise the NSA and FBI, AT&T and the ACLU. We work across the political spectrum to gain access to data from as many power centers as possible. That said, we're not above the occasional hacking foray. Volodya relishes the secrecy, Fiona tolerates it, and I never know what I'm allowed to say. Our lab is in Vienna, where Volodya and I live, and the office is in San Francisco, where Fiona lives.

I clear my throat and begin. "The confluence of the Arab Spring in the Middle East, the political fallout from the Fukushima meltdown, the international impact of Anonymous and Wikileaks, along with continued religious violence in the Middle East, problems associated with austerity policies and associated protests in Europe, and the extreme influences of the Tea Party and this new Occupy movement in America has introduced global instability of historic magnitude. This level of instability almost always leads to some sort of global shift."

Notice how we phrase our presentation in a way that lacks specifics. If I told him that an event that occurred seven blocks from here 22 minutes ago advanced the probability to over 95% of a new historic epoch beginning within months, he might understand the full power of our technology and that could be dangerous or perhaps he'd think I'm crazy. I manage to resist checking my phone to see if our calculation of the time and place of this event has updated.

Gordon says, "You left out capitalist-communist China" and laughs his earthshaking laugh. He recomposes and says, "How will all these changes affect Woodley-Carlyle and America?" He says this as though his corporation and the fate of the United States are identical.

"We've projected Woodley-Carlyle share prices for various scenarios." My report continues into specific predictions for how the company is likely to weather global changes under different executives including Chief Technical Officer, Chief Operating Officer, Chief Financial Officer, Chief Marketing Officer—in delivering the projections, I begin to wonder if native American tribes ever satisfied the egos of tribal elders by designating each of them as some sort of chief. By the time I provide the tiny variation in results for different choices of Chief Administrative Officer, Gordon appears bored and I begin wondering if Occupy's docracy might eventually refer to every member as some sort of chief.

Having dispensed with the subordinate chiefs, I turn to the issue of the ordinate chief and Gordon's fading attention rebounds.

He says, "The reason I commissioned this report is that, well …" He pauses as though weighing what to say, another indication that something has unsettled this usually quite-settled man. "That is, because I'm considering retirement." He looks away and I wonder what he really means. He's at an age where retirement certainly makes sense, but it would have made sense at any point in the last 17 years.

Gordon's retirement is a singular rock among the many pebbles that alter the weave of fate, the only clear-cut event that we've correlated to the coming historic pivot point.

He continues, "I'm not sure Frankie's ready." Frankie is his son, now a senior VP at the firm. I haven't met Frankie but have analyzed his timeweave. "But my dad didn't think I was ready either." He points across the room. "I've been sitting at that desk every day for almost fifty years. I'm not letting everything I built wash away." He looks at his watch, which makes me more nervous. "All right, let me have it."

I need to get to the point, but without providing the details I can hardly expect him to accept my message. I have to cloak my words into a message he will accept. Fiona suggested a specific approach. We'll see how it goes.

He smiles and rests his arms on his crossed legs. I believe this motion indicates that he won't look at his watch again.

I clear my throat. Winter looks at me from across the room. I say, "There are three high probability directions for the Woodley-Carlyle Group depending on when you retire—a Goldilocks phenomenon."

His teeth clench together and for two beats of my heart he looks his age. His perfect gray hair looks a bit thin and his straight posture wilts into the curved-spine of a man who has at most a decade left.

"You mean, too soon, too late, or just right?"

"Yes sir. Woodley-Carlyle could fail if you leave too soon and Frankie takes over."

"That's not going to happen. My grandfather started this company so that America could fight in the Great War before the political situation let us in. Same story with my dad, he had weapons on the ground in Europe in 1939 and then handed off to me during the cold war. I don't want my legacy to be botched wars in Vietnam and Iraq and a mess in Afghanistan. This is my turn. I'll hold it together."

"It?" I ask.

"America."

One of the things I appreciate about this man and all people possessed of, or by, towering egos is their tendency to overstate their importance—I covet this talent. However, on this particular occasion, the timing of Gordon's retirement really is that significant.

I say, "Frankie needs experience standing up to the board, your customers, and the Pentagon—if he replaces you too soon …" Fiona insisted that Gordon would prefer his own answers to ours, despite that he paid us to answer these questions. People rarely make sense to me.

Just as my pause starts to get pregnant, Gordon interrupts it. "Frankie is being groomed. He's on the board; he closes deals; the Pentagon loves him." He looks away and admits, "The Pentagon loves him because we've managed to keep him in line. My son has, well, a rather high opinion of himself."

"Don't you?"

"My son is hard working and dedicated. He's got experience in the trenches of this company, but he doesn't understand the stakes. He's idealistic and naïve." He leans back and let's out another skyscraper-teetering laugh. "My son hasn't failed enough!"

"Fail?" I ask, "I don't recall you accumulating a resume of failure."

"You should have seen me in the Marines." He laughs again,

but he's no longer smiling. "Frankie wasn't in the service. He never had a chance to fail miserably like I did, and my dad, and my granddad." He stands and looks out the window. "I should have spent more time with him as a child." He turns back. "Go on."

"Yes sir," I say. "Our projections prefer the steady, constrained response of experience—up to a point. Gordon," I wait for him to resume eye contact, "Your decision will be more complicated than guiding Woodley-Carlyle through this historical epoch and then passing your responsibilities to Frankie."

"If it is my decision." He crosses his arms and leans against the window. The action stops me for the time it takes to estimate the amount of stress he's applying to that thin pane of glass and then the amount of stress a uniform sheet of glass can withstand. He waits without looking at his watch.

"If you retire too soon, Frankie is likely to overreact when he assumes power. The board will dispose of him and use risk-averse strategies that exacerbate the worldwide recession and increase political tension across the globe."

"That's exactly my fear. The world needs progress; wealth needs to be created. Damn politics."

"If he convinces the board to let him take risks at the wrong time, Woodley-Carlyle will collapse."

"And if I stay too long—assuming that's even an option?"

A hundred years ago the decisions of emperors, kaisers, and kings dictated the timeline of human history. Now, the empires are corporations and the emperors are CEOs, but one thing hasn't changed. Powerful men and women weigh their decision far more on the intuition they have developed through the twists and turns of their careers than on reflective thought. What Gordon doesn't understand and would not accept if I told him is that his business acumen was trained on telephones, nuclear weapons, and mainframes. The might of his intuition has propelled him to this point, but the efficacy of his gut reactions has decayed. The rise and fall of intuitive accuracy happens to every generation and is a primary reason that human history oscillates with a frequency correlated to human lifespans.

I stand and step toward him because I want to touch him, but he's too close to the window. I make it within an arm's length. He used to be taller than me, but he's shrunk in the last decade. If I look him in the eyes, my peripheral vision will impose the reality that this office is a thousand feet above the ground and I'll freak out. So I stare at his chest.

"So there will come a time when I have to throw Frankie right into the fire?"

I nod.

"How will I know when?"

Fiona provided me an answer to this question that she said would be equivalent to: "We'll tell you when to retire." She said that it is easier to feed a man's ego than to starve his pride—I have no idea what that means but follow her instructions verbatim—I say, "You'll know."

Volodya and I had feared that he would follow up with the obvious question—what is the probability that Gordon will time his decision accurately—but he seems to derive meaning from my content-free statement.

He turns, puts his hands on his hips, and looks out at his empire.

There's a knock at the door.

Gordon checks his watch, says "That'll be my two o'clock," steps over, and opens the door.

Three men stand at the threshold. The one who walks in must be Gordon's son Frankie. I hear him introduce me as "Dr. Wentworth" and am instantly confused. Why not use my first name? Why does Gordon rub his chin as though calculating?

I'm not good at this. I don't have the self-control of a spy or the discipline of a diplomat. I'm certain that my expression articulates my concern. Winter yawns. It's the long, open-mouthed yawn that dogs make when a situation becomes uncomfortable.

Fast-triggering neural networks that generate gut-reactions and provide working assumptions for appropriate behavior guide most people's response in social situations. Not me. I have to think my way through everything and it takes time. Masked under the eccentricities of a tweedy academic, people think I'm concentrating and the process usually does generate answers, so maybe that's an accurate description, but it feels more like a soup of confusion and indecision caused by staring at ghosts.

You see, I've never met Frankie Woodley, but the sight of this man catapults me back in time. I was 17 when I met his father. Gordon gave me perspective when my world was falling apart. It's a cliché to say that Frankie Woodley, that is, Gordon Francis Woodley, IV, heir to the Woodley-Carlyle empire, is a chip off the old block. But with the block to my right and the chip standing before me with his arm outstretched, it's all I have.

I look at each of them and they seem to swap positions, swap generations, swap ages. The confusion deepens and seconds pass as I try to climb my way back to the situation. Fashion helps me discern the two men. Gordon's perfect coal suit versus Frankie's edgy executive uniform: a bright green, one-button sport coat over what looks like a long sleeved T-shirt, probably composed of silk, and khaki-colored linen pants. And creases, everything creased and cut to demonstrate that Frankie spends time in the gym. The two men behind him, now just across the threshold, are also creases and tassels but look less natural to the style. It crosses my mind that Frankie might be gay; he looks that good. Still, his hair, the way he walks, and, more than anything, that smile, the open-mouthed welcome with a tiny gap between the incisors, and their lips—identical. I wonder if the mother's genes have been left out of the equation that resulted in this man, this 21st century business icon, this IVth edition of Gordon Francis Woodley.

He takes my hand and squeezes. I say, "Thank you" for helping me break out of the reverie, but he looks at me funny and I realize that my statement doesn't make sense. Another second passes. He's crushing my hand.

I say, "Frankie, it's great to finally meet you." I'm pretty sure that's what I'm supposed to say. The notion that Frankie is Gordon's ghost is now safely stowed.

Frankie's still holding my hand, still has the firm gentleman's grip, but he's looking at his father. "What's going on here?"

"Simon's an old friend," Gordon says. "He just stopped by to chat."

"Oh, *that* Dr. Wentworth," Frankie says. "What brings you to the city?"

With his eyes piercing into mine, I manage a partial truth: "I'm visiting my niece. She's camping in the park for the Occupy Wall Street event."

"Occupy?" Frankie says. He laughs and turns to his colleagues who laugh as though on command.

I wish he would let go of my hand.

He continues, "They'll fade into the background whine in no time." He finally releases me. Winter positions himself between Gordon and his son. "It's ironic, you know?"

"Sorry?" Any irony has escaped me.

"Occupy and the Tea Party are driven by the same distrust of government."

Gordon starts to speak, but before he can emit a word, Frankie continues, now at a higher volume: "Sure, they think their battle is with free enterprise, corporate America, that is, with me, but they're wrong. What they really—"

"No, son, it's the same old threat in different clothes." Gordon speaks with the firm, resonant, but low-volume voice of confident authority. "It's the balance of freedom. Labor is a global commodity and the American labor force costs too damn much—minimum wage in this country is ten times the global market rate. And education isn't the answer. I can hire ten crack engineers in Bangalore for the cost of one overfed Boston software jock. We can't expect the rabble to understand that we, the establishment, the one percent, bear the responsibility for maintaining peace." He walks to his desk and perches on it with one foot on the floor.

Frankie says, "Wrong again, dad. We're on the right track. We just have to get government out of the way."

Then it hits me. The bright green jacket, the comfort he displays but doesn't seem to feel: it's him. The man in the green jacket who caroused with Volodya, the traders, the FBI, NSA, and the police; Frankie is the man who taunted the Occupiers.

He turns back to his father. "They're frustrated and I don't blame them. I was down there this afternoon. They showed up, they have initiative, but they're protesting the wrong establishment. They should be protesting government, not corporations."

Gordon says, "They need jobs that pay enough for a median mortgage, their student loans, and two cars. Until the global working class has a common standard of living, it will be impossible for us to support all of them."

Frankie says, "You're giving up on talent and initiative?" Frankie has a head of steam now. I wonder if he might have a future in politics but don't recall seeing any indication in his time weave. "Government regulations are the problem, not wages, but now that corporations like mine have assets comparable to those of most governments—"

Gordon says, "Like yours?"

"Yes, mine."

"Son, you and I have a lot of work to—"

"As I was saying, since corporations like *mine* have greater assets than most governments, we can let market forces choose the winners, not on the basis of raw power but on the basis of efficiency, resourcefulness, innovation, and talent."

This statement catches my attention. Predicting the likelihoods of different timeweaves requires extensive economic modeling. We use over a thousand models, each of whose parameters have been tuned and back tested to reproduce the various economic realities of human history. I wonder if Frankie and his friends have discovered "forces" that drive human cultures to desirable equilibrium states. Every model we've tried shows that unconstrained supply-demand inevitably lead to monopolies that reduce the creation of wealth and increase wealth disparity. But Frankie's a smart lad, a chip off my mentor's block, he must be aware of this essential facet of culture. Anticipating the revelation of his discovery, I feel like a libertarian. Volodya will be tickled that I've seen the light, and once we subject the hypotheses to data and calculate probabilities with known uncertainties, we can help Frankie unveil this economic serum to the world!

"So stop worrying about the 99%. At least until the next thing comes along."

Now he looks at me. "Do you think that rabble in the park will become a force like the Tea Party? You don't actually think they'll affect a single election, do you?"

My immediate reaction to this question is to pull out my phone and check the calculation. My second reaction is to say, "You were right there! witness to the event that has triggered a historical point of inflection." Fortunately, I've learned not to act on my first few reactions. Frankie's dark brown eyes, the eyes his father wears, challenge me. Anything I say will be rejected. I'm pleased with my choice to say nothing.

"What? Answer me," Frankie says. "Are you, stupid?"

Now I'm less pleased but still can't think of anything to say. Winter steps to my side. His tail is straight and his hackles raised. Hopefully he won't worsen the situation. Winter has temper control issues.

Gordon steps between his son and my dog. He says, "Simon, I wish we had more time. This summer ..." With his hand on my shoulder, he guides me through the door and past the two men, glaring at each of them.

Frankie follows.

A woman in a fine crimson suit steps into the corridor.

Framed in a wealth of silver hair, her green eyes shift from Gordon to Frankie and in that shift, convey disapproval of the younger Woodley.

Gordon says, "Myrna, I'd like you to meet my friend Simon Wentworth."

She says, "We've spoken on the phone." She offers me an envelope, probably payment for our report. Hardcopy strikes me as another anachronism that will bring Gordon down.

"What's this?" Frankie says and then grabs the envelope in Myrna's hand. "You said Wentworth stopped to chat."

Myrna doesn't let go of the envelope.

"Frankie!" Gordon says. "Show some respect."

"To your secretary?"

"To my *executive* assistant."

Their voices increase in volume and the distraction renders Myrna victorious in the tug of war. I accept the envelope from her.

On the thick red carpet of the corridor, I turn and say, "It was nice to finally meet you, Frankie." I'm pretty sure that this is the appropriate social commentary, though it's hard to suppress my desire to quiz Frankie about his obvious lack of control. It's something we seem to have in common and since we're at opposite ends of the social-awkwardness spectrum, it would be interesting to get his take. I start to ask him about it, but he interrupts, which I find even more fascinating.

"My name is not Frankie, it's Francis, or to you, Mr. Woodley."

I smile at his forcefulness.

But then I turn to Gordon who is staring down the empty corridor. His complexion has turned red and, again, he looks his actual age and, with his aging assistant at his side, it occurs to me that Gordon is no longer Mr. Woodley, Frankie is—I mean Francis, wait, I mean Mr. Woodley. Oh, I'll never get this right.

It's another of my deficiencies. As Gordon's mortality appears in my mind, I wrap my arms around him. "Thank you, Gordon, I love you."

* * *

Back in the mirrored elevator, I'm too distracted by all the reflections to check the calculation but can think of nothing else while navigating through the crowded lobby. Finally on the street, I lean against the marble façade and take out my phone. Bother, it still hasn't updated. I dig in deep enough to see that it's processing several key databases that have acquired new information.

Winter and I take a detour up Broadway to circle the Occupy camp on our way to Bowling Green Park where we're to reconnect with Fiona and Volodya. Zuccotti Park is peaceful now. The police milling about Occupy don't have on helmets and their truncheons are inserted in the rings on their utility belts. I don't see Fiona, though double-tapping the Tigger icon on my phone brings up a map indicating that she's inside one of the tents.

There's no sign of Lucy, either. Winter sniffs the line of parked motorcycles. He doesn't like motorcycles, too much high frequency noise for his taste, so he won't pee on one. Lucy rides a 1982 Honda 900 that she rebuilt in high school auto shop. She treats that bike like a pet. Her mother, my dearest friend Gwinnie, exerts tremendous energy fussing over the fact that Lucy rides a motorcycle.

At the apex of Bowling Green Park, Winter lifts his leg and scatters a few drops on the foot of the huge bronze bull. I had no idea he was a shareholder. We pass through a small gate and my phone howls with success. I take a seat on one of the benches that encircles a fountain whose spray forms a cone. I let Winter off the leash and he mingles among the aloof city dogs.

Finally, I take my phone from my pocket and dangle my fingers over it as though casting a spell. Then I dive in. The first thing I notice is that Volodya and Fiona are also walking through the predictions. The second thing is that the second pivot-point, the major shift in human history is 95% likely to occur within five to 15 weeks, peaking in probability 53 days from today.

"That's it?" I say, out loud to no one in particular. Of course, Fiona and Volodya both have their earbugs on, so they hear me.

Volodya says, "Enfatedfaringa," which indicates his displeasure with our technology's lack of certainty.

Fiona says, "Plenty of time, what a relief."

Winter lies down at my feet.

The timing is accompanied by a long list of locations where the event is likely to occur.

I see Volodya approach, staring at his phone. He sits next to me without looking up.

The locations include, in decreasing order of probability: Oakland, Berlin, New York City, and Athens, with ever smaller likelihoods in Amsterdam, Rome, Prague, Sarajevo, or Budapest.

We look at each other and both say, "Sarajevo?"

I add, "That would be nice."

And he adds, "Obvious software bug."

Volodya and I met at a physics conference, the International Physics Symposium-Sarajevo 1983. We were just two nervous graduate students, he from Moscow State and me from the University of California, presenting our first papers. The familiarity of our positions prevented us from noticing that we played similar roles on opposite sides of the cold war. He was an idealist then.

We put our phones in our pockets and stare at the fountain. Fiona comes around the bull statue. She's probably walked five miles today. It must be difficult for her, but she provides no evidence. Standing in front of us, Winter holds a paw up to her. As she crouches down to hug him, he rises on his hind legs and licks her face.

Volodya and I stand and Fiona rises with the help of her cane. She takes out her phone so that Volodya and I can see the soon-to-be famous image of Officer Justin reaching for Lucy's hand; it already has 2,166,152 shares.

With Volodya on my left, Fiona on my right, and Winter a few steps ahead, the four of us follow a path that leads through the gate and past the bronze bull. The flux of people along the sidewalk is less than seventeen encounters per block.

With his lips tightened in dismay, Volodya leans over and speaks under his breath, "The police are circulating Lucy's image and have issued arrest warrant."

Fiona: "Social networks and mainstream media are way ahead of the police in distributing that image."

Me: "For misdemeanor resisting arrest?"

Volodya: "Worse, felony escape."

"That was something." Fiona's smiling now. "Out of the plastic hand cuffs and into the sunset. Brilliant."

Me: "Will there be federal charges, too?"

Volodya: "No, just state charges. Lucy embarrassed NYPD. They search for her. The Mayor's Office will disagree with police. Mayor Bloomberg believes Lucy can crystallize genuine movement. Naturally, they consider political ramifications first. I suspect he'll want his picture taken with her."

Fiona: "Bloomberg will want a ride on her motorcycle."

Volodya explains how he eavesdropped on the authorities by giving the illusion to the police that he was with the FBI and to the FBI that he was with the police. He takes long strides. Winter strains at the end of his leash trying to stay ahead. "If they follow protocol, FBI will infiltrate Occupy to monitor Lucy rather than arrest her. Homeland Security would like her isolated; if not in custody then in known location. And then NSA enters the picture." Volodya frowns and a web of wrinkles forms across his chin. "The NSA, they are a problem."

Fiona says, "The FBI will have little trouble infiltrating Occupy. All you have to do is show up. I walked right into a meeting and they offered me coffee and a bickie. I suggested they focus on forming alliances with minimum wage workers and they made it a 'focus point.'"

Volodya: "The FBI believes Occupy will unite around Lucy."

Me: "They're right, of course. We need to map the probabilities of all possible timeweaves that Lucy's life can follow." While it's an obvious statement, the heart of our job, it is painful to say something like that about dear Lucy.

Volodya: "We still don't know the principals. I'm afraid we have a great deal of work to do."

"That's not exactly true," I say. Volodya hates being contradicted and I have to admit to acquiring a twinge of rotten delight in doing so. "Do you recall the man who precipitated the pivot point?"

Fiona asks, "The wanker in the ridiculous green jacket?"

"None other than Francis Woodley."

"Awwk!" Volodya clucks. "How could I not recognize him? I gave the man my business card! I am getting soft in old age." His chin grows an even more complex configuration of wrinkles. "We rely too much on technology."

"Which is why I spent the afternoon with Occupy," Fiona says. "Paramedics treated Penelope at Zuccotti Park. She's got a bloody nose, perhaps broken, a black eye, some bruises, and is righteously pissed off at the police."

"Yes, well," Volodya says, "another reason our next move should be to California."

"Right," Fiona says. "We have to get Lucy back to California. Penelope, too. If we don't get her out of here, she'll get in serious trouble."

I add, "We'll have to bring their young men back, too. Rob and Bill."

"I should think so," Fiona says. "They'd be lost without their matriarchs."

Volodya: "Bill, Rob?"

Me: "Rob, Bill? I don't know either."

Fiona: "How can you confuse them? One's black and the other is gay."

Me: "But both were admiring Penelope's structure."

Fiona: "Did it occur to you that Rob might appreciate her as more than an object?"

I have no idea how to answer this and she knows it. I suffer under her glare for 13 seconds which I hope will be my sole punishment.

We walk a few more blocks. Volodya steps forward, concentrating on the pavement ahead of him; Fiona, even after so many miles today, now leans into her unique stride with an almost sprightly rhythm. She says, "Simon, I believe Lucy may have found herself after all."

"Yes," I say, "she's really something isn't she? Gwinnie will be so happy to hear."

"We've learned very little," Volodya says. "We know nothing." He finishes with that long, exhausted sigh of his.

I put my arm around him and he permits himself a chuckle. Fiona puts her arm around me and Winter pulls us forward.

3. The Intoxicating Page

2011-Sept-24 Brooklyn
Historic pivot point peak probability: 52 days

Once ensconced in our hotel, I set up in the lobby—hotel lobbies make spectacular away-from-the-lab offices. I query our Vienna-based computing fleet for the whereabouts of Lucy Montgomery and her Honda 900. Our algorithms determine likely locations and then hack into data stored in surveillance systems until facial and motorcycle recognition software locate her. When we access legally dubious information, we risk discovery by other hackers, security firms, and intelligence agencies, which is to say, other hackers so I have to be careful. The process takes twenty-one minutes.

My tablet computer presents me with images from a surveillance camera of a Brooklyn coin-op laundry. I see Lucy's Honda 900 parked at the curb outside. Her timeweave indicates near certainty that she'll spend the night across the street from this Laundromat in a Brownstone that has been leased to the author, Naomi Gross, the youngest of the four people we identified as Occupy motivators.

The next morning, we take the subway, walk three blocks and knock on the door. Rob, the one with dreadlocks, opens it, "What up, yo" or maybe it's Bill. In any case, the door opens to a comfortable, neat home perfumed with delicious coffee and perfectly shaded toast.

Lucy peers around a corner, says "Uncle Simon!" and rushes to hug me.

Volodya hustles Fiona inside and shuts the door. Winter draws me toward the kitchen. Bill perches on the counter and Rob, the one that opened the door, assumes a seat at the table opposite Ms. Gross. Penelope sits across the table with her back to the window holding an ice bag to her face. Fiona maneuvers over, assesses the damage, and commences fussing.

Volodya engages Ms. Gross by asking questions about her published criticisms of capitalism. She responds as though she believes he's genuinely interested, but he's actually probing her motives and deeply held beliefs. Volodya debates patiently, lying in the rhetorical weeds until he spots a contradiction and then launches terse attacks based on the principles of individual freedom.

Lucy and I remain in the hallway. She looks fraught. Fraught with something that includes components of excitement and self-consciousness but also some flavor of anxiety that I can't identify. When I suggest that she return to San Francisco, she shakes her head.

Penelope says, "No, we're marching on Union Square today."

Bill and Rob express their alliance with Penelope through an emphatic "Yar!" or a word of similar content.

Volodya says, "It will likely be more violent today."

Penelope slams her ice bag on the table, revealing purple and yellow bruising on her cheeks complemented by slowly scabbing cuts and abrasions and a slightly bent nose. She says, "No way do I miss a chance to get in that pig's face!"

Lucy's brow furrows and she tugs at her hair. While I'm not particularly adept at reading other's emotions—hence my preference for software—I detect that Lucy is torn between a perception of responsibility and the lingering shock of having been the focus of yesterday's events.

Speaking just above a whisper so only she can hear, I say, "Your contribution yesterday will be magnified by your absence today."

She looks up with those blue eyes and pushes the lock of red hair she'd been tugging behind her ear.

Our hostess, Ms. Gross rises from the table and says, "Penelope, I'm not bringing an agitator to the rally."

Penelope's eyes widen. The effect emphasizes the delicate structure of her jaw line. Fiona must notice the same thing because she runs her hand along Penelope's cheek and says, "It's settled then, the four of us will fly back to San Francisco this afternoon."

"What?" Penelope says. "I spent everything I had on a plane ticket to get out here." The vehemence in her tone is belied by the way she buries her face in the ice bag.

Fiona says, "We'll pay for our tickets on Volodya's credit card."

Volodya's chin tightens.

Lucy says, "If the police want to arrest me for expressing my opinion, they're welcome to."

Volodya, Fiona, and I say "no" simultaneously.

Winter barks.

Lucy's eyes widen.

Fiona says, "Being arrested with a hundred friends is one thing, being thrown into a cage because you've offended a police force won't help anyone."

I've spent 24 years attempting to persuade Lucy to do one thing or another. Just after her parents divorced, when she was little, Lucy would talk to me for hours describing the rights and wrongs in her world. When she was a taciturn ten-year-old, I discovered that I could engage her by asking about her music preferences. She responded with extensive cross-categorized lists of bands, each with a peculiar rationale for why specific musicians or songs merited praise. In her teens, when she wore nothing but black save for white makeup and spoke to her mother in single syllables, she'd phone me. I'd ask one open-ended question and she'd horrify me with her exploits involving intoxicants and sexual partners. She called me 17 months ago and we talked for two hours. As always, she let her passion run free. We talked about existence itself, how the entirety of our lives is nothing but awareness and time and I soaked it up, all the while yearning to have been her father. Still, through all these years, I don't think I've had the least influence on her.

I say, "Lucy, please."

She says, "Okay, I'll ride back on my Honda Nine. I need some time alone on the road—yesterday was kind of a rush."

I'm too dumbstruck to relish the unprecedented victory.

Fiona says, "You can fly with us and we'll ship your bike."

"No. My bike is the only thing I own of any value."

"We're flying first class," Fiona says.

Unable to fully comprehend the increment in Lucy's maturity, nor to convey to Fiona the magnitude of what she's already accomplished, habit guides me to the dead end of attempting further persuasion. I say, "Please? You can sit in coach with me."

"Look, Bill and I rode out here, we can ride back. We'll be there by Wednesday."

Either Rob or Bill, says, "Isn't the important thing that she get yo out of New York State?"

Fiona says, "Straight away."

Volodya says, "I will stay behind and arrange motorcycle shipment. It is not a problem."

Lucy walks into the living room, grabs her helmet, gloves, jacket, and knapsack. She pats me on the shoulder as she walks to the front door.

The component of Bill or Rob who had been perched on the kitchen counter slips into the living room and grabs a second helmet. I concentrate on the remaining young man, trying to connect his face, dreadlocks, and pale coloring to the name "Rob" so as to distinguish the two, I think I've got it now.

Volodya now stands with his back to Ms. Gross, working the user interface of his phone. I take mine from my pocket and hit the Eeyore icon. He's updating Lucy's timeweave. With just seconds to process, the results only extend a few hours but provide a set of probabilities for different routes.

The two of us make eye contact.

Lucy has stepped out the door and Bill only now follows. I rush ahead of him.

Winter barks as we descend the stairs.

Lucy says, "I'll be careful, Uncle Simon."

She pulls her helmet on and then her gloves. I show her a map on my phone. "Once you're through the Holland Tunnel, stay off the interstate until you get to Pennsylvania." I text her a link to the map. Bill's got his helmet on and mounts a black death-trap with a giant tailpipe and the word "Valkyrie" scrawled across a stretch of plastic.

Volodya trots down the stairs. I step out of his way in a direction that causes Lucy to rotate her back to the motorcycle. Volodya attaches a discreet GPS transmitter behind the license plate of Lucy's vintage Honda 900.

She removes her right glove to pull her phone out of her pocket and says, "Okay, we'll stay on the old highways until Allentown."

"Here," I say, handing her all the money in my wallet, two-hundred-thirty-nine dollars, "try not to stay in bad hotels. And eat."

She looks up and says, "Thank you, Uncle Simon, I don't want to be arrested." I step back as she mounts the over-powered monstrosity and, as I turn away, she adds, "Thank you for coming all the way from Vienna to protect me."

My mouth dangles open. Lucy has become an adult. I don't know how to respond. I long for the stubborn child while appreciating the brilliant young woman.

* * *

An hour later, Fiona and Penelope recline in adjacent first class seats in the front row of a United 767. Volodya and Rob are also in first class, though separated by several rows. I take my window seat in coach. I find it more comfortable to share rather than receive the resentment of the institutional class system of air travel. Plus, sitting in economy allots me some solidarity with Winter whose crate sits in the bowels of the fuselage.

We land in San Francisco at 9:03pm. Fiona continues to fuss over the injuries to Penelope's nose and orbital socket. I'm pleased that Fiona has made a friend, though I suspect that their friendship won't be as intimate as Fiona would like. As freshly liberated Winter pulls us away from baggage claim, Volodya gestures at the two of them and suggests that it could be a problem.

2011-Sep-25 Chicago

Lucy's half a mile ahead of Bill in Interstate 90 morning traffic. The suede fringe of her jacket tickles her ribs and the smooth power of four cylinders magnify the intensity of life in a present where the only relevant future is a few car-lengths ahead and the past is limited to what she can see in her rearview mirror.

She cuts between cars in the left and center lanes and then accelerates into the right lane, but then remembers that lane-splitting isn't legal in most states and the notion of being pulled over brings it all back. She attracted a lot of attention yesterday. She knows she did the right thing, but that doesn't wash away the apprehension. Officer Justin did the right thing, too. She's proud of him. Maybe the picture of the two of them can bring peace between Occupy and the police. Maybe other police will learn the lesson and care more for people than property or power. Maybe the police will join Occupy. The thoughts make her feel better about the picture.

They stayed in a hotel outside of Cleveland last night. The two of them drank a twelve pack. Bill kept referring to her as the Occupy Queen. It annoyed her. Bill never seems to get it, how could anyone put Occupy and monarchy together?

When she checked Facebook this morning, there was a post from some people starting an Occupy movement in Chicago. She had no idea how she could help, but it's on the way and it seems polite to visit. She slows to the speed of traffic both to keep the cops away and to let Bill catch up. His Valkyrie aligns with her and they take an off ramp that deposits them under a maze of train tracks and into city traffic. Soon, they're riding next to Lake Michigan. They turn up a side street, park, and Lucy texts the Chicago Occupiers that they're going into a Starbucks and then "checks in" with four-square so that they'll know where.

On a rack just inside the door, she sees the picture of her and Officer Justin on the front page of The Chicago Tribune. She manages to avoid reading the headline. She doesn't understand why it generates so many feelings: humiliation, pride, shame, self-righteousness, or why these feelings culminate in embarrassment. No one gets it. Bill wants her to wave it like a flag.

Lattes in hand, she and Bill sit at a table near the front where they can see their bikes.

Two men wearing gray suits walk by with fresh coffees. The bald man stares at her, says something to the other man, and they stop. In a drawn out movement, slow enough that their intention seems obvious, they pull chairs over to Lucy and Bill's table and sit down.

Lucy says, "Can I help you?"

"No," says the bald man, "we're here to help you."

The other man, with a short buzz cut of jet-black hair, opens his wallet and displays a badge. "We just want to make sure you don't get into any trouble in our fair city."

The bald man says, "And to see you on your way."

Bill starts to get up. Lucy pats him on the thigh and he sits back down. She says, "We're here to meet with Occupy Chicago."

Buzz-cut says, "You're not bringing that garbage here."

"May I see your identification?"

The bald man says, "Why certainly, miss." He takes out the small leather folder and shows his badge and ID card.

Homeland Security. A jolt of adrenalin accompanies the realization. She posted her location on Foursquare.

She calms herself and says, "Would you recommend we protest at the Mercantile Exchange or City Hall?"

Buzz-cut says, "We could arrest you right now for what you did to that NYPD cop."

She holds out her wrists.

Three people walk in the door. She recognizes them as the Chicago Occupiers from their Facebook avatars. Bill gets up. The two Homeland Security Officers remain seated.

Lucy says, "We appreciate your intimidation, but we're going to meet with some people and try to help keep you and your families from being eaten alive by the one percent—no, no, don't thank me. I do this for love. Maybe you could arrest the people who destroyed the economy instead of hassling people who are trying to help you."

At a large table in back, Lucy and Bill join the Chicago Occupy seed group, a generously inked woman named Tanya and two men, one with a Mohawk and the other wearing a hipster vest and boy-capris. Lucy explains how Occupy Wall Street is organized, goes through the basic details of a do-ocracy and why it's necessary to attempt to get permits so that they can at least argue that they tried not to break the law. The woman takes notes, the punk keeps looking back at the door, and the hipster is preoccupied with his phone. Lucy agrees to share and retweet the Occupy Chicago messages to her now hundred-thousand-strong legion of online followers.

The Chicago Occupiers ask Lucy to come with them to the Thompson Center, and she agrees to. The five of them walk toward the door.

The two Homeland Security Officers stand as they approach. The bald one says, "Where are we going?"

In a mocking tone, Lucy describes their agenda, concluding with, "Can you get us discounts for the Art Institute?"

With their new Chicago friends ahead of them and Homeland Security behind, Lucy puts her arm around Bill. He looks down at her and she raises her chin. He leans over and she whispers in his ear, "I want to get on my bike and ride and when we get home, I want to sleep for a week."

Now a few steps from their parked motorcycles, Bill says, "We can go right now."

"Let's help Occupy Chicago and get out of here."

From behind them, "What's that? You plotting against the United States of America?"

Lucy takes a breath and Bill tightens his arm around her waist. She's not sure how much longer she can pull this off. She turns around, "Officer, get this through your head: We are plotting *for* the United States of America."

25-Sept-2011 San Francisco
Historic pivot point peak probability: 51 days

My favorite place to sit in San Francisco is at a dimly lit table in the rear of a combination bookstore, café, and bar on Valencia Street. The Intoxicating Page also serves as TLA's legal offices, labor recruitment center, and hacking sweatshop.

Fiona operates the business from a large elliptical counter set in the center of the store where she can access customers in each section without the aid of her prosthetic leg or cane. She serves soft drinks, candy, pastries, and iced tea in the well-lit area near the entrance that she stocks with mainstream magazines and children's books. The deeper you wander into the store, the more intense the beverages and literature. Right now, she's sitting at a well lit table with Volodya in the young adult fiction and hard lemonade section. Having slept late by virtue of jetlag piled on jetlag, it's almost noon when Winter and I join them.

A young woman adorned with jewelry pierced to her nose, lips, eyebrows, ears, and both cheeks serves Winter a nice bowl of kibble. Though not on the printed menu, Fiona maintains a supply of fine dry dog food. The rest of us get coffee and scones. I request sour dough toast.

Fiona finishes polishing her cane and oiling the stiletto mechanism that releases its blade. Volodya has the historic timeweave on his laptop monitor and is analyzing the correlations that lead to the looming pivot point. I bring up Lucy's. With a few taps on a tablet or smart phone or clicks of a mouse we can see how timelines trace the past to the present, and how timeweaves project the present into possible futures; we can rotate them around, see how one person's timeline connects to another's and how they're likely to intersect. Zooming in on a timeline or weave brings up links to maps, events, and anything else that's correlated to the trajectory.

I say, "Lucy spent the night in Cleveland and just got to Chicago."

Volodya grunts.

Fiona says, "Text her to have lunch at the History Museum—give her Volodya's credit card number."

I click a link on Lucy's timeline that displays the location of her internet connection. "She's at a Starbucks."

Volodya makes an odd sound, reminiscent of an irritated Russian sheep. He clicks an icon that puts his display on all of our monitors. It shows our prediction for history's timeweave. Stable timeweaves grow thicker with small variations as they flow into a reasonably predictable weave of futures. Instead, this timeweave shows the distinct signature of a pivot point. Rather than growing thicker, the weave unravels into branches and twigs four to twelve weeks from now and then blooms into a spray of possibilities in roughly ten weeks—again, due apologies for the metaphor mixing, hopefully this annoyance is compensated by suppression of the headache that would surely result from a rigorous description.

Volodya bellows, "Damn the central limit theorem!" He refers to the foundation of probability and statistics that describes the mathematics of our critical weakness. Since our timeweaves are calculated from the correlations of billions of events, we can rarely divine those few pivotal pebbles in the trickle's path that sway the probabilities of different timelines within the weave or, for pivot points, the unravel. He rubs his eyes in disgust and adds, "How this will happen?"

Fiona turns to me and Volodya frowns. Sensations from my episode prior to the Occupy riot rebound. Occupiers in baseball caps flickered into labor protesters in bowlers and I once again sense the hopeful insecurity in the timeline that I chose. I say, "The many tiny correlations come from the imbalance of prosperity, the changing course of cultural interaction and globalization, the jump in automation—"

Fiona interrupts, "The de-regulation of colossal banks, the return of robber-barons and—"

"Greemph," Volodya warbles, "unleashing individual freedom is solution, not cause."

Winter whines from his spot under the table.

An equally important role I play in our triumvirate is to retrack our allegorical train: "How many far-future branches do you see?"

He increases the scale of the graphic, backing out from a timescale of months to years to a decade. "Tens of thousands of branches, each less than one percent likely—nothing but noise."

Fiona says, "Have you a common results analysis, then?"

Volodya shrugs, "We have no power to distinguish these low likelihood scenarios. We wait for events and see. "

Fiona glares at him.

"You asked. Maybe you don't like answer." Since he knows what Fiona is thinking, he provides the answer: "World wars, further economic collapse, the return of Soviet-style communism, autocratic rule, nineteenth century oligarchy, plague of one sort or another destroying entire continents, plutocracy, nuclear winter from Middle East wars, collapse of civilization—"

"Rubbish," Fiona says. "Surely within that mess you have found at least one utopia."

"I have," he says, but neither Fiona nor I accept this veiled threat of a positive outlook. "The chances for either corporate or socialist utopia are less than chances for thousand year dark age." With that, he removes his display from our monitors and shoves an entire scone into his mouth.

We continue working for another 195 seconds and then Fiona's laptop makes a purring sound. She says, "Right! The ID scan is ready." The scan churned through all the photos and videos of the Occupy protest that have been posted on the internet. She sets her cane aside and manipulates her mouse. "Bugger me dead. Volodya was right."

He snickers but doesn't look up.

"Seventeen of the Occupiers who wore black and covered their faces have participated in activities sponsored by Anonymous," she nods to Volodya. Anonymous is a semi-organized group of open-source software developers and tech-savvy people scattered around the world who object to the unrestrained use of corporate and federal power. Hiding within Anonymous, though hardly anonymous, is a highly organized group of proprietary software developers isolated in one country paid to advocate the rule of a specific autocrat.

The uniquely decorated young woman refreshes Volodya's coffee and brings Fiona and me glasses of water. I ask for a donut. The waitress looks at Fiona who shakes her head. The waitress says, "Some edamame?"

I say, "In what universe could edamame substitute for a donut?"

Fiona says, "If I soaked it in sugar and boiled it in fat, you couldn't tell the diff."

Eleven minutes later, Fiona says, "Of the 17, four have common multiple interactions with sources who—shit, shit shit."

Volodya smiles. His lips go up as if in a smile with some frequency, almost daily, but a genuine grin is quite rare.

Fiona says, "Just say it."

"The common denominator of the anarchists turns out to be anarchy? I'm stunned," Volodya says. "Ties to Germany, Moscow, and Spain?"

"Both," Fiona says, "and I hate you." She sighs as though disappointed, but it's a ruse. "Klaus Schmidt instigated the riot by pushing Mark Froh, the gent in the Giants cap, over the barrier. Klaus is a twenty-seven-year-old head banger from Bremen and you'll fancy this, his aunt was Ulrike Meinhof. Following in his aunt's footsteps, he's an all around rebel who posts deluded anarchy comments on Facebook—or did so until seven months ago when he moved to a hostel in Amsterdam and first intersected the elder man in black who Simon met at Zuccotti Park, Gus Reser."

"Yes," I say. "Something odd about that fellow."

She looks up and says, "Let me finish and you'll see how the pieces sort themselves out." Looking back at her monitor, she continues, "A twenty-three-year-old Dutchman named Adriaan Buijs from Utrecht, another disgruntled, unemployed man with a computer science degree. Stepan Petrov a nineteen-year-old with a degree in maths from Volodya's alma mater, Moscow State. And, most delicious of all, a twenty-two year-old Italian woman, a tree-sitter named Alina Romano—who doesn't love a long lean fiery Italian woman who impersonates men?"

"Are they correlated to Gus Reser?" I ask.

"Well, it's hard to say. The elder man in black—can we call them something else? I feel like I'm in a Will Smith movie—'Gus Reser' seems to be one of several aliases. His actual name, or at least the oldest name on record for him, is Guenther Rader. He's also correlated to Julian Assange of Wikileaks, though ..."

But I don't hear the rest of her report.

Guenther Rader. No wonder he stepped away when Lucy tried to introduce him to me. The name echoes about my skull: Guenther Rader. I can't turn it off.

I reach down and lift Winter up to my lap. Wrestling with him—he doesn't like to be thought of as a lap dog—keeps me from drifting back to that 1977 day in the Bohemian Grove; the day Rader tried to ruin Gwinnie. The day I rescued her.

"That was Guenther Rader?" Volodya says. "He has aged well."

"Let me see, he's linked to Anonymous." Her brow furrows. "Well this is right odd. Call him Rader or Reser, but his timeline doesn't resolve. This bloke lacks an online presence—no email, no smart phone, no social network activity—and seems all but invisible to surveillance cameras. The links are all mentions by others. Without passport records and German arrest reports, we'd have nothing on him. The timeline is rubbish for weaving his futures. We can't even predict his past. Useless." Fiona pops up windows on our monitors showing her display.

Volodya says, "You will find stronger correlation to Baader Meinhof."

"You know him?"

I'm not certain I should say it out loud. Sometimes when you say something out loud it becomes real and I don't want this to be real, but I can't stop the name from falling out my mouth: "Guenther Rader. Yes, we know him."

Winter squirms off my lap and Fiona puts her hand on my wrist making me feel at once reassured and self-conscious.

Rader's timeline looks like a wisp of fog instead of a branch with well-defined stems that ought to describe his past. The width of the fog indicates large uncertainty. Fiona overlaps Rader's timeline on Lucy's and zooms out.

Fiona says, "Until eight days ago, they'd never been in the same place." And then, tightening her grip on my wrist, she adds, "They just met and she has no greater correlation to Anonymous than the average Occupier. Simon, she's okay."

Volodya takes over the user interface. "Odd, less than 5% probability she will be arrested."

Fiona says, "After the photo, no cop wants anything to do with that woman."

2011-Sept-25 Chicago

The long walk to the Thompson Center gives Lucy's Occupy host, Tanya, plenty of time to rally her new followers. When they get there, a few dozen people have assembled, enough to attract a handful of cops. The Occupiers cheer and call for Lucy.

Tanya joins the demonstration with Lucy and Bill following. A police officer of average height but not-so-average width steps in front of Lucy and Bill. His nametag says Lincoln and he says, "Nope. I don't want you here."

"Officer," Lucy says, "I'm not breaking any laws. Your job is to protect and to serve the citizens and here we are!" She curtsies.

Officer Lincoln stands with his feet at shoulder-width, knees slightly bent, and his hand resting on the baton attached to his belt. "Don't tell me my job." He looks Lucy in the eye and his jaw tightens. "Tyvon Justin has a wife and three kids and you got him suspended—I hope you're fucking happy. He's a hardworking man, an honest-to-God union worker. He's the 99%, not you sniveling, irresponsible, entitled brats."

Then several cops move forward and surround her.

One says, "Public nuisance, disorderly conduct."

Another adds, "Resisting arrest, trespassing."

She says, "Resisting arrest?" Bill squeezes her arm and tries to whisper to her but she pulls away. "Arrest for what? Or is that the whole joke?"

A fourth cop says, "You're about to find out." And then, rather than reach for Lucy, he takes Bill by the arm, twists him around and forces him to the ground.

Lucy looks back and forth. The Homeland Security goons seem like her only protection. The tension builds in her chest. The cop presses a knee into Bill's lower back and pulls on his neck. The other Occupiers call the cops pigs, fascists, and other tired clichés that agitate them even more.

She says, "Okay, okay" and thinks of their bikes parked outside that Starbucks. "We'll leave, just let him go."

Officer Lincoln says, "Not so tough are you, now?"

He tries to grab her and she jukes to the side.

Bill groans and his face contorts. He looks up at her and says. "Go. I'll be fine."

"Right," she says, "the cops have a long and storied tradition of fair treatment of young African American men." She pulls out her cell phone and scans her contacts, though she's not sure who to call. Uncle Simon comes to mind and she starts scrolling—not sure whether he's filed under 'U' or 'S.'

A cop bumps into her and she drops the phone. She leans over to pick it up and all she can see are black leather boots in every direction. Except one.

An old man muscles his way through the police, claiming to be her attorney and citing sections of the US Constitution and Chicago Penal Code. He speaks with a European accent that reminds her of Uncle Simon's Russian friend Volodya. She looks up with the seeds of hope in her heart and sees Gus Reser, the one who always wears black. Behind him, she recognizes more of the black-clad Europeans.

"Please arrest me, instead. I will cheerfully bring suit against city of Chicago and state of Illinois. Please, my 401k could use some help." He pushes his way between the cops and offers his hand to Lucy.

Before she can react, he takes her hand and, as he pulls her away from the cops, he says, loud and clear, "Any more officers want their pictures taken with Lucy Montgomery?"

Lucy sees the blond man, Klaus, perched on a bench with a huge camera.

The police give them a wide berth.

She says, "What about Bill?"

"You remember me?" the man says.

"Make them let Bill go," she says, or starts to say, but the words don't get very far. She's run out of whatever it is that has kept her going and feels tears welling up.

He says, "Come with me."

She sucks it up one more time and says, "Let Bill and me go, we'll ride home and there won't be any trouble."

He tightens his grip on her and says, "Lucy Montgomery. Look at me." She does as told. "Do you remember me?"

"Of course, Gus."

"Good. Now think. Will it be any better in San Francisco?"

"Well, I—"

"Every police officer, every FBI officer, every government contractor wants to hurt you."

She can hear Bill nearby pleading.

Gus says, "No, no, Lucy, you need to be careful now." The other European Occupiers form a line between Lucy and Gus and the police. "You can come with us."

"What about Bill?" Beyond the line of Occupiers, Bill is standing, now in handcuffs.

"There is just one of me. When you are safe, I will do what I can for your friend."

"Okay," she says. "Okay. I'm fine."

He leans over until his eyes are at her level and says, "I can help you do this the right way. You achieve nothing from a Chicago jail. But you must trust me." He motions to the side and says, "Adriaan, Alina, would you like to help Lucy?"

Lucy watches Gus Reser jog toward the police as they walk Bill to a squad car. Gus is quick for an old man. He steps between the police and the car, holds his arms wide and smiles. She can't hear him, but can easily read the responses of the police. They look away from Gus and then look at each other. Gus stops talking and pulls his hands together. Still smiling, he cocks his head and waits for a response. Officer Lincoln steps between the cops holding Bill. Frowning, he points a finger at Gus and says something. Gus nods. Lincoln unlocks the handcuffs. Bill starts to step away but Lincoln reels him back in. With an arm around Bill's shoulder the cop pulls him close and speaks into his ear.

Gus walks back to Lucy and says, "Would you like to give me the keys to your motorcycle?" Before she has a chance to answer, he turns to the tall man and says, "Adriaan, Lucy's friend will need some help. Perhaps you could escort him to Ontario Street and see him on his way? If the police bother him in any way, call me." Adriaan rushes off and Gus holds out his hand to Lucy. "Your keys?"

Lucy says, "No one rides my nine but me."

"Of course, if you don't want my help, that's fine." He turns from her as though to walk away, but then steps back, takes a breath, and says, "Lucy, you have the power to change the world. You can repair every problem faced by the ninety-nine percent. You are the center of the emergence of, of, well, I think that you should get away from here." Then in a soft voice and with a gentle smile, he asks, "Please, may I help?"

She says, "I want to go with Bill." Across the street, she sees Bill and Adriaan walking away.

"Your friend has no outstanding arrest warrants. Also, I don't think he understands the Occupy movement. You are in a different position than he is. I have an idea that you might consider."

Lucy doesn't know what to do. She's never been arrested; she's never even had a police officer upset with her before. She wants to go with Bill, but she knows that Gus is right. She has warrants. Homeland security is following her. The facts collide too fast for her to speak.

Gus says, "Yes, the injustices will continue to accumulate until you make a decisive move. Or, instead, you can go to jail."

"But what would I go to jail for? What have I done?"

"Do you understand how the one-percent have defined the word 'terrorist?'"

"Anyone they consider a threat."

"And, Lucy Montgomery," he says, smiling, "you are a threat."

She sees Tanya sitting on a bench with her hands cuffed, sobbing. Officer Lincoln stares back at her and taps his truncheon against his palm.

"Would you like to come with me?" Reser says. "We'll store your motorcycle. It will be perfectly safe until you need it and no one else will ride it. I promise." His voice and smile are calm and, even in tense situations, he's gentle.

"Where are you going?"

"To a place where you will find like-minded comrades and," he motions behind to Officer Lincoln, "the safety and peace necessary to study the methods and politics you'll need to fulfill the promise of Occupy Wall Street."

2011-Sept-25 San Francisco
Historic pivot point peak probability: 69 days

My coffee has gone cold, but that damned name, Guenther Rader, continues to reverberate through my cortexes. I set the mug down and a woman wreathed in tattoos brings me a snifter of brandy. Fiona says, "All right then?"

"I think so."

"Just veg out."

The brandy doesn't have the taut, waxy, formal scent of the Cognac we get in Europe; it's looser, fruitier, easier going, American.

As I settle in to a delightful blend of jet lag and brandy, the bell hanging on the front door jingles and Penelope walks in. She holds the door for twelve other young adults. Her eye is still discolored and her nose is adorned with scabs and bruises. She somehow wears these scars like jewelry; temporary distractions from her otherwise pristine features. Several of her friends carry posters of Lucy and Officer Justin.

Fiona says, "Oh shit, me Intoxicating Page is becoming an Occupy hangout."

Volodya says, "But can they code?" He stands and walks through the growing crowd, offering business cards and suggestions for how to make a few dollars without working for The

Man.

Volodya and I have been writing software since the 1970s. From Algol and Fortran through C# to Python. Still, the two of us cannot produce the entire analysis backbone required for filtering the signals from the vast noise of internet data. Fiona's insights drive our success, but her coding skills are roughly on a par with Winter's so we hire young underemployed adults. We disguise assignments as components of cell phone apps, games, financial analysis routines, or simply research. We pay well, watch after them, provide career advice and references and, while they retain the right to market any commercial apps they create, we get the debugged source code and an informal agreement of future help.

Penelope leans against the oval bar scanning the crowd, her long wavy dark hair swings back and forth. Fiona perches on a barstool next to her.

Now near the entrance, in the Dr. Seuss and juice box section, Volodya surveys potential contributors as they cross the threshold. I pick up my laptop, notebook, and brandy snifter and work my way through the crowd to a table against the rear wall where Fiona serves Everclear with Sartre's *Being and Nothingness*, Camus' *Myth of Sisyphus*, and Kierkegaard's *Fear and Trembling*.

As I integrate the Occupy and anti-austerity movements into our library of economic models so that we can improve the spatial and temporal resolution of the looming pivot point, which we've only managed to narrow down to 4-11 weeks, I glance at Lucy's timeline periodically. Her involvement with Occupy Chicago has been documented across Occupy sites and social nets. That she's attracted the attention of Homeland Security and Chicago police, I tell myself, is only natural.

2011-Sept-26 San Francisco
Historic pivot point peak probability: 64 days

Ten hours later, I make it downstairs at 8:14. A substantial Monday morning queue has accumulated where Fiona operates the cappuccino machine. Seven people populate tables including three of our new subcontractors.

I set up next to Volodya in the hardly imaginative Russian Literature and vodka section, and open Lucy's timeweave. I see that Chicago Occupiers have reached out to Lucy through emails and social networks, but she hasn't responded. We prefer to avoid snooping through people's emails and private postings because it's disrespectful. We also avoid discussing the ethical merits of our software-based snooping.

I say, "No data have contributed to Lucy's timeweave in nineteen hours. She should be on Interstate 80 somewhere in Iowa or Nebraska by now."

Volodya nods twice and starts typing. "Since Lucy was twelve years old, she has never disconnected from internet for more than thirty-five hours. Between phone and laptop, she hasn't disconnected for greater than an hour in last two years. And …" He draws out that last syllable. It's his way of maintaining ownership of a conversation. "Likelihood she disconnected of her own will is less than four percent."

Timelines of her contacts flash across the screen in different colors and widths according to frequency of contact. Four thin lines converged with Lucy's yesterday afternoon in Chicago. My heart sinks. They are Klaus Schmidt, Adriaan Buijs, Stepan Petrov, and Alina Romano—the four Occupiers with strong ties to Guenther Rader.

Volodya says, "Why we didn't see this yesterday?" With a resounding click of Volodya's mouse, a gallery of images appears. Taken yesterday afternoon by a surveillance camera at the Thompson Center, the first shows police surrounding Lucy and Bill, the African American lad with short hair who I should now be able to decipher from Rob, the fair-skinned fellow with dreadlocks sitting with Penelope over in the women's fiction and pepper-infused vodka section.

Volodya says, "Lucy was not arrested," and then clicks to the next image: a gray haired man approaching the huddle of police. His back is to the camera, but I know that old bastard. The next shows Rader guiding Lucy away from the police, though he still manages to keep the camera from catching his face. Another image shows a police officer holding Bill to the ground.

I work the interface of my tablet for a few seconds. "Bill's motorcycle was impounded and …" I catch myself stretching a sentence "… he hasn't the credit required to release it. He's on the phone with his parents."

Volodya opens a window, types for 34 seconds, and says, "It is true about Chicago politics; $1278 to tow and store a motorcycle? Huripoffikle."

"You paid it?"

He puts live video on my monitor: a ragged looking Bill walking through a parking lot to his giant black motorcycle.

My keen sense of denial is doing a wonderful job distracting me from fears of Lucy's fate. I launch search algorithms much as I did two days ago in Brooklyn as Volodya updates the group timeline of Rader and his acolytes.

Volodya says, "Data from her weave say less than 51% she's with him and over 95% that he's associated with her disappearance."

"Disappearance?" The word comes out of my mouth without my permission.

He nods to her timeline, now including the search results. The last update is a picture of Lucy with Rader's arm around her walking into a Hungarian restaurant. There is no image of her emerging and no indication that she left, though Rader's team departed 39 minutes after entering.

"You must tell Gwinnie," Volodya says. He stares at me for a second, the skin of his chin stretched taught. "We've lost her."

4. Gwinnie

2011-Sept-26 San Francisco
Historic pivot point peak probability: 64 days

How can Fiona drive this car? It's got three pedals and she has one leg. Winter stands on the passenger seat with his head out the window. Gwinnie lives in an apartment 29 miles away in the town of Concord at the base of one of California's charming little mountains, this one named after the devil.

How will I tell Gwinnie that I failed her again?

I exit the freeway and drive along a worn looking boulevard. Gwinnie lives in an apartment complex that resembles a 1950s motor lodge. Two levels with exterior concrete stairs leading to a row of identical doors, each marked by a tarnished brass number.

Winter and I stand outside number 209 and neither of us knocks.

I say, "You should scratch, it's more polite than knocking." His tongue dangles from the side of his mouth. The temperature is 7 degrees F higher here than it was in San Francisco. "Fine." I knock four times.

Someone moves inside. A shot of adrenalin pours down my spine. What if she has a guest? What if she was in bed with another man? What if she thinks I'm a burglar?

The door opens.

It's Gwinnie! And she's smiling.

"Simon." It's as if she sings my name. "Is everything all right? You should have called first, I'd have fixed you dinner." The wide expanse of her forehead creases in welcome. She steps out and hugs me. Great masses of red, lilac-scented hair engulf me and her neck smells of Gwinnie.

She kneels down and pets Winter on the head.

"Come in, come in."

I step through the door and search for signs of another man's presence. Then I experience outrage that Gwinnie, the most beautiful, charming, brilliant, and generous woman on earth, lives alone in a one-bedroom apartment on working-class Monument Boulevard. This thought leads me along a well worn path.

On the morning of the 1977 vernal equinox in Monte Rio, a small Northern California town in a hilly redwood forest along the Russian River, I waited for the school bus with Spring, my Irish Setter, when Gwinnie appeared. I noticed her hair first. The breeze wouldn't stop teasing the curling strands, each a unique shade in the spectrum from red to auburn and her eyes were the speckled green of the river. With my skin the pale gray of river rock and my eyes and hair the color of the muddy river bottom, I felt like a bottom-dwelling troll next to this redwood forest fairy.

The bus arrived in a loud blast of diesel and air brakes. She took the first empty bench. I paused there for an instant, hopeless, and then continued down the aisle and sat next to Rod, who I'd known since second grade. The air brakes hissed and gears ground as the bus pulled onto the Bohemian Highway. At the next stop, another floe of students boarded but left the space next to her empty.

When the bus regained full speed, I took a deep breath, stood, and approached. The bus crossed a bridge over the river and I half-fell into the seat. I sat frozen, thoughts cascading through my brain and not a single conversation topic among them. Minutes dragged by. Rod laughed at me. The bus finally stopped in front El Molino High School. I stepped into the aisle and took one gentlemanly step backward to allow Gwinnie to exit ahead of me, but I stepped on Rod's foot and he shoved me ahead of her. Half way to my locker, I stole a look back. She was right there, not a second behind me, and rushing forward.

Where my gray complexion doesn't blush easily, the warm blood flowing just below the surface of Gwinnie's perfect freckles will act on any excuse to flush her into a shade normally reserved for late summer tomatoes. There are many aspects of culture that escape me, but I'm not a total numbfuck. She couldn't have gotten so close to me without intention.

She stopped and looked down at a sheet of paper in her hand. I saw her name at the top of the page and said, "Hey, Gwinnie." It was the first time I ever said her name—try it yourself, two perfect beats.

She held out the sheet of paper, a school map annotated in the red pencil of the front office. I accepted the map. In that instant, far more so than the first time I had sex, which was also with Gwinnie, I knew what it was to be a gentleman—which is something I've experienced far more often than I have experienced sex. "Come with me," I said. We walked side by side and I explained the school's geography. There was an awkward silence for six seconds after I finished my explanation. And then she did another thing that altered my reality. She took my hand.

Now, 43 and a half years later, I try to blame Dick. The bastard who left Gwinnie to raise Lucy all by herself, but I know that it's my fault. Dick was a twig on the tree of her timeweave that I could easily have pruned but instead allowed to grow into the branch that led her here.

"Simon, please."

She knows my thoughts. It's hard for me to be with Gwinnie.

She directs me to an old and tired but immaculate microfiber sofa. I set my satchel on the coffee table next to a newspaper that features the photo of Lucy and Officer Justin on its front page. Gwinnie pours two glasses of wine but nothing for Winter. He stares at me until I let him sip from mine.

Gwinnie says, "Did you talk to her."

"I did."

She waits for me and I clear my throat. Her brow furrows and it makes me hate myself for being incapable of protecting her from every pain she feels.

"How is she?"

"I love you Gwinnie." It just comes out. "Everything is going to be okay."

"What happened?"

That she ignores my declaration is expected; she's accustomed to it coming out now and again, my solitary Tourette's symptom.

"Lucy is probably not in danger."

"*Probably*?"

Her hands flutter to her mouth and I finally acquire a hint of presence. "Lucy is an amazing young woman." I describe my visit with Lucy prior to the Occupy demonstration and relay Fiona's observation that Lucy has found herself.

"But where is she?"

I describe her visit to Chicago but leave out any mention of Guenther Rader. Gwinnie would be terrified to learn that Rader is involved in Lucy's disappearance. It's a burden I'll not share.

Gwinnie says, "You just let her go?"

Winter leaps off the couch.

My voice sputters in response but no word escapes.

"She's just a kid from Stockton. Did you see this?" She holds up the newspaper with Lucy and Officer Justin in full color. "She's on every website, every newspaper, every news channel—how did you expect her to handle this?"

"She's emerging into adulthood."

"Emerging? She's running from the New York Police and you expected her to just la-di-da her way back to San Francisco? Think, Simon, think."

"Fiona thought—"

"What did you think, Simon? Lucy trusts you."

"She's an adult."

"She's a scared little girl."

Rising from the couch, I say, "She was adamant."

Gwinnie turns away.

Winter sniffs her bottom.

She turns back. Her face is streaked with tears. "You let her go."

"I respected her decision."

"I'm calling the police." She takes her cell phone and begins typing.

I'm caught off guard by this most obvious of actions. My hope rises for an instant but then I realize that if we can't find her by weaving timelines, the Chicago police can't help.

She answers questions posed by the Chicago police department. She looks even more crestfallen when she's told that they can't do anything until Lucy has been missing for at least 48 hours. But her crest fully collapses when she explains to the police that Lucy is, indeed, That Lucy. The phone disconnects. She calls back immediately but the officer she'd been speaking with is no longer available. Indeed, no one is available.

I reach out and Gwinnie takes my hand. She sits, sips her wine, stares out the window at a 7-Eleven franchise across the asphalt parking lot. Her eyes are moist. She spills a few drops of wine and doesn't notice Winter tidying up after her. She leans back on the couch and says, "I'm sorry, Simon. I know you're doing all you can."

I put my hand on Gwinnie's cheek. Our lips are an inch apart. I say, "We'll find her."

She says, "Please." And then she starts crying. Each tear is a whip lashing my soul.

1977-July-25 Bohemian Grove

On July 25th, 1977, 127 days after I met Gwinnie, my big red dog, Spring, and I were running along a coastal ridge south of The Grove.

Located 75 miles north of San Francisco, just up the river from the house where Spring and I grew up, the Bohemian Grove is a 2700-acre redwood forest where the most powerful men in the world spend two summer weeks relaxing and recovering from the demands of the world they rule. Like many of the neighborhood kids, Gwinnie and I spent the summers of our youth working for the Bohemians.

At the beginning of each summer the labor supervisor, a man named John who at the time seemed ancient but in retrospect couldn't have been older than 35, drilled us on two rules. First: we could not repeat anything we overheard. He waited until after the girls had gone home to provide his second rule: the safety of the entire world depended on the Bohemians releasing tension. "Men are beasts who must satisfy their appetites in order to relax and if they can't relax," John dictated in a tone appropriate for dire news, "the world will come to an end." Then he'd go into lurid detail as to what it meant for a grown man to "relax." Relaxation, it seemed, entails drinking, yelling, vomiting, wrestling, telling bawdy jokes, performing ridiculous plays, participating in strange rituals, and—this is the part that rapt our attention—various exploits involving their penises. This, we understood without being told, explained why women had to leave the Grove by the cocktail hour each evening.

My job included surveying the forest for lost or confused guests and, during meals, the multipurpose role of gopher. Of course they meant, go-for, but still.

Spring's favorite part of the forest was a small clearing carpeted in redwood needles atop a ridge about a thousand feet above the river. Spring's Clearing is still there, still unspoiled; would that Spring were still here, I miss her so.

The sun was just two hours above the western horizon when my vision went double, then triple, then, like the phenomenon of standing between two mirrors, the world repeated in every direction. My balance began to fail so I sat down, but in lowering myself, multiple repetitions of my shadow followed separate trajectories, and not all of them to the ground. The world began to spin about as my brain processed inconsistent copies of my senses. Shaking my head rendered more images so I tried to stand, but in rising, my brain neglected to invite its requisite blood supply and I fainted.

Spring's tongue brought me back to consciousness. I rose slowly and discovered my ability to navigate overlapping realities. I stepped, quite literally, from one continuous action that melted its own blue-green edge into another. And did it again. Each reality brought a set of primordial feelings positioned on the scales from contentment to dread, joy to misery, and assurance to despondence. It would take decades for me to accept that these emotional responses are the only measures I have of a timeline's desirability.

We took a winding path down into the forest. We heard multiple, echoing copies of laughter from the campground below. I caught a whiff of cigar smoke. Spring wasn't allowed among the guests, so she took off, her long legs and flowing red hair blurred together as she picked up speed on an old deer trail. I launched up a tree. Since people rarely look up, I was privy to many state secrets from that vantage. Two men passed below. I recognized the former President by his ski-slope shaped nose and the other man was the short fat Russian who had been his Secretary of State. When they passed out of sight, I dropped from the tree, ran through the forest dodging fallen branches, alarming robins, and annoying several copies of a raven, to the valley floor.

Benches and tables sufficient for nearly 2000 people formed concentric arcs facing a pond beyond which was an orchestra pit and stage whose backdrop consisted of a 40-foot owl statue. The Bohemians stood in groups or sat at tables talking, drinking, laughing, smoking, and "weaving not webs"—a phrase that adorns the entry gate and is spoken frequently among guests but rather lacks meaning. My 17-year-old mind thought it an odd way to prevent nuclear war, even for beasts.

I weaved my way through the beasts. A conversation at a

nearby table began to reverberate, the words overlapped, displaced by a fraction of a second like an echo. The interactions of the men acquired the ethereal qualities of flames. Rather than substantial beings of water and carbon, they flickered into and out of existence, there but insubstantial, until there again. I stepped toward the grills rather than the kitchen, and was overcome by regret, as though I had just made a mistake that I would spend my life trying to overcome. I stepped away from the grill, toward the kitchen and felt immediately better even though my foot separated a short, severe looking man from his cane.

I steadied the man and stepped back to the grill, but a wall of trepidation pushed me away. I took a full step toward the kitchen and experienced the feeling you get when you've identified a moral imperative and have chosen to pursue it despite looming difficulty.

Walking into the kitchen, I heard Gwinnie talking to the chef. Oh, the perfect soprano notes of that voice, like an oboe with a soggy, thin reed, slightly shredded so as to excite every harmonic within the instrument's resonant cavity and the musician's throat. I almost stopped to listen, hoping that I might hear her laugh but, standing in the doorway, a boy carrying a bag of trash nearly bowled me over.

Unlike Gwinnie's voice, that of the chef, a skeletal German named Guenther Rader, made jagged connections with syllables and abrupt intonations of vowels. That none of the sounds had that multiple-copy reverb escaped me in the overflow of loathing for this man. Though, to be fair, I couldn't decipher whether my loathing resulted from what I considered his lecherous nature or from jealousy of the time he spent with Gwinnie.

I dashed around bags of potatoes and onions, between the freezer door and the giant sink of the dishwashing station. There she was, Gwinnie, her back to me, leaning over a counter covered with hundreds of small plates decorated with olives, salami, peppers, and wedges of cheese.

"Gwinnie," I said. I hadn't quite caught my breath and it came out louder than I meant and my voice sort of cracked on the second syllable. She reached up and tucked in one of the red curls fighting for release from her hair net. I said, "It's after five, you have to leave the Grove!"

Rader said, "She is not finished yet."

Gwinnie said, "Mind your own beeswax, Simon." The way she said my name, extending the syllable on the central m, struck the bravado out of me and I stepped back toward the door like a scolded lamb. But in taking that step, my shadow disengaged from my foot. Reverb built up and that sensation of impending regret nearly knocked me over.

Staggering backward, I saw Gwinnie in a horrific light. In that step, in that reality, she had no spirit, no fortitude, nothing, no Gwinnie at all. However beautiful, she appeared as an empty vessel. A tuft of sound from her voice sounded fearful, sounded ruined. Yes, that was it, Gwinnie was ruined.

Stuck in the intersection, shadows of my hands argued with the positions of my fingers. The ruined reality tugged at me.

Rader handed Gwinnie a bowl and she scooped a beige creamy substrate onto one dish and then added slices of tomato and cucumber. She looked at me from the corners of her eyes. Well, one of her did. The flickering overlap started to give me a headache and with the headache, I felt a sad resignation.

Rader stepped to a cupboard, removed a small unlabeled jar and brought it to Gwinnie. "Four color and spice, is special pepper for the hummus—mixes with tahini just so." He pursed his lips and closed his eyes as he said it. Gwinnie smiled at his gesture. I hated him even more.

She took the jar and dashed red powder across the beige substrate.

"More than that—be generous."

Gwinnie dashed more and more of the powder.

With each scoop, that reality of ruin and chaos took greater hold and I very nearly surrendered to it. But then I noticed something. Something that really was wrong, something that had no double, no echo, something set precisely at the intersection of realities. As the powder sat on the hummus, it lost its color. It turned pink and then disappeared altogether. Stranger than that, where the powder accumulated, the hummus dissolved into tiny yellow pools and exhaled wisps of steam.

I said, "That's not right."

"What do you know?" Rader yelled in thick reverb as though he spoke from inside a tunnel. "Get out of here."

Gwinnie set the powder down, lifted the plate and headed toward the door.

"But the reaction …" I said.

Gwinnie paused in front of me.

"You know nothing," Rader said.

I said, "You can't take it out there, it's almost 23 minutes after five."

"God, Simon, you're so paranoid."

As she passed, the feeling of ruin crested in a wave of despair.

I stepped after her and stayed ahead of that wave.

She worked her way through the crowd, to the row of tables closest to the lake. I was a good ten meters behind when someone grabbed my shoulder—Rader. He said, "Go back in and wash dishes. Stop bothering pretty girl."

I could see him grip my shoulder, a solid hold, but also an overlapping image of me slipping out of his grasp.

Fifteen meters ahead and separated by two circles of men standing between the first and second row of tables, Gwinnie set down the plate. Slipping away from Rader, I looked back and saw him wrap his other arm around the neck of my shadow.

I ran toward Gwinnie.

A man stepped in my way and we collided. His drink fell from his hand and his cigarette caught in my shirt. I kept going, though I heard him fall behind me.

Voices in my wake: "Stop that kid," "come back here," "what's he doing?" Multiple voices, not echoes, I felt separation, felt myself closer to the more desirable timeline. Then, a single, loud voice, "Someone get Frank a fresh drink."

Gwinnie set the dish before a gentleman and turned back.

The gentleman scooped hummus with a slice of bread. Gwinnie frowned at me. I stepped around her, bumping a man in the back of the head as I did so. Someone grabbed my arm. Jerking away, I stumbled into echoes and shadows and multiple visions but clenched my stomach muscles and managed to recover enough to make it two steps closer to the table. Now my legs caught up in Gwinnie's and she tumbled behind me—several of her fell, my vision could no longer be trusted, but I didn't stop.

Another three steps and the feeling of solidity returned.

The name "Frank" finally penetrated my mind; knocking over the chairman of the board could have unpleasant repercussions.

I finally made it to the table. The gentleman watched me, the hummus-laden bread still in his hand. He didn't appear upset, merely curious. His eyes were dark and warm. He looked as though I'd entered his study without an appointment. Most wonderful of all, though, there was just one steady figure of him and one steady feeling of me.

Of course, I had no idea of the significance of this first meeting with Gordon Woodley. The spotlight of significance shines on pivot points only in retrospect—unless Volodya and I write your software.

I said, "You mustn't eat that."

Someone reached around my neck and pulled me off my feet.

In the commotion, I couldn't tell if he heard me. The man who I would come to know as Gordon Woodley separated into two overlapping images, one calm and comfortable, the other writhing in agony.

With my back pinioned against the chest of whoever held me, I swung both legs up and managed a sufficient lever to knock over the table. The plate landed in the dirt.

They pulled me away. John, my boss, yelled at me—I don't know what he said. I could feel Gwinnie to my left, heard her blaming me for the disruption.

I watched a single image of Gordon Woodley standing over the plate looking back at me. The short dark-haired man who walked with a cane stepped over to Gordon. With some effort, he leaned down and picked up the fallen plate. He set the plate on another table and took a slice of lemon from a gentleman's drink. With a calm but stern look, the man squeezed lemon juice over the hummus. The first drop flashed back in a puff of steam. The steam of succeeding drops smoked off the plate like tiny geysers.

Gordon pointed at me. The dark-haired man held out his cane in my direction and for an instant I thought he'd say something to John, or Rader, or the guards who held me. More voices demanded my attention, and as my captors pushed me to the ground, it occurred to me that poisoning a great industrialist would surely have ruined Gwinnie.

I spent that night and the following morning in a locked room at the server-boys camp waiting for justice. John stepped in seven minutes before noon and said: "You're expected at the Clubhouse after lunch." Then he walked away.

The Clubhouse juts out from the side of a steep hill. Trees, whose roots are set in the valley hundreds of feet below, pass through the wide balcony and broad eves. Bernard Maybeck built it in 1903. I climbed the stairs and crossed the threshold into a nearly square room about 29 feet on a side. Along with the sandstone and granite fireplace, the furniture consisted of several throne-like redwood chairs, a couple of rockers, and a table. Fifty-four minutes later, Gordon Woodley and the short fellow with the cane arrived.

Gordon said, "You must be Simon, I am Gordon Woodley." He put his left hand on my shoulder and offered his right. I took it and his hand clenched about mine.

"No, no," he said. "Apply a firm grasp, when you shake hands—hasn't your father taught you this?"

"He's dead." I hated admitting my father's lack of existence because people's responses, wherever on the scale from shock to compassion, made me uncomfortable.

I matched the pressure he applied.

"Better, but look me in the eyes."

"How can I judge the appropriate pressure without watching the muscles in your forearm?"

The man with the cane spoke with an accent: "Pressure is force per unit area, you can't observe it with your eyes, you need a pressure monitor, for example, your hand."

Gordon let go of my hand and said, "This is Professor Edward Teller."

With blood rushing to my face, I shook the professor's hand.

Gordon said, "Good. A man must have a firm shake to be taken seriously." He motioned for me to sit. I did and he lowered himself on the hearth at my side. The other man rested his cane against the table and sat in a chair next to me.

"About yesterday," Gordon said, "you may have saved my life. Tell me, how did you know? Did you see who poisoned my plate?"

"It wasn't Gwinnie!"

"The serving girl? Of course not."

"Well, Gwinnie sprinkled the powder over the hummus substrate, but she didn't know it was lye. She thought it was a spice. It was that Guenther Rader." I spoke the name with such vehemence that three specks of my spittle landed on Gordon's cheek.

He pulled a hanky from his pocket and said, "What makes you think it was lye?" He wiped his cheek.

"I didn't know what it was until Professor Teller applied the lemon juice. I could tell the PH was way off by the way it reacted—but I couldn't tell whether it was acid or base."

The two men looked at each other and I wondered if I'd said

something stupid.

Gordon said, "You're a very intelligent young man, where are you going to college?"

"I'm going to be a mechanic!"

He turned and smiled at Professor Teller who said, "You will attend a university and take physics."

Then Gordon said something that I'd never heard before and it stuck with me: "Simon, you have a bright future." He stared at me for another few seconds and added, "I want to help you." He took out a business card and a pen. He crossed out the phone number on his card and wrote in a different one. "This is my direct line. I want you to call me collect every Wednesday at 6pm. If I don't answer or don't return your call, call me again the following Wednesday and if you ever need anything, any money, any advice, any help, I want you to tell me."

At a loss for words—due to my fear of the telephone—I said, "Mechanics."

Gordon said, "Every Wednesday."

2011-Sept-27 2:18am Concord CA
Historic pivot point peak probability: 63 days

It is not the first time I've slept with Gwinnie, but it is typical. Still on the couch, she's to my right with her cheek on my shoulder and Winter to my left with his chin on my thigh. Winter snores once every two seconds and Gwinnie once every five seconds; every ten seconds they snore at the same time. If I move too much, it will disturb both of them. I work my tablet free of the satchel with my feet and then reach forward, careful not to shift my right shoulder, and take it in my hands.

Lucy has now been disconnected from the internet for thirty-six hours. Her timeline still ends with the picture of Rader's claw around her shoulders as they enter a Hungarian restaurant. I turn away, seeking out the front page photo of Lucy with Officer Justin, if my brain insists on capturing an image, I prefer this one.

I tap the Eeyore icon to bring up Volodya's display. He's got two windows up, the aggregate timeweave of Rader and his gang and, in the other, new software that he's stepping through the debugger. I look over his figurative shoulder and read the code. It's a follow routine, software that anticipates Lucy's movement and expands the search radius out to smaller and smaller correlations.

The timeline for Rader's gang is pretty simple. They left the Hungarian restaurant, went to Chicago's O'Hare Airport and flew back to Europe. Volodya has obviously poked and prodded and supplemented the calculation with all the available data, but it gives no indication of what has happened to Lucy. The images show Rader's crew checking luggage, shopping in the airport sundry shops, and boarding the plane. I don't know whether to feel worried about Lucy's continued disappearance or comforted that she is no longer with Rader.

Apparently my subconscious prefers the latter. The next thing I know, Winter's paws are digging into my belly. I don't recall reclining on the couch or removing my coat and shoes, much less my socks. Winter lies on his back crammed between the couch and me. My tablet computer is on the coffee table next to my satchel. The screen comes to life when I touch it. A window pops up with a message from Fiona: "Good morning. Shower, brush your teeth, and comb your hair before you do anything else. Anything!"

I check to see if Fiona activated the camera on my tablet computer but no, she knows me well enough that it wasn't necessary. I smell coffee and hear Gwinnie humming to herself in the kitchen. The desire to recline and sink into this world is overwhelming. As I lean back on the couch, guilt stabs me: Lucy.

She's still offline, but her timeweave has split. One branch shows the same fog of uncertainty it had last night and the other branch gives a 47% probability that she's in Aurora, a Chicago suburb. Zooming in, I see that this likelihood rests completely on the fact that her motorcycle is now parked in an Aurora garage.

We still have no unambiguous evidence of her location; her phone's off, she hasn't used a credit card, and Volodya's follow routine has done nothing but violate privacy laws. However, her timeweave does offer one certainty: she is in the United States. Volodya took the risk of accessing the multitude of cameras at all boarder crossings and airports within 700 miles of Chicago. She's also on the FBI's no-fly list. I find this comforting and disturbing and I'm further disturbed that I find it comforting, but not as disturbed as I am by this damn picture that's burned into my cornea: Lucy with Guenther Rader's tentacle around her shoulder.

I set the tablet carefully aside. Winter hops up and dashes into the kitchen where Gwinnie sounds happy to see him.

As the water washes the night from my eyes, I feel encapsulated in Gwinnie's world: the lather of her shampoo, the soap on her loofah, the plush rug on the bathroom floor. I sink into in a reality where I am Gwinnie's husband, but it slips away, as it always does, into a pile of could'ves and should'ves that compose a scrap heap of opportunities unfulfilled.

In the tiny apartment kitchen, Gwinnie prepares for her job at an insurance company in an office where she is beautiful and the people she works with are blessed to share her time. She offers me drip coffee and is beautiful and I want to experience this every day of my life, both past and future –though in my dreams we have a cappuccino maker. There are hints of red seeping through the powdery substance below her eyes. The wide expanse of her forehead is creased with worry, but she greets me with warmth and smiles and raisin-dotted oatmeal.

She says, "Have you found Lucy? Can I talk to her? When is she coming home?"

"We're pretty sure that she's probably in a Chicago suburb."

"Pretty sure? Probably? Pretty sure *and* probably?"

"Her motorcycle is parked in Aurora."

"Well, she wouldn't leave her bike—but why does her phone go straight to voice mail?"

"She's asleep?"

"My daughter does not turn off her phone. Do they have cell phone coverage in this suburb?"

"Yes."

"Simon, something's wrong."

"I need to get back to work." I sip the coffee and take a step into the living room to pick up my tablet computer and then realize that if I show her the photo, she'll recognize Guenther Rader and freak out. I step back toward her.

"What are you hiding from me?"

"Gwinnie …" the two syllables slip off my tongue and make me sound like the spurned lover I have always been to her. Shame colors my face a deeper gray. I fear that I'll never be Gwinnie's hero.

She cups my chin and, as I look up, I see hope in her eyes. I double-check to make certain that it's not pity—which would probably kill me—but it's hope. She says, "Simon, please find her."

A hint of steel works its way up my spine and it once again becomes clear that my height exceeds hers by five inches.

5. Gordon Francis Woodley, IV

2011-Sept-27 Yerba Buena Island
Historic pivot point peak probability: 63 days

The Bay Bridge approach empties into the business end of San Francisco. I sense the many obligations my traffic jam colleagues must tend to before they make the return commute. I am compelled to straighten my tie in solidarity.

It is no different at The Intoxicating Page. Volodya has three flat-screen panels configured in the urban anthropology and fortified wine section. Fiona sits on a mat in a pool of sunlight meditating in the self-help and vitamin water section. Each claims to be in their most productive environments.

Before the door closes behind me, Fiona breaks her trance: "Lucy has come back online."

Concealed by the backs of his three monitors, Volodya adds, "Lucy's social networking accounts are active, it is not clear that Lucy is person operating them."

Fiona folds her leg into a sort of mono-lotus position with her arms extended over her head and hands as high as she can reach, touching in a prayer configuration.

His voice on edge, Volodya says, "Three posts in the last hour, made from her NICs, but not so much her style." Our timeweave calculations use NIC, network interface controller, addresses to determine the location from which social media posts are made, a comparatively low risk hack.

With my satchel on the bar where I can see his face between two of the monitors, I set up in the light beer and sports section. "Is she still in Chicago?"

His head quivers as though it's preparing to lift off. He barks out a syllable, "No." He looks like he's struggling to breathe. "We discovered only now, no fewer than seven hours after her arrival, that she is in," he takes a breath in a way that conveys self-loathing. "She is in Amsterdam."

"Impossible," I say.

"She traveled in disguise. Makeup. Wig. A cap. Hunched over." He struggles with each word.

I say, "But the no-fly list?"

"A bug." He coughs up these two words as though he's swallowed one. "A bug in our software over-weighted her presence on the no-fly list. With makeup, facial recognition was too weak to overrule her use of fake passport and presence on no-fly list." His hands cover his eyes. "No fly-list. We weighed efficacy of the FBI over facial recognition. We had retinal identification! We IDed Rader's gang; knew she was with him." His voice trails off. I wonder if he's weeping.

I open my laptop. Lucy's timeweave has updated and is firm. A link takes me to an image of a black-haired, freckle-free, middle aged woman at O'Hare airport; then another in Amsterdam. I can see why our facial recognition failed. But then I hit a link that brings up video of Lucy looking like Lucy at a bakery in Amsterdam eating a croissant at a table with two of Rader's protégés, Stepan Petrov and Alina Romano.

Volodya puts a satellite shot of Amsterdam on my monitor. "Lucy is with Rader in this building that faces the Prinsengracht canal. Mmm, two kilometers from train station."

Zooming in, I examine the building. We can usually isolate a person's location to a given room, but this only indicates that she's currently in the specific building.

Volodya is aware of my puzzlement; I must have made a "tsk" sound. He says, "She's in a cold spot."

A cold spot is the antonym of a WiFi hotspot. That is, the building has no internet service; neither wireless nor wired. He switches to stale satellite imagery. The roofs of neighboring buildings are gardens of small satellite dishes, antennae, and cabling. This roof has updated ventilation, but no cabling, no technology.

Volodya says. "It would seem that Rader has configured modern equivalent of a hideout. The windows are not blocked, the doors maybe are not locked but is not accessible by software."

"Is it shielded?" I ask. By covering the walls and ceiling of a room or building with a conductor like aluminum foil, wireless transmissions can be blocked.

"The cell-phone base stations provide insufficient resolution to determine if phones inside transmit or receive. I can determine neither who is there nor what are they doing. We know, essentially, nothing."

"Garbage," Fiona says, moving toward us. "We know where Lucy is, we know she's healthy, reasonably safe, and have no reason to believe that she's not perfectly happy. We actually know everything we need to know. What we don't know is none of our business."

"You suggest that we discontinue surveillance?" Volodya asks.

"I didn't say that." Now behind the bar, in the center of it, really, she maneuvers to my right, where the cappuccino maker sits opposite Italian literature, and makes herself an espresso.

I ask, "Are you coming with us?"

"I'll stay here and mind our programmers."

"You will watch Penelope," Volodya says. "But you will not convert her."

In response, Fiona does that thing with her eyelashes that manages to convey a message that is at once innocent and wicked. Beyond those themes, the message escapes me.

Opening my email, I see the itinerary for our flight to Amsterdam, Volodya in first class, Winter and I in coach—KLM has greater respect for dogs than United. The flight leaves in six hours and we'll be staying at a lovely bed and breakfast situated on a tiny island in a broad canal.

My calendar has generated a reminder. Our next deadline is in a fortnight: updated predictions for Gordon Woodley. Sipping a demitasse of espresso sweetened with three teaspoons of honey, I watch Gordon's timeline evolve from its state four days ago when we last met. It should grow from the past to this moment and weave into potential futures, but one hour ago it stops. Just stops, no weaves into the future or even completion to the present.

I say, "Something's wrong with Gordon's timeline." The time-weaves of his secretary and his son Frankie—I mean, Mr. Woodley—diverge from Gordon's into their futures. Refreshing the calculation doesn't make a difference. I zoom in on Frankie, err, Francis's timeline and espresso catches in my throat.

Attacking the keyboard like a bibliophile hitting the highbrow fiction rack near Fiona's extensive selection of single malt scotch, I assume control of the 38 surveillance cameras within a block of Francis. I maximize the priority of the process to enable our Vienna servers to run the computationally intensive facial recognition software so that I can find and watch Francis in real time.

Volodya looks up. Raising my priority reduces his. Such an intrusive search also leaves breadcrumbs that can be tracked back to us. Volodya steps over and stands behind me.

It takes almost 97 seconds for the servers to isolate the cameras along Francis's path. He's walking through a corridor. The tagline in the upper right of the display indicates the camera's network interface controller identifier and physical location. In a separate window I do a Google search on the address, though I don't really need to, Francis Woodley's location is obvious enough. I suppose I just hope that I'm wrong.

I feel Volodya's hand on my shoulder encouraging me to step aside and let him drive the user interface. Fiona comes around the bar, hops over and drapes her arm around my neck.

Volodya directs the orientation of two cameras. Fiona leans over and taps my tablet display, bringing up a monitor that will tell us if anyone tries to override our actions, that is, let us know if we get caught.

One camera shows Francis stooped over with his hands on his forehead. He's wearing a plum colored coat. Tears drip down his face, off his chin, and land on his yellow shirt where they form splotchy-shadows.

The other camera points at Gordon Woodley lying on a gurney in the corridor of New York Downtown Hospital. Fiona says, "Gordon Woodley was taken to a community hospital?"

Nurses in multi-colored scrubs surround a woman who has a stethoscope dangling from her neck and is writing on a clipboard. In the background, two emergency medical technicians in highly reflective jackets lean against a wall. The lack of activity and the frustrated countenances of the healthcare workers reveal the situation.

Fiona says, "Bugger all," and both displays close. Someone with legitimate access to the cameras has overridden our command and she got us out of there.

I'm left with the image of Francis looking at the dead body of his father, Gordon Woodley, the man who, more than any other, made me who I am.

2011-Sept-27 San Francisco
Historic pivot point peak probability: 50 days

For nine months, Gordon Woodley has been inextricably correlated to the coming historic pivot point. His death should shock the system—an unpredictable major perturbation—but it doesn't. The opposite has occurred. Since he died, our prediction of the pivot point's timing has become more precise. What had been a range of 5 to 11 weeks has narrowed to six to nine weeks, peaking 50 days from today and now Berlin dwarfs Oakland in probable location. I look deeper and see that Amsterdam is still possible but not likely.

Gordon's heir, Gordon Francis Woodley, IV, is a 29 year-old man with a negligible database of high-level decisions. His timeweave is now inextricably tied to future history. I need to talk to him.

Volodya and I go to the airport together; he flies to Amsterdam and Winter and I fly back to New York City. The funeral is set for four days hence.

2011-Sept-28 New York City
Historic pivot point peak probability: 49 days

At six minutes after midnight, Winter and I work our way between well-dressed couples into the Gild Hall Hotel Lobby. My itinerary informs me that we're staying at the "coolest hotel in the financial district." I cock my head to the side and throw down a vibe.

"Sir? Are you all right?" a woman asks from behind. Dressed in professional formal clothes, her nametag says Sheila and identifies her as the concierge. Her black and yellow hair matches the lobby's tan leather couches and black tables. She appraises me as though wondering if she should contact the authorities.

I straighten my visage and hold up my itinerary. She guides me to the check-in desk.

The next morning, Winter and I assemble ourselves in the delightful lobby of the cool hotel and set to work. For some reason, Sheila-the-concierge prefers that Winter not avail himself of the splendid couch. He curls up at my feet and we settle into our tasks. He snores and I write software and examine timeweave links. The death of Gordon Woodley derails my thoughts at least every 7 minutes. I try to arrange a meeting with Francis Woodley, but he seems to have become a hermit with his office on the 99th floor his hermitage.

Our second day working in the Gild Hall lobby feels routine. I nod to Sheila and she avoids eye contact with me. Everyone else looks at me as they walk by. Winter takes a spot in the direct path of the elevator where hotel guests can't help but pet him.

Francis finally emerges from his office 51 hours after his father's death. He enters the elevator at 2:03pm. His timeweave gives no indication of his destination; no meetings, just a ranked list of his favorite restaurants, delis, and exclusive clubs. I assemble my laptop, tablet, smart phone, notebook, ink, and quill into my satchel. When I stand, it comes to my attention that a television is affixed to the wall behind the couch. I can't help but chuckle at my own self-absorption. I thought the interest paid to me by passersby resulted from my sophisticated appearance. I am then struck by the fact that I've missed a major news story. There, in closed-captioned headlines is the report of the death of another great American tycoon.

Brandon Birch, CEO and President of Stamford Oil, died this morning of a "a massive heart attack." The statement makes me wonder if he had a massive heart. Photos of Brandon Birch and Gordon Woodley fill the screen and are then replaced by photos of their heirs, Francis and a young man named James Birch with the caption: "New age tycoons."

Winter hops up and down in anticipation of an outing. It's hardly appropriate behavior for a "service dog" and I can feel Sheila's indictment.

My phone displays directions that will put us in Francis Woodley's path. Out the door and a few blocks along, we approach the nickel and gray marble veneer of the building whose top floors house the Woodley-Carlyle Group. Winter tugs at his leash, so I quicken my pace. He begins to trot. As I trot, he gallops, and as I gallop, he sprints.

We turn the corner at Wall Street and nearly bowl over a man. He's wearing a coal suit with narrow pinstripes and a white oxford shirt with a beige and black striped tie. It is Francis Woodley in the costume of his dead father.

"Frankie!" I say. The word escapes me without thought, so I correct it. "Excuse me, I mean, Francis, Mr. Woodley."

He looks down and his eyes pass my face. He glances at Winter and then his gaze stops, fixed on the ground between us.

He says, "My father used to call me Frankie."

"Yes, I apologize for using that endearment."

Still looking at the sidewalk, he says, "No, it's fine. I wish—no, never mind. It's fine, please call me Frankie."

"Thank you, you have no idea how much easier that is."

He looks up at me for an instant. "You knew my father, didn't you?"

"I loved your father."

Had I known the effect of my words, I'd have never uttered them. He chokes as though I've hit him in the solar plexus and bends to a knee. Winter, his long brown ears hanging down, looks up at the man.

Frankie says, "I never told him I loved him. Never. Not even once."

Winter licks his forehead.

The model of Gordon Woodley that still lives in my brain is displeased by this display and before I think to modify my words, they're out: "Frankie, stand up. Wear your garish clothes, be your loutish self, your father did not raise you to be the sort of man to pronounce 'I love you,' he raised you to be a titan of industry."

"What?"

With my statement loose, I can hardly reel it in, but I certainly won't repeat it.

"My clothes?" He says and I cling to the unlikely hope that he didn't hear me. "This is a five-thousand dollar suit."

"But it's not *your* suit," I say, again, seemingly out of control. "It's your father's suit."

"You knew him well, didn't you?"

"He was my mentor, as close to a father as anyone I've ever had." I'm pleased with this sentence but make the mistake of continuing. "So we're like brothers."

Frankie shakes his head. "I keep thinking that he'll show up in a dream so I sleep a lot."

Gordon has now been dead almost 52 hours, which puts a

hard upper limit on how much sleeping he could have accomplished. I ask, "Why now? You could have talked to him any time."

"Because I never listened to him."

"I found his advice quite sage."

"Can you tell me about him?"

Everything about this scenario seems inadequate. My confusion works its way out of my mouth: "What happened to you?"

He stands and looks around as though he doesn't know where he is. "My father died."

It's not what I meant and in my effort to avoid asking the question again, I say, "Frankie, pull it together, you have a critical mission." My hand flies to my mouth and I add, "I apologize for being so forward."

But he smiles and, for the first time, his face appears animated. "That's what my dad would say. You even sounded like him." From this angle, the bags under his eyes are more obvious. It's difficult to believe that he has slept at all.

"Yes, I'm so sorry."

"No," he says. "It's good." Then he looks skyward. "Critical mission. Yeah, that's him All right. Hey, you want to get a drink?"

I look over my shoulder to see who he might be addressing. No one behind me seems to be listening. He guides me along Wall Street, past the Stock Exchange, to Broadway. I can't help looking up at him, even staring; death brings changes, but this is a different man.

He holds the door for Winter and me to enter a tavern. It's dark inside and cluttered. The furniture is worn and the mirror behind the bar hasn't been cleaned in perhaps a generation. A man solicits us in an Irish brogue.

Frankie says, "Tullamore Dew—two."

Two small glasses appear before us. The smell brings to mind James Joyce, Morgan Llywelyn, and Jonathon Swift.

Frankie raises his glass and says, "To my dad."

We drink and Frankie motions for more.

While I do drink frequently, I don't drink much. Two drinks in less than two minutes is quite a bit for me, but I feel compelled by Frankie's momentum and discover that we've each consumed four doses of Irish Whiskey in as many minutes.

Winter yawns and makes his irritated whine.

Frankie asks, "Is your dog okay?"

"Well, he feels a bit left out and he can smell beer everywhere, so naturally …"

"And a beer for the dog!" Frankie says.

"He's partial to hoppy ales, if you have one."

"Hoppy ales?" Frankie laughs and, in the dim light the bags under his eyes disappear.

We exchange stories of his father, conjecture on his goals and the state of his business, a wealth of trivia regarding sports that I don't understand, economic statistics, political predictions, and vile discussions of highly personal acts. The drinks come slower but show no sign of ceasing and my sense of time follows neither a linear nor logarithmic progression.

With the alcohol wending its way through our bloodstreams, I find myself making ill-advised statements and asking questions of dubious value.

"How come you never listened to your father?"

He contemplates before answering and then speaks clearly. "Because I'm stupid."

"But you and your two men, you seemed to have a plan. I rather thought you were intent on your father's resignation and now you have it …"

"Be careful what you wish for."

"You wished Gordon dead?"

"Not dead, just out of the way and now that he is, all my plans seem stupid. But I know they're not. I just, damn. I need his advice." He orders yet another dose and I can hardly refuse, though I've done something that I've never done before: I've lost count.

He says, "Tell me what he'd say. Come on, talk to me, you said he's alive in your head, let him out."

A resigned sort of blissful nausea settles behind my eyes and I start to cry.

"No, no, don't do that. Snap out of it! I've had enough crying."

He takes the back of my neck and pinches me.

"That's what my dad used to do when I pissed him off. Just like that, I used to think he'd lift me up and carry me around by my neck. I hated him for it."

He lets go.

"Gordon Woodley does not want you to become him." Hidden among the debilitating effects of alcohol are seconds of utter clarity. "Look at you, you're dressed like him, you walk like him, now you need his advice? The man is dead. The time to emulate him has passed." And just as it came, the clarity departs.

We sit in that bar for five more hours. I tell him stories about his dad and he says that he always wanted to go to The Grove, but his father discouraged it. He'll start going now in his father's place.

He asks about the meeting I had with his father in a moment of inebriated lucidity that wholly lacks wisdom and I provide numerical details of how Gordon's premature retirement would have affected Woodley-Carlyle's share price. I conclude with: "I'm still trying to calculate how his death affects these results."

He says, "You *calculated* that I couldn't do it?"

"No," I say, aware that I'm missing something but unaware of what, "it was the timing of the handoff. Too soon and either you wouldn't be ready or the company wouldn't be ready and too late and …" but now the alcoholic fog has overwhelmed me and I can barely squeeze out: "It doesn't matter, his death changes the parameters, it changes you, it changes expectations." And it sounds so good that I try to mark it down in my notebook, but the ink sloshes and the quill bends and the paper is smeared.

"You think I can't do it," he says. "You laid odds that I can't do it."

"Maybe, but death changes how your employees and colleagues will—you see, the dynamic is—" I'm nearly thankful that he interrupts me because this sentence has no point.

"What you said was right."

"What I said?"

"Yes, when you were channeling my dad." Now he takes a deep breath. He starts laughing and, as he does, he puts an arm around me. With the other he reaches down and encourages Winter to hop onto his lap. Embracing the two of us, he says, "You're right. I won't become my father. And you know what? I'll take that bet. I say that Woodley-Carlyle shares double within my first three quarters. What do you say to that?"

"You'll do quite well, Frankie."

He wrinkles his face and says, "Call me Mr. Woodley."

2011-Sept-29 Amsterdam
Historic pivot point peak probability: 48 days

Volodya sits on a bench in Amsterdam gazing across the Prinsengracht canal at a block of well-adorned 19th century structures. He pays particular attention to the plain six-story building where Lucy Montgomery is staying, whether or not of her own free will. Where its neighbors have ornate décor, gargoyles, color, and taste, this building reminds Volodya of Soviet architecture, just square windows and brown plaster; nothing to encourage bourgeoisie taste.

Vladimir "Volodya" Kazimer grew up in Moscow, served in the Soviet Army, and studied at Moscow State. His emergence followed the path of his childhood hero, Andrei Sakharov, the Russian physicist who developed the first hydrogen bomb: from admiration for the communist principles of classless equality to tolerance for its seemingly pragmatic bureaucratic exceptions. Then he sought the advice of his hero on a tricky problem in plasma physics and discovered that Sakharov was an enemy of the state being held in internal exile. Volodya's idealism evaporated like so much perspiration and the patriotic lad became a skeptical enemy of a hypocritical, autocratic state.

Young adults come and go from the Soviet-style building. A sign above the door says it's a hostel. Volodya surveys the surrounding block with a radio frequency scanner and confirms that no radiation is transmitted from this building; no WiFi, not even cell phone signals. It's positively prehistoric.

He heads back to the bed and breakfast. Unlike the hostel, the B&B radiates as much charm as it does RF. Situated on a tiny island in the Kasiergracht canal, the many-gabled house is painted a similar brown, but the eaves are decorated with unicorns, dragons, Pegasus, and at the peaks, the Dutch Lion. Flowering plants hang from gutters, and chimneys of stone or brick rise from each room.

Volodya jogs from street level to a stone dock, climbs into a small boat and rows to the island. He steps in, wipes his shoes on a mat, grunts to the proprietor when she offers him coffee, and proceeds to his room. He closes the door and opens a cardboard box that holds a hundred webcams. They're about half the size of a ball point pen and could be much smaller but for the AA battery. The lot of them cost less than a thousand Euro. He opens each part, connects wires to the tiny processor chip, and downloads encryption firmware. After reassembling them, he attaches strips of double-sided foam tape to their housing. Since the little cameras can't transmit their signals farther than twenty meters, he also configures a dozen routers, each about the size of a coffee mug, to retransmit the camera signals through cell phone connections to the lab in Vienna.

The proprietor knocks on his door and presents a pot of coffee. She's at least a decade his senior but where his wrinkles pull his lips ever downward, this woman bears lines from her eyes and mouth that testify to a life spent smiling. He asks to borrow a bike and she offers her own.

Volodya ascends the stone steps to street level and rides to Rader's hostel. The whole city is littered with abandoned bicycles—flat tires, missing wheels, broken chains, rotted seats—locked to every immovable object. He wedges the bike between two others opposite Rader's front door and attempts to stretch a cable from the railing to the bike. Dropping to a knee, he attaches cameras to abandoned bicycles and their corresponding routers to the canal-facing side of a telecommunication patch box. He works quickly and complains with enough guttural sounds to appear like any other grumpy Dutch bicyclist.

Pretending to give up on the prospect of locking his bike here, he moves farther along, attaching cameras to abandoned bicycles, atop a garbage can, and the underside of a bus stop bench and atop its canopy.

Rader's bound to discover the surveillance hardware eventually but will probably assume it was positioned by the CIA, NSA, MI6, BND, Interpol, or FSB, certainly not TLA.

Volodya spends the next three days studying Rader's building. It's more like a dormitory than a hostel. The four younger Occupiers who accompanied Rader to Occupy Wall Street come and go along with a dozen other young adults. They spend a lot of time at the train station. Lucy doesn't emerge from the building, though she occasionally appears in a second story window. The TLA server fleet in Vienna churns through the video and identifies people coming and going. Like the four Occupiers, most have technical degrees and computing experience.

Volodya puts RF and microwave sniffers in front of the building, in back, and in hallways of adjacent buildings. He hires a Belgian student to enter Rader's building with a sniffer and ask for a room. The student reports that they had no vacancy and the sniffer reports no sign of any network or cell phone emissions.

How can hackers survive without wifi?

2011-Sept-30 New York City
Historic pivot point peak probability: 47 days

Winter and I make it back to the Gild Hall Hotel and through the door without falling. My intoxicated haze has turned to an ache and I yearn for the dreamless sleep of the drunkard. I stumble to the couch that has served as my office. The TV above acquires my attention. The same story seems to be running as when I left here in glorious sobriety seven hours ago: death of a tycoon.

But wait, wasn't it an oil Tycoon named Birch who died this morning? My head is too foggy to recall. The closed-caption display reports the death of Charles van Bibber, CEO of Investment America, Inc. Bibber or Birch? Oil or finances? It all runs together. Isn't it all finance?

Our charitable concierge, Sheila, emits a Volodya-quality whinny which draws my attention to Winter who is also reclining on the couch. I rub his belly, look back up, and see images of Gordon Woodley, Brandon Birch, and Charles van Bibber on the TV. Lined up like this, the three men are very similar in appearance; lightly tanned, brownish-gray hair, lovely dark suits with colorful ties, winning smiles, and strong jaw lines. The similarity brings to mind the inbred monarchies that ruled Europe from the enlightenment to the First World War.

The anchor says, "Three powerful men, dead in four days, every one a victim of massive heart failure with no previous history of illness, what are the odds?"

The numbers assemble in my head but for only a second before being washed aside by alcohol, I'll let Volodya tend to the algebra.

The anchor adds, "An FBI source reports that the simultaneous deaths of three corporate icons are not a coincidence. Could an Occupy faction be responsible?"

"No," I mumble. "If Occupy were involved, we'd have seen a branch on their timeweave."

My phone says, "G'day mate," indicating that Fiona would like me to enable my earbug. Before I can emit so much as a "hello," she says, "Have you seen the Woodley-Carlyle timeline?"

"I'm drunk."

"Really?" I can hear the smile in her voice. Fiona is of the firm belief that my drinking habits are insufficient. "Well, look at your tablet, the timeline should be displayed—who got you bombed?"

"Frankie Woodley."

"He'll have enjoyed a much finer afternoon hitting the turps with you than on the stock exchange floor watching his dead father's business collapse."

"What?" I pull my tablet computer from my satchel. The display comes right up, but Sheila has emerged from her desk and now stands beside me.

She says, "What sort of service does this animal provide?"

This question always throws me because I'm uncomfortable lying and the truth never seems to generate a desirable response. Fortunately, Winter experiences no such constraint. He stares up at her and, tail wagging, sits. When she looks at him, he raises his paws, balancing on his haunches in the classic begging posture. As the concierge's expression softens, he falls slowly backward. The concierge reaches out to catch him. Winter's ears flop into his most sympathetic visage. The concierge scratches behind his ears and Winter rubs his muzzle into the space between her breasts.

"Never mind," I say, "Winter has it under control."

"What a good dog," Fiona says. "Now, do you see the timeline?"

"Oh my!"

"Right."

Not only has Woodley-Carlyle stock dropped 50%, but its timeline seems to have merged with that of the other two companies with fallen executives: Stamford Oil and Investment America—whose stock prices have also lost half their value.

"You're in New York City and unaware that the bottom has fallen out of Wall Street?"

I stammer.

"Excellent drinking, Simon."

"Yes, well …" And now the TV monitor shifts from the dead tycoons to the effect of their deaths and the suspicion surrounding their timing: The Dow Jones dropped 1500 points today and the SEC stopped trading. "Oh my."

"Right," Fiona says, "your country has lost 10% of its value in the last two hours."

2011-Oct-1 am New York City
Historic pivot point peak probability: 46 days

I collapsed on the hotel bed nine hours and 11 minutes ago. I describe my plight to room service and they recommend their hangover special: Eggs cooked in fat, potatoes cooked in fat, pancakes covered in butter, bacon and sausage. I prepare a bowl of kibble for Winter prior to gorging on the cholesterol feast.

It hits me as I emerge from a languid shower that Gordon Woodley will be buried today. I look down and sigh. Then it occurs to me that a crashing stock market is a rather fitting tribute.

Foregoing the hotel lobby and Sheila's scrutiny, I set up on a desk-like table in my room, configure the television as a monitor, and populate it with four screens including Bloomberg, CNN, Fox News, and Al Jazeera, all with captions. Each feed has its favorite presumption of the group or groups behind the deaths of Woodley, Birch, and van Bibber—socialists, rival capitalists, Islamists and/or the Russian and/or Chinese governments, or Occupy. The common theme, though reported with varying levels of gloom and glee, is that the corporate infrastructure of the western world is under attack.

I see that Volodya is online so I activate my earbug.

He says, "It is a problem."

"Indeed."

"They are lying or they are fools."

"The media?"

"Of course."

"Have you done the calculation?"

"I see problem, I solve it." He harrumphs. "The deaths correlate to stock market collapse but are precisely the sort of random occurrences in which people find nonexistent patterns. Three men died within one week and they see pattern." He harrumphs again.

I tap the Eeyore icon and see the timeweaves of the three heirs. They barely know each other, but their weaves merge today with large probabilities of ongoing interactions over the next few months indicating that the three are likely to merge their corporate power. I spend an hour stepping through the calculations. Why would these young men, each one an heir to power, collaborate rather than compete?

I pop up a text balloon with the results on both Fiona and Volodya's monitors. Fiona has just come online. She's marking up a menu for the day's drink and literary specials including a Pabst Blue Ribbon-Wall Street Journal combo plate she calls "Pour the suds on the duds."

Fiona puts a note on my display: "The funeral is in one hour."

* * *

My black suit is hopeless. The lapels don't lie flat, the pocket flaps stand up, the pants have myriad creases, none vertical, and my tie is stained. Only now do I recall Fiona telling me to drop the suit off at the Men's Wearhouse when I arrived in New York. Sheila brings a handheld steam iron to my room, but when she realizes that it's me, she recommends that I stand in the bathroom with the shower running. Doing so has little effect.

Police officers line Broadway outside Grace Church, some in riot gear.

Frankie stands at the door accepting condolences. As I approach, it happens again. This time I see it coming and allow myself to surrender for an instant. It is Gordon two decades before we met; a man who owns the world and carries his wealth as responsibility. As it passes, my breath catches in my throat. I'll miss my mentor.

Frankie takes my hand in both of his and it happens yet again. I say, "Mr. Woodley, care well for your empire."

He releases my hand and passes me to his mother. Since women aren't allowed to visit The Grove, I never met any of Gordon's wives. Frankie is the offspring of the third. She's a tall woman with, I recall Gordon saying, "legs up to HERE." The sound of Gordon's voice in my mind generates a sob that triggers a hug from the new widow.

The pews are lined with the most wealthy and powerful people in the United States. Three former presidents sit in adjacent rows and the Secretary of State sits with her husband.

Jack Welch offers me a seat beside his wife, Suzy. He's an intimidating man when sober, but today he's a somber gentleman. Winter hops up and sits between us. Suzy's taken aback until Winter rests his muzzle on her thigh and peers up to her with his most winsome gaze.

Frankie walks his mother to a front pew. A trail of whispered outrage forms in his wake. He's wearing a form-fitting suit of astoundingly non-reflective black; no doubt a synthetic carbon material. His tie is equally black but shiny and his shirt is black, too, with a coefficient of reflectance midway between the suit and the tie. It seems like well-chosen clothing for a funeral, ideal really. But then Suzy Welch indicates Frankie's shoes: purple Converse All Stars. Rather than outrage, I find the contradiction in form appealing. Frankie should mourn, but he should not succumb. The rivalry between bull and calf deserves respect and the rebellious choice of shoes demonstrates this respect. I look at my own shoes. Brown oxfords a decade old, reasonably scuffed—and, oh my, they clash horribly with my black suit.

Sixteen men stand and tell tales that demonstrate admiration for my mentor; stories of golf, board rooms, and the exercise of power that generate a mix of melancholy and laughter, a dance of denial and inevitability. As the mourners adjourn and an interval forms prior to placing Gordon in his final resting place, Winter and I lag behind, never more than ten steps from Frankie. Wallace van Bibber joins Frankie first. Then, right on queue, James Birch steps over.

Watching my timeweave calculations take shape in the present, I nearly feel as though I've scripted this meeting.

Wallace, the oil heir says, "No way do a bunch of lazy, latter-day hippies have the ability to pull that off." His jet-black suit is complemented by boat shoes and he carries a fedora.

Wallace, in a conservative dark suit designed for funerals says, "Ridiculous. Dad had the best security money can buy."

Wallace and Wallace turn to the coffin and look at Gordon's corpse. Wallace says, "He ran a tight business."

Wallace adds, "You think Islamo-fascists did it?"

Frankie: "It just seems weird that they all died at the same time of the same thing."

Wallace says, "The bozos in blue sure won't help."

Wallace: "Did you know that the police only solve 40% of murders and less than 10% of reported crimes?"

Wallace: "And that 80% of statistics are made up?"

Wallace: "Unless some terrorist group takes credit, we'll never know."

Wallace: "Cops are incompetent because they're unionized: no competition, no efficiency."

Frankie: "Jim, you nailed it."

The other two had been standing with their back to the coffin, but now the three of them form an isosceles triangle with Frankie facing his dead father.

Shuffling closer to their triangle, I'd like to assure them of the lack of correlation between their fathers' deaths. But Frankie rotates in a way that blocks me and I don't feel assertive enough to disrupt their conversation.

Frankie: "As long as governments stand in the way of corporate progress it will just get worse, regulations, regulations, and regulations."

Wallace: "That's what the Occupiers should be protesting, but they can't see through that ninety-nine percent versus one percent propaganda."

Frankie: "If supply and demand were left to do its innovative magic we could eliminate war and poverty."

Wallace: "Until one country goes broke and attacks another."

Wallace: "No. That's a 'we've got the bomb' concept, get over it. Obsolete thinking."

Frankie: "For a country to attack, it has to have soldiers who don't question generals. But with the market unleashed, there would be no generals, just employers. The only way employers can motivate workers to risk their lives is if they pay really well. See? The wealthy countries wouldn't need to fight and the poor countries couldn't afford to."

Wallace: "Mercenaries?"

Frankie smiles and puts his arm around Wallace. "Wally, my friend, as long as there are governments, there will be war. Governments don't make sense in globalization."

Wallace: "He's right. Governments are quaint relics of history."

The funeral director approaches and whispers to Frankie who nods to the other two young men. They exit the church on Broadway where a long line of expensive cars, plus a few taxis, and of course the hearse, prepare to guide Gordon Woodley's corpse to Green-Wood Cemetery in Brooklyn. Confusion arises over the procession route. It seems that the Brooklyn Bridge has been Occupied. Freshly printed maps are distributed directing the procession through the Carey Tunnel.

A fellow software ace invites Winter and me to join him and his wife in a limousine. Were he not so fond of Winter, I'd find it difficult to refrain from suggesting that Mr. Gates' employees pay proper respect to memory management.

At the cemetery, Winter and I maneuver close enough to

Frankie to continue eavesdropping. He takes a list from his pocket and calls three men over. He does a double take at the list and then waves to James Birch and Wallace van Bibber. "Your dads were supposed to be pall bearers, will you guys stand in?"

Gordon Francis Woodley, III, is buried at the feet of Gordon Francis Woodley, Jr. who is buried at the feet of Gordon Francis Woodley and there is plenty of space to continue the trend.

6. Utopia

2011-Sep-26 to 2011-Oct-3 Amsterdam

Guenther Rader monitors Lucy's reactions as they walk from the train station to the hostel. She laughs at the Torture Museum, gawks at the coffee shops, and pauses to take in Amsterdam's beauty at the Herengracht. He leaves her at a café to have coffee and croissants, a chance for her to settle down before her reeducation. Two hours later, Rader guides Lucy upstairs to a small, windowless room. Other than ceiling-high bookcases that cover three walls and a knit oval rug, the room is unfurnished. Rader believes that removing consumer goods helps people realize the irrelevance of such comforts to a well-lived life.

He stops one step inside and takes Lucy by the shoulders. Looking down into her eyes, he says, "Have you had a teacher who you disliked at first but who later became your favorite?"

Lucy says, "Ummm, I guess."

"Please try to remember that." He releases her shoulders and sits on the floor with his back against the bare wall. "We call this the library. It has everything you need. You'll come to love this room, everyone does. There's a bathroom across the hall."

He taps the spot next to him. Lucy leans her backpack against a bookcase, takes out her laptop, and sits next to him. She opens to a blank internet browser.

Rader holds out his hands. "Give me that."

"What?" Lucy says.

"You won't need it." He pulls the laptop out of her grasp and sets it aside. "The internet is a portal and we can't let anything in that's uninvited, nor can we let anything out that we haven't released." He takes a spiral-bound notebook and a pen from a bookcase and hands it to her. "You need to concentrate. To save the 99%, you must understand how movements like ours have succeeded and failed in the past."

"You want me to read hardcopy? Actual books?"

He nods.

"All of these? But, Gus, we need to act now. Right now, while we have media buzz."

"You are, of course, free to do anything you like. I have no more authority over you than you have over me. But if you leave, they will find you." Starting from her eyes and working downward, he looks her over, taking in her T shirt and her jeans. Her cute little boots, designed to mock genuine utilitarian footwear. "Lucy, you have no idea what you're doing and no concept of the forces against you. You are a stupid little Bourgeoisie girl desperately in need of enlightenment."

She glares back at him and rises to her feet, a small act of defiance that kindles his hope. His expectations soar even as he realizes how much work will be required for her to learn self-discipline.

Lucy says, "The 99% is behind me right now but won't be forever. We have to act!""

Rader takes two books from the shelf, *The Formation of a Persecuting Society* and *Anarchy Harmony*, puts them in her hands, and says, "I suggest you get started." He walks out, carrying her laptop and phone, and closes the door.

Behind him, he hears Lucy try to turn the knob.

He says, "The door sticks a little," and proceeds along the hall to a kitchen where a dozen young men and women sit around tables or perch on counters talking and laughing. Like Lucy, they know him as Gus Reser, a kind, wizened gentleman who they can rely on for shelter, food, and, when they need it, bail. Rader appreciates and relies on them, too.

Guenther Rader was born during the Soviet liberation of Berlin two kilometers from the ruins of Hitler's bunker. His formative years were spent admiring the emotionless efficiency of the Soviets. As the ruins grew into a utilitarian city, he developed faith in the power of a classless state built on respect for the honest, hardworking producers of the world. On his 16th birthday, the Soviets erected the Berlin wall. Two years later he patrolled it as a guard. He shot three traitors as they tried to escape and earned a post in the German Democratic Republic. As part of the apparatchik army, he began to see that the political elite treated common people no better than the Nazis had before them or the capitalists did on the other side of the wall. It disgusted him, but he never gave in to it, always managed to see the possibilities. Rader shares this idealism with the young people who make up his Council, his own personal Soviet.

He walks into the kitchen, smiles at Alina Romano and she slips off the counter. He found Alina in Palermo protesting Mafia-corrupted environmental policy. Rader exchanged a long-overdue favor for her freedom, probably saving her life.

She heads down the hall where she'll spend the day with Lucy studying *No Gods, No Masters* and *Anarchy, State, and Utopia*. They'll discuss how Europe's anti-austerity movement and Occupy fit in the history of popular rebellion and the mistakes that have destroyed movements in the past. After Alina, Stepan Petrov will work with Lucy through the night. Rader helped Stepan escape the FSB after he hacked a Russian government website and posted gay rights propaganda. Where Alina has political savvy and a keen understanding of the tools of revolution, Stepan brings pacifism and geek-credibility. He'll show Lucy some of the computing tools they've developed for poking the monster of world order. If she works hard, he'll also bring her a chair.

Members of Rader's council continue their rotation, keeping Lucy awake and immersed. After 24 straight hours, she's given a glass of water. After 48, they bring her a desk. Every time she complains or dozes or asks for food or drink her resolve is questioned and every time her resolve is questioned, she spends ten minutes alone, after which she is awoken for another lesson.

Finally, after three days awake with only water to drink, Alina brings her an altogether different tool.

"You are tired of history and politics?"

Lucy rubs her eyes.

Alina holds out a small black pistol.

Lucy shakes her head as though trying to clear her mind. "A gun?"

"Of course."

"But I, we, how can—God, I can't think straight. A gun? No. This is too weird."

Alina puts the gun in Lucy's hand. She accepts it but holds it by two fingers as though it could infect her.

"Why? What for?"

"For revolution," Alina says.

"No, no, no, this is, no, I don't think so." Lucy sets the gun on the far corner of her desk.

"Stupid Americans, you think you know everything. You don't know how to shoot. You don't know how to build bomb. Why you waste my time." She stands and walks out.

Rader steps in.

"Gus," Lucy says, pointing at the gun. "What's that for?"

"Guns are instruments, that is all. Don't fool yourself about who you're up against. Don't forget Chicago. If I hadn't been there, they would have found an excuse to kill you."

"But, Gus, Occupy isn't about hurting people. We'd lose our credibility—"

"Not about hurting people?" He says and thrusts a laptop at her. "Really?"

He clicks an icon that starts video of a special TV report on Officer Justin.

"You hurt this innocent man. He's been suspended from the police department for aiding and abetting a prisoner—you. His children can't walk three blocks to school without being harassed so his wife moved out and took the kids with her."

Her voice quivers. "How could they do this to him?"

Rader says, "You ruined his career. You destroyed his family. Had you understood the world, you could have engaged him without destroying him."

"Why? Why would they be so mean?" Her voice dissolves into weeping.

"Not about hurting anyone?" He switches to video of the cop clubbing Penelope while she lies on the ground and then the man in the Giants cap being yanked over the barricade by two cops. "This was your fault. Your lack of preparation brought this on these innocent people."

"Me?" She chokes out the syllable.

"You tricked that poor cop. Your friends were there to back you up and you abandoned them."

"I did? No, I was with them—"

"No, you ran away. You got on your motorcycle and rode to safety while the cops beat the shit out of your friends."

She can't hold back the tears any longer. Maybe if she'd had some sleep she could find enough bravado to push back, maybe if she weren't so hungry she could think of a question, but she's too confused and everything Gus says makes sense. The big picture she's been studying is all about the subtleties of messaging and symbolism. And she rode away. She ran away.

"You did this. If you continue in ignorance how many more must suffer?" He pauses the video and points out her friends being beaten and cuffed. "Do you understand what you have done to these innocent people?"

She nods and he repeats the question again and again. The video shoes more blood, pepper spray, and injustice and then ends with the police protecting that man in the bright green sport jacket as he shakes a fist at the Occupiers.

Finally, she screams, "Yes, it was my fault!" And finally cries for someone other than herself.

"You think the 1% will submit to your will because you're right and they're wrong? Do you think they will accept change merely because it's just? Do you think they will not hurt people, kill them to protect their empires?" He hugs her and whispers in her ear, "Of course not, but if you study and learn how to use a scalpel, then you can cut out the cancer without hurting the innocents. That's my advice." He takes the laptop and snaps it shut. "Do whatever you like."

A few minutes later, he returns with a cot, a sleeping bag, and a sandwich.

2011-Oct-3 Amsterdam Centraal Train Station
Historic pivot point peak probability: 45 days

Volodya greets me at the Amsterdam train station. Even before we emerge from the glorious old building into the stately city, he says, "Probability now peaks at 45 days, distribution average is 49. The clock ticks and we know nothing."

"Nothing?"

"Nothing."

We take a streetcar to the Kaisergracht canal where the three of us climb into a small rowboat. Winter advances to the bow and Volodya rows us a dozen meters to our tiny island-based Bed and Breakfast hideout. I succumb to jet lag, sleep through the afternoon, and wake at dawn to Winter demanding his morning constitutional. He annexes the island, and returns in 70 seconds. Volodya meets us in the common area and I set up on a sofa and Winter takes a spot in front of the gas fireplace. The matron of the B&B brings me coffee and provides four sugars and plenty of cream at my request and without criticism. I love the Dutch.

Volodya's working on a new algorithm to decipher Rader's timeline. It integrates information from the cameras he set outside Rader's hostel, cameras that get clear shots of him, and intersections with his contacts and his contacts' contacts, rather like trying to build someone's personality by how others treat him.

Volodya says, "There is something that I don't like."

"The coffee is wonderful."

Volodya sips his black, unsweetened coffee—the very thought makes me cringe. "We cannot operate without access to their system." He stares into the darkest corner of the small room. "I am buried in software development." He looks at me. "You must solve other problem."

I say, "The problem of how a band of hackers operates without an internet connection?"

"Yes. Should be trivial." Volodya defines the word trivial in the tradition of Russian theoretical physicists: unsolvable problems are challenges, solvable problems are trivial.

I hack into the Dutch Telecom network and search for signals that access Rader's building. After two days mining the tedious layers of routers, repeaters, and add/drop equipment, I've found no connections. If Rader has internet access inside the building, it is not through a cable, it is not wireless, it is not through a satellite link, and it is not associated with Dutch Telecom.

Unwilling to admit my failure—just as Volodya has not reappeared in the common area of the B&B in these two days indicates that he's making no headway with Rader's timeweave—I surrender to Winter's suggestion of genuine legwork. To start off on a positive foot, I pack a network interface controller, a router, and several cheap video cameras in my satchel.

We cross the canal, trot up the stairs, and walk to the Prinsengracht, the canal facing Rader's hostel. We sit at a tiny table outside a café where I can see Rader's doorway and my laptop can survey wifi signals. With the knowledge I've acquired from Dutch Telecom, it's easy to trace the signals to buildings and to the people connected.

2011-Oct-7 Prinsengracht, Amsterdam

Lucy wakes on the floor next to the cot in a pile of books and notes. She stretches her legs and rubs her neck. At first she thinks she's back at college in Berkeley, but as the dreams dissipate and she looks around the room, she sees the pistol on the desk and it all comes back to her.

"Good morning, Lucy."

Gus's voice startles her. He's sitting on the cot behind her.

"Oh, hi." She yawns and rubs her eyes. "What time is it?"

"Time to overthrow the one percent, my friend!"

"Oh. Yeah. I can't seem to get over the jet lag."

"It's time to get back to work, sleepy head." Gus stands and offers her his hand. She takes it and he guides her to the kitchen.

The kitchen is packed with people and now she knows them, some of them pretty well. Stepan pulls out a chair and she sits next to him. Gus fixes her a cup of coffee and she helps herself to a croissant. The room buzzes with ideas. Adriaan wants to rescue his hero, Aaron Swartz, the computer scientist who faces 30 years in prison for making academic research journal articles available to everyone for free.

Klaus, the only member of the group who hasn't spent a shift studying with Lucy in the library—at 27, he's the oldest and is always coming and going—suggests they hack into court computers and replace Swartz name with that of Dick Cheney. Everyone laughs.

Lucy can't remember ever feeling like a part of such a close knit group of people who get it. She eats and drinks and listens and talks.

Gus comes back an hour later and takes her upstairs to another windowless room. This one is easily ten times the size of the library. A huge round table is centered in the room with a dozen wooden chairs. Each place is set with a keyboard, mouse and monitor, like a computing dining room. Most of the seats are occupied and the ticking of keyboards accompanies laughter and conversation. The walls have chalkboards covered in flow charts and calculations.

Adriaan asks her to sit next to him.

Lucy says, “Finally, internet access—I’ve been getting withdrawal.”

Stepan says, “No, we develop and test code here, but deploy it from one of our hotspots.”

“What? No internet here, either?”

“Security,” Stepan says.

Lucy looks up and sees Gus looking back from the door. He smiles at her, a warm grin that reminds her of her grandfather.

2011-Oct-9 Amsterdam
Historic pivot point peak probability: 39 days

Young adults come and go from the hostel in the way of young adults, conversing, joking, flirting. Lucy is not among them. Klaus is the only one of Rader’s gang that comes and goes alone. I spend three days working from this table watching the flow of Rader’s gang while I install and back test new economic and behavioral models that promise to improve our timeweave predictions by a percent or two. Finally, that bastion of solid advice, my beagle, demands escape from the tedium.

The Adriaan Buijs exits the hostel with two others. They walk past us, I rise from our table and follow. By peeing on every stationary object, Winter provides the means for them to acquire enough of a lead that they’re unlikely to detect us. During one such urination, I realize that my seat at the café might be visible from a window in Rader’s hostel.

For a moment I feel altogether busted, but then I survey the scene. Another man, roughly my age, and wearing a similar comfy suit strides past with a small dog, then I see yet another man in a tweed jacket across the river with a terrier. I cheerfully conclude that Winter and I are positively incognito. Of course, the other men are considerably taller than me; the Dutch are a race of giants.

We follow Rader’s protégés to the train station where they enter the Burger King adjacent to the inner platform. Winter and I maintain our nonchalance by taking a seat on a bench facing track 4 where we have a clear view of the thin giant and his two normal-sized colleagues. They set up their laptops at a table. A train arrives and obstructs our view. With four tracks between us, it's amazing we had those few minutes of direct observation.

I launch a program that scans wireless internet connections within the train station. I'm puzzled by the random flux of dozens of WiFi signals until I realize that every passing train provides its own unique network to its passengers. Narrowing my analysis to the station's network, I search for the three hackers' connections. I spend the day invading the privacy of 1007 people, none of them related to Rader's gang.

Back at the train station the next day, I stare at the fluctuating Ethernet connections of passing trains. One delayed train sits on its track for hours and I notice that three computers connect and then disconnect and then connect again at random but short time intervals.

"Brilliant!" I say and Winter hops to his feet. "Why have Volodya and I never thought of this?" By switching among networks, never staying connected to one for more than 128 seconds, they can't be hacked unless the hacker knows the sequence of connections in advance; a form of meta-encryption. More than an encrypted signal, it is an encrypted connection.

We wait for Rader's apprentices to leave and then Winter and I saunter to Burger King. While Winter distracts the diners, I attach cameras to the bottoms of tables and along the frames of fast-food art—I'm stunned at the realization that the introduction of the BK Broiler has escaped my attention—and affix the router and network interface controller under a central table. We should now be able to access Rader's system, solve his timeline, and predict his timeweave.

2011-Oct-10 New York City

Gordon Francis Woodley, IV, opens the door of his penthouse apartment to welcome his new business partners: James Birch and Wallace van Bibber. "Thanks for coming."

"I want to hear your idea," James says. "And drink your scotch."

"Stick with the Lagavulin 16, don't dip into the good stuff."

"Mind if I light a cigar?"

"Mind if I fart in your face?"

"Come on guys." Wallace frowns. "We're here to do business."

"Wally is right," Frankie says, pouring himself and Wallace glasses of wine as James helps himself to a full measure of scotch. "Remember what we talked about at my dad's funeral?"

James says, "That government is obsolete?"

"I think I have the solution." Frankie keeps a close eye on Wallace. "What if governments could be replaced by corporations?"

Wallace says, "That's crazy."

"You know that competing corporations are more efficient than governments; better at solving problems, better at administration, better at everything." Frankie sips his wine and stands in front of the couch where the other two men now sit. "The three of us have more money, and therefore more power than many governments."

"My dad used to say that democracy requires compromise and compromise destroys great ideas." Wallace speaks slowly. "But some things can't be done in the private sector: military, highways, the justice system, those will never be profitable."

"Corporations are perfectly capable of taking on everything you listed. Government does a horrible job building roads and bridges, providing police services, and fire protection."

"Privatized police and fire? Are you crazy? A fire department that invoices its customers?"

"Well, if you don't like that approach, move to a country with a different one."

James shifts to face Wallace. "I've always thought police and fire should operate on an insurance model."

"Now hold on," Wallace says, "No military means no freedom. The Chinese and Russians will be invading at about the time the Muslims get their dirty bombs in your capital or your headquarters, whatever you call it."

"Solvable," Frankie says. "China and Russia don't have democracy in their way and both countries are ruled by successful businessmen like us, they'll love this idea. And why not corporate-religious countries? Try it, see if it works, if a theocracy becomes utopia, sign me up." Wallace looks more dubious. "But I've gotten ahead of myself," Frankie says. "The idea is pretty simple. We want to unleash the forces that drive progress in nature—evolution, natural selection, law of the fittest—the same forces that drive markets in economies gave people the biggest brains in nature. Getting government out of the way will unleash the natural forces of competition and drive innovation like never before."

"But only the rich will survive," Wallace says. "We have an obligation to the working class. It's one thing for the weak and stupid, but we can't sit up here and watch hard working people fail."

"Let's talk about failure," Frankie says. "A healthy fear of failure made sense in medieval times when failure meant death, but it doesn't anymore. And failure is the only way that we learn. Right?" He waits for Wallace to nod. "Now, if a thousand different types of governments competed for citizens, we'd learn more about the underlying forces of economics in one decade than has been learned in all of history."

James says, "But governments don't compete, they hold their citizens hostage."

"Governments evolved from tribes," Frankie says, "and tribes formed to protect people from the elements."

"And from other tribes," James says, swirling the amber liquid in the light. "Governments are paranoid and their fear of failure holds everyone back."

"James, let me finish. Everyone has the same goals: peace, prosperity, and freedom, but no one knows how to achieve them for everyone, every country and every citizen. Everyone. I don't have the solution but I know that the way to find solutions is to try different approaches. If people could choose the countries where they live—totally open borders—then they would choose to live in the best countries."

"Open the border?" Wallace says. "Let Mexico overrun the US?"

"Only as long as the US has better living conditions than Mexico."

"That would just bring equal misery to everyone."

"If all of the world's wealth were fixed, like one pie that we all tried to take a slice from, then sure, equal misery for all, but it's not fixed, it's not a pie, it's a fertile field. We create wealth all the time: inventions, solutions to new and old problems, increased productivity." Frankie raises a hand to keep James from interjecting while Wallace considers. "The country that provides the most desirable living conditions would attract the strongest workforce. Once unemployment rises or wages decrease, people would move to a better country. It's simple, we do it all the time. Unleash market forces on political problems."

Wallace picks up his wine glass and takes a sip. Frankie watches him work through the concept. The brow furrows, he rubs his chin, shakes his head, and then his brow relaxes, like tumblers falling into position. Finally, Wallace smiles. He says, "What will we call them? Countries? Corporations? How about 'Corporatries'?"

"Corporatries," Frankie says. "I love it !" He feels like he's imitating his father. "We need to act now and the first step is to buy the land where we can start building corporatries. The great recession has given us an opportunity we'll never get again. Between the three of us, we might be able to buy Greece."

James says, "Do they sell countries on Craig's List?"

"You guys in?" Frankie points at James who nods and then

Wallace who shrugs and says, "I'm buying real estate by the square mile right now anyway."

Frankie reaches under the table and pulls out three folders. He hands them around and says, "Turn to page three, I've already got a team studying the finances of collapsing European countries. Greece, Ireland, and Spain get the media attention, but some eastern European countries are starving for capital. We can buy hundreds of square miles of lush hillsides with old-Europe charm, subdivide and then: may the best corporatries win."

"Sounds good," James says. He swallows the last drop and adds, "But there are big fat elephants and donkeys in the room."

"Of course," Frankie says. "Turn to page seven. In the last three years we've seen exactly how to get the politicians out of the room. Kill the economy and people will give up their addiction to government. We can trigger a recession that will make the so-called Great Recession look like a night on the town. And we can do it with in a way that increases our wealth. Then, we'll be able to buy whole countries. We have to start first, though."

"Sure, need prototypes." James pours another scotch. "Crashing a market is easy, stampede the herd. Nothing panics easier than the mob and then everyone will sell everything all at once. Boom. End of economy, ready to start over."

Wallace says, "The SEC won't allow us to dump our holdings."

"We'll have sold long before the panic. The SEC won't even exist by the time anyone clues in to what we've done. If we plan it right and get the right allies …"

"But so many people are suffering through this recession," Wallace says. "If we make it worse, people will die."

Frankie walks around the coffee table, sits next to Wallace, and takes his hands. "There has always been suffering, but this will be the last time. Market forces have to be allowed to work their magic or people will continue as they always have, oppressed and impoverished, our corporatries can bring real civilization. We can do it."

"Jesus said, 'The poor you will always have with you,' but if you're right, I mean if there's even a chance that you're right," Wallace raises his glass, "we have to try. Decency demands that we try."

2011-Oct-10 Prinsengracht, Amsterdam

Guenther Rader and Klaus Schmidt, the old man from East Germany and the young man from West Germany, sit in Rader's office. Schmidt is the only one in the hostel who knows Rader's real name.

Rader sips black coffee and ponders the best way to broach the subject. "You did well in New York. You created Lucy Montgomery."

"What? I couldn't get close enough to take down that pig."

"No, Klaus, dear boy. You don't understand." He sips the coffee. "You created the phenomenon of Lucy Montgomery by catalyzing the process."

"What do you mean, catalyze?"

"By pushing that man across the barricade, you created the conditions for Lucy and that pig to respond. A catalyst enters a system and instigates change but emerges unchanged."

"The deed?"

"Yes, the deed that generated the propaganda—and what a message she delivered. Klaus, I have been searching for a symbol like Lucy all my life. She presents a momentous opportunity that we must not waste."

"You have a plan?"

"Why did you push that man at that time?"

Klaus leans forward and his blonde hair hangs over his face. From behind that veil, he says, "A hunch, I suppose. That man, a bit older than the others, white, he had on a nice watch and wore the cap of an American Football team—"

"He was a symbol."

"Yes, and he seemed already agitated. Then a man across the

barricade, the Wall Street capitalist, you know, the one in the green suit, pointed a finger at him and the pigs moved in to protect the damn oligarch." Klaus pushes his hair back. "I could feel it. I just knew that he was the trigger so I pulled it."

"You see, that one action catalyzed the creation of Lucy as a symbol of our struggle. If you had overreacted, joined the battle, she wouldn't have happened. Oh, there would have been a battle, plenty of turmoil but nothing would have emerged but bad press. Instead, Lucy is loved even by people who hate us. She gets nothing but favorable press—and lots of it. That, my friend is 'propaganda of the deed.'"

"How do we make the next leap?"

"Just as you did. We expose our symbol to the political elements and search for that one deed, a single action that will wake the masses to action." Rader strokes his chin. "Symbolism must be simple. Lucy must remain innocent and the establishment must commit an act of obvious injustice."

2011-Oct-11 Prinsengracht, Amsterdam

Lucy has now been in Amsterdam for two weeks. She moved out of the library and into a room with Alina this morning. She stretches out on her bed and stares up at the sky through the window next to her. Alina sits at the desk with a laptop.

Lucy says, "I get the distinction between organizing and leading, but I don't see how we get from to fair, classless, do-ocracies."

Alina says, "Authority, she is imposed on people by fascists—autocrats, oligarchs, plutocrats, presidents—all same thing. Remove them and the natural goodwill of the people emerges."

"Won't there always be charismatic figures with a desire for power?"

"Blast authority out of the system all at once by a great explosion."

From the doorway, Stepan says, "*Nyet*, use finely tuned algorithm, not explosion. Finesse not bloodshed."

Alina laughs.

Stepan sits on Alina's bed across from Lucy. He says, "You have learned about the propaganda of the deed—how to shock the system. Violent revolution is one way, and maybe that's what it will take. Alina thinks so but I don't. I think we can bring down the beast with technology."

Alina says, "Stepan is a pacifist." She slides onto the bed next to him. "Were he not so cute, I should break him."

Stepan: "Lucy's a pacifist, too."

Lucy: "Gandhi, King, even Nelson Mandela—I mean, eventually—all the successful revolutions of the twentieth century were pacifist revolutions."

Alina: "Like Tiananmen Square? The Bolsheviks? Mao's cultural revolution? No such thing as peaceful revolution."

Lucy: "The Velvet Revolution."

Stepan: "Soviet Union already was in turmoil by the time Vaclav Havel organized his revolution."

Alina: "Havel, I spit on him, a Western pawn."

Lucy: "Hey, Vaclav Havel is my hero, okay? He believed in freedom."

"Capitalist freedom," Alina says. "You need more time in the library." She wraps her arm around Stepan, but his attention remains focused on Lucy. "Self-interest must be destroyed for a classless system to happen. Property cannot be owned. It cannot be private."

Lucy: "That's why people think anarchy is chaos."

Stepan: "Lies that the establishment has fed us for centuries."

Lucy looks at each of her new friends. Stepan smiles back at her. Alina looks frustrated, as usual. This room, the conversation, the camaraderie reminds her of college. Except, in college these discussions were purely figurative. These people are serious and it scares her. Just because the FBI has decided she's a terrorist, doesn't mean she wants to become one. She says, "Okay, say we manage to cripple authority and de-establish the establishment. And let's assume we can do it with a finely tuned algorithm." She smiles at Stepan and he smiles back. "How do we keep new bosses from taking over?"

Alina: "The Bolsheviks removed the oligarchs just to follow charismatic figure. French revolution led to fascist Napoléon."

Stepan responds to Lucy as though Alina hasn't spoken, "Do you understand the concept of emergence?"

Lucy: "You mean like beehives and swarms?"

Stepan: "*Da*, complex, self-organized systems emerge when large numbers of components follow simple rules. Bees are stupid insects, but within hives, they communicate, tell directions, choose a queen—"

"Ah, a queen!" Alina interrupts. "She is authority."

Stepan glances at her and says, "No, she's not." Then he turns back to Lucy. "In a hive, the workers choose one egg, feed it royal jelly, and it becomes what is called the queen, but she never leaves the hive. She does just reproduce. She does not command others. The hive emerges as a well organized entity without leadership. Same thing led to you. A planet formed from stardust made of chemicals that interact through simple rules of electromagnetism and then, four billion years later: a photo of Lucy Montgomery with a New York City cop changes world. This is emergence."

Alina: "*Ecco*!"

Lucy: "So if we can shock the system enough to disable the foundation, then we'd have to make people follow some rules? I still don't get it."

"No," Alina says, moving back to the desk. "You don't get it because you are—"

Stepan: "The rule is simple, we do it already. We do it in this house. We do it in families and people have always done it. One simple rule: we respect each others rights."

Alina turns away.

Lucy leans back on the bed. "But there has always been authority. If we could have been a hive, how did we get here instead?"

With her back to Stepan, Alina says, "When people stop respecting authority, there will be no Napoleons, no Caesars, no Presidents. To get there we must destroy establishment."

"Or, we destroy money," Stepan says. "Money is faith in authority. If we destroy its value then all capital disappears and with it, all authority. No rich people, no poor people, just equal people." He turns to Alina but she doesn't look back at him. "And no need for dynamite."

Lucy: "Is that what you guys are doing? Are you hacking banks and—what are you doing?"

Stepan: "Money is erasable. Debt and wealth are nothing but numbers stored on computers, networked computers."

Alina: "By destroying the conmen and their power, we can stop this religion of consumerism. When we respect each others rights we will come together and understand what we need, what we really need."

Stepan: "Imagine a place where everyone can be free to express their own talents."

Lucy: "You mean where we can all get high and make art?"

The three of them laugh, but their laughter is interrupted by a deep voice from the doorway. Gus says, "Would that be so bad?"

For an instant, Lucy feels like she's been caught smoking by the principal. In the next instant, she recognizes the knee-jerk reaction to a lifetime of accepting authority. She sits up straight and says, "Gus, come on in." He steps in and Lucy pats the bed next to her and he sits. Lucy says, "Alina, Stepan—come on, see how we react to Gus? We can't help but respect his authority."

Gus says, "I have no authority. Don't need it, don't want it."

Lucy turns back to Stepan. "I get it, but I think it will take generations for people to stop respecting authority."

"Maybe not," Gus says. "You have heard of the *Wiehnachtsfrieden*? During World War One, the week before Christmas, German and British soldiers stopped fighting, climbed out of the trenches and came together. They talked. They played football, they buried their dead together. They were brothers for almost a week, until the high command began to punish 'fraternization' with execution and ordered them to resume killing one another. You see? It can happen." He smiles at her and adds, "It is up to you."

"Me?"

"Yes, the leader who does not lead, the organizer who people respect instead of fear." Gus takes a breath and looks at Lucy, looks deep into Lucy's eyes as though challenging her in a staring contest. She stares back. The room is silent for minutes and then he blinks first. "Lucy, if you work hard enough and use your tools wisely, you can recreate civilization." He looks away from her, scanning the room, as though weighing his thoughts. He nods and turns back to her. "I think that it is time for you to meet a very important friend and to discover the extent of the tools available to us."

7. Webs

2011-Oct-12 Kaisergracht, Amsterdam
Historic pivot point peak probability: 36 days

From a sofa in the common area of the B&B, I watch Lucy and Rader through the second story kitchen window by virtue of a camera positioned on an abandoned bicycle across the canal. Volodya has set up at the other end of the couch and Winter's between us. The proprietress provides a steady supply of coffee, cookies, and dog biscuits. Volodya grunts at her kindness. Her cheerfulness increases in proportion to his annoyance.

My tablet shows Lucy rising from the table. She looks out the window and I'm gratified to see her smile. Stepan Petrov stands next to her. She looks up at him and he touches her cheek. I feel like a voyeur, a relieved voyeur, to be certain but a voyeur none the less.

At the end of the couch, Volodya chuckles, always an unnerving sound. "Installing network controller at Burger King was brilliant move, Simon. Trojan horses now gallop through Rader's system. When they next connect we will have treasure of information. Everything we need to solve puzzle of Guenther Rader."

Seven minutes later, our laptops emit a low-pitched whine. Winter sits up and growls. Our laptops pop up windows from one of the cameras outside Rader's hostel.

Lucy steps out of the building with Rader at her side.

I say, "Is this the first time she's left?"

He makes a disapproving tsk sound. "We could pick her up."

"Hmmm," I say, "she seems quite content. I don't think she wants to be picked up."

"Her safety would be assured."

"That's hardly a desirable state for someone her age." As the phrase "pick her up" echoes around my cranium, I realize that the phrase is equivalent to the word kidnap. "No," I say, "until she wants to leave him she will stay with Rader."

"They will be going to the train station Burger King," Volodya says and raises video feeds from the cameras that Winter and I placed there.

2011-Oct-12 Amsterdam Centraal Train Station

Lucy sits at the table Gus indicates. The Burger King has three televisions along with dozens of people eating and waiting for trains.

She checks her phone. It's the first time she's connected since leaving Chicago. Gus chats with some of the geeks working at another table while she scans the posts to her accounts. She figures the person who covered for her must be Alina, since some of the messages sort of convey an Italian accent.

She posts on Facebook that she's occupying Amsterdam. Comments pop up immediately: mostly jokes about coffee shops and the red light district but an interesting thread, too. A bunch of her friends from high school have joined Occupy Oakland. They ask what she wants them to protest. One suggests they march on the Port of Oakland. She types: "Sounds good to me!" Penelope's page is like a running history of Occupy San Francisco. Looking at the photos of her friends—she stares at an image of Bill for a while—she feels funny, not homesick, which is weird enough, but displaced, like she's different now, a part of something else.

Gus brings her a glass of Campari and soda from the bar upstairs.

Lucy asks, "Who has been posting on my Facebook and Twitter feeds?"

"Yes, we had to keep those up while you studied. You took

longer than I expected. I thought you had a stronger constitution. Good thing we are here for you."

"Sorry," Lucy says, "good thing."

He says, "Let me show you a few tools. You'll find them powerful."

Lucy types the URL as Rader instructs. A flash animation of a pirate flag waving in the wind covers a password field. Rader leans over and types into the field. "When you are ready, you will have complete access." Telling her to use tools that are password protected is a typically Gus thing to do. He has a way of pushing and pulling at the same time.

The next page has no header, no banners or frames, no graphics at all, just a command prompt: ">" like on old-fashioned computers. He says, "Do you understand what this is?"

"Some sort of database?"

"No. Not 'some sort of database' this is far more important than that. Can you not see?"

"Sorry, maybe if you could tell me what I'm doing."

He says, "I thought you had studied computer science," and follows with a sigh. "Adriaan will help you. There is not time for me to spoon feed you right now. We have a meeting."

"Sorry," Lucy says. This time, though, she wonders exactly what she is apologizing for.

Gus stares at her again.

"What is it?"

"This is how you access Anonymous."

"Really? *The* Anonymous?"

Gus nods with no lingering trace of disappointment. "You will learn how to access information and request action. Your user name is Lucy and they will know who you are. I suspect they will do anything you ask because you would not ask them to do anything they don't want to do anyway. You see? You organize, not lead."

He stands and walks the perimeter of the room, examining

each person that is not a member of his council. The others have luggage at their feet and are reading, playing with their phones, eating, watching television, or checking the monitors for arrivals and departures. Something on a wall catches his attention. He leans over and examines an advertisement for the BK Broiler, mumbles to himself, and returns to the table. He reorients Lucy's laptop so that it faces that wall and opens a Skype window.

Lucy recognizes the blonde man in the display. Julian Assange, the Wikileaks founder.

* * *

"Aaacckkfaug!" Volodya says.

I nearly pop out of my seat.

He holds up his tablet with a still image of Guenther Rader looking directly into the camera that I put under the frame of the BK Broiler print. Volodya clicks the play icon and Rader cocks his head as though looking at the camera from different angles.

Leaning closer to the camera, we hear Rader whisper, "There you are. Good. You, too, should see this."

Volodya: "We have to shut down."

Me: "No, Volodya, we don't."

He looks at me in shock.

Volodya: "They know we have hacked them. Our horses are not Trojans, they are not zebras, they are elephants that will surely be turned against us. We must shut down."

Me: "And we will, but we need to see this first."

Volodya: "You think it is worth risk."

Me: "I do."

Volodya: "It will be on your head, but I will have to perform recovery."

Volodya and I both start at the sound of Fiona in our earbugs: "You gents need to pay attention."

Me: "You think we should shut down?"

Fiona: "Pay attention!"

Me: "What are you doing up so early?"

Volodya's face tightens into a wrinkle-free sheet of tension as he leans over his laptop and types furiously.

Every bank can be robbed, every athlete can lose, and every system can be hacked. Our security system consists of a simple trap. A single fiber connects our lab to the internet, a physically tiny but figuratively fat fiber-optic. At the entrance of that fiber, a hardware circuit—that is, a circuit with no software component—counts every bit of information that comes into and goes out of that cable. At the other end, we count every bit that is received by the phones, tablet computers, and laptops that Fiona, Volodya, and I carry. The circuit compares the counts every millisecond; if they don't match, the circuit disconnects the cable and our server fleet becomes inaccessible to everyone.

* * *

"Hello Guenther—aaah—Gus."

"Good day, Julian. It is my pleasure to introduce Lucy Montgomery."

Lucy says, "Umm, hi."

"Very nice to meet you, Lucy," Assange says. "You might be the most recognizable person on earth right now." Lucy can see his hands folded together on a table and the white walls of an office behind him. "I'd like to help you understand your place in history." He flexes his fingers and looks back at her. "You should now realize that the Occupy movement in America is the same movement as Anti-austerity in Europe and that they grow from the same roots as the Arab Spring movement. The roots are free exchange of information.

"Everyone has the right to hold opinions without interference. To form opinions, people must have access to the actions of governments. But politicians, generals, bureaucrats, and corporate executives control information to their advantage, they determine what is secret and what is open. When you examine the secrets, you see that secrecy is used to protect political advantage, power. Almost all 'top secret' documents do nothing but conceal corruption and criminal acts perpetrated on the public." He shrugs and adds, "I think people have a right to the truth and I am persecuted for it. I am comfortable with this. People understand."

The statement jostles Lucy's bullshit meter. Without thinking about who she's talking to, the power he wields, and the help he can provide, she says, "Don't pretend that there are no legitimate secrets. There are *real* terrorists." He raises his eyebrows as though he's been interrupted by a child. She says, "Did you assault those women in Sweden?"

"I am not the first person that so-called representative governments have charged with falsified crimes."

"Why Sweden? Are there no women in Britain or Australia that could falsely accuse you?"

"The US is trying to extradite me for exposing their crimes, so they conjure false charges of rape. Do you see the irony? The United States has raped its own people and they charge me." He takes a breath and adds, "Gus, she may not be the right person."

Gus puts his arm around Lucy and pulls her close enough that their cheeks touch. "Our Lucy questions authority—would you prefer a docile rebel?"

Assange leans back and shakes his head. "Of course, you're right." He rubs his eyes as though wiping away doubts. "Lucy, you're welcome to judge me by my actions. I have nothing to hide and hope that you'll see that I committed no actual crimes in Sweden or anywhere else."

Lucy says, "I have a Wikileaks t-shirt." Then she laughs and adds, "It's probably pirated."

"Yes, back to the point," Assange says. "You have heard about the deaths of three rich Americans? The corporate media is using the coincidence of their deaths to convince people that you and Occupy are terrorists."

"Me? But I—"

"So that they can discredit you while distracting the public from the crimes the three men have committed against the people. Lucy, you must be careful. Occupy will be infiltrated and shut down unless you accomplish something big. You have limited time."

Lucy feels his words in the tension that runs from her neck to her belly. She leans forward and sighs.

Assange says. "Gus, it's time to show her. I will disconnect now so you can speak freely. Goodbye Lucy, nice to meet you, you can change the world." The video window closes.

Gus stands and Adriaan steps over from a neighboring table. Adriaan opens the window with the black background and white text. The curser blinks next to the prompt. He types a series of commands that brings up a list of companies owned by Stamford Oil, Investment America, and the Woodley-Carlyle Group. There are two lists for each company, one is marked "Classified Organizations."

"These are actual WikiLeaks files?"

Gus stands behind her, leaning over with his hands on her shoulders. "Yes, there is something you should know that can help you distinguish your friends and enemies."

Adriaan clicks one of the classified Stamford Oil holdings, Central American Relief, Corp, and opens another PDF document. He scrolls down to a page titled, "Profit/Loss Development Risk Analysis."

"This is an internal document. Notice the date? That's two years prior to the contamination of Oriente, Ecuador. Go ahead, read it."

At first Lucy has trouble working through the business-speak but then realization dawns. "They actually list 'acceptable levels of contamination'?" She looks up at Gus. "Acceptable by what standard?"

"Continue reading."

Now her jaw falls open. "Oh my God. They have a budget for bribing local officials based on the number of deaths? They did a cost-benefit analysis? Profit per birth defect?" Her jaw clenches.

"They planned to contaminate that site. They destroyed those people's lives to cut costs?"

"Now continue to the end of this section so that you can see who performed the calculations for them."

She skips to the end and sees a familiar logo: Time Line Associates, GmBH.

"Uncle Simon did this?"

* * *

I leap up from the couch. "We did no such thing!" My tablet falls and Winter barks. "It's a lie. We calculated only legal, decent assumptions. We told them they would fail."

"However, we did work for them," Volodya says. "Lies cast in half-truths are most believable."

Fiona says, "Pay attention!"

We hear Lucy say, "It can't be, can it? Uncle Simon wouldn't do this."

Fiona says, "See?" And Volodya says, "Quiet!"

I watch Rader put his arm around Lucy and show her another bunk document. This one comes from an analysis we performed for Investment America. We can't see the text, but if the acid boiling up from my stomach is any measure, my guts can. As she reads it, her expression evolves from shocked to horrified.

"Oh dear," I squeak. "How can this, this, this *poppycock* appear in Wikileaks?"

Volodya: "Either Rader doctored the documents to further his control of Lucy or the documents were altered within Stamford Oil—perhaps as cover-your-ass exercise. Wikileaks sources are as vulnerable to deception as any other news organization."

Me: "Do you think Lucy will believe it?"

Volodya: "People believe things—it is solvable problem."

Fiona: "Simon, she'll come to her senses. She knows you."

Winter lies back down.

"But Gwinnie. What if Lucy tells Gwinnie?"

My heart clenches up again. Winter stares at me. My mouth is open but I can't speak.

"Oh Simon, surely you don't think that in her heart of hearts Lucy believes this rubbish. She'll sort it out."

"It is informational time bomb in Rader's hands." Volodya shrugs. "Is solvable problem, we defuse it."

"Volodya's right. Nothing to worry about here, old chum, just some work to do."

I understand their words. I love these two people more than I can say, but my mind is going in too many directions to contemplate a solution.

And then, as my stomach boils and my mind spins, my display turns blue.

"We have a problem."

We have been breached and the system has shutdown.

Volodya's frown etches deeper into his chin, the lines reach up to his eyes and forehead. It strikes me that he will become even more severe looking as an old man than he was as a young man.

My laptop comes back up first. I say, "It's just a laptop now. What good is that?"

Fiona doesn't offer an insight or sarcastic quip and I realize that our earbugs are also useless. I put mine in my coat pocket and its absence makes my ear feel funny.

Volodya taps his right index finger against his teeth. "Will you come with me to Vienna?"

We decided how to handle the situation long ago: The system will remain disconnected from external networks until we return to Vienna and can determine the damage and to what extent the hackers can access the system should we reconnect it. We are hopelessly disconnected from our timeweave technology

Volodya says, "We must phone Fiona."

"Do our phones have the 'telephone' app?

He stares at me.

"It seems so archaic." I enable the speaker-phone feature of my no-longer-so-smart phone, select her number, and put it on speaker.

Fiona says, "Since I'm using the telephone feature of this device, I take it that the situation is not so good."

"It is grave problem."

"Ah! Damn, I just bet Penelope that you'd say it was 'serious'—where did you get 'grave?' Now I owe her a drink."

"You have informed a contract employee of our problem?"

"Just that we'd been hacked. People get hacked all the time. No one knows what it means to us. Relax."

"Fiona," I say, "We have no way to tell what Rader is doing to Lucy."

Fiona: "We have no way of knowing when it will happen."

Volodya: "Last update gave 32 to 43 days."

Me: "Then we have to be online in less than 21 days."

Volodya gives a confirming caw.

Fiona: "Can't you access the cameras and microphones you put outside Rader's Hostel without the servers?"

Volodya: "Wholly upgraded gateway, authentication process–"

Me: "Determine damage done, trace to—"

Volodya: "Set booby traps, build wyrms, viruses and—"

Me: "Revenge?"

Volodya: "I have ideas."

Fiona: "Stop your yabber. What can we do without the servers?"

Volodya: "We cannot monitor all hundred of systems that I've installed. We have lost ability to identify faces and voices, to remove noise and sharpen images, to access surveillance systems, we—"

Fiona: "You're thinking of this the wrong way. A certain set of tools has been, well, suspended. It's about time we did some legwork."

"Fiona, you don't understand. We are not detectives, we are scientists. You suggest we use tools that we do not have."

"I said 'legwork.' Both of you posses a complete pair of legs—

but no matter, I'll tend to the legwork with just the one."

Neither of us know how to reply. Discussions of Fiona's missing limb can make her quite irritable.

"You know," she says, and I can hear a smile in her voice, "I recall a story about two blokes a long, long time ago—wasn't it 1984 ? Anyway, one of these lads hacked into American Telephone and Telegraph Corporation's system and the other hacked into the Soviet telecommunications system. And why did these two hackers compromise the security of the opposing forces of the cold war?"

Volodya says, "That was different."

I say, "We were interested in the same physics. The governments wouldn't let us collaborate. We had to do something."

"Yes, but you hacked the two most secure systems in the world at the time."

"That is true," Volodya says, and as he says it, the frown lines embedded in his chin disappear in reflection across 27 years.

I add, "And they never found out."

Fiona: "You committed treason at the height of the cold war."

Volodya: "They still do not know that we could access everything they said."

Me: "Gorbachev used to call Reagan at the most amusing times and complain about wheat, rain, and star wars."

Fiona interrupts, "Who do you think hacked us? Maybe the NSA, MI6, or some other government agency?"

Volodya and I make eye contact. He says what we're both thinking: "It is absurd notion—a government agency could hack us—absurd."

I contribute, "It is to laugh."

"Then who do you think did it?"

"Rader's hackers, of course."

"Rightio! It's the next generation, just like you were. I think it's adorable."

* * *

Lucy's deep in another document, The Future of American Wealth Distribution, a strategy document dated February 2001 for the Woodley-Carlyle Group.

As she reads, her eyes narrow and fists clench. It's packed with graphs of employment rates, GDP, and economic growth for different regions of the world with emphasis on the US and China. She's studied enough economics to have a clue, but the date of the document must be wrong. She pulls up an internet browser and compares with up-to-date charts on Google Financial. They look the same as the charts listed in the document, predictions from 10 years ago.

It takes another hour to confirm her suspicions.

Lucy grew up in a two-bedroom house in Stockton, a small city in California's central valley. In 2005, Gwinnie refinanced the house to pay for Lucy's education. Along with part time work, Lucy managed without loans through her first two years at UC Berkeley. Those two years were like a college recruitment video: great education, huge conversations, and laughter, romance, and parties. In 2007, Lucy's mother's job was outsourced to China and the money dried up. Lucy switched to student loans and worked full time. Then the economy imploded, the value of her mom's house dropped to half of its outstanding mortgage, and within a year foreclosures made the whole development a ghost town.

"It was all planned in 2001."

Gus nods.

"They planned it." Lucy shakes her head as though the concept can't quite settle into place.

Gus points to a paragraph. "It is here."

It seems crazy, like faked moon landings or fabricated 9-11 attacks. She can't understand how anyone could be so rotten. She's already read the paragraph twice, but reading it aloud makes it real: "Standards of living for working Americans will drop to a level that the global market can sustain. As America can no longer support a middle class, it is necessary to consolidate American power where it can exert the most influence. Power will be consolidated in the judicial and executive branches of government by massive campaign financing and wealth consolidation, increased taxes on all but the highest earners, a corresponding decrease in services, and increase in personal debt." She sips at her Campari and soda without realizing the glass is empty. "This can't be."

Gus says, "Read the next paragraph."

She does: "Two tiers of society will form. The financial class will provide for their own security and transportation. The working class will support public police, fire, and transit through taxes. The two consumer tiers will simplify marketing demographics. Entertainment prices will exceed the accessibility of the working class. In order to maintain peace, the financial class must provide access to all lower-tier forms of cultural entertainment, like sports events, at least through alternative media."

Lucy stops. She lifts the glass and sees that it's empty. She stares across the room at the televisions, one fixed on a soccer match, another showing a fast food advertisement, and the third advertising an exotic car that features a tall, thin, fashionable, middle-aged white couple.

She turns to Gus. "Why isn't this in the news?"

"Come now," Gus says, "Why do you think?"

"They did it on purpose," Lucy says. "They fucking planned it."

"Look at the last page."

She does and sees the TLA logo again.

Lucy's eyes start to well up. "My mother worships Uncle Simon. He's not like that. How could he …"

Adriaan leans over and starts a video, obviously taken with a smart phone, showing Simon Wentworth with his dog Winter sitting next to Jack Welch at the funeral of Gordon Woodley. After a poor edit, the video jumps to a scene with Simon talking to the heirs of Samford Oil, Investment American and Woodley-Carlyle beside Gordon Woodley's open grave.

Lucy can barely breathe.

"Look closely at this man." Gus stops the video on a still shot of the man standing next to Simon. "It is important that you learn everything you can about Francis Woodley."

He starts another video. It shows a teenage Simon sitting in a forest between Gordon Woodley and Henry Kissinger talking to Edward Teller and Dick Cheney."

"That's at The Grove," Lucy says. "Simon worked for The Bohemian Club. So did my mom."

"It is where spiders weave webs."

"But how could …"

He starts another video. Lucy recognizes it as the Occupy riot at the New York Stock exchange. It shows the riot unfolding and Penelope being beaten. It also includes a view of the iconic image of Lucy and Officer Justin but taken from a different perspective. This image has Lucy and Officer Justin in the background. The foreground shows a man in a bright green blazer taunting Occupiers from behind the police line.

"That was Woodley?"

8. 99 ± 1%

2011-Oct-13 Vienna
Historic pivot point peak probability: UNKNOWN

TLA's worldwide computing lab is an apartment on the second floor of an elegant 18th century building in Vienna, Austria. To conceal our computing fleet from infrared searches, we installed the lab over the freezer section of a grocery store and connected our ventilation system to the refrigeration system's exhaust

Volodya and I sit at a pair of two-meter long tables facing windows that look over the Naschmarkt, a kilometer-long outdoor marketplace. Volodya uses all six of his monitors as a single mammoth display. Mine are configured according to my eyesight: the two monitors closest to my keyboard for my workstation, and the outer four for high-resolution display of timeweaves or video.

We employ the Gorkems, a lovely couple who live in the building and operate a Turkish deli in the Naschmarkt. Though they are not technologically savvy, she loves to turn screws and route cables and he is a topflight chef who finds pleasure in divining recipes, which is to say, algorithms. The couple tend the hardware maintenance of our server fleet in our absence. They also provide gyro, hummus, and baklava of magnificent quality along with coffee so wonderful that one can hardly bear the temptation of bathing in its muddy glory. I'll not mention the pomegranate brandy that Mr. Gorkem distills in the rear of their market stall for fear that you'll dash off to Vienna and expose this minor offense to the law.

Volodya and Mrs. Gorkem spend three days checking the connections of all 1024 server blades, individual computers that slide into racks rather like books fit on shelves, every disk drive, and every power source for hard, firm, or soft invasions. I read through log files matching Ethernet addresses to internet addresses and on up the protocol stack to find the entry point employed by the hackers. When we find no sign of a breech, we disconnect the database disk drives and connect the system to the internet. It's hacked in minutes and our spiders get lost trying to follow the source.

Our competitive spirit demands that, first, we secure our system in a way that is both impenetrable and responds to hacking forays in such a way that, second, we play a counter-joke on Rader's hackers that they'll never forget. The long hours caught up in the puzzle distract me from ruminating on the fact that Lucy considers me, her doting pseudo-uncle, the enemy.

As the days pass, we create software that both searches our system and harasses each other. By the eighth day we have accumulated a knee-high stack of takeout food containers and find ourselves so absorbed in chasing each other that we crash the system.

"Yes," I say, "the task at hand."

Volodya grunts agreement.

Three seconds later, a cartoon of Winter chases me across every display, complete with him yelping for his supper and the odd sound that I'm accused of making while concentrating.

Winter howls. Volodya laughs. I scowl at them.

On the tenth day we configure a dummy database and let the bot hack in. The upgraded system determines that its usage pattern is inconsistent with ours and kicks it out in 9 minutes. A new file also appears in the root directory of the hub server. It's a jpeg image of someone standing in a city street wearing a Guy Fawkes mask holding a sign that says "LULZ!"

At first it's a polite chortle. I overlay the photo on a picture of Volodya and throw together a script that melds the two together. Now Volodya is on every monitor in our lab, but with the goofy smile, cunning eyes, and odd facial hair of Guy Fawkes.

He advances to snickering.

Struggling to contain my own chuckles, I manage to say, "If you ever smiled, there'd be no difference."

He emits laughter unlike any I've ever heard from him, a legitimate, "Har, har, har."

Leaving just the arched eyebrows of the Guy Fawkes mask and the odd chin whiskers, I animate the image to alternate Fawkes's grin and Volodya's scowl. Between shrieking fits of laughter, he says, "Stop, now. Please. Halt!"

I impose a wink on the animation. Now it's scowl-grin-wink-arched-eyebrows-scowl …

Tears roll down his face. "It is as Fiona said."

Nearly sobbing, I send a continuous stream of Volodya-Fawkes images to the printer. As the sheets drop into the tray, the two of us race about the lab posting them on walls, server racks, doors, the floor, and, in the hilarity, I even tape them to the windows. Volodya convulses on the floor. The joke achieved, I realize my stupidity and take them down from the window.

"Yes. They were good times, Volodya. Back then, we were the only ones, but now …"

"They are our people, surely we find a way to employ them."

* * *

On the morning of our eleventh day of computing purgatory, my phone says, "G'day mate." Fiona's cheerful voice dusts off a shred of sanity. "They've left Amsterdam, off like a bride's nightie. The building's empty, lads, we're blind."

Volodya and I look at each other. Winter yawns, whines, and curls into a tighter ball.

Fiona continues, "But we're not deaf. Her social network posts are hopping. She's got almost ten million Twitter followers. It looks like she's going on an anti-austerity/Occupy tour of Europe."

2011-Oct-24 Europe
Historic pivot point peak probability: UNKNOWN

Pursuing Lucy across Europe, from one city to the next, airport to train to bus, delivers exhilarating catharsis, though not without several minor vertiginous instances of timeweave confusion.

Europe's gothic architecture, whether in glorious colors, drab gray, or dusty coal, is most majestic this time of year. Europeans belong in coats, sweaters, and scarves. London feels somehow misleading without prevalent umbrellas. The flourish of Berlin diminishes under blue skies, though I can easily imagine Socrates arguing with Plato on a summer day in Athens.

Without timeweave prognostication, I feel like an explorer without a compass. Winter and I walk through Brandenburg Gate an hour after Lucy has departed Berlin. We see her on a news report from a lounge at the Hauptbahnhof: She stood on a remaining segment of The Wall and, for the first time suggested, "Democracy when? Get out of the way or get on board—democracy now!" As the image leaves the screen her Twitter feed alerts me of her next stop: Athens.

The Greek government has just initiated drastically austere budget cuts to services and government employment. I'm at the edge of the crowd when Lucy announces, "Governments wring their hands and say austerity is the only path to recovery. The 1% isn't going hungry, they're not losing their homes, they're not being harassed by cops. They're the criminals, but the system they set up makes us pay for their mistakes. When will the 1% suffer? When will they share the burden? Democracy when? Get out of the way or get on board—democracy now!"

She goes to Madrid when Winter and I visit Barcelona. I think she'd have preferred Barcelona. In London, throngs overflow Trafalgar Square. Lucy stands knee deep in the fountain and delivers her speech. In Dublin, youths welcome Lucy, startle Winter, and express hatred for the English. Some things never change.

At every stop, Lucy acquires another ten to hundred thousand social media followers. According to her social networks, Oakland is her next stop.

2011-Oct-31 San Francisco
Historic pivot point peak probability: UNKNOWN

Winter has taken a seat atop my roller suitcase which increases the difficulty of manipulating the bag through the glass door of The Intoxicating Page. Fiona holds the door.

"She's a celebrity, Simon."

Fiona's wearing a tall, black pointy hat with a wide brim, a tight black dress that barely covers her torso, and black stockings constrained by bright red garters completed by a red stiletto heel, and makeup: black eye shadow, black lipstick, and a small obsidian nose ring.

"I get it—Halloween!" I say. She's dressed as the very witch who appears in the tattoo between her breasts and the nose ring is meant to be her wart. "You're like a picture within a picture."

She sets aside her cane, which is disguised as a broom, and takes Winter in her arms. I park my bags in history/blended whiskey. The growing Halloween rumble of The Intoxicating Page threatens my state of consciousness. Fiona guides me to the love seat in the romance corner and pours me a glass of Champagne. The bubbles go down my throat like an internal shower.

She puts the bottle in an ice bucket and lifts Winter onto her lap. "Have you heard about The Sons of Industry?"

"The who of what?"

"That's what the media is calling the three of them, The Sons of Industry—Frankie Woodley, James Birch, and Wallace van Bibber." She sips her champagne. Winter drools on the sofa.

Remember your drinking partner in New York City? He has a new venture. I had to learn about it from CNN. CNN, Simon!" She scratches behind Winter's ears and gets a back leg going.

"I should be helping Volodya. We have no idea when Lucy is

getting here, no idea what Rader is doing. I'm not doing any good chasing Lucy around the world."

"For a hacker, you're not very good with over-the-counter technology." She holds up her phone for me. "See? She posted that her flight has been diverted—Homeland Security is less than enthralled over her visit."

"She stopped using a false passport?"

"But of course, Rader knows how to please the media." She sets the phone down and swirls a finger in the champagne and offers a few drops to Winter. "It doesn't take teraflops to see what Rader's doing." Winter licks the bubbly juice and sneezes. "Rader is creating a personality, preparing a media storm. Right wing commentators want Lucy arrested, leftists want her sanctified." Winter makes his harrumph sound and pushes his nose into the gap between Fiona and me.

"I should call Gwinnie."

"So far the media are leaving Gwinnie alone. Though paparazzi are camped out in front of Officer Justin's walkup in Queens. He's right gobsmacked, that one."

"Officer Justin?"

"Right, the fellow in the photo with Lucy, he's stuck in the middle of all of it."

"You don't suppose Rader will make him a sacrificial lamb."

"It depends on what he's doing," Fiona says. "She's the tool, but what is he trying to accomplish?"

"Up until we lost access, it didn't seem as though his goals had changed since he escaped East Germany in 1974. They're rather altruistic in a sense."

"Except for the bloody trail he'll leave behind."

"Yes, except for that." The champagne opens windows of thought that morality would prefer shuttered. "The ends, I mean. It's crossed my mind that he could be grooming Lucy for politics."

"No, Simon, that's pixie dust. He's going to get her killed."

That I don't drop my glass at this statement should serve as further testimony to the value of moderate intoxication. "Why would he do that?" As I pose the question, the concept of denial crosses my mind.

"Is the last timeweave calculation too out of date to get a probability?"

"Hopelessly. Lucy is well out on a specific branch, it would be an extrapolation of an extrapolation."

"Relying on commercial tech is bollocks. I'm calling Volodya," she grabs her phone. The motion upsets Winter enough that he plops down to the floor, shakes, and wanders about the evening crowd of costumed, intoxicated literature lovers.

"It's three in the morning in Vienna."

"I don't care." She has already selected his number.

With Fiona otherwise occupied, thoughts of Gwinnie enter my mind. She must be beside herself, which is where I'd like to be. Though I fear the blindness of telephony, I make the call.

* * *

"How could you do this to me?" Gwinnie says. "Our home. Our neighborhood." Her anger drifts to sorrow, but it's her disbelief that breaks my heart. "You helped them plan it. They did it on purpose."

The fact that Lucy could have phoned her mother and shared the distorted version of our work without my knowledge gives me a wholly inappropriate sense of outrage.

She adds, "How could you do it to Lucy?"

I manage to squeak out, "We're helping Lucy."

"You expect me to believe that?"

Between the dream of her affection and the fear that she'll dispose of me—a fear that has been realized temporarily many times since the day we met—I can never find the right words. I want to say: Gwinnie, I love you but only manage "I do," which is sort of similar.

She says, "You haven't even talked to her."

"We're keeping a close watch. She's been misinformed. We would never help a company or government do anything mean to you. Remember, we work with the Sierra Club, too." Everything comes out so jumbled; what does the Sierra Club have to do with Gwinnie?

"So you're stalking my daughter."

"No, no, of course not. We'd never—"

"You know where she is, who she's with and what she's doing, but you haven't contacted her?"

"No, she's being manipulated by umm," if I tell her that Lucy's with Guenther Rader, she'll worry even more, but what else can I say? "this group of people who, umm, and they lied to her about us." Then an instant of clarity, a stone to cling to in the emotional rapids, I say, "But Lucy is safe. That's what matters, isn't it?"

"Lucy never sounded better, she's got direction and enthusiasm. She told me about her mentor, a gentleman named Gus Reser who is doing everything for Lucy that I asked of you."

I discover that I've paced my way across The Intoxicating Page to the horror and port section.

"I think it would be better if you left us alone." She disconnects.

* * *

Winter's muzzle pushes into my cheek. Buried in the would'ves, the could'ves, the should'ves, I've melted onto the floor at the base of the horror case. His tongue covers the distance from my chin to my forehead and on up to *The Book of Cthulhu*.

Fiona offers me a glass of port, the syrupy, red fluid of zinfandel and syrah raisins looks like blood. She says, "Why didn't you tell her that 'Gus Reser' is actually Guenther Rader?"

"If she knew it were Rader, she'd panic."

"You have to stop protecting her." She takes a drink from the bottle and says, "Volodya's working on a whole new firewall, implementing something he said you invented forty years ago."

I built my first clock based on a simple biological oscillator, my heart. The waveform differs slightly for each person, like a thumbprint or a retina or a face, but we'd thought that it couldn't be used as a biometric signature because it varies with mood.

The thought brings resolve to my spine.

9. Winter's Tail

2011-Nov-2 Oakland
Historic pivot point peak probability: UNKNOWN

Fiona appears at my table in the engineering and unflavored water section of The Intoxicating Page and announces: "She's here."

"Lucy?" I lean to the side and scan the store beyond my monitor.

"Yes."

"At The Intoxicating Page?"

"They're going to storm the Port of Oakland."

"She brought rain? But how could—"

"Simon, she's a celebrity. Penelope and the others are acting like The Beatles have reunited for a free concert."

"They're Beatles fans?"

"It's a simile, Simon!"

"Fiona, you're being awfully short with me."

Rather than the pre-concert tension that I felt at Occupy Wall Street, Oakland provides the historical backdrop of the Black Panthers and the tradition of political upheaval in neighboring Berkeley. Gritty tension mixes with an atmosphere of raucous goodwill. Roughly 12% of the Occupiers march beneath clouds of sweet, skunky ganja smoke.

Mob mentality infects me, or perhaps it's a contact high, in any case, I purchase a "Fuck The Man" T-shirt from a kind young gentleman with an impressive dreadlock mane and eyes as droopy as his trousers. Fiona holds my coat while I put the T over my shirt and tie. With her short, spiked hair, tight fitting jeans, and T-shirt advertising The Intoxicating Page torn at the neckline to reveal her crescent-moon, witch tattoo, Fiona fits right in.

Fiona, Winter, and I stay on the periphery. With 18,674 people, it takes 78 minutes to walk to the port; both amiable and angry people chant, bang drums, and play musical instruments.

At first, I can't tell from where the disembodied voice emanates, but then realize that it's coming from the phone in my pocket. I remove it and see that Fiona is holding hers, too. The display shows Volodya: "… of the Bonapartes. But I warn you, if you don't tell me that this means war, if you still try to defend the infamies and horrors perpetrated by that Antichrist—I really believe he is Antichrist—I will have nothing more to do with you and you are no longer my friend, no longer my 'faithful slave,' as you call yourself!"

The crowd wends around us.

"Are we sorted?" Fiona asks.

Volodya looks up from *War and Peace* and says, "I have solved the problem."

"Brilliant!" Fiona says, "I'm sick to death of this blindness. We're at Occupy Oakland, can you get video of—"

"I know where you are." Volodya sounds offended.

The display switches to video of the march viewed from a helicopter. I can see several helicopters hovering over the port; one with a TV channel logo and two others, presumably law enforcement.

Fiona and I take out our earbugs, mine from my inner jacket pocket, Fiona's from her jeans, and insert them in our ears. I require several seconds to reacquaint myself with the intricacies of our user interface and then, like the bicycle-riding cliché, I'm back. The ever-present banter among the three of us is like acquiring a new sense.

I ask, "Where's Lucy?"

"The system has only just come up," Volodya says. "Data are being assembled, we should have her likely position in a few—yes, it is solved. Lucy is in a taxi on a side street near the port, presumably with Rader."

The great monster-shaped cranes come into view. Over 70 meters high with neck-like structures that lean over container ships to lift railroad-car sized containers with their mouths, it is industrial activity incarnate. Five cargo vessels line the harbor with another three in the bay accompanied by tugboats.

The march has blocked a queue of semi-tractor trailers from entering the port; some with engines running and drivers at the wheel, others parked.

The police form a wall along the sidewalk to our right. Where the New York City officers were mixed between those in white shirts with the customary short-brimmed pointy hats and those in riot gear with helmets, the Oakland police wear helmets with clear facemasks and stand with their hands on their belts ready to employ their side arms, truncheons, dangling gas masks, and/or Tasers. A few carry shotguns and still fewer carry large bore weapons suitable for firing tear gas and flash bombs.

"Over here," Fiona says, using her cane to access a gap between the line of police and Occupiers. The crowd's motion occasionally jostles an Occupier into the wall of police who respond by pushing back with truncheons held like staves. I button my coat over my rebellious new T-shirt and, for the moment, my conservative suit and advanced age, at least compared to most Occupiers, generate largesse among the police. Similarly, Fiona's cane and limp render her, I presume, a non-threat in the officer's minds.

Nearer the port, the crowd becomes too tight for Winter. I reach down to lift him. In so doing, my posterior nudges into the police line. An officer presses his club against my back, pushing us into the crowd. I lose my footing and start to tumble. A young woman tries to step out of my way, but with no vacant space, she also stumbles.

Winter feels safe in my arms, though as long as that club

presses against me I'm incapable of standing. I shift my position to both provide Winter further cover and the stumbling woman something soft to land on. The club slips away. The officer's balance wavers. Trying to recover, he steps forward. His heavy leather boot swings into my line of sight. Just as he attains stability, Winter lets out a beagle-quality yelp of pain. I tighten my grip on him and realize that the officer is standing on Winter's tail. Winter lets loose a scream mixed with a howl—he sounds like a coyote under assault by a roadrunner.

An unfamiliar voice yells, "The pig is trying to kill the dog!"

Calculating the response of both crowds and paramilitary organizations to this sort of stimulus is trivial. Preparing for their response is equally trivial: keep your head covered and maneuver away from the action. But as long as the boot remains on Winter's tail, I'm stuck where I am. Preparing for Fiona's response to the perception that Winter is being attacked is considerably more complicated. On my knees with my right arm cradling Winter and my left hand propping me up as well as gripping my phone, I can't stop her.

Three police officers push into the crowd to form an island around the officer, but with no space for an island, the crowd pushes back. The officers push forward. The crowd pushes back; the force with which the police and crowd push increases with each oscillation.

A baton comes down and misses my head by inches. Rather than swinging back up, the baton continues beneath me and is used as a lever to pry me up. I'd welcome this action except that it causes me to pull Winter which stretches his tail. He let's loose another wail, this one more like the mirthless laugh of a dying hyena.

From my crouched position, I don't see Fiona's cane but I do see its blade swing through the thick black leather boot just a foot from my eyes. The officer's scream joins Winter's. The two howls are nearly in the same key. Blood seeps from the officer's ankle.

Winter comes free and I attempt to rise.

As the officer falls, I vault up and forward with Winter held tight against my chest.

The act of observation employs several sections of the mind that are not synchronized. The sections of the brain concerned with fight and flight require about a quarter of a second to respond, but evaluation of the scene takes at least a full second. So it is that the two officers who witnessed Fiona's assault on the officer who stepped on Winter's tail are only now processing the images from which they will later assemble their accounts of this incident. Fiona is well versed in how to use the timing of such processes to her advantage.

As the two officers step to their fallen colleague, Fiona releases her prosthetic leg. As her leg falls in one direction, she leans against her cane and falls in another direction. The pressure with the ground retracts the blade into the cane. As she falls, the officer who helped pry me up drops his club and reaches for her and the other officer catches her by the shoulders.

A second before, the police officers' thought processors were on track to identify her as the aggressor, but in the course of that second, Fiona provides an experience inconsistent with the officers' expectations. Instead of internalizing that Fiona cut the fallen officer's Achilles tendon, they're protecting a handicapped woman from a rioting mob.

The three mobile officers guide us to safety on the sidewalk behind the wall of police. Five people are arrested for the attack. Since none of them have knives, they'll be released uncharged.

However, the injured officer will never forget the odd little man with a beagle and his one-legged associate.

* * *

I crouch down to examine Winter and Fiona uses me as a bench while she reinstalls her leg. Winter maneuvers his rump away from me as I try to assess the damage. His tail is bent in the middle and sensitive to the touch. I fear it's broken, but his attitude is fine. Indeed, his friendly demeanor poses a problem: it hurts when he wags and with people offering him sympathy, he wags quite often.

Fiona says, "We should make way."

We move to a sparsely populated region of the crowd. A young woman to our left beats a drum and, behind us, a man with a tuba lends a cheerful bellow to each upbeat of the percussion. Flags of many colors and slogans wave in the ocean breeze.

Volodya, who was been quiet through the melee, says, "That was a mistake."

Fiona says, "He broke Winter's tail!"

"Yes, well," Volodya says. "The systems are not fully engaged. We struggle to monitor Lucy. Now I must search for video of your attack. It is a serious problem."

"Piece of piss," Fiona says, "program a spider to scrub it."

"The video will be cached and likelihood is high that police will find it."

The drummer comes to an abrupt stop and yells, "Tom Morello!"

The crowd repeats the name, generating greater fervor. Though I'm unfamiliar with him, Tom Morello must be a well-known figure. Others yell "Rage!" and "Fuck the machine" and "Where's your guitar?"

The man behind us lets loose a single-breathed tuba solo.

Now I can see Mr. Morello atop a container just this side of the port property. He's not a large man, but he carries himself with the confidence of someone with extensive experience addressing large crowds.

An amplification system has been assembled and he speaks into a microphone.

"That's illegal," Fiona says, referring to the amplification. "The cops can move in now."

In my earbug, Volodya says, "No, they are not so foolish."

The police remain in place along the sidewalks and at the gate to the port.

The crowd acquires moderate silence and Morello announces, "You, the 99% have shut down the Port of Oakland!"

He waits through the predictable expression of pleasure before continuing, "The Port is closed and the Teamsters are with us! Listen, a lot of shit went down last week. The cops made a mess of things and it's nice to see them on their best behavior today."

Fiona says, "Last week the police critically wounded a war veteran."

A black-clad occupier yells, "We'll fuck them up!" in the silence between sentences.

Morello points at the occupier. "Whoa—this is about injustice, not war. We don't need more war. These guys over here," he motions to the sidewalks and lines of police, "they're not the multi-billionaires who steal your bread." He pauses for a beat and then raises his voice to a level between song and scream to say, "Rage, people! Rage against the machine!"

The crowd cheers this line as though they'd been expecting it. Volodya says, "That statement refers to the man's rock band."

The drummer picks up the beat for four bars, the tuba lets out one great oompa.

Morello motions for silence and gets it. "Occupy doesn't have leaders or celebrities, but we've got someone better." With a rock star's intuition of stage timing, he lets another beat pass before looking down and to his right where, even from here, I can see the crowd parting. "We've got Lucy!"

This time the crowd erupts. Rather than beating a cheery rhythm, the woman to our left hits her drum as fast and as hard as she can. The tuba player blows as hard and loud and as high of a note as he is capable.

Volodya says, "Look at your phone."

The display is a live local television feed of Lucy being lifted by the crowd. Morello reaches down and pulls her up on the container. The way she looks up at him distinguishes which of the two is the rock star and which has just been thrust into the public eye.

Lucy takes the microphone and speaks to the crowd as though these 19,564 people embody her best friend: "Oh my God! I just hugged Tom Morello!"

In the mix of laughter and cheers, the crowd expresses a BFF's empathy and Lucy accepts that affection with neither effort nor presumption. Lucy is one of the 99%, part of the crowd, even as she stands above it. A hundred different YouTube versions of her hugging the rock star will eclipse the words she'll speak in the next ten minutes.

Fiona says, "Oh my, she really is brilliant."

I'm overwhelmed by the realization that Lucy is no longer a youth stuck in the recession-rut of stagnant career development. She's a woman in full control of her identity, comfortable with millions of people tuning into her contemporary version of folksy kinship.

I say, "Do you have video of Rader?"

Volodya doesn't answer, but in the silence I can almost hear him shaking his head in the negative.

With the sun dipping across the bay behind the San Francisco skyline, its golden light reflecting from the Transamerica Pyramid, Lucy casts a long shadow on the crowd. She's alone up on the container now. It's rusty but looks black in this lighting. Lucy turns away from the crowd, holds her hand over her eyes like a visor, and surveys the port. She points at the cranes, leans away from the microphone and speaks to someone the crowd can't see, gauging the situation, the port, the impact of Occupy, and her purpose.

Whether it's choreographed or not, it's working. The crowd settles down, cheers wane to murmurs. They're almost ready to listen.

Volodya says, "I believe Rader stands south of container in

shadows. He's always in the shadows. I loathe this man."

Fiona points to the center of the crowd about twenty steps from Lucy. "Penelope and Rob are over there with Occupy San Francisco."

Lucy taps the microphone as though checking to see if it's turned on. The effect brings the crowd to silence. No drumming, no music, not even a murmur. She speaks softly, as though talking to herself.

"So this is it," she says. "This is where consumerism starts. This is where the shit comes ashore to fill Walmart and Target." She indicates the port behind her and speaks in a sedate, melancholy tone. "Container ships cross the sea bearing crap made of plastic for us to use and throw away. We've been trained to exchange 40 to 60 or 80 hours a week of our lives for garbage. Our time, our lives. You know, time is all we get in life. And they've trained us to throw it away." The last time that Lucy and I properly visited, this is what we talked about: Awareness and time and how nothing else really matters. It's a precious message, but I don't understand what it has to do with international trade.

"We give our time to corporations in exchange for money and then we give that money back for a few hours of distraction. A TV, a can of Coke, Chicken McNuggets, an energy-wasting SUV. They poison our bodies and minds and leave hundreds of miles of garbage floating in our oceans. We're helping them strangle this planet. They control us through government and police.

"A week ago, just blocks from here, the cops went kinda crazy and a man was seriously injured." Elements of the crowd disparage the police. "The police have been conned into protecting the 1% so that they can get paid. We gotta stop fighting among ourselves."

With the crowd rumbling, Lucy raises her voice. "The system is rigged. Consumerism has failed." She pauses and starts slowly: "Democracy when?" The crowd joins her chorus: "We're changing the world so get out of the way or get on board—democracy now!"

The tuba joins the fray.

"Some things have to be destroyed before they can be fixed. That's where we are. It's time to bring down this corporate-ocracy. This government must be destroyed to be repaired!"

2011-Nov-2 Port of Oakland

As Lucy says the last words, "This government must be destroyed to be repaired!," she looks into the crowd and sees Penelope, Rob, and Bill. Penelope jumps up and down and screams. Lucy pulls out her phone and takes pictures of the crowd even as they take pictures of her. Gus will have someone post them on Facebook later and tag them as "friends."

Lucy has never sought attention. Riding a motorcycle means riding alone and she likes it that way. The first time she gave her speech had been terrifying. She's accustomed to it now, accustomed to being terrified in front of oceans of people. She had a poster of Tom Morello on her bedroom wall as a teenager. It would probably still be there if the bank hadn't foreclosed. She can't get over it: Tom Morello introduced her today—and he gave her backstage passes to his concert tonight!

Klaus helps her down from the container and people move in. They want to talk, they want to hug, they want to help, but she wants to say hi to Penelope and hang out in Berkeley with her friends and have dinner with her mom and go to Morello's concert—except that, no, that's not quite what she really wants, it's what she thinks she ought to want; what Lucy before it all happened would have wanted.

Klaus drags her away from the crowd and, just as Gus trained them, Lucy shows affection for the people while Klaus makes apologies.

"Just a few minutes more," Lucy says, "I was talking to them" and waves toward the crowd, to everyone but no one in particular. She keeps taking pictures and listening, repeating enough of what she hears to leave the lasting impression that she not only cares but will remember. She does care, but it's too much to remember.

After what happened to Officer Justin, the police stay clear of her.

She, Klaus, and Alina run the last few blocks to the taxi. Klaus gets in front with the driver and Lucy gets in back with Alina and Gus who says, "We have a huge opportunity!"

"No kidding," Lucy says, "I have backstage passes."

"What?"

"Tickets to Tom Morello's concert and backstage access."

Gus says, "I have a better surprise for you."

"Hmm?"

"You're going on TV."

"What?"

"You're going on Rachel Maddow's show, MSNBC, national TV!"

"When?"

"We go to the studio right now." He takes her phone from her. "We have ten minutes to prepare."

2011-Nov-2 The Intoxicating Page
Historic pivot point peak probability: still UNKNOWN

"You have the same hair and similar eyes as Rachel Maddow," I say. "You could be—"

"Sisters, I know."

Volodya says, "That Fiona emulates Rachel Maddow is not coincidental." It's four in the morning in Vienna and Volodya's still scrubbing video of Fiona's assault from the internet.

"Thank you, Volodya. Having a Russian hacker interpret my ambitions is a dream come true."

We're back at The Intoxicating Page, sitting in the science fiction area dedicated to Old Crow Whiskey and the three Bs: David Brin, Ben Bova, and Gregory Benford. Winter's curled up on the floor licking his bent and swollen but probably not broken tail.

When I mention the veterinarian he runs to the children's section and hides behind a doll house.

My laptop shows Maddow teasing her audience with references to "Occupy's poster child" and the network cuts to commercials.

Volodya says, "Parallel contradictory broadcasts insulate the populace from paradoxical statements."

"What are you talking about?" Fiona asks.

"A second relevant broadcast."

Volodya directs another television stream to my tablet computer. This one shows Frankie Woodley shaking hands with Sean Hannity on Fox News.

Fiona sets a copy of *Kiln People* on the table that I use to prop up my tablet.

She says, "Equal and opposite broadcasting."

"All but guaranteeing that conservatives and liberals will be insulated from offending opinions," Volodya says.

"Punch to the gut of pluralism," Fiona says.

On the monitor, Maddow uses her patented voice of reason to ask, "Here's the question everyone is asking: what does Occupy want?"

"We want a chance." Lucy looks frustrated. "Global corporations have rigged the system against us. They've rigged it against small companies, too, and homeowners. Everything they do, no matter how rotten, turns out to be legal. Legal doesn't mean justifiable, you know, it means the rules are written to favor the 1%. We just want a chance." Lucy takes a breath and adds, "And I have a question for you."

"Okay," Maddow says, letting the last syllable hang in the air.

"How come the police always side with the banks? The sheriff who threw my mother out of her house was our neighbor. Why would our friend evict us so that the bank could let our house bake in the sun unoccupied for over two years? Who will throw the sheriff out when they foreclose on his house? Why don't the police support the people instead of the banks?"

Maddow says, "New York City's Chief of Police was quoted saying that you destroyed the man's career."

"Officer Justin?" Lucy says, now her voice has an edge to it. I've heard this edge before. "That's what I'm talking about. All the other cops enforce the will of the 1% and then one good cop, the best cop we've seen at an Occupy protest, actually takes on the role of a Peace Officer, and they charge him with a crime. How is protecting me from being Tased and stung with pepper spray 'aiding and abetting' my 'escape?'"

"Fox News says that you made Officer Justin an Occupy martyr."

"You listen to me, Rachel Maddow. Officer Tyvon Justin is not an 'Occupy martyr,' that's a lie, he's being used as an example of what happens to cops who don't bow to the one-percent."

Sean Hannity's polished voice comes from the tablet. "Frankie Woodley, you are the one percent. What do you have to say to the protesters?"

"Working hard and succeeding should be rewarded," Frankie says. "I'm proud to be in the top one percentile."

"The Occupy Wall Street clan thinks you owe them a job."

"Look, Sean, unemployment is right around 10%," Frankie says, "which means that employment is 90%, not so bad. The protesters need to realize that being unemployed is a choice. Start a company. Create apps. Work fast food, clean houses, pull weeds if you have to, but get some capital and make your own opportunities. The goldmine of opportunity is infinite."

"They have no initiative," Hannity says.

"No, that's not it, Sean. It took initiative to put together the Occupy Wall Street movement. I'd hire Lucy Montgomery in a second. She's got talent and I have capital—that's how it's supposed to work."

"Hang on Frankie," Hannity says. "Look what she did to the police officer in New York City—destroyed his career."

"Well, she got her fifteen minutes of fame," Frankie says.

Both monitors now show the iconic photo of Lucy and Officer Tyvon Justin.

"Officer Justin should have Tasered her," Hannity says. "But if he had, she'd sue him."

"That's the problem with whiners and moochers who think the world owes them something. Instead of creating their own opportunities, they destroy other people's opportunities—but I think we can change that."

Hannity says, "I had him on the show last week—a great guy, good American, a Democrat, in fact."

"What do you expect?" Frankie says. "He's in a union."

The monitor shows Lucy with rouge from the Oakland sunshine and eyes as wide open for Rachel Maddow as they were for Tom Morello. She says, "As long as unemployment and college debt are high, there will be no shortage of Occupiers." She looks away from the camera for an instant, then back with a smirk and adds, "But as long as our country is set on disaffecting youth, we'll have plenty of good music."

Maddow laughs and says, "You met Tom Morrello, today—how was that?"

A star-struck smile tugs at Lucy's lips, but then she shifts gears. Her brow furrows and she leans into the microphone. "At first, I just couldn't believe Tom Morello introduced me. I mean, seriously, Tom Morello." Maddow indulges her with a grin. "But then, it kinda hit me, you know, Rage Against the Machine, right? And I realized who it is."

"The machine?"

"Yeah, I realized that The Sons of Industry—they are the machine. Rage Against the Sons."

On the tablet, Frankie Woodley says, "Initiative and talent aren't the problem, government is the problem. If we could remove the minimum wage, reform bankruptcy, eliminate entitlement programs, I could help the protesters create their own opportunities."

"Of course," Hannity says, "but how do you solve the problem of government interference?"

"No one wants to say it, but everyone knows it's true: corporations should replace government and the only way for that to happen is to put government out of business."

"Out of business? What does that mean?"

"It means that government has to be destroyed so that corporations can take over for the benefit of everyone."

"Destroyed? Come on, you don't really mean that do you? Destroy the US government?"

"Along with all the rest."

On the monitor, Rachel Maddow says to Lucy, "A few hours ago, you gave a speech at the Port of Oakland where you said that government must be destroyed. Did you really mean that?"

"Is that what I said? It's so exciting to be a part of the Occupy movement. Everything is happening so fast. Umm, government isn't doing its job—that's pretty obvious. When the 99% have to prop up the 1%, capitalism isn't working. It's not even capitalism. Yes, government needs to be destroyed before the will of the people can replace it."

"You don't really mean that, do you? Destroyed?"

10. Rage

2011-Nov-2 San Francisco

Rader watches Lucy's performance on monitors from the studio lobby. With her red hair, pale skin, and blue blouse she looks like an American flag. No one could watch this and doubt her sincerity.

Sitting next to him, Klaus looks up from his phone and says, "I tweeted 'Rage against the Sons' from Lucy's account and it's already trending."

"The time is close," Rader says. "Come with me."

The two men walk out to Market Street. Rader scans the surroundings for surveillance cameras, leans against a building out of direct view, and says, "You remember what we spoke of a few weeks ago about catalysts and symbolism?"

"You mean Francis Woodley? The Sons of Industry?"

Rader nods.

"We wait for him to commit injustice?"

"We don't have time to wait."

Lucy steps out of the studio positively aflame.

"You finally get it," Alina says. "Rage against The Sons!"

"We need to take those bastards down," Lucy says. And on she goes, listing friends she'll text to spread the word, posts and tweets to bring Occupy and austerity fighters into the game. Then she holds up two bookmark-sized pieces of paper. "… backstage passes! And the Fillmore is like a mile from here. We'll get Tom Morello to spread the word."

Rader takes Lucy by the arm. "When did you get this idea to take out your frustration on The Sons of Industry?"

"This afternoon, when—"

"And you'll act on impulse? Again? Whose life will you destroy this time?"

"Gus, those guys represent everything that's wrong. Three spoiled brats who've never had to work for anything and are too rich to fail. We can organize—"

"We will take taxi to airport. Our flight leaves in two hours. We have an important meeting to prepare."

The glow leaves Lucy's face. For an instant she looks as though she'll scream at him. In that instant, Rader feels sympathy for her. She's tasted the candy of fame, of course she wants more.

Before she can speak, he stops and leans down. "You have worked too hard to regress so fast."

"I need to talk to Tom Morello."

Rader let's out a disgusted guffaw.

"Gus, he's worth a million followers. I want him on my side."

"You want him. Your side. Lucy, listen to what you're saying. You are nothing." He looks up at the sky and then back at her. "But I am nothing, too. I have no authority over you or anyone else. Do as you wish, but if you're interested in justice, you'll work rather than play."

"Alina and I will meet with Tom Morello."

"Two pretty girls backstage at the rock concert?"

Klaus lets loose hardy laughter.

"Oh shit. He won't think of us as groupies, will he?"

Klaus says, "If you get near him, maybe he'll talk to you, but security will see you as his toys."

She looks at the backstage passes in her hand, turns to Alina, who shrugs, and then puts them in her backpack. "Well, I should really visit my mom."

"You're mother?"

"She must know I'm here and if I don't call or visit—"

"You can do anything you like," Rader says. He nods to Klaus who steps into the street to flag a cab. Without looking at her, he adds, "Why don't you call your mother from the airport?"

Klaus gets in the front seat of the cab. In back, Lucy sits between Rader and Alina. Rader takes the makeup kit from his bag and hands it across Lucy to Alina. On the flight from Dublin, having the TSA mistreat Lucy worked to their advantage, but it won't on the way home. Alina applies foundation first, covering Lucy's freckles and darkening her skin just enough to hide that fluorescent Celtic luster. Then she adds shade to hollow Lucy's cheeks and give angles to her jaw line. She finishes by penciling in crows feet.

Lucy talks to her mother for nearly fifteen minutes, describing her experiences at rallies in Europe and Oakland as though it were a spring break vacation. When Lucy struggles with an answer to why they have to return to Amsterdam, Rader holds out his hand and Lucy hands him the phone.

"Hello? Ms. Montgomery? Yes, it is Gus Reser, here."

He walks out of Lucy's hearing range and says, "Lucy is in danger here. Those horrible people, Simon Wentworth and his friends at TLA have mobilized the FBI against Lucy. There are warrants for her arrest and they have assembled circumstantial evidence tying her to the murders of those three industrialists." Lucy's mother sounds like the lead dupe in any American situation comedy. "Don't worry, Ms. Montgomery, Lucy will be safe in Amsterdam, and the FBI will soon learn that it was really Simon Wentworth, Volodya Kazimer, and Fiona Black who murdered those three men. I'll see to it that they're arrested and then we'll all be safe. I promise."

A few minutes later the airline begins boarding. Rader takes an aisle seat in the row behind Klaus, Lucy, and Alina. An hour into the flight, Lucy comes and sits next to him. She says, "I'm sorry, I just realized who we're up against and I wanted to fight."

He puts his arm around her. "We all do. I've been fighting this war my entire life."

"When we get back, I'll study the propaganda of the deed."

"Maybe it's time for Alina to teach you how to use that special tool, the one you said could destroy our credibility?"

2011-Nov-2 Above The Intoxicating Page
Historic pivot point peak probability: still UNKNOWN

I'm settled in at the roll-top desk I use from my room in Fiona's flat. Winter sleeps on the floor at my feet with an ice pack taped to his tail. Fiona comes in and sits on the corner of my bed with her head in her hands.

"I took it out on him," she says. Winter stands with his paws on one of her knees and licks her neck. "I attacked a police officer—what a twit."

"You were avenging Winter."

"Vengeance isn't really my style." She runs her hands down Winter, when she touches the swelling he looks back at it.

I say, "He'll be okay in a few days."

"We'll take him to the vet tomorrow."

"He doesn't like veterinarians. We'll wait three days and if he can't wag, we'll take him in."

"He can't wag?" She sighs and leans back.

Following her third sigh, she asks, "Can I see the police officer's timeweave?"

"Sure, I'll launch the calculation, but you know what to expect. A fork in his road, he'll either recover and rejoin the police or go on disability, the timeweave won't resolve which until the surgery is performed."

"Surgery?" She sighs. "Bloody hell. I want to see his likelihoods. I might need to help him."

"Okay," I say and configure the calculation. The satisfaction of my work pulls me in and the next time I look up, Fiona's curled around Winter on my bed and they're both asleep.

Volodya has already identified the man as Officer Michael Davis of the Oakland Police Department. His constant exposure to surveillance systems provides ample data and a distinct timeweave forms in a few minutes. Most timeweaves of people with established careers and family lives consist of a solid branch with a few low probability twigs tied to external effects of the economy, possible illnesses of a spouse or children, or, for a police officer, a job-related injury. Officer Davis's timeweave isn't like that.

This man's past illustrates the pain caused by the financial collapse of the early 21st century: Officer Mike Davis's father lost his job selling mortgages in the real estate collapse three years ago. His sister suffers from multiple sclerosis, was denied health insurance, and had to declare bankruptcy. She died eleven days ago, the same day that his wife moved out. Now he lives with his mother.

I look over at Fiona, sound asleep in the comfort of this nice home. She will do all she can for him. I zoom in on his timeweave to search for a concrete way that we can help this unfortunate fellow. An odd confluence of data dominate his future as a police officer. One particular link, blinking to indicate that this one datum should be checked for error because its impact on the calculation is so large, a temporary kluge that we implemented to prevent another no-fly bug, takes me to a video taken at Occupy Oakland one week ago.

The video shows a tear gas canister fired into a crowd of protesters from behind the police line. Our software calculates the trajectory of the canister and the likelihood that this particular trajectory could have been random. The video repeats, but pauses at the instant the canister enters the frame. A dotted line indicates the trajectory: it will hit a decorated veteran of the Iraq war.

A second video of the same event comes up, this one from a camera on the opposite side of the street. It too pauses on a still. A dotted line traces the trajectory of the canister back behind the police line to the rifle that fired it. A third video from yet another point of view—this one from a surveillance camera in a neighboring parking lot—doesn't include the tear gas canister at all, but the dotted line extends to the man holding the rifle. I click the play icon. After shooting, the officer walks to the parking lot. Light reflects from his badge and nameplate. Pattern recognition software reconstructs the name, Michael Davis, and brings up an Oakland Tribune stock photo of the man who suffered a severed Achilles' tendon for hurting Winter's tail.

I back up and work through the primary links in Officer Davis's timeline. On the first night of Occupy Oakland protests, a video shows Officer Davis talking to Occupiers, joking around with them, even helping a few set up a tent. He told them to give The Man hell.

Why would he shoot a tear gas canister at such an important Occupier, eight days later?

When I finally get back to the video showing Officer Davis after he's fired the tear-gas canister, I notice something about one of the people standing in the shadows. Something about the way the man holds himself, the way he walks—no, that's not it, it's the way he never looks in the direction of any of the surveillance cameras! Zooming in on the image, I know, in the pit of my stomach, the very base of my gizzard, that this man is Guenther Rader. While my gizzard is certain, my frontal lobe is equally certain that Rader was in Amsterdam at that time. Wasn't he?

I pull up Rader's timeline, such as it is. A time-thread whose only firm links are from video we recorded outside his Amsterdam Hostel. I loosen the face recognition criteria and turn the software loose on our library of video covering a four day period around the date Officer Davis fired that tear gas canister. None of the images show Rader.

Did Rader recruit Officer Davis? Convince him that sacrificing the Iraq war veteran would incriminate the police? If so, it worked. Occupy's popularity jumped after the report. Could Rader be behind Davis's attack of Winter's tail?

2011-Nov-3 Above The Intoxicating Page
Historic pivot point peak probability: still UNKNOWN

Three hours and seventeen minutes later, my phone sings *Somewhere Over the Rainbow*. It's Gwinnie!

"Simon." Gwinnie's voice is drenched in fear.

"What is it?" I've fallen asleep on the precarious edge of the bed next to Winter. Fiona is asleep on his other side.

"Lucy is with Guenther Rader."

"Yes, I know." Winter rolls onto his back for a belly rub. Fiona stirs. I struggle to maintain balance here on the edge.

"It was him. She's been with him the whole time and—why didn't you tell me?"

"But Gwinnie, how could I? You said all those things. He convinced you that TLA caused your foreclosure and, and, and you said you thought it would be better," and now my cursed voice cracks, "if I left you and Lucy alone."

"You need a stronger heart, Simon. You're my best friend—you should know when to ignore what I say!"

Fiona sits up and whispers, "She wouldn't have believed you anyway."

I say, "Gwinnie, you wouldn't have believed me anyway."

"You should have told me."

"No," I say, experiencing what I know from previous experience will be a short-lived sense of confidence, "you were better off believing Lucy was fine while the three of us monitor and protect her."

Gwinnie sighs.

"Lucy called you yesterday?"

"Yes. She's going to Europe again—but I suppose you already know that."

"How did you figure out that Gus Reser is actually Guenther Rader?"

"Lucy put him on. She said he'd make me feel better. He's very slick, you know. He made it sound like she's on a business trip."

"Tell me what they said."

"Umm, I don't really remember."

I think I hear her crying, a sound that brings to mind images of her beautiful forehead contorted in misery and tears flowing down the ideal slope of her nose.

"She mentioned Brussels and Berlin, I think."

"She's already been to Berlin. Did she say why?"

"Wait, Simon, I forgot the reason I called." The dear thing sniffles, bringing to mind her perfect nose leaking into a tissue that had no idea of its good fortune. "Simon—you and Fiona and Volodya, you're in trouble."

Gwinnie says something else, but I'm distracted and it doesn't register. I ask, "Why do you believe we're in trouble?"

"Reser, I mean Rader, Guenther Rader. He said that you and Fiona and Volodya murdered those three businessmen in New York City and that the FBI is going to arrest you, that then we would be safe. Simon, I knew something was wrong, it didn't feel right. To doubt you, it didn't feel right. I'm so sorry."

"Murder?"

"That's what he said—and I believed him—Simon, maybe you're right, maybe you're right about everything. If only you'd listened to Fiona that night, I'd have never gone out with Richard. Maybe we ..."

After hearing those words, none of the others matter. Calm comes over me, a feeling of exultant joy that Fiona quashes by slapping me.

"... it did make me feel better, hearing from Lucy, knowing she was okay, so I went to bed, fell right to sleep, but when I woke up I knew it was him. I dreamt that we were in The Bohemian Grove. I was working in the kitchen and Rader was there and Winter came and barked at him and he tried to attack Winter with a cleaver—it was so weird, like a Disney cartoon villain—and you were knocking on the door but couldn't get in—then I woke up. And it all fit together. Gus Reser—Guenther Rader. And he's got

Lucy."

2011-Nov-3 Above The Intoxicating Page
Historic pivot point peak probability: 13 days

"We have a new problem."

Fiona, Winter, and I convene in the living room of her flat. Me in my soft, brown terry robe, Fiona in a long T-shirt, and Winter, of course, in his fine fur coat. The image of Volodya shows him in a black sweater, collar up as usual, at his desk in the Vienna office.

Fiona says, "How did I know he was going to say that?"

I ask, "Has it converged?"

"Yes, calculation says now that we have more than nine but less than 17 days. But that is not the problem." He looks at his camera so that the image on our screens indicates he's looking at us. "Someone, and I believe little research is required to identify whom, has assembled evidence that ties the three of us to the spurious murders of Gordon Woodley, Charles van Bibber, and Brandon Birch. The ersatz evidence has been neatly installed in an assortment of FBI databases—our guilt should be assumed within a few hours."

He puts the display of his monitor on my tablet. Fiona squeezes between Winter and me on the couch so she can see it too.

Volodya launches a spider. "This is new code, very efficient. Nice trick, uses a vector that follows cookie crumbs through Anonymous, it will determine who assembled the evidence against us—perhaps our best chance at identifying computational strengths of Rader's gang."

"A correlation gradient?" I ask.

"Yes, Penelope wrote this. Nice code, too." Volodya posts a software source code window on my tablet. "See? Comments, a lost art."

"Excuse me, gents," Fiona says. "Stop pissing around with

software and tell me what evidence the FBI has that makes me a murderer?"

"Yes, well," Volodya says. "A circumstantial electronic trail, a bit of real and plenty of artificial evidence that places each of us in contact with the three men within 24 hours of their deaths—sufficient for authorities to arrest and hold us, well, you, I rather doubt the evidence is sufficient for sovereign state of Austria to extradite me."

Fiona climbs her cane to a standing position. She leans to the point of falling but with the furniture arranged to accommodate her, she catches herself on a bookcase, hops to a desk and takes a seat. In one seamless motion, she boots up a desktop computer, opens a drawer, and pulls out a thick file.

"Crinklspiragocious. The FBI has just begun processing the information," Volodya says.

"Can we travel on our own names?" Fiona says, though she's holding up two Australian passports.

"That could be a problem."

I lift my laptop from the coffee table and open a Lufthansa booking window. Fiona tosses me the passports and I book us on a flight to Vienna.

Volodya chuckles. "The press will call us rogue security contractors."

2011-Nov-3 SFO
Historic pivot point peak probability: 13 days

"G'day, mate," I say in my most boisterous Australian imitation. "No worries, Bob's your uncle."

Fiona's already through security. Winter is in the soft x-ray booth, they didn't even make him take off his collar, and Lufthansa lets him travel in a carry-on crate.

"We'll be having shrimp on the barbie tonight in Austria."

The security agent, motions me through.

"Oops," I say, holding up my boarding pass, "Right then, bit of a mistake, no kangaroos in Austria."

The TSA agent does a double take. Fiona bursts into artificial laughter and says in her loudest voice and thickest accent, "Right then, we'll bring our own joeys."

I laugh all the while, putting on my belt and shoes, collecting my change, keys, phone, and carry-on, feeling that Australian is one of my best impersonations until I look up and see Fiona glowering at me. The TSA agents seem to agree with me, though. Waving us through with smiles and good wishes.

"No," Fiona says when we're well clear of security, "if the FBI asks, they'll never remember the outspoken Aussies with the beagle."

"My accent is that good?"

She doesn't answer.

11. The 1% Solution

2011-Nov-4 Vienna
Historic pivot point peak probability: 12 days

Back in our lab overlooking the Naschmarkt, Volodya rises from his desk to greet me. We shake hands and pat each other's shoulders. He complains about impending snow flurries and I brag about my Australian accent. Once we complete this ceremonial if awkward expression of affection, we're back at full speed.

Volodya indicates graphics on two of his monitors. "Here is the timeweave for The Sons of Industry, and here, the timeweave for Rader's gang. Both desire economic collapse."

I say, "Why would Frankie and his friends bring down the economy? It's their economy. And what would motivate Rader to? Frankie might lose more money, but the poor lose everything."

"A happy 99% becomes fat at the trough. Comfortable bourgeoisie do not desire change. On the other side," he indicates another monitor, "look where The Sons are investing: precious metals, short calls on large corporations, real estate in downtrodden regions of Europe. None of these accounts are directly owned by Frankie, James, or Wallace, but the sequence of bank transfers leads back to them. They stand to profit a great deal."

"Anonymous might be able to bring down the monetary system by corrupting enough databases," I say. "But The Sons of Industry can't sell enough shares to start an avalanche without triggering SEC safeguards."

He points to another monitor, a stock market timeweave. "If Dow Jones falls 1000 points in fifteen minutes, SEC will stop trading, but eventually trading must resume and collapse continues. Stop orders add to landslide. We predict 10,000 points down in one week."

I mumble, "Total collapse."

Volodya says, "Should Anonymous move against even one financial institution, the effect avalanches, a situation whose repercussions will require much study to predict."

A sigh escapes my lungs, inflates my cheeks, and deflates my shoulders. Hunching over, I peer down at the Naschmarkt. People go about their lives, exchanging currency for food, goods, and services. What gives a person the audacity to think that their personal goals are worth the misery of millions, even billions, of others?

Dropping into his ergonomic desk chair, Volodya says, "We must translate the myriad possibilities into precise probabilities for each conceivable action of Rader and his Occupy-Anonymous coalition and Frankie Woodley and his Sons of Industry. Tremendous challenge, but we will find the pivot point and prune the timeweave."

We calculate. It is what we do.

Volodya says, "It will be our World Cup!"

The sole advantage to pessimism is enthusiasm in the face of bad news. I find it infectious and announce, "Our Super Bowl!"

Fiona, who has apparently been standing behind us, adds, "Our Olympics."

"We have great deal of data to work with," Volodya says. "The Sons of Industry's plan to replace countries with corporatries will require new models."

"Corporatries?" Fiona asks.

"Fascinating concept," Volodya says. "Unadulterated corporate freedom. No such states have ever been tried. The freedom to attempt different solutions to complex problems, in a way, it's what we do."

"We simulate them," Fiona says. "No one gets hurt in simulations."

Volodya says, "Imagine the freedom to pursue your own goals without the burden of pointless laws and jealous tax collectors."

Fiona says, "Imagine global famine."

"There is potential for giant gains."

"There is potential for extensive suffering." Fiona raised her voice. "They're trying to destroy civilization!"

Winter whines.

"Stop it," I say. "You're bothering the dog."

"Gromfrinkin-apologize-frick," Volodya offers.

"I still love you," Fiona accepts.

"Thank you," I say. "Now, do we model corporatries as monarchies? Oligarchies? Plutocracies? Feudal states?"

"No, corporations have run mining towns and manufacturing centers that include housing. We modify those models to allow free movement from one to another like employees in eras of high employment and combine with models of small countries."

Fiona says, "Do you really need computers for this?"

We both turn to her.

"Come on, what do you think will happen when one of these corporatries starts to fail? And they will fail, right? The point of allowing competition—though God knows Wall Street seems to have forgotten this part—is that some companies lose. The same thing will happen that happens every time an organization fails. The people at the top will protect themselves at the expense of the people at the bottom."

Volodya says, "A mere opinion."

I say, "We have to calculate the probabilities."

Fiona pushes her chair to the corner of the room, grabs her cane, stands, and walks out. Winter yanks his leash from the coat rack and rushes after her.

Almost exactly three hours later, Volodya's laughter rouses me. It is Volodya's default laughter: impending *schadenfreude* composed of equal parts amusement and malice.

He says, "By end of week, Rader's group will replace us as suspects in the murders of the elder Woodley, Birch, and van Bibber."

"I knew you were up to something." I say, and as I look toward him, a new structure catches my eye on the timeweave of Rader's gang. "They're going back to Berlin?"

Volodya rotates the timeweave and clicks on a link. "It would seem."

I pop up humanity's timeweave. "Amsterdam is all but out of the running."

"Probability of pivot point occurring in Berlin has not risen proportionally." He brings up a list of names and photos of people who had not previously been associated with Rader's gang.

"Ah," he says. "Old-school anarchists. Socialist utopians who either live in Berlin or have reserved accommodations."

From behind us, Fiona startles me. "Like a reunion of 1970s terrorists, survivors from Baader-Meinhof, Red Army Faction, IRA, the Weather Underground, Revolutionaere Zellen."

"Yes, but no one linked to Anonymous, no Occupy motivators," Volodya says. "Why convene the old guard failures?"

Me: "To use old-school methods?"

Fiona: "How can they afford these hotels?"

Volodya: "Most of them assimilated, developed careers, became petty bourgeoisie."

Fiona: "Look, they've hired a caterer. I bet it's a fundraiser."

"Ahh," Volodya says. "I'll set alerts on their accounts."

2011-Nov-5 Vienna
Historic pivot point peak probability: 11 days

Jet lag put me to sleep early and woke me four hours prior to sunrise. Winter-the-sleepy-headed dog has no such issue. I carry him down to the lab.

The latest timeweave for humanity bursts into a geyser-like spray in 8-13 days. The spray consists of 67,958 tenuous futures and none of these 67,958 predictions—oops, it's updated to

67,873—has greater than a 1% chance of occurring. Since the precision of our timeweave technology is at best 2%, we have no handle on which of the 67,873 timeweaves—sorry, 68,011 now—are meaningful. This classic signal to noise problem comes from the butterfly effect of chaos theory amplified by the bane of our predictive engine, the central limit theorem of probability and statistics.

I literally roll up my sleeves and figuratively dig into the weedy timeweaves, as indistinct as blades of grass from an airplane, with an abstract shovel. I start on one with 247:1 odds; economic collapse followed by a billion-strong worldwide Occupy/anti-austerity movement; as western governments fail, they ally with corporations to suppress Occupy and the resulting oppression spawns full-scale revolution. With Europe, North America, India, Brazil, and the Pacific Rim in turmoil, Russia, China, North Korea, Iran, most of Africa, and Mexico mobilize—World War Three. I leave that thread and try another: the huddled masses turn to the few surviving corporations for food and shelter, the corporations replace government, an era of plutocracy begins, the prosperous few live in gated communities while those who offer no corporate value become, by definition, outlaws, and, soon the impoverished billions rebel: a different approach to World War Three.

Drops of perspiration sting my eyes. I force a smile and say, "Frankie and Lucy both promised utopia!" Winter's tail thumps against my feet—its swollen in the middle but seems to have healed enough for him to laugh at me.

Here's one where fear of unbridled corporate power leads to government overreaction: wide-scale nationalization, planned economies, bureaucratic corruption, decades of oppression, and a century-long dark age. I tag this one for Volodya, he might find it nostalgic.

Working faster, I see famine, plague, pandemic, peak oil. I expected climate change to rank higher. What? No swarm of locusts? Oh, here it is.

I examine 978 timeweaves in five hours but still can't find one where the world struggles for a few years, even a decade, before resuming its altogether imperfect chaotic path into a mostly tolerable future for at least half the planet's population.

2011-Nov-5 New York City

James and Wallace sit across from Frankie at a low-slung glass table in the Woodley-Carlyle office suite sipping thirty-year-old cabernet.

The shift of their less visible portfolios to precious metals and short calls on major corporate stocks, including their own, will be complete when the first corporatries are ready for launch in two years. All they'll have to do is flip the sell switch, bring down the world economy, and provide a safe, productive haven for the world's most talented people.

A team of Woodley-Carlyle real estate specialists found the right place for the first corporatries : Bosnia-Herzegovina. Beautiful rolling hills, fertile land close to the Mediterranean steeped in European culture. The Sons channeled cash through dozens of untraceable subsidiaries to Bosnian businesses and government officials. The transaction only burdened the public with the word "investment," which, in this economy, was sufficient to assure acceptance of the Sons' terms and conditions. The huge capital infusion guarantees a thousand square miles within three years—the time needed to relocate current residents—but the first hundred square miles are being quietly cleared right now.

Five leather-bound proposals lie on the table before them. Each describes a unique corporate-society. James Birch designed a sink or swim free-for-all: no regulations or taxes, profit-based insurance ventures instead of police, fire, and emergency protection, every road a toll road, every service pay-as-you-go, free of any concept of welfare.

Wallace van Bibber went the other direction and designed his based on conservative Christian values: heavy regulations on what is taught in schools and what passes for entertainment, gun ownership required for every male citizen over 16, single-family homes with a church on every block, and low taxes with charity-based social safety nets.

Frankie's corporatry will cover food, shelter, restaurants, and entertainment so citizens can concentrate on their work; like a giant startup that gives its employees no reason to leave.

Eviction of people who fail is the one component all three have in common, though the definition of failure varies—from bankruptcy to specific crimes and, for Wallace, immoral acts. The two remaining proposals are modified plans from sea-steading think tanks.

Frankie says, "If you needed proof that business is the ultimate art form, it's in those five documents. Or at least in the two or three that acquire the greatest market share slash population."

James says, "Each one will draw people with different talents. I'll get all the risk takers and big thinkers." He points at his two friends and adds, "I'm going to win big."

Wallace says, "The Bible says that my design will still be growing stronger as your new-age concepts flame out."

"All right, boys," Frankie says. "My bean counters and bureaucrats offered some advice that we have to discuss." He hands out copies of a report.

James says, "What's it say."

"Aren't you going to read it?"

"No. What's it say?"

"You guys," Frankie waves his copy at them. "To let market forces do their thing, they recommend that we guarantee free movement across corporatries. To do that they say we should require common debt relief and bankruptcy laws that cross borders."

"What?" James says. "If someone makes a bad investment or gets too far in debt, that's his problem. No way. Free-loaders shouldn't be allowed to walk."

Wallace says, "If someone is in debt to a corporatry they shouldn't be able to leave until they work their way out."

"If the corporatry fails, the citizens should fail with it?"

James sits up straight. "Absolutely! They're shareholders."

"Okay, we're on the same page," Frankie says. "But we'll have to bring it up at the meeting." He sips his wine. "The idea will sell itself."

James: "The only billionaires who won't join us are the ones who feed at the government trough."

Frankie: "We have the right people lined up. Once we show them the land …"

Wallace: "We could unite the world."

James: "And isolate anyone who won't play."

Wallace: "We could start a new era of peace and prosperity."

Frankie refills their glasses and then stands and raises his in the direction of the Atlantic ocean. "To the Sons of Industry."

James: "Rage against The Sons."

Frankie: "The Sons are the machine."

Wallace: "I'm happy to be The Machine."

"I'd rather be The Man."

They drink.

2011-Nov-9 Vienna
Historic pivot point peak probability: 6 days

Four days caught in the metaphorically rapids of 42,086 conflicting and intersecting timeweaves of doom leaves me exhausted. I've concealed my work from Volodya because he would insist that we automate the task, but writing and debugging automation code would take longer than the maximum 8 days we have left. I hide it from Fiona because she wouldn't understand the value of sifting through noise. There is simply no other way right now.

After I work my way through the 42,985th timeweave, Winter growls. He doesn't like me to get frustrated and this mishmash of timeweaves has taken me to my limit. I stand and he bolts to the coat rack, grabs his leash, and brings it to me. We walk downstairs and into the heart of Vienna.

Austria's infrastructure glistens with the legacy of the Hapsburg Empire. These streets, the great square at St. Stevens' Cathedral, and the monumental halls once throbbed with the glory of 470 years of oligarchy. Prior to the Great War, the world was dominated by interlinked empires. We take the train to Shoenbrunn palace and tour the offices where Emperor Franz Josef spent 14 hour days for over 60 years running the Austro-Hungarian Empire that he inherited.

Emperors suffered the indulgences that typify all oligarchs, but those flaws are not what made them blind to their imminent decay. The twigs formed around civil unrest that took root from a new industrial class and ever increasing wealth disparity—disparity between those who did the work and those who collected the wealth. And then, on a summer day in Sarajevo, a twenty-three-year-old man who was dying from tuberculosis assassinated the emperor's nephew and heir and brought those four centuries of empire to a close.

History does not repeat itself, at least not perfectly. No two swings of a pendulum or two beats of a heart are identical. The forces that drive pendulums and hearts don't change from one oscillation to another, though random fluctuations in the surrounding conditions distinguish different periods. What we mean when we say that history repeats is that the traits of different eras recur as the surrounding conditions evolve.

Winter and I return to Vienna as flakes of snow swirl between Belvedere Palace and the Heroes' Monument that commemorates the Soviet army for liberating Vienna from Nazi rule in 1945. At first, the descendents of the Hapsburgs embraced the Nazis, but they cheered six years later when the Red Army liberated them. Like so many snowflakes in the wind, history sways with the breeze of time.

I feel that my best move is to take a nap with my dog.

* * *

I awake in my bed with Winter serving as my pillow in that odd state where it feels like morning but the clock insists that it's evening. Despite the physical comfort, I'm left with a dream-vision of my experience at the intersections of realities prior to the Wall Street riot: the Occupy protest and the Haymarket riot merged and no direction brought contentment, just different levels of dread.

I feed Winter his supper, work through another 645 timeweaves—every one of them impending disaster—and join Volodya and Fiona for dinner. Mr. Gorkem has provided an array of Mediterranean delights, gyro, kebab, tabbouleh, fresh-baked pita, and kofta. I recount my walk with Winter.

Fiona suggests that history repeats at a frequency of three human lifetimes, "just long enough for the mistakes made by one generation to be forgotten so that they can be repeated."

Volodya agrees, an event which nearly causes me to choke. He says, "Vienna has often been at the center of history. I wonder how the geometry of the 47 year period from the long depression of 1873 to onset of the First World War correlates to 36 year period from 1970s inflation-driven recession to this Great Recession."

"Well," Fiona says, "we'll find out in 6 days."

"Six plus or minus two days," Volodya says. "As few as three, maybe tomorrow, maybe next week—probabilities are given by *distributions* not integers."

Me: "Pass the baklava."

Fiona: "Simon, eat your tabbouleh."

Volodya: "In 1914 change was inevitable, but emergence of capitalism-based democracy and autocratic communism was hardly foreseeable."

Me: "Nature of a pivot point."

Fiona: "They were all well intentioned, you know."

We both look at her and she says, "At the turn of the 20th century, democracy, communism, and anarchy—no one knew how the revolutions would turn out. They meant well."

Volodya: "Couldn't overcome human attraction to nationalism, racism, xenophobia which led to large-scale fascism as the transitional state we know as World War Two."

After a cube of baklava, I gorge on lamb gyro.

Volodya says, "Did you know that mayors of eleven American cities will hold a conference call in four hours ?"

Me: "The likelihood of a coordinated shutdown of Occupy has always been high."

"Police in each of these eleven cities will raid and remove Occupy camps at dawn tomorrow. One of two timelines emerges. Probability of Occupy deconstruction is twice probability it blossoms under this pressure."

Fiona: "That could be our pivot point."

Volodya: "No. Pivot point probability is now isolated to Europe: 43% chance in Berlin—"

Me: "Where Rader is taking Lucy."

Volodya: "—and 39% chance in Sarajevo where Frankie is holding his corporatry meeting. Remaining 18% distributed among Athens, Dublin, Madrid, North Africa, tiny chance in Moscow."

I choke on the word Sarajevo.

Volodya: "What? Sarajevo? Where I met my friend Simon Wentworth? Lovely city for a pivot point."

Me: "You know what happened in Sarajevo."

Volodya: "Similar epochs, similar results, but lightning is unlikely to strike twice in same place."

2011-Nov-9 New York City

Frankie likes to tell people that he started working on Wall Street when he was ten years old. He doesn't mention that his first job was selling newspapers. At 16 he washed dishes in a diner in the Bronx. He did it for the money but not the paycheck. He took the checks home and gave them to his dad who then deposited his allowance. His allowance averaged a hundred times the value of the paycheck. When Frankie turned 18, Gordon Woodley sat him down and showed him the pile of paychecks—none had ever been cashed. Frankie remembered his dad's words: "Son, these are hard working people who paid you a fair wage. Do you know why it's not right for us to cash these checks?" At first, Frankie had been indignant. He'd earned that money, but under his father's scrutiny, he came to understand. The people who employed him deserved a break and the sums involved didn't amount to pocket change to the Woodleys. Frankie recalls saying, "It's about respect." More than the words, he remembers his father standing up and offering to shake his hand.

But Wallace van Bibber and James Birch never did dishes, never worked retail, never stamped a time card. Frankie considers both good men, deserving of their wealth, but it was Frankie who built The Sons of Industry.

The empty bottle of cab is still on the table next to three empty glasses. Frankie has spent this week working through every detail. He was flippant about the bean counters' report because he didn't want it to frighten the others, but he took it seriously.

Now that the sales meeting is set up in Sarajevo, he can't stop thinking about what Wallace said: "We could start a new era of peace and prosperity." It brings to mind a comment his father used to make about Communists and utopia, that they neglected reality. "Bunch of clowns," Frankie says aloud to himself.

He stands and looks out the window. "I don't want to be a clown." He steps to the desk and picks up the report from his bureaucrats. He finds a paragraph suggesting bylaws that will guarantee transparency and smooth exits for executives. "No fuckin' Enrons." He tosses the report back on his desk and paces the length of the office.

"Corporatry." He likes the name. The focus group hated it so he fired the marketing director. He laughs at his own hubris.

There's a knock on the door. His father's admin, Myrna. She walks in two counts after knocking. She doesn't need permission. Hell, Frankie thinks of her as his boss. She's well past twice his age and has more than twice his experience.

"Mr. Woodley, everyone has RSVPed." She peers up at him over her reading glasses.

Frankie wonders if his dad ever had sex with Myrna. Such a dynamo, he'd go for it if he weren't essentially afraid of her.

"Who's in and who's out?"

"It's an impressive list."

"You think?" Frankie asks. Impressing Myrna feels like he's impressed his father's ghost.

The day he moved into this office she brought him a resignation letter. He offered to triple her salary, but she wouldn't budge. She wanted to be with her grandchildren and to travel. He told her to hire a staff and offered her unlimited paid vacation. She still wouldn't budge. Then he created trust funds for each of her grandchildren and told her that he'd put a million dollars in each one for every year she continued working for him. She budged.

"You will have the fifteen most powerful people in the world outside of government—have you reconsidered my recommendation?"

"Of course. I've struggled with it. I know you're right, but I think your timing is off. Once we get through this meeting, you can set the agenda for the next one and invite anyone you like."

She raises her eyebrows.

Frankie adds, "You can chair the meeting, if you want."

She laughs and cuffs him on the chin. If she were taller, she'd probably ruffle his hair.

"Behave," she says. "You will need protection from the Middle East—you'll need Egyptian generals, Arab Sheiks, Dubai executives—"

"The next meeting—anything you say. Let's get the west and

east on board first, okay? Who's in and who's out?"

She reads off the names from memory. "Larry Ellison, Elon Musk, Peter Thiel, Meg Whitman, Mark Zuckerberg, Richard Branson, Tom Siebel, Michael Dell, Charles Koch, Amancio Ortega, Christy Walton, Phil Knight, Stefan Quandt are all in. Steve Jobs is tentative, of course, he's sick you know, but said he hopes to attend. Craig Walmark and Warren Buffet are out, didn't expect them anyway. And the Russians ..."

"Yes? Yes!"

"Both Sergei Popov and Oleg Deripaska are coming and they both know the other will be there. The Chinese were in until they found out the Russians will be there, and Kim Dotcom said he might surprise you."

"Fan-fucking tastic!"

"Frankie—your language."

"I love it when you scold me."

2011-Nov-10
Historic pivot point peak probability: 5 days

When Winter and I enter the lab the next morning, Volodya has different timeweaves and calculations on all twelve of our monitors.

"I've been waiting for you." He stands, Winter walks between his legs to the pillow under my table. "These are timelines of Franz Joseph I, Kaiser Wilhelm II, Nicholas II, King George V, President Poincare, and, of course, Vladimir Ilyich Lenin."

"Why?"

"Correlation with pre-world war one epoch." He uses a laser pointer to indicate the monitor closest to me. "Look here, timelines of Joseph, Nicholas, and Wilhelm connect and reconnect to each other, quite stable. And on this monitor, Lenin smears across history from 1900 to 1916, random walk about Europe with attractor in St. Petersburg." He moves to the monitor closest to his keyboard. "And then the pivot point: assassination of the heir to ancient and exalted empire, Archduke Franz Ferdinand by a Serbian teenager, Gavrilo Princip."

The monitors above and behind these show the timeweaves for the Sons of Industry, Rader's gang, and, of course human history. A lump climbs up into my throat.

"Yes," Volodya says, "conclusion is obvious. So I did the numbers. Very peculiar, let me show you."

We sit in our respective chairs and I roll over next to him.

He says, "Correlation between Rader and Lenin is 0.76."

A correlation measures the similarity with which two parameters behave under the same circumstances. Numerically, they run from minus one to plus one. A correlation of 1.0 means that two parameters experience the same degree of change under the same influences; zero correlation means the two are unrelated; and correlation of -1.0, called anti-correlation, means that the two variables respond in opposite ways to common stimuli. Correlation of 0.76 is about what I'd expect for someone who emulates his hero as Rader does Lenin.

Volodya says, "No surprise. The highest correlation ties Franz Joseph to Frankie's father, Gordon Woodley: at 0.94."

"Certainly," I say. "Two hard working men born to power."

"Frankie Woodley and Franz Ferdinand correlation is 0.74, lower than I guessed. If history replays, Frankie may survive."

"Volodya, I don't like where this is going."

"Ignorance will not help us care for Lucy." He clicks his mouse and a timeline appears next to Lucy's.

I say, "Gavrilo Princip?"

"Yes, Lucy correlates to Princip at minus 0.92."

"*Minus* 0.92?" I activate my earbug and call Fiona downstairs. I find it difficult to breathe. She appears in 77 seconds.

Fiona: "Doesn't make sense, mate. Lucy's timeweave puts her in Berlin and Frankie's puts him in Sarajevo. Both of them experience pivot points, but nearly everyone on earth will be affected by this event, whatever it is."

"No," Volodya says, "there is causal link."

He offers his chair and she sits, takes his mouse, and zooms in on Frankie's timeweave.

"Holy dooley! He's bringing the greatest concentration of financial power since the Hapsbergs, Windsors, and Romanovs, to Sarajevo three days from today—Silicon Valley tech giants, Wall Street icons, European business moguls, and, of course, no swindle would be complete without a couple of Russian oligarchs."

"The history of the 20th century was launched by the assassination of a petty nobleman by a sick and confused young man." It feels more like I'm listening to these words than speaking them. "Two World Wars and a Cold War, no fewer than 80 million violent deaths."

"You overlook key point," Volodya says. "Correlation between Lucy and Gavrilio Princip is *minus* 0.92, anti-correlated."

"What does that mean?" Fiona says, "That Lucy becomes friends with Frankie Woodley and they prevent World War Three? Anti-correlation."

"Mmmhm," Volodya warbles, "correlation or anti-correlation so strong means something. Determining course of action will require a great deal of work."

"Look, lads, she'll be in Berlin and he'll be in Sarajevo, how can they be correlated, or anti-correlated, or whatever if they don't even interact?"

"Butterflies cause but don't correlate." Volodya frowns in disgust. "Skirts correlate but don't cause."

Fiona looks confused.

"Fashion is correlated to the stock market," I say. "Skirts rise and fall with the market—strong correlation, maybe the stock market causes skirts, but do skirts cause stock prices?"

Volodya: "We know nothing."

Me: "We know that Lucy and Frankie are the keys to preventing disaster."

Fiona: "And we know where we'll be spending the weekend."

Volodya: "I will go to Berlin."

Me: "I should be with Lucy."

Volodya and Fiona look at each other and shake their heads. She says, "No, you're coming to Sarajevo with me."

12. The 99% Solution

2011-Nov-12 Amsterdam

Lucy sits next to Stepan eating yogurt with blueberries. Alina's across the table drinking coffee.

Klaus comes in and leans over Lucy. He says, "I haven't seen you lately."

"You can find me in the library or the hacking room—or in the basement."

"You've been practicing?"

"If I ever need to," Lucy says, "I should be able to shoot—"

"Not enough time in the basement," Alina interrupts. "She doesn't practice; she reads instead."

"I can hit the broadside of a barn almost every time."

Klaus says, "Handguns have their own personalities, you have to practice to get to know them." Then he motions to the others and leads them out of the kitchen. Stepan rubs her shoulder as he leaves and Alina frowns at her—all is normal in her world.

Gus likes to talk to Lucy in the kitchen but not always with everyone around. It's ironic, of course, he never tells anyone to do anything, but everyone does what he wants anyway.

She sits alone thinking about What To Do Next, but her thoughts wander across her studies—she figures that she has the equivalent of a Masters in the History of National Rebellion by now. She's come to believe that it's all about emergence, the same phenomenon that leads to swarms of birds and schools of fish and the behavior of hives. So close to the answer, it's like she can feel it bubbling up inside. It's there, she just has to recognize it.

Gus comes in, sits next to her, and rests a hand on her shoulder. "Lucy, it is nearly time."

"I know, Gus." She pulls apart a croissant as though looking for the answer. "I'm working on it. I just need—"

"You must find it soon and act while the world still recognizes you. Soon, Lucy, soon. I'm ready to do my part."

"Really? You're that close?"

"You perform the deed and I can destroy the monetary system and it will happen."

She sighs and looks away. "How will I know?"

Gus stands and steps into the hall. "Come with me."

Lucy follows.

"We have something for you."

They walk downstairs and step outside. Everyone is there. Stepan takes her hand and Gus continues across the sidewalk. Klaus, Alina, Adriaan, and their newest member, the American whose foot is in a protective boot, stand in a row blocking something.

"Lucy," Gus says, "we know how much you're sacrificing and we want you to have this gift."

He motions and the others step aside, revealing a motorcycle.

Lucy does a double take. It's not her motorcycle. It's the motorcycle of her dreams: a vintage 1979 Honda CBX1000 with a red gas tank. The CBX was the predecessor to the Japanese crotch-rockets—just as fast, more chrome but less flash. "What? Am I? Why …"

"Go ahead," Gus says.

"Really? It's mine?" She rushes to the motorcycle and puts one hand on the throttle and the other on the clutch.

"Yes," Gus pulls her close to him. "You need the freedom to travel."

Klaus hands Lucy her leather jacket. She puts it on and the fringes dangle from her arms reminding her of who she used to be. She takes her helmet, too, but instead of tucking her hair behind her ears and pulling it on, she stops

Looking at the motorcycle, she doesn't feel the excitement she expects. No, she feels a surge of guilt and shame. It's just an object. Any freedom that this over-powered machine offers is an illusion. Sure, she'd like to go for a ride but isn't that just another consumerist urge? Another distraction?

Gus smiles and nods like a proud parent on graduation day. "Lucy, think of it not as a possession but as a tool. When you arrive and when you depart, people should know it is you."

He sounds sincere and that makes her angry. He should know better.

She says, "It's consumerist crap."

Gus's expression doesn't change.

Klaus says, "Maybe it is art?"

"Art? From a global corporation? It's not art, Klaus, it's an opiate."

Gus puts his arm around her and whispers in her ear: "You passed. Now you're ready." Then, to the council: "We go to Berlin."

2011-Nov-12 Vienna
Historic pivot point peak probability: 3 days

I've now worked through 52,664 of the timeweaves that spray out of this pivot point. Disaster abounds, the timeweave noise fluctuates, and my sorting algorithms don't help. Volodya's next to me, his frown lines deepen as he struggles to comprehend what it means for Lucy to be *anti*-correlated to the assassin who started World War One.

As I open the 52,665th timeweave, Fiona speaks through our earbugs, "You'll want to see this." She puts a video window on a monitor. She's upstairs in the apartment with Winter. "Lucy has a new motorcycle."

It's a live feed from one of our cameras by the canal. Lucy stands outside Rader's hostel in her leather jacket holding her helmet.

Fiona: "Seems odd that Rader would let her ride a motorcycle to Berlin."

Volodya: "Illusion of freedom is last stage of brainwash. We may need to take her."

Fiona: "Right, kidnap a major international figure. Rader would never think to use that for propaganda."

We watch in silence as Lucy steps away from Rader, opens the rear of a white Peugeot cargo van, and sets her helmet inside. Then Rader and his crew load the van with backpacks and boxes. In a matter of minutes, six of them board the van. Klaus Schmidt, the man who instigated the riot on Wall Street, puts on a helmet, mounts the motorcycle, and takes off as the van pulls onto the street.

"Fiona," I yell, "press pause!"

The still image is only partially in focus.

"That's Michael Davis—the police officer who stepped on Winter's tail," I say. "He's driving the van without a safety belt."

Fiona: "Right, at least his ankle seems to be healing."

2011-Nov-12 Europe

The van seats three comfortably so the others have to lounge on backpacks and boxes in the cargo bay. Lucy parks herself against a wheel well. Stepan makes his way to her. She tells him that she wants to be alone and he moves back to Alina.

The others talk about the meeting and Berlin and What Comes Next. Alina goes on about explosives and weapons. Stepan insists that software is more powerful. Alina chides him for being a pacifist and he replies that all fanatical women with a crush on him say that. Everyone laughs.

Lucy falls asleep.

Hours later, Lucy steps out of the van into chilly, overcast, evening Berlin. The others grant her a wide berth. She stretches her back against a light post and takes in the unremarkable urban neighborhood along a river.

"The Spree River," Gus says from behind her. Adriaan and

Klaus carry luggage into an old three-story building. She looks at the CBX parked beside the van. Two months ago that bike would have been a dream come true. It's embarrassing to have worshipped corporate symbolism.

She follows Stepan inside and up three flights of stairs to a large flat. The two of them set their things down and then walk through the hall to a common area with old, worn couches and easy chairs.

Gus approaches from the opposite direction, steps aside for Stepan but blocks Lucy. He holds out a paper file and says, "Read this."

She takes the file and wonders why old people feel compelled to print everything. Guiding her to a bedroom, he indicates specific pages. "The fascist Woodley has been busy."

She sits in a chair with a view of city lights reflecting from the river. The top sheet has the logo of "Hotel Central"—a reservation page for Francis Woodley. He'll be arriving tomorrow and is staying for a week. She searches for the address: 8 Cumurija Street, Sarajevo Bosnia-Herzegovina. The "Preliminary Agenda" is on another sheet of Woodley-Carlyle letterhead with arrival times for 18 people and their guests associated with 18 separate flight plans. She recognizes most of the names—Richard Bran son? He wouldn't be part of this, would he? She sees one of the Walmart heirs and thinks, yeah, this is the list, all right.

The third page is a map. At first she thinks it's a map from the Sarajevo airport to the hotel. She looks closer. No, the map provides directions to a valley in the Bosnian countryside. The whole valley, from mountain ridge to mountain ridge, is shaded in yellow and labeled "173 square miles." In its center, next to a lake, a place is marked "chateau"—they're having a picnic in the country? It seems silly. The next sheet has a map of Sarajevo. Gus marked some notes on it with a blue ballpoint.

Going through the agenda brings tremors of shock. *They bought an entire valley where they're going to build corporatries? What the hell is a corporatry?* She reads the rest of the file with her mouth hanging open. When she finishes, she stares at the map. *No person should have that much money.*

She reassembles the file and walks down the hall. The others are hanging out in the common room. Alina, Stepan, and Adriaan sit on a couch kidding around, planning forays into Berlin's nightlife, acting like bourgeoisie teens. She feels old. Gus leans against the door. He smiles and pats her on the back as she passes.

She says, "Hey everyone," and the room goes silent. That she can kill a party so fast makes the load heavier. She describes The Sons' meeting and hands around the map showing the valley that they have already acquired.

"That's not acres," she says. "Those are square *miles*."

Klaus says, "*Shite im Himmel*" and hands the map along.

Adriaan says, "Bastards."

Stepan says, "They're the machine, what do you expect?"

Alina says, "I'd like for them to suffer."

She passes around another sheet. "Here's the guest list, twenty of the richest assholes on earth will be there."

Adriaan: "If Lucy tweets an invitation, a thousand people will show up."

Alina: "We should blow them up."

Stepan: "Would it not be more effective to video the meeting and show to the world?"

Gus takes Lucy by the elbow and guides her back down the hall. He says, "Let them brainstorm."

Now back in the room she's sharing with Alina, Gus closes the door and says, "Do you remember Julian Assange saying that we have limited time?"

"He said we'd be infiltrated and Occupy would be shutdown if we didn't act."

He looks at his watch. "As we speak the police are raiding Occupy Oakland."

She takes a laptop from the nightstand. She checks for the

green icon in the task bar before opening the Occupy Twitter feed. "They already raided New York, Chicago, Boston—oh my God."

"Unless you make a huge impression very soon, Occupy will fade into the night."

"Everything we've done? How can it just fade away?"

Gus says, "The time for peaceful protest has passed."

2011-Nov-12 Europe
Historic pivot point peak probability: 3 days

Fiona, Winter, and I are on a train headed in the general direction of Sarajevo, we'll have to transfer in Bratislava and Budapest. Traveling first class by train doesn't trouble me. I fear that if I don't have to watch others pass through on their way to steerage, their plight no longer offends me.

All set up, I open the 56,843rd timeline. My hope rises. My stomach settles. I feel a smile forming. Along this thread, the world meanders along with the usual inadequacies of democracy and regulated-but-reasonably-free market economies, the Oakland Raiders are even poised to win the Superbowl! But then, as though the gods of computation are testifying to the pointlessness of this exercise, the timeweave fluctuates deeper into the noise and out of existence. All I see are different paths to destruction.

Fiona says, "Think of it, Simon, we're in the very heart of history, traveling the world, drinking fine coffee. We are blessed."

"I have trouble seeing it that way."

"Don't worry about Lucy. She'll be finished with Rader soon."

"You said that he's going to get her killed."

"I could be wrong."

2011-Nov-13 Berlin
Historic pivot point peak probability: 2 days

Volodya first came here 26 years ago when West Berlin was an island in a sea of East Germany. The city haunts him and, like the twisted home-sweet-home of a fairy tale, he can't resist it.

Though Volodya Kazimir and Guenther Rader share no opinions, no hobbies, and no interests, they have one thing in common: they both crossed from East Berlin to West Berlin and emerged here at the Central Berlin train station. He walks slowly through this shiny new version of the *Hauptbaunhof.*

After he and Simon hacked into the telecommunication systems of the superpower rivals, the two physics students debated physics analyses and argued the merits and failures of centrally planned, single party socialism and competitive, two-party capitalist democracy. Volodya conceded when he discovered that his country had betrayed the man he most admired, Andrei Sakharov. Once he awoke from idealism, he began planning his escape.

When the Deutsche Democratic Republic constructed The Berlin Wall, they blocked the U-Bahn subway stations on the east side and patrolled them with armed guards, much as they did The Wall. The trains kept running through the tunnels, carrying people from point to point in West Berlin, but without stopping at the East Berlin stations. The Alexanderplatz subway station was one of these ghost stations.

In 1985, believing that his true feelings were unknown to the KGB, Volodya arranged for his wife Viktoriya and daughter Ulyana to accompany him to a physics conference in East Berlin. The three of them took a Sunday stroll. When they came to the Alexanderplatz Station, Volodya bribed a guard. The guard stepped aside and Volodya's family snuck into the ghost station. It would only require a mile of hustling through tunnels to emerge here at the Hauptbahnhof in West Berlin. The guard waited until they were thirty meters away to open fire. Volodya turned at the first sound of the guard's boots on the station's tile floor. His wife and daughter were just steps behind, shielding him from the gunfire. He watched as his daughter was cut in two. He carried Viktoriya's corpse all the way to the Hauptbahnhof. The smug look on the guard's face still haunts him.

Today, he takes the opposite trip on the U-Bahn from the Hauptbahnhof to Alexanderplatz. He tells himself that it's the most direct route but knows that he'd have taken it anyway. The only role that nostalgia plays in Volodya's world is self-torture.

Rader's fundraiser meeting will be held in the Alexander Plaza Hotel. Volodya walks past the entrance, around the hotel, and into an adjacent park. A sign indicates that dogs aren't allowed on this shaded patch of grass. He thinks of Winter and it helps wash away some of his memories. Crossing through the park, he walks behind the hotel, and then around, attaching wireless cameras at each corner with a dab of epoxy along the edges of overhanging masonry. He enters the hotel lobby, takes a seat, pulls his laptop out of his knapsack, and configures software to monitor the cameras.

He crosses his legs and positions himself with a clear view of both the hotel entrance and the check-in desk. To anyone walking past it looks as though the severe looking middle-aged man is surfing the web. It's almost true. The web he's surfing happens to be the hotel database.

A couple checks in and Volodya watches their information populate the various database fields. The fleet of computer servers back in Vienna takes a few minutes to assemble models of everyone staying at the hotel. The seven people who checked in with false names are identified by relating the times that they checked in with images from surveillance cameras at those times. Guenther Rader checked into a suite under the name Gregor Ritter and collected the card key but has not yet used it.

Volodya alters a few fields in the hotel database and writes a short script that swaps card key data between the suite and the next room to be booked. In 30 minutes the script will automatically put the data back in order.

He stands, puts the laptop in his pack, walks to the check-in desk, and books a room. Volodya shows his ID. The clerk runs a plastic card key through the encoder and gives it to Volodya. With his pack over his shoulder, carrying a router and a dozen tiny cameras, Volodya proceeds up to the suite where Rader will hold the meeting.

Thirty-five minutes later, Volodya returns to the front desk and explains that his card key isn't working. The young man at the desk cheerfully recodes it and Volodya proceeds to his room for a nap. He rises two hours later, checks the camera feeds and sees that a white Peugeot cargo van is parked in front of the small park neighboring the hotel. He alerts Simon and Fiona, who have settled in their Sarajevo hotel room, and the three of them wait.

2011-Nov-13 Sarajevo and Berlin
Historic pivot point peak probability: 2 days

Fiona says, "They disappear in the woodwork, don't they?"

"They seem to have assimilated happily enough," I say. "Look, that gentleman was with the Revolutionaere Zellen."

Fiona says, "That woman was a Red Army Faction assassin."

In my ear buds I hear Volodya say, "The people in that room who are over 60 all have roots in Cold War terrorism. The swarthy fellow near the punchbowl was once an aid to Daniel Ortega."

Fiona says, "Is that the chap who tried to overthrow the Sandinista National Liberation Front for being insufficiently socialist?"

"The very one, Ortega jailed him for crimes against the state."

Fiona and I checked in to the Hotel Astra Sarajevo 77 minutes ago. We're a block from the 5-star Central Hotel where Frankie is staying.

The three of us watch Rader's party on our laptops. Fiona's lying on one of the beds and I'm sitting at a small desk. Volodya's in his room at the Alexander Plaza Hotel in Berlin, several floors below the party suite.

Volodya: "The woman crossing the room—"

Fiona: "Oh honey, those shoes."

Volodya: "She claims to have been Che Guevara's lover."

Fiona: "I take it back; a woman that age looking that good can wear any shoes she likes."

Me: "It's quite a reunion."

Fiona: "When do you think they last saw each other?"

Me: "They don't appear threatening."

Fiona: "They're threatening that tray of caviar.

Volodya: "The youngest person in the room is sixty-one, how threatening can they be?"

Fiona: "I plan to be plenty threatening in ten years."

Me: "Why is Lucy still at the flat?"

Volodya: "I suspect that Rader has prepared an appropriate entrance for her."

Fiona: "And would like his guests appropriately lubricated prior to submerging them in twenty-first century culture."

The party continues. An hour of punch and hors d'oeuvres with laughter and storytelling and more punch gives us time to determine the combined resources of the crowd and an estimate of Rader's working budget.

Volodya: "I believe it is time for feature attraction."

Lucy walks in wearing a skirt and an Occupy T-shirt—the same clothes she had on in the iconic picture with Officer Justin.

Rader asks for attention and introduces her. The elder rebels applaud and those who had been sitting, stand.

She gives a short speech on the Occupy and anti-austerity movements. It's got the same details as her other speeches but with a marked edge. This time, she uses names when she refers to the 1%: Francis Woodley, James Birch, Wallace van Bibber are mentioned often; she guides them in the "Rage against The Sons"-"The Sons are the machine" chant and finishes in ten minutes with her other trademarkable statement: "Democracy when? Get out of the way or get on board—democracy now!"

Rader then assumes the floor and describes Francis's meeting in Sarajevo. He depicts corporatries in detail. As he speaks, the aged revolutionaries grumble about the fascists and Rader encourages them. "They hold the capital, they hold the power, and they are going to use it against the people."

Me: "He knows as much about Frankie's plans as we do."

Fiona: "He must have hacked The Sons."

Volodya: "To be expected, if he can hack us …"

"My friends," Rader raises his voice and his hands, "we have an unprecedented opportunity. The internet has made true democracy, genuine anarchy possible. Every person can now vote on every issue—the ultimate promise of community is within our reach. Authority is now indefensible. The fascists Woodley, Birch, and van Bibber are the obstacle to everything you have spent your lives working for. It can finally happen. Look at this young woman! She is in constant contact with over a hundred million people who respond to her words and reinforce her actions."

Rader walks Lucy through the room for personal introductions.

Volodya: "And now they write checks."

Simon: "Checks? Who writes checks anymore?"

The meeting reverts back to a cocktail party and Volodya's right.

With the din of revelry, it's difficult to distinguish individual conversations unless they occur right next to a smoke alarm, thermostat, painting, or heating vent, but Rader's expression indicates that he's getting what he came for.

Fiona: "Lucy is their princess."

Volodya grunts.

Me: "Look how she carries herself. Gwinnie would be so proud."

Volodya: "Gwinnie would not appreciate her daughter's participation in armed revolution."

Fiona: "There's no evidence of anyone arming anything."

Volodya: "They want blood."

As the meeting winds down, the hardcore rebels, the survivors of Baader-Meinhof and the Red Army Faction, corner Lucy and ask for specifics. Rader maneuvers himself into position behind her.

A bald man with a scarred forehead says, "You're prepared to trigger the revolution?"

Volodya: "Fuck."

Fiona and me: "What is it?"

Volodya: "Quiet."

The bald man says, "I'm not talking to you. Your symbol must answer."

Lucy looks from him to Rader and back.

Volodya: "Movverbastid, it is Helmut Braun."

Fiona: "Facial recognition IDed him as Bruener Holz. He works for Daimler Benz in Stuttgart."

"No, is Braun." Volodya's voice drops an octave in pitch and two decibels in volume. "I saw him only once but …" I can't hear what he says.

"Volodya, are you okay?" Fiona says. "Who is he? I'll double check."

Back at his standard volume, Volodya says, "He was STASI—we must pay attention."

Lucy says, "The revolution already started."

Braun says, "Naïve. You must mobilize before the fascists shut down your communication."

"They can't."

"The instant you become a serious threat, they will turn off your internet toys. You have this moment to mobilize."

Rader raises one hand and says, "We should discuss these details in private, come with me."

The images on my laptop, which sits on the small hotel desk, dance about in ways that contradict Newton's laws. I shake my head and the sensation worsens. Time slows, bile climbs. I hold onto the desk chair and try to focus, try to find the timeline boundaries. In focusing, I realize that I've oversimplified. The image of Rader doesn't dance or split or echo. He steps deliberately toward the door. Lucy, on the other hand, flickers into multiple images. The bald man doesn't move at all. I lean to-and-fro and side-to-side but no direction alters my sense of dread, though it climbs with every step Rader takes. One Lucy walks at his side, another Lucy dawdles behind, yet a third announces something about videoing or occupying the party.

Looking up from the monitor, a wholly distinct sensation overcomes me: utter helplessness. Separate timelines dance all around the room. I can see each one, but they all feel the same. It's like being stuck in an elevator with mirrors on opposite sides. So many similar realities.

The images of Lucy coalesce as though I've just watched a physical manifestation of her making an ominous decision. Time resumes its steady pace.

The bald man follows Rader and Lucy out of the room.

Fiona: "Where are they going?"

Volodya: "Out of our reach."

Fiona: "Do you have access to the hotel database?"

Volodya: "Please."

Seven minutes pass in silence. No one has noticed my experience but Winter.

Volodya: "One door opens on seventh floor—cross-referencing registration—hotel has shit software—it's not them. Another door accessed on third floor, five doors down hallway from where I sit. Yes, is Braun's room."

Me: "Any way we can tap in?"

Volodya: "Ummmm—no—none of them carry a cell phone. We are blind and deaf."

Fiona: "It is a problem."

I look back at Fiona on the bed. She shrugs and says, "Someone had to say it."

Rader's party continues. Fiona shuffles about the feeds of each camera like a television director hunting for the best angle. Volodya digs into the hotel computing infrastructure, looking for ways to activate telephones or smoke alarms, anything to get Rader, Braun, and Lucy somewhere that we can listen in.

Forty-six minutes pass.

Volodya: "Braun's door just opened from the inside and then closed."

Ten minutes later, Lucy reappears at the party.

Fiona: "She's alone?"

Volodya: "It would seem."

Fiona: "Look, she's flushed. Something's not right with her."

Me: "Switch to the third camera. There."

I capture a full facial image of Lucy. On another monitor, Volodya scans video from before she left the party and captures a similar before image. Facial analysis software compares them in seconds, posting results in a separate window: increased heart rate, galvanic skin response up 500%, pupil dilation and eyes open 22% wider.

Fiona: "What did those devils do to her?"

Me: "We need to find out what happened."

Volodya: "Fuck it, I go up there."

Fiona: "Don't be a ning-nong."

Me: "She's right, Volodya. You won't be able to hear them and if they recognize you we lose any advantage we might have."

Volodya: "Gmm. Of course, I mustn't allow Braun to displace my judgment."

Lucy walks straight to Stepan and hugs him. Klaus whispers in her ear. The party guests converge on her and she announces: "I can't give you the details, but we're going to do something decisive."

Me: "I hate that word."

Fiona: "We have no idea what she's talking about."

Me: "It has to be somewhere in her timeweave-geyser."

2011-Nov-13 Berlin

In a room five doors down the hall from Volodya's, Guenther

Rader and Helmut Braun stand face-to-face.

"The entire power structure will be in one place," Braun says. "One well-placed explosive. Everything cannot rest on that one girl. What if she misses? A massive explosion would be easier, more effective, and far less likely to fail than a stupid American girl with a gun."

Rader says, "Helmut, my friend, you don't understand—"

"Your work impresses me—all this information, the zeal of your Soviet and ability to infiltrate without being traced—but all the fascists in one place? How can you pass up this opportunity?"

"Please listen, you truly do not understand."

Braun crosses his arms and takes a seat. Rader sits in a similar chair.

Rader says, "If we bombed Woodley's party and killed the capitalists, we would accomplish nothing more than scaring the 99%. These deeds do not create propaganda, have never worked and never will."

"Anti-terrorist police improve, so must we improve."

"We have improved, but that is not the issue." Rader crosses his legs. "To catalyze the emergence of genuine democracy, we must enrage the people, not the power structure."

"Killing Francis Woodley will have this result, assuming it is possible for this American girl to succeed."

"Woodley is not going to die."

"What? Why then are we here?"

"If Lucy kills Woodley, or if we manage to kill all of them, government forces will become ever more paranoid, the people will support them, and this chance will be wasted."

"No, the people would push back. With the fascists out of the way, there would be a power vacuum and we would raise the consciousness of the masses."

"That has never worked. Let me explain what will work."

Braun exhales and uncrosses his arms.

"The people love Lucy," Rader says. "Everyone loves Lucy.

Even people who worship the fascists and disagree with everything Lucy represents, they love *her*. Even the police who fear being in a photo with her, they love her." Rader laughs. "Helmut, even the people who hate Lucy love her! The tiny, pretty-but-not-beautiful white girl with the unmanageable red hair, big smile, and straight teeth whose sincerity is unassailable—everyone loves her. Our comrades upstairs love her. They hate everything America stands for, but they love this red, white, and blue child."

Braun starts to smile.

"You understand?"

"You have no intention of killing Francis Woodley, do you?"

"I intend to protect him."

* * *

Lucy's commitment to a vague but "decisive" action satisfied Rader's friends at the party last night because they understood the need for secrecy. But afterward, sitting in the kitchen, Alina, Stepan, Adriaan—everyone wanted details. Lucy stares at the ceiling all night, caught in a tornado of doubt, questioning every decision she's ever made, especially the decisions that led her to join Occupy. By sunrise she feels nothing but the unrelenting momentum of her choices forcing her in one direction.

She lies on the bed and stares out the window, watching the river flow past.

Klaus walks in the room without knocking. "Lucy, are you prepared?"

"Then you know?"

The way he pulls back his hair is enough of an answer.

He says, "We will be right behind you. Stepan and Adriaan are preparing the van now. We'll be right there the whole way."

"Do they know?"

"No, we can't tell anyone—we have no way to be certain that we haven't been infiltrated. I'm the only one who knows. The others believe that we're installing equipment in the van to video Francis Woodley's meeting so that we can expose them. Preparations are the same for cameras as for guns—shooting is shooting, whether video or bullets."

"Where's Gus?" Lucy asks.

"He will be there."

"What? He's not here?" The emotional tornado threatens to touch down again, surprising her with a rush of affection for Gus Reser.

"Calm down, Lucy, Gus had a meeting. I will prepare you and see you on your way."

"I'm not sure I can do it. I've never done anything like this. I've never even vandalized anything. My mom, my friends, I don't think I can do it."

"Of course you can. You have come so far. It will be fine."

"Fine? How can it possibly be fucking fine?"

"Keep your voice down, we mustn't alert the others."

"What if I can't do it? What if I miss? What if I get caught? I don't want to go to jail. I don't want to disappoint my mother." The tornado twists up to her throat. She fails to hold back a sob. "I don't want to."

"We will make certain that you don't fail. The important thing is for the world to believe that you, Lucy Montgomery, the woman who stood with Officer Justin on Wall Street, has acted."

"I don't want to!" She tries but fails to hold back the sobs.

"The people will follow your actions."

"Are you sure?"

"You have studied the propaganda of the deed. You know what I say is true. Gus wouldn't help you into this position if he didn't believe it would work." Klaus rubs a tear from her cheek. "Lucy, we don't want you to go to prison, but if you do … well, think of Nelson Mandela. You're stronger than you think."

She cries until the sobs and tears quell her inner storm. She finally manages to swallow. Klaus looks so certain. She wants that certainty, too.

"Let me walk you through the process." He offers her the pistol. "You know this tool. You're a good shot."

"I am?"

"You know your weapon. Another weapon, maybe not so good, but this one, you know."

He speaks with such confidence that her resignation starts shifting to resolve.

Lucy loads and unloads the gun and Klaus quizzes her on aiming techniques and ways to steady the weapon even as she moves at high speed. They spend the next hour studying a map of Sarajevo and the pros and cons of acting at different places. Then they work through a variety of escape routes, how to cross the border from Bosnia to Croatia and the town where Gus's friends live. The people she'll stay with until the revolution gains momentum.

"Lucy, just think, the next time we meet, you'll be a historic figure. Right up there with your hero, Vaclav Havel."

Too many people are relying on her. The pressure of millions of followers doesn't permit her, one worker in an emerging hive, any choice. She wipes her eyes.

"Lucy, look." He flips through the printouts of maps, instructions, the agenda for The Sons' meeting, and finds a full color printout of the photo that has defined her life. "You don't want this to go to waste."

She stares at the picture. The moment has grown so huge, but right now, she remembers what it was really like, the feeling when Officer Justin put down his Taser and took her hand. He's a good man and he's suffered. A thought floats to her like a life raft: she owes it to him, too; she can't let Officer Justin's sacrifices go to waste.

13. Divergence

2011-Nov-14 Berlin
Historic pivot point peak probability: 1 day

Volodya walks along Oranienburger Strasse, a long, narrow, tree-lined street through the former East Berlin. He remembers walking along here with his wife and daughter long before the trees were planted. For the millionth time he wonders how a state can so overstep its role that people would rather die than live under its oppression. Why this side of the wall and not that?

The vibration of his phone delivers him from the reverie. He wants a few more minutes of solitude.

He steps into the Oranium café and shakes off the cold and the memories. He sits near a window so he can see down the street to where Rader and his crew are staying. A tall Aryan woman brings him an espresso. She's confused him for a regular customer and he corrects her but welcomes the espresso.

Sipping the hot, bitter syrup, he stares out the window. His phone vibrates again. He considers re-engaging with Simon and Fiona. Self-torture has little practical utility and he's a practical man, but right now he prefers this melancholy privacy.

He keeps an eye on the white cargo van a block down the narrow side street and relaxes.

Two additional cups of espresso and a strudel later, he sees activity around the van and decides to take a closer look.

Leaving the café, he takes out his phone; maintaining his privacy in this situation would be a mistake.

* * *

Fiona and I face each other across a small table in our hotel room. Sitting here, even so far from Volodya, empathy engulfs me. I know what he lost in Berlin.

Twenty-six years ago, Volodya and I devised a crude messaging system that deposited files on each other's computers—just text with a silly encryption scheme: anyone checking would think we were sharing bad translations of Sartre's play, *Nausea.* One morning in my lab at Lawrence Livermore, I opened one such message. It described Volodya's plan to escape the Soviet Union with his wife and daughter by crossing from East to West Berlin. The thing I remember most about it, the least Volodya-like attribute, is that he asked me to wish him "luck." I replied with an offer to help and he used one of our hacked phone lines to call me. Through the crackling noise of the line and our analog encryption scheme, I remember listening to my friend sigh and then the vertigo and nausea overcame me. His voice came in echoes. With the noisy connection and the weave of timelines, I couldn't understand his words. I leaned in different directions, concentrating on slightly different realities—wait an hour, go right now, stay where you are—but each brought a sense of horror.

He was a different Volodya then, more emotional, not just younger and unseasoned but of a different mettle. If you'd known him then, you'd only recognize him now by the determination in those icy blue eyes. When the timeweave jitter settled down, I heard him say, "Not a problem. Come to Berlin, my friend, we'll meet you at airport." He waited another second, as though expecting me to say something before hanging up. From the instant that phone line went dead, I've regretted that I didn't wish him luck. Not that it would have helped, of course. Another in a long line of would'ves, should'ves, and could'ves: if we could have calculated timeweave probabilities back then, we would've known that the Soviet Union would collapse five years later.

Fiona shakes me from the past. "He just enabled his earbug."

Volodya: "They modify the van. Watch."

I hear despair in his soft words. I ask if he's okay but he just grunts.

Fiona: "Don't be distracted."

It bothers me that Fiona has to take the serious role, Volodya's role. Holding the phone to his ear, he orients the camera so that Fiona and I can see, but he doesn't speak.

He crosses the street and strides along the opposite sidewalk, past an apothecary, opposite a brick building and passes the van parked in front of a beige building next to the red motorcycle. Stepan and Adriaan are working inside the van with power tools but we can't see what they're doing from this side of the street. He continues to the river, crosses, and doubles back. He passes the CBX and pans the phone as he passes the van.

Fiona says, "They're installing equipment in the van."

I see Klaus holding a cordless drill. "Surveillance equipment?" I ask.

"Right, and look at this." Fiona magnifies two images, one captured when Volodya walked along the opposite sidewalk and one taken just now, images from both sides of the van. The street-facing side shows two slight oval shadows and, from the inside, a spring-loaded cover.

I say, "What are those?"

"I don't know."

I sigh, "The lower hole could accommodate a rifle barrel."

"Oh, I see, and the upper hole for its scope."

I indicate the boxes still loaded in the van. "What's in those?"

"Simon, how can I possibly tell?"

Fiona and I look at each other.

Volodya's silence bothers us as much as the images we've just seen. I say, "Volodya? Are you okay?"

* * *

Volodya hears Simon but doesn't respond. He sees no point in saying that he's not okay, that he'll never be okay, that his sense of sentimentality largely perished with his wife and son. Why would he share this feeling that the world is a thief and all people can do is fight for periods of peace and joy in an ocean of hopeless turmoil?

His teeth grit together. Something in his peripheral vision catches his eye. He turns at the end of the block, 40 meters from the van. He scans the entrance to the drab, Soviet-era building and sees what caught his attention.

Lucy's freckles make her look younger in person than on video. As he watches her walk toward the van, he feels a hint of paternal sentiment, the sort of memory-feeling that surfaces when you catch the smell of flowers that grew in your long-dead wife's garden, the garden where you played with your long-dead daughter.

Carrying her helmet and dressed in the leather jacket and boots—or maybe due to the contrast between the leather and her innocent appearance—he's drawn to her. The overwhelming sense of wrongness wears on him. He's tired of injustice. He's fed up with ideologues coercing people to surrender their chances for peace and joy.

Watching Lucy walk to her motorcycle, her head downcast and shoulders shaking, he sees something in her that reminds him of someone else. He whispers to himself, in the moment forgetting that Simon and Fiona can hear: "I can stand to see the world fall and fail and wither and die, but I cannot stand to see this woman go with it."

Lucy looks back at the hotel. Her eyes are red and her mouth is set in a frown. She looks like a little girl who has just been scolded.

From his earbug, he hears Fiona yell, "What are you doing?" And Simon: "Volodya-No!"

He jams the phone in his pocket and runs to Lucy.

She pulls her hair behind her ears and puts on her helmet. She snaps the chin strap, mounts the bike, and pulls on her gloves. She hits the ignition as he reaches for her.

He yells over the engine noise, "Lucy, please!"

Her head jerks toward him. She says, "What are you—"

"It's me, Volodya. Simon's friend."

She tries to push him away.

He wraps his arms around her waist. Even with her knapsack, she barely tops a hundred pounds. He figures that he can run with her over his shoulder, run away and protect her. He lost his daughter, he'll be damned before he lets his friend Simon lose Lucy. She tries to kick the bike into gear, but he lifts her. She clings to the throttle.

"Let me go."

"It is mistake—Rader is not who you think he is!"

She lets go of the throttle and reaches into her jacket. She pulls out a pistol; a compact 9mm Beretta. If she pulls the trigger, the odds are as good that she'll hit herself as that she'll hit him.

He lets go. She gets back on the bike.

"Lucy, please." He holds his hands up in surrender. "Let me help you—you don't understand what—"

Lucy kicks the bike into gear and bursts onto the street, the front wheel half a meter off the ground.

As Volodya lunges at her, the air is punched out of his lungs from behind. Then two kidney chops and he hits the pavement facedown. Someone grabs his wrists and twists one behind him in the classic, incapacitating grip of a police officer making an arrest.

* * *

"Simon," Fiona says, "we've lost the signal, can you—"

"No, the phone is engaged and it's moving." I show her the GPS indicator moving north from the center of Berlin. "The video is dark and the sound—let me try something." I try some filters to enhance the audio, but I can't dig out any voices. "The phone must be in his pocket. He's in a car or something. See? You can hear the engine." We're quiet for 19 minutes, concentrating on the noise from our earbugs.

I whisper, "Should I go to Berlin?"

Even in the worst of times, Fiona's lips flirt with a smile, a grin, or at least a smirk, some indication that she appreciates the humor of life. Right now, her lips are set in a line.

She starts to speak, "One thing at—"

"Quiet!" The engine sounds from Volodya's phone go silent.

Someone says, in German, "Helmut will be most happy to keep you company. I believe you have met before?"

"Braun?" It's Volodya's voice and as she hears it, Fiona's lips perk up.

"Yes, a STASI comrade you once knew."

Volodya says, "I'm not a pleasant guest."

I say, "Why does he always drop articles in English but has perfect German grammar?"

Fiona says, "He learned German as a child, English in his teens."

"Yes, but English is a Germanic language."

"Right," Fiona says. "Try to focus. Your best friend is being held captive by terrorists."

2011-Nov-14 Prague

Lucy hits 5th gear and settles in for a long ride. The CBX glides along the smooth autobahn pavement, six air-cooled cylinders in perfect harmony carrying one rattled young woman.

If someone had told her two months ago that she'd be riding across central Europe with a loaded Berretta in her pocket, well, she probably would have packed up and moved into her mom's crappy apartment in Concord.

With no phone and no computer, the knowledge that no one can contact her and no one can stop her brings a feeling of freedom and power. She bites down, leans into a turn, and zips past a BMW at 115 miles per hour.

The Autobahn narrows as she approaches the Czech Republic border. She rides into a tidy German travel center, gets eight liters of gas for 40 Euro and walks to the travel center café. She hasn't looked at a hardcopy map since third grade and even then it seemed ridiculous. How do you fold these things?

The map shows 1400 kilometers from here to Sarajevo. Once the Autobahn ends at the German border, it's archaic highways through Hungary and two lane roads from Croatia to Bosnia. She takes a few bites of a croissant but can't force it down. All she wants to do is ride and sleep, either full speed or out cold. She crams the rest of the croissant in her pocket and gulps the espresso, burning her tongue, but even that feels good, deserving.

The Czech border guards wave her through without even looking at her. The road curves from town to town. The cars aren't as fancy and the going slows.

All signs point to *Praha*; she gathers that it's Czech for Prague. Winding along a forested road, slowing to get around livestock, seems so romantic. If she could start over, that's what she'd do. The image of how it could have been: Stepan and Bill, Penelope and Klaus, even Alina, all working together at The Intoxicating Page.

But that little fantasy just brings Uncle Simon to mind. They used to spend hours talking about the vagaries of fate and destiny. She misses him. No, that's not it, she misses who she thought he was, not the bastard who helps the Francis Woodleys of the world rig a global economy so that they can legally steal the house where she grew up.

She gets to Prague at sunset. The cobblestone streets and gothic architecture enhance her mood. The map has a little star marking the café where Vaclav Havel planned the Velvet Revolution over coffee and cigarettes.

She works the bike through traffic and slush.

She stops at a statue of Franz Kafka and realizes her own metamorphosis. Another sob tries to climb into her throat. The poor man in that story woke up with the body of a cockroach and disgusted everyone who once loved him. Loved became hated and the only person who would talk to him, betrayed him. She cracks open a vent in her helmet to keep the faceplate from fogging up.

Café Slavia is bigger than she expected. She sits in a corner and a waiter requests her order. Lucy points to a placard on the table and he leaves. Vaclav Havel must have had lots of friends or they could have planned their revolution in a smaller café.

The waiter returns with a glass of cappuccino covered in whipped cream. She rests her head against her helmet, stares out the window at the gothic bridges that cross the river and tries to picture the Velvet Revolution. The tanks rolled in and somehow the Occupiers stopped them. She feels like she should have been able to accomplish that sort of thing on Wall Street. She should have been able to stop the man in the green suit. She shakes off the thought and imagines Vaclav Havel smoking in the booth next to her.

The next thing she knows, the waiter makes a loud sound near her ear and she wakes up. The coffee is cold and the whipped cream has melted down the side of the glass. She goes out, sits on the motorcycle, and pulls her helmet on but doesn't bother to attach the chinstrap. The road along the river is thick with traffic and pedestrians, but she winds back the throttle and works through the gears. She fishtails in a patch of slush but doesn't slow down.

2011-Nov-14 Sarajevo

Frankie faces the mirror as Gijjelle adjusts his bow tie. She is perfect for this trip, perfect for almost anything. Perfect for the cover of Vogue, perfect for Sports Illustrated, perfect to sit beside at dinner, too. If she weren't so beautiful, she'd have been a comedian. She tells stories about her experience doing standup at The Improv. She had to apply makeup that detracted from her appearance to get people to listen—the perfect setup for him to say, "It's tough to be beautiful" and kiss her.

Everyone is here but the elusive Kim DotCom. Myrna, the executive administrative assistant he inherited from his father, insisted they invite a few local government officials and once the invitations went out, the extravagance appeared.

"Europe," he says, "even Bosnia can make New York seem rustic."

"I tell you," Gijjelle says in that ruffly Belgian accent, "the smaller the country the greater the hotels." Then, imitating the version of Ricardo Montalban Billy Crystal performed on Saturday Night Live, "Let me tell you dahling. You look mahvelous."

"The sooner we go, the sooner we get back. Shall we?"

"We shall."

He holds the door for her—a gilded, three-meter high door—and she wiggles as she passes. Larry Ellison and his new girlfriend hold the elevator doors for them. Elon Musk leans against the rear of the elevator. He has that sparkle in his eye that indicates he knows the answer.

Ellison says, "Fantastic."

Frankie says, "The real fun starts tomorrow."

"This better not be the Amway version of Thiele's old sea-steading idea."

Frankie laughs.

Gijjelle says, "You brought extra luggage?"

"What's that?" Ellison says.

"If it is soap that Frankie sells, you'll be carrying gallons of it home." Then she rests one of her long slender arms across Frankie's shoulders. "Frankie could sell a FORTRAN card reader to a database company."

Frankie squeezes her hand in gratitude.

"You know," Ellison says, "it's not that sea-steading was such a bad idea, it was just impossible to implement."

Elon Musk says, "No, it could be implemented, but it's a tiny horizon idea. We're here because Frankie is thinking big. I came to find out how big. To the sky or beyond?"

"You'll have to judge for yourself," Frankie says. "Tomorrow morning, guys, I'll show you how to get government out of the way of entrepreneuring."

2011-Nov-14 7:51pm Berlin
Historic pivot point peak probability: 15 hours

Volodya awakens without moving. He keeps his head down and tries not to alter his breathing tempo. Surveying his body, he realizes that he's tied to a chair. He cracks one eye long enough to see Braun across a table; he's reading a newspaper and shows no indication that he realizes Volodya is alert.

His wrists are tied behind him by what feels like a cable tie. His ankles are tied together but feel otherwise free to move. To test the assumption without alerting Braun, he raises his heels from the floor and discovers that he's also tied to the chair at the knees.

One eye feels swollen. No bones are broken, though a couple of ribs might be cracked. He'll know for certain as soon as he takes a deep breath. Feet, ankles, knees are all good. He's got a cramp in his neck and a bruised shoulder; all in all, not too bad.

He understands that he will be lucky to get one chance and right now he has as much of an advantage as he'll ever get.

For a career scientist, Volodya has spent a lot of time tied up and bruised. It's a strange moment to discover optimism. This isn't a problem. No, he's sought this opportunity for 26 years. Of all the ex-STASI thugs in Germany, what a stroke of luck to be Helmut Braun's prisoner.

Helmut Braun was the guard who Volodya bribed that morning at the Alexanderplatz subway station. Decades later, when Volodya and Simon perfected their face-recognition software, Volodya hired a police sketch artist and used their software and the drawing to identify that guard. Since then, he has resisted the temptation to hunt Braun down.

To capitalize on the situation, Volodya needs Braun close to him. Without being able to test how far he can move, Volodya can't know just how close Braun needs to be. Given the angle of his knees, he estimates that he has a range of less than a third of a meter, maybe ten inches. Adding up the situation results in a simple tactic: he has to wait until Braun loses patience and checks his physical condition. Then they'll be close enough for Volodya to exercise his advantage.

Volodya sucks the inside of his right cheek between his teeth and bites down. When he tastes a good stream of blood, he parts his lips ever so slightly and exhales through bloody saliva. He manages a few bloody spit bubbles.

Braun still doesn't move.

The bloody saliva drools down Volodya's chin. He blows more bloody spit bubbles but they don't draw Braun's attention either. He adds wheezing to the menu of symptoms and keeps his eyes closed and the angle of his head unchanged.

As Volodya internally debates whether the next symptom should be a cough, a moan, or a gag, he hears the newspaper ruffle.

"*Ack so*," Braun says. "Klaus got you good in the chest. Maybe he cracked a rib into your lung. I'll have to tell him. He'll be pleased."

Volodya keeps his eyes shut and continues to wheeze and blow spit bubbles. He hears Braun stand and step over. In concentrating on the sounds, Volodya realizes that he's neglected to maintain his breathing tempo.

Braun says, "How long have you been awake."

Volodya opens his eyes wide, feigning shock at waking to Braun. "What is this? What have you done to me?" Then he gasps as though in excruciating pain and, through clenched teeth and in Russian, squeaks out: "Can't breathe." He chokes and hacks up a gob of blood.

"Do not worry," Braun replies in Russian. "I will relieve your pain and you will be released in good time." He walks to a counter.

Volodya watches him prepare a hypodermic.

"Don't worry, you will not die today. I don't need that kind of trouble."

Volodya coughs again, groans some more, and says, "Please,

why are you doing this? I'm just a scientist."

Braun laughs, taps the hypodermic and a small drop forms at its tip. "It's okay, I know what you are and don't care. Truly, I don't want this trouble." He approaches Volodya with the needle poised.

Volodya looks around, groans and spits for effect but doesn't see anyone else in the room. His survey reveals a concrete floor and metal shelving stacked with hoses, belts, gaskets, and tools. He hunches farther over and whines, then tries to sound as though he's crying. It sounds more like laughter though, so he fakes a convulsion, rolls his eyes up in his head and tries to blow another blood bubble.

Braun stops and leans down. "*Shite*," he says, "come now, be all right, I cannot have this. Come back now, good Russian, be strong. I'll fix the pain for you."

Volodya makes a choking sound, holds his breath and lets bloody drool drip down the side of his mouth onto the table.

"Fuck," Braun says, now a step closer. He puts his free hand on Volodya's chin and lifts. Volodya is dead weight. Braun moves closer.

That one more step worries Volodya. Surely Braun hasn't forgotten everything he learned from STASI. Or is he just a soft old man? Whatever it is, Volodya's chance has arrived.

In letting his head fall forward, Volodya positioned his center of mass over his feet. Yes, they're cabled together, as are his hands. But it's a wooden chair, not too heavy.

He thrusts his feet against the floor and pushes. His head snaps into Braun's chin. Volodya whirls around. The legs of the chair catch Braun off balance, knocking him to the floor.

With his ankles tied together, Volodya has little control and his spinning motion continues until, at the point where he thinks his back is to Braun, he pushes off again.

Rather than flopping on top of Braun as he intended, one of the chair legs hits first causing a crisp snapping sound. At first Volodya thinks that the chair leg has broken, which suits him fine, but then, as the chair continues its fall backward. Volodya realizes that the chair leg must be intact or he wouldn't be falling in such a slow teetering motion. Still, something snapped.

Braun screams. Volodya wonders whether it was Braun's ankle or leg.

The back of the chair finally comes down against Braun's chest. Braun struggles for breath. Volodya pushes his feet against the floor, exerting whatever leverage he can assemble against the back of the chair to maintain pressure on Braun. With the advantage of free limbs, Braun grasps the chair and tries to push Volodya off. But he makes a mistake. Instead of rolling out from under the chair, he pushes straight up against the seat where Volodya's hands are tied.

Volodya gets a grip on Braun's arm with both hands and twists, torquing Braun's forearm. Braun pushes on the seat. For an instant the two men are locked together, motionless.

In this moment of equilibrium, Volodya smiles at the absurdity. He's got the advantage. The scoreboard says that Volodya has constrained feet and wrists and is bruised from head to toe, but he also has a measure of leverage and no broken bones. Braun's scorecard shows that he's trapped and has a broken ankle or leg.

Volodya tightens his grip on Braun's arm. He leans left, rotating the chair, while maintaining pressure. A popping sound precedes another scream. Add dislocated elbow or shoulder to the scoreboard.

Volodya keeps hold and keeps twisting. Braun screams louder. Volodya twists the arm that held the gun that cut his daughter in half. Then, gritting his teeth, Volodya rocks back and forth until he gets enough momentum to rise a few inches and crash back down on Braun. He rotates and rocks, twists and pummels, using the chair back as a weapon while maintaining his unrelenting grip on Braun's arm.

When he feels Braun's will relent, Volodya stretches out his legs and wedges his feet against a table leg. With the added leverage, he works the top of the chair-back into Braun's neck. He walks up the table leg, slowly, managing just enough friction to get his feet to the table-top. He concentrates the combination of his weight and the force against the table on that one point of contact with Braun's body.

After hundreds of seconds, Braun goes limp. Volodya keeps pushing. Keeps pushing until he's exhausted and Braun is dead.

2011-Nov-15 12:01am Croatia

Lucy knows better than to ride without sleeping. But where would she stop? The air in her face and the road under her wheels feel like her only friends.

Gliding along Hungary's country roads, she spaces out, misses an off ramp, and drives through Budapest. When she gets back in the countryside, she relaxes on a long, straight, two-lane road. It's past midnight and rain dribbles across her helmet, but she doesn't slow down. The scant light of the moon behind cloud-cover illuminates flat, empty, boring fields on both sides of the road. An iPod would sure be nice; Amy Winehouse would be a perfect accompaniment to the smooth power of the CBX.

A guard at the Croatia border waves her to the side, but she doesn't feel like dealing with people. Besides, who knows what no-fly list or no-pass lists she's on? She digs into a pocket and takes something out. In the dark, with raindrops across her helmet she can't tell what it is. Either the bogus passport Rader gave her or the map. She flashes it at the guard and leans into the turn to get around the lowered gate. He reaches for a sidearm. She pretends not to notice, waves to the man, and accelerates forward. No one bothers to follow.

It'll all be over soon enough. And "over" feels like the right word. Once she does this, everything changes.

Bam, she kicks down a gear and cranks the throttle. The front wheel comes up and she holds it for a good hundred meters.

When she levels out, she sees flashing lights in the rearview.

The pursuit is at least a quarter mile behind when she hits the brakes, shuts off her lights, and takes a gentle turn onto a side road. After the car passes, she turns her headlamp back on and continues along the back road. A minute later, she discovers a small town that's sound asleep. She parks the bike next to a soccer field and finds a dry place to sit in the grandstand.

14. Convergence

2011-Nov-15 12:26 am
Historic pivot point peak probability: 10 hours

The lights are out in our hotel room. Fiona's in bed behind me. Winter's curled up on my pillow. I'm at the desk. I haven't seen them all, of course, but I've seen 70,952 of them. I check them as they pop out of the information aether but there's nothing new to them. I have found three that do not lead to depression, famine, oppression, plague, feudalism, and war, always war—like a revised old testament and I'm tired of it. New weaves flicker in and out of existence every few seconds, but none of them cast light on the situation. No, the light has already been cast.

There is only one non-calamitous though hardly utopian timeline. It has been here all along, hiding in the noise since Officer Justin reached for Lucy's hand.

Fiona says, "Simon, don't sacrifice sleep. Your work requires-"

"Mental acuity, I know."

I scan the timeline again. Nothing has changed but the probability of it occurring, now up to 0.13%—strictly speaking, it's meaningless as a prediction, but now I know what has to happen.

I've found that crucial pebble that can reroute humanity.

Worse still, I now understand what it means for Lucy to be anti-correlated to Franz Ferdinand's assassin.

My eyes close and, though it feels like seconds, five hours pass before they open. My shoulders are tense, my back stiff, my neck bent. A surge of adrenalin pulls me out of the chair. I stare into the shadows of our room.

Lucy was the first and only baby I ever held. Her skin was like thin paper lightly covered in tiny red hairs that rendered it a delicate orange-tinted pink. And when she laughed, it came out in a series of titters shaking her little belly. When she learned to walk, I pretended that I'd forgotten how and she taught me to navigate about her parent's living room using furniture to steady myself. She laughed then, too. When she learned to talk, I told her that her hair was actually tiny inverted carrots. She said, "Is not!" But later, I saw her trying to chew on a strand. When Lucy got her first motorcycle, Gwinnie called me in a panic and I came right over and taught Lucy motorcycle physics: how motorcycles stay up right, how they fall down, and the role of friction between the tire and the road. She asked brilliant questions and absorbed the entire lecture. And then seventeen-year-old Lucy said, "Yes, Uncle Simon, but you left something out." She took me outside and taught me how to ride her motorcycle and I came to understand her affection for overpowered, two-wheeled vehicles.

The greatest gift that Lucy ever gave me came when Autumn died. Autumn was my Border Collie friend. Lucy sold her computer to get enough money to fly to Vienna and hold my hand at Autumn's funeral. It seems that my affection for Lucy's mother brought me a far greater friendship than I'd realized until this very minute. I used to be Lucy's Uncle Simon. I'm not much to her now.

I bump the table.

Fiona says, "Turn on the light before you break something." I ignore her.

I reach down and hit the Eeyore icon, half out of habit and half out of hope. When the program confirms that he's not connected, it searches for credit card or bank transactions, images from surveillance, and so on but finds nothing.

Lucy's timeline has updated. She's in Croatia right now and her timeweave intersects Frankie's in four hours. Not coincidentally, the pivot point countdown has narrowed to 4 to 10 hours.

"Stop torturing yourself, Simon," Fiona says. "Volodya was

right. This has gone far enough. We'll stop her as soon as she gets here."

"No, Fiona, we can't stop her."

"Of course we can. You distract her and I'll disable her motorcycle—six air-cooled cylinders, amazing it hasn't already overheated."

"No. We have to let her do it."

"What are you on about?"

"Anti-correlation. I understand it now. I found the timeline." I take a breath to settle myself and say, "Fiona, not only do we have to allow Lucy to kill Frankie, we have to assure her success."

She makes a Volodya-like sound of distress.

"If Lucy fails, then millions of people will die, billions will suffer." The words come out dry of emotion, as though I don't control my own voice. "I found the pebble, the butterfly, the one thing that has to happen."

"Oh, Simon, no." She stands up and takes one cane-aided step over. "There has to be another way."

"Fiona, listen to me. I've been through every thread of the timeweave. She's anti-correlated. Anti. She has to—," a lump clogs my throat.

"You checked them all?"

"By hand, yes."

"But they're still changing."

"The details, yes, but the one way out of this calamity is stable."

"It could change."

"It hasn't in 51 days."

"If you're not absolutely certain. *Absolutely* certain, you can't … you just can't!"

"Fiona, Lucy is *anti*-correlated to Gavrilo Princip." Winter hops up and whines at me. "Your lack of understanding of basic statistical principles—"

"Arrogance is not argument!"

"—prevents you from understanding this essential, simple fact: just as Gavrilo Princip assassinated Franz Ferdinand and triggered World War One, Lucy Montgomery must assassinate Frankie Woodley in order to *prevent* World War Three."

She stares at me. Winter whines.

"I'm sorry, Fiona. I don't want my beloved's daughter to ruin her life. and I don't want my mentor's son to die. But," I take a breath, "not only must we allow these two things to take place, we must assure that they do. Don't you see? We have the opportunity to prevent a calamity that could destroy life on earth, for this would truly be the war that would end all wars."

Fiona smiles at me, a toothy, condescending smile. "You take your work too seriously. You and Volodya, you both do. I'm sorry, Simon, but your technology is not as good as you like to believe. But you are."

"We predicted the terrorist attacks of 2001 and 2007. We predicted the housing bubble and Great Recession of 2008. Our techniques pass back tests and future tests at every scale. At Occupy Wall Street, we predicted an iconic event—it happened. Volodya and—"

"No you didn't. You predicted the time and place of the pivot points and the repercussions, but you weren't so good at what caused them. Sure, you predicted that terrorists would fly airplanes into the World Trade Center Towers—but they left such a big internet footprint you couldn't miss it. You didn't predict that terrorists would bomb the London Underground and you didn't predict that Lucy would launch an anarchy movement by posing with a New York City Policeman."

"But we did predict that Shearson Lehman would fail first—we got that one, too."

"Whoop-de-fuckin'-do."

Winter walks a circle that includes my pillow and lies down. I climb in next to him.

"Simon, we've never been this close to a major pivot point before, but you've been preparing your whole life. Your special talent is honed and ready."

"Oh." I wonder if she's right. It feels both strange and comforting that someone else believes that my episodes are anything more than modest seizures or schizophrenic incidents. I look at her. She puts her arm around me. I have to admit that I'd respect her opinion more if she understood the Central Limit Theorem.

She says, "To do this, you need your sleep."

"Laying the responsibility for the future of humanity on my shoulders isn't exactly a lullaby."

"Simon, look at the computer monitor."

"Want me to shut it off?"

"That timeweave looks like a lawn sprinkler."

"I suppose we can add that metaphor to the bin, lord knows we have enough."

"Lucy is correlated to Gavrilo Princip, right? How did Princip kill the Archduke?"

"Anti-correlated!" I speak altogether too loudly. "In this epoch of history, her actions will lead to the *opposite* results of Princip's."

"Whatever. What did Princip do?"

"Well, it was a team," I say. "A Serbian Colonel, named Dragutin Dimitrijević but they called him Apis, armed a group of boys by manipulating them into a nationalist fervor. I bet if I ran a correlation analysis between Apis and Rader, it—"

"Get to the point."

"There were seven of them. They waited along the parade-route of the Archduke, each armed with different weapons—the route took them along the street next to the river, one block from here. First, a nineteen-year-old named Nedeljko Cabrinovic threw a bomb but he forgot that it had a ten second delay and, rather than killing the archduke, the explosion injured a dozen innocent people."

"What happened then?"

"Cabrinovic ate cyanide and jumped in the river."

"No, what happened to Archduke Franz Ferdinand?"

"They drove away, right past the other would-be assassins. Cabrinovic's failure shocked the others and they didn't do anything."

"The Archduke drove right past Princip and Princip did nothing?"

"Yes."

"Then how did Franz Ferdinand die?"

"Well, after the failed attempt, Princip went to Moritz Schiller's deli. Some people think he had a sandwich, pastrami seems unlikely, I suspect he'd get a kebab or dolma or maybe—"

"Get on with it!"

"Well, the archduke's driver took a wrong turn and ended up in front of the deli. Princip came out and his target was right there. The driver had trouble putting the car in reverse and Princip took out his gun and fired two shots; one hit Franz Ferdinand in the chest and the other hit his wife Sophie in the belly."

"What was the probability that Franz Ferdinand's driver would make a wrong turn? Or that he'd have trouble shifting gears? Or that Princip would choose that deli? Or that Princip would decide to put the precise amount of mustard on his sandwich so that he'd step out at the perfect time?"

"I don't believe the sandwich theory. Sandwiches aren't native to Bosnians or Serbs so why would Moritz Schiller serve—"

"Simon! Pay attention. Don't you see? If you'd been here with all of your computing hardware on June 28 in 1914, you could never have predicted what Princip did."

"No," I say, my voice dropping an octave and at least three decibels. "Fiona, don't you see? You've listed the pebbles that directed that stream to global conflict. I've found the one that can divert this stream: Lucy must kill Frankie or …"

"No, Simon, it's up to you. You, not an algorithm, not mathematics, it's up to you."

2011-Nov-15 5:44am Berlin

In a garage, tied to a wooden chair and lying over a corpse like a turtle on his back. The better part of an hour has passed since Braun died—no, Volodya needs to be honest with himself—since he killed Braun. Volodya never wanted to be a killer. He just wants to analyze data with his friends Simon and Fiona.

His legs are tied to the chair just below his knees. His ankles are cable-tied together, but his feet have enough play to push across the floor, though he may not be able to turn and his average speed won't compete with that of a turtle, unless the turtle is inverted. He scans the shelves above him, the table in front, and the walls beyond it.

Loathe as he is to concede to good fortune, a garage is quite a convenient place to find oneself bound to a chair. He lets go of Braun's arm and works his way off the man's corpse. His hands are tied behind him at the wrists with a cable tie. There's no chance of breaking it without a blade.

A clock above the gray metal door reads 3:44. To this point, he'd assumed it was daytime, but what he'd thought was light from a window turns out to be a long fluorescent tube that had been behind him.

Sliding along the floor, he works his way past air filters, oil filters, radiator hoses, and cases of transmission fluid. Two shelves up, he can see racks of tools and can nearly taste the presence of wire cutters, sheet metal snips, hack saw blades—all out of reach. Eventually, he works his way into a corner. The top of the chair-back gets caught at the base of a shelving unit. He tries to move in the opposite direction but can't break free. He tries rocking the chair out of the grasp of the shelving unit base to no avail. It's trapped.

"It is a problem." He says this out loud. Fiona once said she was going to have it engraved on his tombstone: "Here lies Vladimir (Volodya) Kazimir, he no longer has a problem."

The thought of remaining here for hours or days waiting for

someone to show up angers him. The anger builds. He arches his back and tries to burst the ties from his wrists through sheer pressure. That the cable ties won't yield increases his anger. He kicks the cartons on the bottom shelf to his right. His feet attain purchase on a shelf support with plenty of leverage but only in one direction: straight back into the base of the shelving unit that has caught the chair.

He pushes, more out of anger than hope. All it seems to do is work the top of the chair deeper into this trap. By rocking back and forth, he might be able to bring the whole unit down. He considers the odds. There are hundreds of pounds of tools above him, solid steel that could crush him. On the other hand, if it doesn't kill him, he'll be wading in tools, some with sharp edges.

He yells, "No problem," and pushes in and rocks back. Again. And again he pushes in and rocks back. If he's making progress, it's measured in microns, but he pushes and rocks anyway. Sweating, panting, straining, he pushes and rocks again.

The chair bursts free.

The shelf rocks back and forth.

He shuts his eyes and braces, but it steadies and nothing falls.

The dynamics don't make sense. If the chair-back had been wedged beneath the shelf, then his pushing-rocking motion should not have freed it. Millimeter by millimeter, he rotates the chair until he can see the point at the base of the shelving unit that had held the chair.

No, it wasn't caught under a bottom shelf. It was wedged against a seam in a support pole. The shelves and poles are built of thick-gauge sheet metal. The poles are made by rolling the sheets into cylinders with a seam that runs their length. The chair back got caught on the tiniest opening in such a seam and, as he pushed, that seam unfolded, exposing a sharp edge.

It takes another hour to position his back against that pole and work the cable tie along the bare edge. Seconds later, the cable tie snaps open and falls from his wrists.

Ten minutes after that, Volodya's running along a deserted Berlin sidewalk. He's got his wallet and passport with cash and credit cards, everything modern civilization requires for freedom of movement, but no cell phone, no tablet computer, no laptop. He feels naked.

2011-Nov-15 6:31am Bosnia-Herzegovina

The freezing wind and ancient bleacher seats, not to mention her fear and loneliness, prevent Lucy from sleeping more than an hour.

Shivering, she gets on the CBX and heads back to the long, dark highway. It's colder on the bike, but the rush of acceleration on the empty country road warms her. The Una River defines the Croat-Bosnia border. The guards wave her right through and onto a bridge. She'd been prepared to demonstrate the dragster-quality acceleration of the CBX had they tried to detain her.

A two-lane road leads her through a sequence of mountains and valleys. She passes an old mine with a warning sign showing a skull and cross bones. Villages nestled in valleys look isolated and cozy, like Hobbit shires. After two hours along country roads, from one shire to another, she comes to a freeway and takes the onramp to Sarajevo where she joins a steady stream of traffic. The road climbs another mountain. The sun is well over the horizon when she crosses the ridge and drives into Sarajevo on a street parallel to a river.

She stops next to a mosque with a copper dome, takes off her helmet and gloves, and scrapes gunk from the corners of her eyes. She pulls the pile of documents out of her backpack: printouts, always printouts. The mundane thought, in the face of the task before her, brings a smile to her lips.

Along with the agenda and a description of the hotel, she finds a map. Gus scribbled some notes on it with a blue pen. A little star marks the Central Hotel where the Sons are staying. He also marked the course they'll take through Sarajevo to get to the road that leads out to the countryside where they plan to build their massive gated communities. She unfolds the map of Eastern Europe she bought at the gas station back in Germany, cross-referencing Gus's printed map. She works through different options, memorizing four separate escape routes to get a feel for which small roads connect to large roads that lead to Croatia and Gus's friend's house.

2011-Nov-15 9:27am Sarajevo
Historic pivot point peak probability: 27 minutes

Fiona and I walk through the lobby and out the door. The door is edged in brass whose patina testifies to its age. This door was here when Gavrilo Princip killed Franz Ferdinand.

She grips my shoulders and says, "Okay, Simon, let it come, fall into the flux. I'll be right here."

The door, the image of the city street before me, the people, the cars, the river—everything flickers, position and motion oscillate between possibilities. If your brain lost its ability to assemble sensations into a coherent timeline, this is what it would feel like. I know the door opens before me and closes behind, but that's not how it looks or feels. Instead, every sensation jitters, cause and effect grow confused.

No, cause and effect aren't confused. Reality is. Which tiny cause interrupts the flow of history? Some pebbles alter destiny and some boulders have no effect at all. Along one timeweave thread, a trickle flows onto a field and evaporates. On another, it carves a canyon.

I try to move forward, try to be smooth and continuous as I step from strand to strand.

I say, "This is like searching for a metaphorical pebble on the rock face of a figurative mountain." Fiona says something in reply, but I can't hear her over the rapids of time.

Winter pulls me forward and I struggle to keep my balance. I drop to my knees and take a breath. The vertigo, the rush of blood in and out of my head—my arteries can't seem to decide which way to direct the flow. One Winter pants tiny bursts of steam, another lags behind with Fiona. I step this way and nearly bump into her. Then I glance back and see her next to me, her cane at my side.

There is one constant in the noise, one simple signal above the background: I can rely on Fiona, every version of Fiona will care for me no matter how deep I fall into the cracks of fate. Gratitude passes over me and leaves a wake of confidence. I'm free to drift, relax into all the sequences, all the weaves, all the possibilities. Instead of resolving into individual channels, the flux of timelines merge and switch with a dynamic I've never experienced.

I don't recall rising from that crouched position, but I'm walking forward, opposite traffic. I cross a street and turn a corner. We pass a line of black cars, sunlight dances on their waxed finishes. From one angle they look like a parade, a procession; from another angle they look like taxis. Nearing the river, we pass a van and I have to look away because it's too bright, painted in dazzling shades of anger and fear. Fiona tugs on my arm and I step into a faster version of myself. I wonder if she knows that she's just favored a specific reality over another. Like all timelines, it's a blend of dread and hope, but this one is slightly less dreadful.

At a corner, I feel as though I'm diverging, splitting into different states of confusion and for no reason that I can discern, I lean into the sunshine and find at least one of me walking toward the river along the parade route that carried Franz Ferdinand to his death.

Would history have differed if Ferdinand had died here where Cabrinovic threw his bomb? Would Gavrilo Princip have survived his tuberculosis, perhaps lived a long, boring life? Would the Hapsberg empire have survived? Would democracy have emerged across Europe?

What pebble diverted the course of Princip's timeline from

conspirator to assassin? Would some other pebble, or maybe a boulder, have put an end to Imperial Europe?

A car honks and I jump out of the way. My shadows look confused, but as the car continues along the riverfront street, they reassemble into a single well-behaved shadow mimicking my steps. A Fiona or maybe a Winter tugs on my leash. I look back and see a horseless buggy, it flickers into a Mercedes sedan.

We pass a cluster of people. The cluster fluctuates between three and ten people as if they're dancing in and out of themselves.

Fiona stops—or, I think she stops, certainly one of her stops. She says something and pulls on me, dragging me from the rapids to a single timeline; it feels like being pulled onto a raft.

Holding me up and steady, she says, "He's coming this way. He's going to see us. Do you know what he'll do?"

"Frankie?"

"No, Rader." She speaks much louder than is warranted, what with my ear no more than three inches from her mouth.

"He'll kill us."

2011-Nov-15 9:27am
Historic pivot point peak probability: 27 minutes

Fiona hovers over Simon. People walk around the odd little man being protected by the tall woman leaning on a cane.

Fiona believes in Simon's ability to see into time. She understands that this belief, this faith in her friend, is not wholly rational—a point which Volodya has made many times—but the worlds are strange places. The notion that someone could be born with a different appreciation of time's passage seems no different to her than the fact that some people have perfect pitch, some can balance on a wire, some can taste sounds and smell music; talent is strange. That one person in seven billion could have the talent to feel the crossing of different realities doesn't seem so strange to her. Even Volodya admits that with so many people on earth, a few must have one-in-a-billion talents.

She has doubts, of course. Can Simon see through these timeweaves with Gwinnie's daughter in the mix? Twenty-first century culture has come to appreciate the intellectual prowess of geeks, but in the 20th century, people like Simon were nerds and losers. If it had been like this back in college, The Idiot Gwinnie would have latched onto this man who would do anything for her.

Simon leads them toward the river. Fiona follows several steps behind. They pass the Hotel Central where six black Mercedes limousines line the curb. She sees the white Peugeot cargo van parked across the street, next to the river. The three tiny openings along the left side would be difficult to see if she weren't hyperaware of them. Rader's sidekick, Klaus Schmidt, huddles over a sheet of paper with Stepan Petrov, Alina Romano, and the Oakland cop, Mike Davis. Davis limps to the van. Klaus motions to Stepan, who jogs along the river, and then points at the limos up the block. Fiona identifies Adriaan Buijs standing next to the Hotel Central entrance.

As Fiona turns back to watch Rader's gang position themselves, a little warning goes off in her mind. She looks back at the line of limos and sees Rader. If he hadn't been wearing black, she wouldn't have recognized him. He stands next to the leading limo. The only other time she's seen him was at Occupy Wall Street and then she didn't know who he was. He looks smaller and older than the model of a villain in her head.

As they pass the van, she pulls Simon by the arm, orienting him so that Rader can't see his face—if he hasn't already. By pulling him, she changes Simon's direction and rather than continuing along the sidewalk, he steps in front of a car. The car honks and veers around him. Fiona rushes forward. Simon steps back on the curb and shakes his head. The shaking continues down his torso all the way to his calves. Winter shakes in an almost identical fashion.

Orienting her back to Rader, she tries to conceal Simon. She rotates him so that she can watch Rader without letting go. She combs her mind—has Rader ever seen her? Does he even know she exists?

She positions her finger over the button in the handle of her cane, ready to release the blade.

Simon mumbles to himself again, which is good if he's getting closer to the solution, but bad because it causes people to give him a wide berth.

Rader scans the area.

Fiona guides Simon into the sun and away from Rader. Walking with her back to Rader feels too vulnerable, so she drops off to the side. Pausing as a cluster of people walk by, she steals a glance back at Rader. Then she checks Simon and Winter. Concealing a mumbling man walking a beagle is a silly notion, but as long he keeps pace with the crowd, he might go unnoticed.

The crowd thins around him. Maybe it's a random fluctuation, like those moments in traffic when one lane gets a few seconds at full speed; maybe the crowd senses tension, maybe they're just freaked out by the weird little man. Coincidentally, or maybe not, Simon steps away with purpose. She looks back at Rader, but he's gone and the white van is pulling away from the curb.

Simon nearly jogs as though following something in his own shadowy world. Winter trots along beside him. Fiona increases her pace, but her leg slows her down.

"You will stop interfering."

It's Rader, half a block behind them. Simon doesn't seem to notice.

Rader breaks into a full sprint at Simon. He moves well for an old man. He doesn't seem to notice Fiona, but as he closes, they make eye contact and he moves laterally away from her. She sees that he holds a gun inside his coat. She lunges forward, running in her own style with her real leg propelling her and the cane preventing her prosthesis from slowing her down too much.

Simon is focused on something at the end of the block. He

even pushes past a pedestrian—an action he would never contemplate were he not only partially here.

Her cane can either get her to Rader before Rader gets to Simon or she can convert it to a weapon, but she can't accomplish both.

Rader closes on Simon.

That decides it. She has one chance to prevent Rader from killing Simon.

Fiona, now two steps from Rader, sets her cane in the ground in front of her, leans into it and swings around with her prosthetic leg outstretched, gaining momentum. She continues spinning as her real leg comes down. Now with both her prosthesis and cane swinging, she triggers release of the ten-inch blade, reaches out and stretches, twisting as she falls.

Rader dodges into the street. A car veers around him.

She's certain that he's too far from her, certain that she'll have to let go and hope that the cane can become a spear. She feels her prosthesis come free. If she lets go of her cane, she won't even be able to stand, much less help Simon.

She lets go.

The blade slices through Rader's pants, through his kneecap, into the meniscus and cartilage. The counter-torque of impact sends the cane spinning into the street.

Rader's forward momentum throws him to the pavement.

Simon continues walking, oblivious. Winter, however, is not oblivious. He whips around, barking and growling. The motion pulls his collar over his head. Simon continues with Winter's leash and collar dragging along behind.

Fiona scrambles for her cane, but her leg is closer so she grabs it.

Rader rolls onto his side with the pistol in both hands. Its long barrel includes a silencer. He aims at Simon.

Fiona hurls her leg at Rader, but it's so damn unwieldy. The thigh-end hits the tire of a parked car and the leg bounces to the side. She can see Rader take a breath and steady himself, the action of a practiced shooter preparing for a kill.

But instead of a clear shot at Simon, 30 pounds of snarling, teeth-gnashing beagle fly at him. The gun makes a substantial spitting sound. The dog screams.

The white panel van careens onto the curb straight at Fiona. She rolls out of its way.

Winter screams again.

Klaus Schmidt jumps out of the van, glances at Fiona who is sprawled in the street, struggling for her cane. He lifts Rader and puts him in the van and starts to climb in behind him.

Rader says something in German and Klaus hops back out, grabs Fiona's cane, and gets back in.

The van accelerates away.

15. A Metaphorical Pebble

2011-Nov-15 9:51am Sarajevo
Historic pivot point peak probability: 11 minutes

Where is the serendipitous pebble that can prevent both the minor calamity that will kill Frankie and ruin Lucy and the major calamity that will punish billions? How can I nudge Lucy-Princip into Lucy-boring-nobody and push the world back onto the path of utterly imperfect but at least partial civilization of somewhat good intent? Or are my goals too ambitious?

Time's whirlwind induces nausea. The uncertainty of my footsteps staggers me, but urgency pushes me forward.

The cacophony crystallizes for an instant. A familiar, heart-wrenching sound penetrates my mind. A cry, a shout, a spitting sound, like a mechanical cough, and then a scream. I look around, but as my heart rate climbs, so does the volume of the visual noise. I have to cover my eyes. I don't know what has happened; I do know that whatever it was could well break my heart. I have to go on. I'm tied to the timeline in which it occurred. I can't make it unhappen.

The ruckus fades behind me. A small truck drives by and, as it passes through a building's shadow, I see a tank piloted by enraged Serbs. It transitions from shadow to light and, for just an instant, I see a parade of horses ridden by men in helmets. I'm distracted by the notion that the image should be in sepia.

Turning up a street away from the river, I stop where Moritz Schiller's delicatessen once stood.

Cars come and go, jittering among possibilities. A man steps out of the museum—no, now it's a deli—with a paper cup of coffee, perhaps a latte, maybe a Frappuccino. Behind me, I hear a car backing into a parking space. The man reaches into his coat pocket. He takes out his phone and walks around me. As he passes, his short leather jacket turns to black wool, he becomes thinner, loses his healthy pallor, and his phone becomes a Browning pistol. He raises the gun. I take two certain steps toward him. He looks at me and pauses to let me pass, but I stop between him and the car. Another wave of vertigo passes over me. He raises the gun to his ear and speaks into it.

Obstructing this man as he talks to someone on his cell phone is probably not the destiny-diverting pebble for which I search.

I shake from the tip of my nose to the tip of my tail. I look down, expecting Winter to repeat this motion, but rather than a floppy-eared beagle there's just a leash attached to an empty collar.

2011-Nov-15 9:54am Sarajevo

Lucy stands on the sidewalk in front of the Mosque and studies the map Gus gave her. The breeze ruffles the edges of the paper and light shines off the tarnished copper dome behind her. She closes her eyes and visualizes Francis Woodley's route into the countryside. She pictures herself riding up, shooting him, and then unleashing the CBX on country roads. Caressing the red gas tank, she smiles because the only thing on this road that can keep pace with her is a faster motorcycle.

Excitement wells up from the despair that convinced her to do this deed. She's ready to go, ready to start this revolution. The word "murder" never percolates up into consciousness. If it did, she'd probably turn around right now. Instead, she nurtures anger at all the injustices the plutocrats and oligarchs perpetrate on the innocent hard working people of the world and focuses it all on the image of Francis Woodley in that green jacket shaking his fist at an Occupier.

She mumbles, "Bastards," unzips her jacket pocket and takes out the pistol. Holding it under the map so no one can see it, she checks the magazine, releases the safety, hefts it in her right hand, and puts it back in her pocket, this time leaving the zipper undone. She practices taking it out of her pocket. It catches on the zipper the first time, but she finds an orientation where it slips out cleanly. The process gives her a little badass, gangsta buzz.

She takes a deep breath and finds the agenda for Francis Woodley's meeting. It shows the time they're supposed to depart the hotel. She doesn't have a watch, of course. Watches are like printouts, why bother when it's all on your phone? She doesn't have a phone, either, but there is a clock tower. How quaint. It's all very quaint. The clock tower says she's late. Story of her life, late for the revolution.

She puts her helmet and gloves back on. She rides slowly at first, comparing street signs on the sides of buildings to those she memorized from the map.

2011-Nov-15 9:55am Sarajevo
Historic pivot point peak probability: 26 minutes

Fiona lies prostrate on the sidewalk with her cane gone and her prosthesis out of reach. She can see Simon up the road. He turns toward her for a moment but instead of seeing her, he shakes his head like a blind man saturated in sound. Then he resumes his march into a future. Fiona loves Simon, but knows exactly what she can and cannot rely on him to provide.

Rader's gone now, his minions carried him to the van and they drove off. Winter lies with his head dangling from the curb into the street.

A small crowd forms around her. A woman and her son step forward. The son carries her leg and the woman helps her sit up. Another woman and two men lift Winter from the street onto the sidewalk.

Winter snarls and snaps at them. The relief that he's alive is replaced by the realization of how much he must be suffering –the only thing Winter ever snaps at are Milkbones.

Fiona indulges the mother and son as they help her attach the prosthetic leg at her hip. They lift her up and she steps to Winter. A young woman cradles his head in her arms, rubbing the space between his eyes, down his forehead all the way along his muzzle and then again. The motion calms him. He licks his chops, exhales a long breath, and pants.

The woman says something in Bosnian. Fiona replies in French: "*Désolé, parlez-vous français ou en anglais?*"

The woman replies in English. "Did you see the car who hit him?"

One of the men says, "Were you hit? Or just the dog?"

Winter's coat is torn open along the left side of his chest, marking the path of the bullet. Pink muscle shows through the gap and blood seeps but doesn't flow from the tear.

"That van," Fiona says, "the white cargo van hit him; did you see it?"

The woman translates and people look up the street, there's no sign of it now.

Fiona has lost sight of Simon, too.

It takes several minutes for Fiona to figure out that the woman, whose name is Ena, has offered to help Fina get Winter to a veterinarian.

With Simon out of sight, Rader and his gang gone, no idea where Lucy is, no notion of what has become of Volodya, and feeling hopelessly vulnerable without her cane, Fiona struggles with the concept that all of civilization could be collapsing. No, she thinks, that's not it, *bugger civilization.* She doesn't want to play anymore. She wants to serve drinks and literature and laugh with Simon and Volodya and Winter.

Winter's ears are back, his tail curled up between his legs like a second penis, and he breathes the short, rapid, panting breaths born of fear. He looks up at her with sad brown eyes and exhales a heart-rending whine.

Fiona walks alongside the woman. As they turn up a street,

Fiona looks at the line of limos and sees Rader standing just where he was before, maybe 15 minutes ago.

The only sign that he's been injured is that he's leaning against a cane—her cane!

2011-Nov-15 9:56am Sarajevo
Historic pivot point peak probability: 25 minutes

Having shaken off Gavrilo Princip's ghost, I step away from the assassination museum that used to be Schiller's deli. I walk up Appel Quay parallel to the river. It's not nearly as shallow now as it was that day in June of 1914 when Nedeljko Cabrinovic tried to drown himself in four inches of water.

The morning traffic flickers and that 1911 Graf & Stift Double Phaeton convertible seems to follow me. I can almost wave to the glowing, joyful woman, Sophie, and her doting, high-born husband, Franz.

My world blurs and smears. Sometimes people look as if they're stepping out of their bodies, though their bodies do catch up. I shake my head and yawn to clear my ears.

The previous century horseless carriage flickers into a procession of Mercedes limousines with Frankie Woodley in the back seat of the first car. My initial thought is to wave at him, but he's laughing with Gijjelle.

The mid-morning quiet, the relaxed flow of traffic, the autumn sun reflecting from the river—other than the rather clichéd notion of calm prior to storm, none of this portends a shift in history.

Frankie's Mercedes procession stops in traffic two blocks ahead in the left lane of the two-lane, one-way street. Picking up my pace brings another wave of queasiness. I anchor myself in the present by staring at a bright green motorcycle that has the word "Ninja" scrawled in a graffiti-like font across the fuel tank.

The sound of two women chatting on the sidewalk nearby repeats itself in an echo. A man in a green canvas jacket carrying a matching green helmet approaches from the other direction, but his shadow precedes him, pauses, rejoins him, and then leads again as though he's illuminated by some errant strobe light.

As the last Mercedes in Frankie's parade moves forward, the Peugeot van passes. I duck into one of the oscillating shadows of the fellow carrying the green helmet and the queasiness becomes pure vertigo: like I'm standing on a bridge, high over water, afraid that I might jump and equally afraid that I won't.

The van now paces the trailing Mercedes in the six-car procession. Wait. No, it's parallel to the center car. No. Damn my vision. It's as if the van swings between two places. A trick of the light? A symptom of my madness? The intersection of two branches of destiny?

The green-clad fellow steps up to the Ninja motorcycle.

A winding, high-pitched scream approaches from behind. I step around the man and look back. I see a flash of red hair beneath her red helmet. At first it's a blur, but I take another step and as she passes and the engine Doppler shifts to a low frequency roar, the vintage red CBX comes into focus.

I don't know which way to jump.

Lucy slows in the traffic ahead, now two blocks from the convoy. Rader's van passes another car. The van has solidified into a single entity.

That green tint finally appears between timelines, like the edge of thick glass separating here from there. The nausea, the double-vision, the echoes have all been replaced by a visceral sense of foreboding, a complete lack of hope, that feeling we get when the shit hits the fan; that pessimist's paradise of sour relief when our worst expectations come true.

The pain of that reality sucks me in, but I push out as though trying to swim upstream in a torrent of rapids. The green tint yawns between here and there.

The echoes return. Lucy's motorcycle oscillates in my vision as though oozing in and out of its own image. Everything shifts back and forth. Time's progression comes to a crawl.

The man next to me is all but frozen in the process of taking his keys out of his pocket.

Crossing the widening gulf between timelines feels as though I've escaped the rapids only to go over a waterfall.

I say, "I have to steal your motorcycle."

Time launches forward, that foreboding disappears, and I emerge from the pessimist's refuge into a world of pure movement.

He looks at me as though I've asked for the time and he doesn't wear a watch. He says something in Bosnian and then tries French.

In what I presume is passable French, I say, "No time to chat, I'm afraid." He looks at me funny. Maybe it was Italian.

The man leans across his bike, helmet perched on his forehead, staring at me.

Grabbing the keys from his hand, I say, "Terribly, terribly sorry about this."

He lunges at me.

While I am certainly not the sort of man who would willfully bring harm to another human being through a physical act, my tenuous grasp of anatomy combines with my deep understanding of dynamics to provide the tools necessary for immobilizing this unsuspecting, wholly innocent man: just as his center of mass passes from a stable to a metastable point, I poke him in the kidney and kick his left leg into his right leg.

My experience with motorcycles is just a bit more tenuous than my grasp of anatomy. That is, Lucy once taught me how to ride her 900.

Throwing my leg over the seat, I put the key in the ignition, pull in the clutch, start the bike, and wind back the throttle. The instant my rear touches the seat, I kick the gear lever. Releasing the clutch, the motorcycle emits a low-pitched complaint and, rather than vaulting forward, it begs to stall. The innocent man—

maybe he's not innocent, maybe providence has provided me a guilt-ridden scoundrel—pulls my arm from the clutch lever. I wind the throttle all the way back and the bass complaint becomes baritone subservience. The bike climbs onto the sidewalk and the man releases my arm.

People leap to the side. Turning parallel to the street and the river, I pull in the clutch and kick the transmission lever downward. Leaning into a gentle turn so as to exit the sidewalk onto the street between a passing car and a parked car, I release the clutch.

Ahh, I think to myself, this must be first gear.

In a wobbling burst of acceleration, the angular momentum of the wheels compensates my dubious sense of balance and the sheer exhilaration of seemingly multi-g acceleration vaults me forward, right into a timeweave seam.

A car gets out of my way. The front wheel rises in front of me. I pull the clutch, switch to a higher gear, and the wheel bounces back on the pavement. The acceleration is nearly uncanny. Surely Newton had no idea the disregard that motorcycles would demonstrate for his law of conservation of momentum.

Weaving between cars amounts to a dance of leaning in one direction, then the opposite, then the opposite to that, a delicious slalom. Lucy's passion makes sense to me. That exuberant young lady goes wild with every journey she takes.

I can see her ahead, now. She's executing the same dance, though not quite at the same rate. It occurs to me that, in my lack of experience as a motorcycle enthusiast, I could be taking excessive risks. Well, desperate times, measures, and all that. Besides, this is not only great fun, it has achieved something that no other experience ever has: my head is quiet. This second. And now, this one. It is quiet in here. I've never heard this before.

The traffic slows, and in slowing, creates a perfect alley between lanes through which I can accelerate with even greater abandon than I so far have abandoned.

Ahead, now on the same block, Lucy slows for a small clot of traffic at an intersection. The magnificent City Hall building stands to our left, the very building where Franz Ferdinand delivered a speech he hoped would inspire loyalty to the Empire prior to his doomed parade.

The right lane offers the options of crossing the river over a medieval bridge, continuing out of town along a one-lane road, or, together with the left lane, turning uphill. The limo procession follows the left lane, taking a sharp, hairpin-like turn.

Lucy looks back for an instant and then slices between cars. I can hear her going through her gears at a pace that can only be described as practiced to the point of perfection. She leans into the arc of the turn, accumulating velocity through unvarnished acceleration.

I follow at an unjustifiable, indeed, an unwise speed. Leaning into the turn, a vision of the geometry of my acceleration vector appears in my mind. If I decrease my speed, my acceleration vector will point in exactly the wrong direction. I lean farther into the turn, trying to optimize the road's radius of curvature, my speed, and the angle that I'm leaning so that the acceleration vector will push me up the hill—a precise calculation performed in roughly 270 milliseconds. But there is a problem. The road is not banked. Nor is it flat. Instead, it leans slightly downward to the right requiring me to make an even more acute leftward angle. I find myself rapidly merging into the right lane. Alas, I discover that tram tracks also follow that right lane through the curve.

A great scraping sound precedes the sensation that my pant leg is being torn. My rear tire touches the tram track and shifts abruptly right. That shift both sharpens my turning radius and reorients the motorcycle upright and, just like that, I find myself shooting up the hill as though fired from a proverbial cannon; the only remnant of the serendipity of the act is a to-and-fro wobbling motion.

Ahead of me on this rather dreary, closed-in block, despite the perfection with which I navigated the turn, Lucy has managed to increase the distance between us. She closes on the line of black cars and decelerates. I accelerate.

There are six cars. She's three lengths ahead of me as I pass the caboose of Frankie's parade.

She reaches into her jacket and pulls out a gun.

At this speed, had I not been expecting it, I doubt that I'd have recognized the weapon and expect that the people in these cars—drivers, security, and one-percenters alike—won't see it until it's too late or right on time, depending on the outcome you desire. The cars modify neither their speed nor direction. No, they seem to be oblivious to the threat Lucy poses. To them, she's just a youngster passing at an unsafe speed in the way of youngsters.

It occurs to me that my plan of action lacks details. While acutely aware that the data support Frankie's assassination at Lucy's hands, my plan is to follow my whim, to stay in this greenish hue at the intersection of realities until I find one that feels right. "Feels right?" Oh how Volodya would disparage that concept.

Lucy reaches the first car. She points the gun at the rear window.

I don't know what to do. Nothing feels right, except riding motorcycles away from strife on winding mountain roads.

The window of Frankie's limo is open. Other than the possibility of his impending doom, it's a crisp, pleasant morning. I imagine Frankie extolling the wonderful climate and geography.

I twist back the throttle and kick the transmission to a lower gear without touching the clutch. The combination jolts me into the gap between Lucy and the car.

Over the din of motorcycles, I hear a weapon fire, and then again, but see no sparks emerge from Lucy's gun.

My left handlebar scrapes the car. My right handlebar passes below Lucy's left handlebar. I can't put it off any longer. Do I let her kill Frankie? Do I help her? Or do I rescue both of them and give up on the rest of humanity?

People scream inside the car.

The scraping friction decelerates my motorcycle to Lucy's speed. With Lucy on my right and the limo on my left, I peer into the car. Frankie has pushed Gijjelle against the opposite door, shielding her. His eyes are wide but not focused in my direction. He stares at the seat in front of him, at the driver.

Another shot rings out. I see the sparks this time. The driver of Frankie's limo is shooting at me or at Lucy or at both of us.

At first, the driver's action strikes me as reasonable, after all Lucy poses an obvious threat to his passenger and how could he not believe that I am somehow her ally? Then I make a second observation.

The driver of Frankie's limousine is Guenther Rader. Ours eye lock. Recognition shocks us both. Dozens of thoughts try to push their way into my consciousness. The first to work it's way to the surface is relief: I don't have to decide, Guenther Rader has done that for me. The second thought is confusion: how did I miss this timeline? Why would Rader kill Lucy? Even in this hectic instant, a third thought comes to the fore: I need to discuss this with Volodya. And that thought generates yet another: Fiona was right, our technology is wanting.

Rader fires three rounds in succession. A chunk of lime green plastic shreds off the front of that probably-innocent man's motorcycle and bounces off my knee.

I reach for Lucy's gun, not to prevent her from using it, but to take it and shoot Guenther Rader. It's not that I lack compassion for him. Rader is as much a prisoner of time as any of us. I believe that he means well, that his vision of and desire for anarchic utopia is sincere. My problem is that I abhor this man. The animal that resides in me, the undomesticated component that we all carry, sincerely wants to harm this rotten son of a bitch. So I grab for her gun.

Lucy leans away from me and into the path of the white van.

The van provides yet another distraction to magnify this unseemly long instant. What we had thought were holes in the side of the van meant to accommodate rifle barrels and sights, are filled by camera lenses. Three separate cameras point at the scene. I feel a desire to yell "cut" or "that's a wrap," anything to get us out of this act.

From inside the car, I hear Frankie call my name. It comes out with a question mark. I don't blame him for wondering what I'm doing on a motorcycle in Sarajevo. I turn to him and the motion causes my motorcycle to wobble left which encourages me to shift my weight to the right. The motorcycle leans back to the right, and left. I have no control.

Frankie reaches for Rader.

Lucy accelerates ahead of me and leans into a right turn. Still reaching for her gun, my hand comes away empty. Her hands are both on her handlebars.

I find myself concerned that she has dropped the gun and that someone might find it and hurt themselves. Then I notice that the road onto which she's turning is a one-way street and she is headed in the wrong direction. Then, as though to quell that concern but ignite a more immediate one, her rear tire rubs against my front tire. Lucy leans farther into the turn, making an ever more acute angle. My front tire climbs her rear tire, pushing her to the ground. Lucy's motorcycle slides out from under.

On her side, Lucy skims across the pavement and her motorcycle slides directly into my path. No acceleration vectors appear in my internal heads-up display this time. I try to maneuver into a turn that can't possibly avert my hitting her bike but quite likely will prevent my motorcycle from hurting Lucy.

The motorcycle I stole slides out from under me. My momentum projects my body across the rough pavement. Shards of fine flannel tear from my most comfortable suit. Shards of fine skin tear from the only body that I have with me. My satchel, which I've somehow managed to retain, tears from its shoulder strap.

My laptop and tablet smash into the curb.

I hit a bump and come to a stop. The bump is Lucy. Her helmet, in particular. She pushes me off her head. Her jeans are less torn than my suit and, while I'm uncertain whether or not all of my limbs function, hers seem to. She sits up. Her leather jacket, torn along the sleeves and shoulder, expose pieces of the plastic lining that protected her skin. Just as I expect her to look around or take off her helmet or get up and survey the damage, something altogether separate diverts our attention.

Local traffic has pulled to each side of the road, allowing the procession a high speed escape. A car screeches to a stop behind us.

Making the unconfirmed assumption that I've retained my ability to locomote, I grab Lucy by the head, the helmet, that is. Despite my lack of exercise and general lethargic nature in the physical if not intellectual sense, I'm quite strong and Lucy is quite light. In an adrenalized burst of power that would make Superman proud, I drag Lucy to the curb by her head.

Lucy gets her feet beneath her and her helmet comes off in my arms. We make eye contact for no more than a third of a second. She shoves me back into the street and runs up the hill toward the white van, which has stopped at the street's summit. Her shredded jeans expose much of her skin but everything seems to be functioning.

A burst of automatic gunfire shatters the pavement in front of Lucy. She stops and steps back toward me. When she sees me, she turns and sprints into a gap between buildings. I follow.

Whoever fired the automatic weapon at us must have been on the street; a second shooter, perhaps a third, yet I don't see a grassy knoll. We emerge onto another street. I tug on Lucy's shoulder, indicating a narrow side street.

She shrugs me off and rears back as though to strike me.

Another burst of gunfire marks the pavement we just vacated.

She heads down the side street and I follow. We emerge into

the finely landscaped patio of a lovely yellow brick home.

I point to a centuries old live oak and say, "Up the tree!"

Lucy ignores me.

I grab a low branch, hoist myself up and yell, "People don't look up. They're essentially two dimensional creatures, we'll be safe here."

But she's not listening. She bends over and runs along the side of the house. She stops and peeks around the corner. She calls out, "Alina!"

"Lucy, that is you?" Since the words come with the extra vowels that Italian accents pose and in the range of a woman's pitch, I presume it is Guenther Rader's tree sitting colleague, Alina Romano.

Lucy replies, "What happened? I couldn't get a shot at the bastard."

I climb higher toward a limb that reaches out over Lucy.

Alina says, "The plans, we have changed them."

I work my way out on the limb, pass over Lucy and see Alina. As I suspected, she carries a firearm. Though I'm hardly an expert, I've seen enough movies to recognize it as an automatic handgun, an Uzi. From the look of the weapon, I can't imagine its magazine holding more than 40 projectiles.

Lucy steps out from the cover of the house.

Alina points the weapon toward her in a nonchalant fashion, as though she's unaware of its orientation.

Lucy says, "I dropped the gun and trashed that bike. Let's get back to the van."

"You can't. The polizia look for you."

"What happened? It almost seemed like Gus was shooting at me." Lucy's voice trembles.

"*Si*, and he missed. But I won't."

Lucy holds up her arms. "Alina, I know we haven't always gotten along but you wouldn't."

I scream like a banshee. Alina jumps back and sprays the house and tree with gunfire.

I drop from the limb. While it's not the most graceful landing, I manage to project myself forward enough to acquire sufficient momentum to land on my feet and then roll into Lucy, knocking her down. I spread myself like a tarp over her. Alina fills the air above us with another burst, this one much shorter in duration and it ends with curses in Italian. At hundreds of rounds per minute, it's about time the magazine ran dry.

She reaches into a pocket of her short, green, military-looking jacket. The sort of thing you'd buy at the Che Guevara revolutionary gift shop. Instead of pulling out another magazine, she resumes cursing.

Lucy crawls out from under me.

She says, "Where's Stepan? Gus is gonna kick your ass when he finds out …"

But Alina runs back the other direction.

Sirens wail with European accents, the dissonant clanging of two tones.

"This way," I say, tugging her back in front of the house. She's dazed enough to obey. A flash of light catches my attention. I push Lucy into a shrub, reach around and cover her mouth. She thrashes a bit, but I impose my weight and whisper in her ear: "Quiet, just for a second."

A man runs past carrying a weapon. Lucy's eyes go wide in disbelief, or shock, perhaps pain, maybe disillusionment, and she whispers, "Klaus?"

We wait a few minutes in silence. She seems to acquiesce to my authority, my interest in her care, or maybe she's simply given up. With my hand still on her collar, I encourage her to follow me to the edge of the well-maintained yellow brick building. We see Klaus jog up to the white van and Alina.

Lucy jerks her shoulders, twisting out of my grasp. She steps around the house and calls out, "Klaus, over here."

He turns and says, "There you are, we've been looking—"

But he's interrupted by another burst of gunfire. This one louder and with greater authority. Chunks of brick smack into my torso. I reach for Lucy. This time she falls into my arms. Convinced she's been hit, I carry her as gently as I can. She collapses on the wet leafy ground beneath a boxwood shrub. She's making a pathetic sound. I fear the worst. Leaning over, I survey her torso and limbs. That she doesn't resist my medic-like probing does nothing to settle my nerves. Her skin is white, as though hundreds of freckles have simply turned off their pigment. She whispers the same incantation over and over. I ask where it hurts and push my ear close to her mouth.

"Stepan," she says, "Stepan shot at me. Stepan. He's a pacifist. Why would he shoot me? What did I do?"

I sense Klaus and Alina encroaching.

Lucy is uninjured, but she needs motivation. That thought gives rise to another: One day, long ago, when Lucy was a toddler, I had promised to take her to visit some baby goats. Lucy had the sniffles and it had just started to rain when Gwinnie said that we should stay home instead. Lucy collapsed in a sobbing fit. I tried to console her but, once convinced that their worlds are collapsing, toddlers cannot be dissuaded. Or so I had thought. Gwinnie stepped up and did something that I thought was indefensible but was also quite effective. One loud, firm slap to Lucy's behind—a behind, mind you, that was well shielded by a diaper—and Lucy's fit stopped. Like that, as though woken from a dream, a sort of "thanks, I needed that" instant.

With a cupped palm to compress sufficient air upon impact to maximize sound and shock value while minimizing pain or harm, I slap her right cheek. The loud smack will surely draw Klaus and Alina to this boxwood shrub. Lucy's eyes focus on me, incredulous.

I whisper, "You have to get away from them."

She whisper's back: "I need to talk to Klaus."

"Right now, you have to get away from them."

"Why would they shoot me?"

But before I can answer, she gets to her feet and takes off in the far more prudent direction, away from that white van. Staying in the shadows of the tree and the house, we manage to reach the corner before we're spotted. Klaus yells something in German.

Ahead of me, Lucy hurdles a short fence and runs into a cluster of buildings. We emerge in a courtyard where a covey of women huddle around small children, clearly terrified from the prolific gunfire. Lucy leads me through an arch. We turn left onto one street, right on another and find ourselves on a long, narrow street paved in flagstone and lined with shops. A sign in several languages, including English, says "Old Town Sarajevo."

I slow to a walk and say, "We can act like tourists now. Just maintain."

Lucy stops and stares at me, as though questioning my presence.

"He misled you!" I say. "I can explain—"

We both see Alina come around the corner. She carries the Uzi at her side.

We run for it.

Cities like Sarajevo that emerged from centuries of civilization without rational design don't follow a grid-like structure. The roads twist about, seemingly always uphill. We duck into a shop. Women's clothing hangs from various hooks on the wall as well as from hangars on rails. The proprietor, a woman roughly my age, greets us with dubious looks at our torn clothing. I smile broadly and say, "Hi! We're looking for a bathroom." She looks at the two of us in the befuddled fashion of Europeans immune to the actions of American tourists and resumes her needlework.

Lucy looks out the shop window. "They're shooting at me because I'm with you."

The concept takes me by surprise. I can't help but pause to entertain it. In that pause, Lucy runs out of the shop. I follow, but she's well ahead of me. Dodging shoppers, she makes her way back in the direction we came. I run along behind, impeded by the wares set outside shop doorways. Lucy is an intelligent young woman and I trust her judgment. Perhaps they are shooting at her because of my proximity. Perhaps they weren't shooting at her at all, perhaps I am the target. Weighing the possibility slows me down.

Klaus stands at the end of the street, waving to Lucy. She slows to a walk and calls his name. I can tell from here that she's releasing a pent-up breath.

I trip on a gap in the flagstone. As I stumble, I see that Klaus holds a gun at his waist, out of Lucy's line of sight. Regaining my balance, I also see Alina approaching from behind Lucy.

The consequential dose of adrenalin accelerates me to top speed. Lucy is ten meters from Klaus. He raises the handgun. Lucy stops. Her mouth falls open and, trembling, she says, "Why?"

I hit Lucy at full speed and the two of us slide along the flagstone.

Alina lets loose another wild spray of automatic gunfire, chunks of which fly into shop windows and old stone walls.

Lucy rolls into a crouch and runs along the building. I stand to my full height and yell, "Klaus, how about a little love for me?" I don't know where I acquired that vernacular, but he turns in my direction. Lucy runs past, behind him. She calls out to him, too, though her call involves a disparaging epithet accusing him of incest with his mother. He turns and trots after her. Raising the pistol, he fires. A clay tile on the roof of one of the shops disintegrates.

Leading with my forearm held vertically, I hit him at full speed from behind in the general area of his kidney. He hits the ground and wails. I land on him and slide onto the street, get up and keep on running.

Still at least half a block behind her, I follow Lucy out of the Old Town tourist zone, through an old neighborhood, and onto a busy street, then down an alley.

It had to happen eventually: a dead end.

2011-Nov-15 11:10am Old Orthodox Church

The building to our left is built of pre-industrial age bricks that I reckon for the 15th century. Stones at its base could be a millennium older still. Arched doorways shorter than me line the wall with doors built of hardwood and iron.

We enter a courtyard onto a manicured lawn lined with small trees whose gnarled trunks testify to their advanced age. Following the lawn between the ancient buildings, I see a square tower on my left. A black cross tops the tower. I do a double take and identify the building as a church. As I make this identification, Lucy pulls open a door and enters the church. She sits in a pew and looks down at her hands. I fear she's crying. I sit next to her and catch my breath.

Three bearded men wearing black robes and large cylindrical hats look at us. I lower my head as though in prayer and they return to their conversation.

I whisper, "He misled you."

"Why would they shoot me? I did everything for them. Everything. I—"

"Shhhh, I can explain." The words feel inadequate, as if offering Franz Josef the right to vote would compensate for his assassinated nephew and destroyed empire. I mumble, "We need Fiona" because she'd know what to say.

"What are you doing here?" Lucy asks.

"Rescuing you?"

Her hands start to tremble and she struggles to take a breath. At first I think she's crying, and she is, but it's worse than that. I touch her cheek. "I'm sorry I slapped you." My hand comes away moist. Her skin is clammy and even paler now. She can't catch her breath.

She stands and makes her way back outside.

At her side, I say, "Never accept an unwanted fate."

She leans over and vomits.

I take her hand, it's cold and moist, too. She doesn't resist; she doesn't seem to realize I'm there. I pull her to a building across the courtyard and a door beneath an exterior flight of stairs. It's locked, so we continue along a brick path.

The courtyard, the ancient church and ancillary buildings and gardens are enclosed in a brick wall. Standing on my toes, I can see over the wall. A white van passes slowly. From this vantage, I can't identify it as Rader's, or even as a Peugeot. Then we hear Rader's voice. Lucy starts in the direction of that voice. I glance back—we're still alone in the courtyard—and then run after her and grab her arm. She doesn't try to tug free or even pull away.

Scanning the yard, in a state of what I must admit is utter panic, I notice a border garden of roses and deciduous shrubs overgrowing a short door at the rear of the church. I tow Lucy toward it. She doesn't speak or look in the direction of my coercion, she merely submits. The small door is locked, but the lock appears to be among the first products of the Iron Age. My finger fits in the rusty keyhole and, though I attempt to dislodge the single tumbler-like mechanism, the guts of the lock crumble into bits of rust. Ramming my shoulder into the door pushes it open. The hinges emit the low whine of a suicidal rodent.

I pull Lucy into what seems like an old, abandoned closet until we stumble down stone stairs. I let go of her on a landing and she resumes studying her hands. I scramble back up and pull the door closed. The absolute darkness combines with the dank smell of stale, dry air seasoned with iron and stone dust.

I feel my way down the uneven steps. Lucy's still on the landing, still standing. I pass her and go farther down the stairs. I can feel Lucy following. We continue below the level of any reasonable basement. The floor at the bottom has the consistency of a layer of ashes and every step kicks up dust.

She whispers, "I don't think I can do it anymore."

"It's okay Lucy. We might be safe here and if we're not, there's only one way out so we might as well relax under the assumption that we are safe."

16. The Old Orthodox Church

2011-Nov-15 1:27pm Hotel Astra Sarajevo

Fiona carries Winter into the hotel room. He's still sedated. The entire left side of his body is shaved and he's got 32 stitches in a long line from his shoulder to the end of his rib cage. She sets him on the bed and attaches the Victorian collar so that he can't chew on his stitches. The veterinarian's English wasn't so good, but he printed English instructions for the drugs: antibiotics to prevent infection, doggy-morphine for pain, and a tranquilizer to reduce his desire to play.

She'd hoped to see Simon when she got to the room but isn't surprised that it's empty.

The television news is in Bosnian, but it's abuzz with a criminal act perpetrated on wealthy American tourists. She gasps at the sight of two wiped out motorcycles and searches for the TV station's web site. It doesn't have one, so she goes to a local newspaper site and looks at photos of the scene. Two mangled motorcycles marked with traffic cones and police investigators. One of the bikes is obviously the red CBX Lucy rode. The other consists of a gnarled black frame with pieces of lime green plastic all over the road. She zooms in on the photo and sees blood; just a few patches, not too bad, plus some torn gray flannel. Her sense of denial does its job until she sees Simon's satchel against the curb. She tries to convince herself that it could be anyone's satchel.

It doesn't add up. How did Simon's satchel get there? Who rode the second bike?

Winter moans behind her. He stands on the bed, staring at her with his head lowered and a look she's never seen before. He wavers and she lunges on the bed to catch him.

"It's you and me, pup." A feeling of loneliness and self-doubt surfaces—should she have left Winter and chased after Simon? She returns to the laptop and configures software that will search for signs of Simon and Lucy across any and all networked devices, time-stamped within the last ten hours. It feels strange to set up the system without Simon or Volodya in her ear, as though she's flying solo for the first time.

Barely a second after hitting the run icon, a video comes up that has gone viral. It's less than a minute long and includes three different camera angles as though staged. It opens with Lucy riding along a street parallel to a black Mercedes limo. Frankie Woodley is visible in the back seat with his supermodel girlfriend. As Lucy rides up to the car, Frankie appears to go into a rage. The camera angle switches to a broad lens that shows Frankie firing a gun at Lucy. She ducks, turns and wipes out. It ends with an ominous voiceover: "What the 1% does when the 99% doesn't behave."

Fiona doesn't get it at first.

She starts at the beginning and steps through. The video doesn't actually show Frankie holding a weapon; it doesn't show anyone with a weapon, just gunshots from the car at Lucy. Nor does it show Lucy being hit by those shots. The implication that she was shot is obvious enough from the motorcycle crashing. It also only shows one limo, not the procession of six; Lucy appears to be riding along, minding her own business; and there is no sign of Simon at all.

Fiona steps through the video a third time. Now she compares each frame with photos on the local news site. Certain objects in the video have been blurred out. Without the comparison to the after-incident still photos it would be easy to believe that they're just stationary objects behind the moving camera. But hints of the green motorcycle remain in the video. Plus, in the first several frames, Lucy has something in her hand pointed at the car window. It's easy enough to guess what it is, but where did the green motorcycle come from? What role did Simon play? And where the hell is he?

The timeweave has generated more links. Fiona works through them one-by-one. They're all references to Lucy as a martyred hero.

Fiona finally gets it. She wonders how she could be so stupid, but Winter whines behind her and she forgives herself the oversight. Lucy's dead. One of the links points to a video posted seconds ago from Occupy Oakland: a candle light vigil mourning Lucy.

With the software searching and Winter comfortably sedated, Fiona straps on her leg and heads outside to search for Simon the old fashioned way. Traffic flows on the streets next to the river and in front of the Hotel Central and City Hall as though nothing has happened. Up the hill behind City Hall, police have blocked the street. The motorcycles are gone and a man in a hardhat has just finished sweeping up the last pieces of plastic, broken glass, and oil. She walks past slowly, examining the pile of refuse—no sign of Simon's satchel.

She steps toward the cop to ask about the green motorcycle rider, but her phone vibrates. It's an actual call, though she doesn't recognize the number. "Hello?"

"There is a problem."

"Volodya! Where are you?"

"On a pay phone at Medunarodni aerodrome."

"What?"

"Airport in Sarajevo—you are in which hotel?"

"Hotel Astra."

"Put on Simon."

"He's not here."

"He doesn't answer his phone."

As Fiona explains the situation, she realizes how few facts she has: Frankie survived the attack, Lucy's been killed, and there's no sign of Simon. She describes the scene before her in detail and then the trending video.

Volodya says, "Have you calculated Lucy's timeline?"

"I'm trying to find Simon!"

"You recall white van?"

The discrepancies now cascading into place. Leaning against a building up the street from where the motorcycles crashed, she describes her encounter with Rader and concludes with, "Rader was driving that car. The others were in the van. They framed Frankie and killed Lucy."

"Propaganda is expensive," Volodya says and then quizzes her on the other details.

Fiona concludes with, "Shit, Volodya, Rader and his thugs must have Simon."

Volodya says, "Rader shot Winter?"

"He's okay, a lot of stitches, but he's okay."

"I'm coming."

2011-Nov-15 2:36pm Old Orthodox Church

My Timex Indiglo watch sheds the only light and I must say, once your eyes grow accustomed to utter darkness, that little green glo is quite effective.

It's cold and dry down here beneath The Old Orthodox Church. Lucy's sleeping on the floor with her hands between her face and the dust. I lift her head and slide the remains of my coat underneath. She ignores my every move but coughs less.

Holding my Indiglo watch up to the beams, I can see what must be graffiti, probably from the most recent Serbian war and both world wars. I look for Holy Roman Empire graffiti to complete the set. Given this history, I hardly expect to be discovered. On the other hand, something akin to refugee room service would be nice.

Each time Lucy stirs I emit some Indiglo, hoping she'll provide company. Being alone with my thoughts serves to amplify my worries about my dog and my friend Volodya. I try to focus on Fiona who I'm confident is out there searching for us. I know how to get her attention, too, but to do so, I need to slip away for several minutes. Looking down at Lucy, I can't imagine how she can be comfortable in the dust, gravel, rocks, and dirt. I feel about for some structure on which to sit and, barring that, something that we can use to displace enough of the detritus to create a region of comfort. Reaching up and around, I discover shelf-like structures. Reaching into one, my suspicion is confirmed: bones. "Do you think the dead would mind sharing their space?"

To my surprise, she responds, "Perfect fit."

"Among the long forgotten dead?"

"This is where I belong."

I clear enough space for us each to lie down in relative comfort. "I suspect the dust is quite sterile—the utter lack of moisture wouldn't bode well for bacterial growth—we're fine here until thirst and hunger and cold begin to affect us." I reach down to help her up and onto the shelf

She pushes me away.

She says, "Let me rest in peace." It's too dark to see, but I stare in her direction anyway, wondering what has become of the young woman who stood on the container at the Port of Oakland. That Lucy seemed so strong, so compelling and fresh.

I move down to sit in the dust next to Lucy and listen to her breathe. She's not asleep or crying. She's just lying there doing nothing. I listen to people up in the courtyard, bells from the tower, traffic, birds, all the sounds of day-to-day life make me feel more isolated.

I say, "We should check each other's injuries."

After a respectable duration without response, I add: "My left leg stings quite a bit and this dust aggravates it."

Still nothing.

"Don't you find the darkness oppressive?"

My monologue continues one sentence at a time for 31 minutes. I cover topics from the need to clean our wounds to the eventual need for food and water, including my growing desire for a latte. Her only response is a groan when I define a space at the far end of the stairs as a latrine.

Though I was talking to myself, she finally replies in a whisper that I can't hear but suspect raises a dust mote.

I lean down to get an ear close to her mouth and say, "Sorry?"

"Simon, I don't care. I truly do not care.

"Lucy, please talk to me."

"Leave me alone."

"I can't."

"Shut up. Please. Please shut up."

"Oh," I say, "right. Sorry, I meant that I can't leave. Rader's still out there and I suspect he'll kill me if I appear outside."

"I'm trying to sleep and I don't want to talk to *you*."

"Oh," I say again, "right. *Me*." I stand and try to wipe the dust from my clothes and wounded skin. "Do you mind if I sit up on the shelf?"

"I don't care about you. About the shelf. About anything. I don't care."

Now perched on the shelf, I rest my elbows on my knees and chin in my hands. "Do you find it liberating to not care?"

"What part of 'I don't care' and 'leave me alone' do you find unclear?"

"Oh," I say yet again, "right." My effort to remain silent lasts only as long as it retains my focus: less than seven minutes. Then I say, "The man you think of as Gus Reser is actually named Guenther Rader. He's not a good man." I begin to explain how Rader misrepresented me but Lucy's breath settles into the loud steady rhythm of sleep.

I settle into the darkness and the voice of doubt tries to convince me that my actions have instigated a hundred year dark age and/or World War 3. Leaning into the cracks of reality doesn't help. Maybe it's just here in our underground lair, but as far as I can tell, we're on a stable timeline, no intersections, no vertigo. Sure, I feel queasy, but the queasiness of hunger, thirst, and chill come in quite a different shade.

Hours pass. Lucy doesn't move. I listen to people walking about the courtyard above, talking to each other in Bosnian, French, or German. The Old Orthodox Church must be a tourist destination.

Lucy lies motionless for six hours, not even a shift in the angle of her legs. I'm torn between sitting here and protecting Lucy or going out to alert Fiona. Night finally falls. The church bells ring and six minutes later I hear a chorus. I check Lucy with my Indiglo, her eyes are open, staring at nothing, ignoring the green glow, ignoring me, ignoring the universe.

I ask if I can check her wounds. She doesn't say anything so I Indiglo her extremities. Her scrapes are dry but caked in the fine dust. I gently tug on her hips and roll her over. That she allows this bothers me. Dirt cascades from inside her coat.

"Aren't you hungry?"

She's quiet.

"Thirsty?"

The people leave the church and the quiet of night encroaches on the quiet of this tomb. The temperature drops.

"We have to wash our wounds." I try to speak with authority. I stand and bump my head on a crossbeam. "I'm sure there's a faucet in the garden. Will you come with me?" She says nothing. "Fine. I'll find a vessel and return with water to clean your wounds. It will be cold and the spillage will convert the dust into mud, but if you won't come to the water, the mud will come to you." The impatience accumulating in my belly feels liberating.

I scamper up the stairs, listen at the tiny door, hear nothing, and push it open. The courtyard is dimly lit by streetlights beyond the wall. I crawl out and pull the door shut. Still on my hands and knees, I wait behind a shrub, listening. Having studied these sounds for eleven hours, I'm confident that I can recognize inconsistencies. A car drives by beyond the wall. Its headlights cast long shadows in the courtyard.

An inconsistent sound alerts me. I tuck myself deeper behind the shrub. I hear a shuffling, like a team of mute coyotes tugging the corpse of a giant rodent, from behind me, or perhaps above. I concentrate on the sound. Then, immediately to my right, I hear the rodent whine.

No! It's the hinges of the small door to the catacombs right next to me. Lucy starts out, sees me, and pulls back. I can't tell you the relief I feel that Lucy has shown some initiative. But, that relief dies an immediate and tortuous death when the door shuts and she says, "Leave me alone."

I move back to the door and try to open it, but she's wedged it shut.

2011-Nov-15 6:53pm Hotel Astra Sarajevo

Fiona opens the hotel room door to greet Volodya. He comes in, sets a box on the bed—a new laptop. His left eye is bruised and swollen, his nose looks slightly asymmetric, but his chin is taught with concentration.

Fiona says, "It's nice to see you, too."

He sets the laptop on the desk and plugs it in. "I must configure new computer."

Winter's tail thumps the bed. It's no longer swollen but does have a slight bend in the middle.

"He must wear the collar?"

"It keeps him from bothering his stitches."

"The dog saved Simon's life?"

"And mine."

"I'd have never thought," Volodya says. "He is suffering?" He scratches Winter behind the ears and Winter's rear leg picks up the tempo, but the action strains his stitches and he whines quietly. "You tough little beagle."

"Volodya, we have to wash up your abrasions before anything

else." She steps into the bathroom, wets two hand cloths, and rubs soap on one. "Come in here and sit down. You can tell me what happened while I fix you up."

"Little to tell. I killed Helmut Braun."

She leans out of the bathroom. "Come in here. Now."

Volodya sits at the chair watching the new laptop boot up. He raises an index finger to indicate that he's not to be disturbed—perhaps his most annoying gesture, but today she finds it comforting. "We are connected to TLA servers. While new laptop loads software, may I drive yours?"

"After I tidy you up."

He takes a deep breath and stands. The motion is that of an old man. Fiona has known Volodya for over twenty years. He has always maintained excellent fitness and always had that ingrained scowl. The combination gave the illusion that he didn't age. She brings the washcloths to him.

The wounds are worse up close. Stitches would help, but she knows better than to suggest them. He tells her what happened, starting with his attempt to restrain Lucy in Berlin, "My lack of discipline is as bad as Simon's," to escaping Braun, "revenge only emphasizes regrets," and flying to Sarajevo. He speaks in a monotone. Fiona notices that he tells the story in perfect English without dropping any articles until the very end: "And I come here to find wounded beagle, missing friend, and world on precipice of disaster."

"What are you talking about?"

"You do not recall the probabilities we calculated? The anticorrelation of Lucy and Gavrilo Princip? We spend our lives developing greatest prediction technology in history and then, at time to act, we don't have necessary patience to watch timeweaves emerge from data."

"No timeweave predicted that Rader would murder Lucy and frame Frankie."

"Timeline had to have been there. Simon and I missed it. Our mistakes may have taken humanity on path to annihilation."

"The egos on you two—amazing you can fit in the same room."

He pulls away from Fiona and returns to the laptop. "You did not configure timeweave calculation for Lucy or Simon? Neither of them?"

"I set up searches isolated to Sarajevo and time-stamped since I last saw Simon."

"You do not understand nature of correlation. Actions far away and long ago can affect where he is now. We created timeweave software to superpose all possible causes no matter how tiny their effects."

"Piss off," Fiona says. "I did my best." Images of throwing her cane at Rader flash back. It's hard to believe it all happened this morning. Then Simon disappeared. She should have gone after him. But Winter. She sits silently, examining her actions, trying to reconstruct any detail she might have overlooked.

Volodya attacks the keyboard. He doesn't sit with his usual stiff but perfect posture.

"Volodya?"

"One minute." He types in an editing window.

"I couldn't get up. Rader was pointing that gun."

"One minute!"

"I've never told anyone this before. Maybe it's obvious." Fiona leans back next to Winter, closes her eyes and reconstructs the image. "I am afraid that someday I'll fall down and not be able to get up. Damn leg. But I had to use my cane, I had to—"

"Fiona, please."

"Bloody hell, Volodya, I'm spilling my guts to you."

"Your guts can wait—almost finished."

"Sod off."

"There. I have control of Frankie's phone. He was not injured."

She moves to the end of the bed and takes her laptop. "Where is he?"

"This new laptop is not bad." Rows of data scroll across the screen but no timeweave yet. "Nice of Frankie to leave his GPS on. It appears that he tried to continue his plan, but his guests abandoned him." He switches to another window. "Let me just hack this little … Ah, yes. Sarajevo air traffic control. Run this through translation software and—nice. Now search on every name in Frankie's guest list." Seconds of typing pass. "Wallace van Bibber has already left, the others have filed flight plans, and," switching back to the phone data, "Frankie will be feeling the shock of failure in the next few hours." Volodya looks back at Fiona, his face reflecting satisfaction at the small hacking job.

"You're hopeless," Fiona says.

"We have much work to do." Now he's back on the computer. "The timeweave Simon calculated last night are out of date. Everything has changed." He scans the stale timeweave, looks up, and bleats, "Mmm. I see. He had nothing to work with. We must upgrade our software."

"What? Bugger all. We must find Simon!"

"Best if Simon logs onto system and tells us where and how he is."

"Are the police still out there?"

A few minutes later he accesses a surveillance camera. "Like so many confused cattle."

"What about Rader?"

"Hacking Rader is considerably more difficult. Perhaps you can stop interrupting?"

"I got Rader. He won't run again, he may never walk."

"But apparently he can drive and shoot."

"What?"

"Look closely at photos tagged in Frankie Woodley's timeline."

Fiona hits the Trotsky icon on her laptop to bring up Volodya's display: a photo of Guenther Rader leaning on a cane shaking hands with Frankie Woodley.

"He infiltrated Frankie's security detail. Evidently Frankie's driver failed to show up this morning. Guenther Rader drove instead and now is sort of ironic hero."

"But I got his knee, they had to carry him away."

"It is at least swollen." Volodya zooms in on the image. "That is your cane." Volodya finds video of Rader walking away. "He puts little weight on it."

"They just let him go?"

"Of course. He performed security job, why would they detain him?"

"Because he stole my cane."

2011-Nov-16 1:12am Old Orthodox Church

I'm stuck outside the Old Orthodox Church Catacombs hiding under a bush.

I whisper, "Lucy, please." The only response is the sound of Lucy descending the stairs, back to her crypt. "Oh no!" I say, more in response to my morbid thoughts than Lucy's rejection. I lean against the door for eleven minutes debating whether or not to continue my quest for a bucket and a source to fill it. I hear a grunting sound behind the door, not weeping or sobbing, but the sound of someone exerting force followed by a short grunt and a long unhappy sigh.

I push against the door. Then pull. She's managed to lock it tight. I picture the door in daylight and recall the corroded lock and whining hinges. I take the measure of the hinges in Indiglo and then search through the mulch below my shrub for a tool. I audition sticks and small rocks.

A muffled crashing sound behind the door followed by an abrupt groan jolts me with adrenalin. I ram my fingernails into the hinge and pull. The top hinge comes first and it's enough for me to reach inside to remove the object Lucy used to wedge it shut—a femur.

I drop the bone, vault down the stairs, hit my head on a beam, slip in the dust, and fall into the pile of bones I cleared off of the catacomb shelf. I shine my Indiglo far and wide, but its range of six inches is neither far nor wide. "Lucy?" I whisper. "Are you all right?"

Now scanning the floor, I see the Lucy-shaped impression in the ground where she spent the day. Nearly panicked, I search across the floor but can't find her. "Lucy, please. Say something. Are you all right?" Visions of this dear woman hanging from a noose invade my soul, my only comfort comes from the notion that any rope she might find down here would be so decrepit that it couldn't hold her weight.

"Lucy, please?" I beg. "Please say something."

"Leave me alone."

She's behind me, up on the shelf that I cleared.

I hold up the Indiglo. She glares back at me, the very glare that she wore in the difficult years of her early teens, the tortured look of someone imprisoned by her own decisions.

"I just want to be left alone."

"But I heard a sound."

"I bumped my head. Please leave me alone. Please, please, Simon. Please—now I know why my mother has dumped you so many times."

She has found my off switch. I contemplate her words in the cold sobriety of a lifetime of rejection. The bitter cold of this winter night piles atop the emotional chill. I drop into the dust.

She said it over and over and I didn't listen. She doesn't care. And now, I don't either. I lie in the dirt. It's soft, like ashes. I close my eyes, expecting sleep but it doesn't come. Instead, I'm bombarded by visions of Lucy: the stubborn red-headed toddler who questioned every statement her mother made, the bright and kind but skeptical child, the adolescent who died her hair black and hid her freckles under corpse-white makeup, the college student who challenged every presumption of society—as Lucy grew from an infant to an Occupier, she tried on many different costumes. Her costumes, her roles, had a common center. Like the moon orbiting earth, she auditioned roles that revolved around the core of who she is and will become. At her core, Lucy cares about injustice. Without that, I don't think she has anything and Guenther Rader beat it out of her.

I can't let Rader ruin Lucy.

When Rader tried to ruin Gwinnie, I knew what to do. The lye reacted with the hummus and I reacted to it. What can I do now?

I ask again if she's hungry or thirsty. She says nothing. I take her wrist, check my watch and count her pulse rate. No obvious sign of trouble, except that she endured my prodding without complaint. She doesn't care—these three words repeat inside my brain like an unwelcome jingle.

My stomach rumbles. But for coffee this morning before Fiona, Winter, and I left the hotel, I haven't eaten in 22 hours. The thought of coffee percolates my memory of Lucy in the café where Vaclav Havel planned the Velvet Revolution. Even then, she didn't care. I should've stopped her. I should've ignored the presumption of our predictions. I should've listened to Fiona.

The should'ves pile up in the darkness of my soul, creating a heap of shame regarding our use of technology. All our spying, monitoring, and analysis have done nothing to help Lucy. And if she found out! Oh my, I would not want to participate in that debate.

The sun rises and people start coming and going in the courtyard above. I start to say something, but stop, not wanting to kindle Lucy's anger. My sensitivity to her temper kindles an internal debate. I perch on the shelf. Lucy climbs down and returns to the dusty floor.

After 89 minutes of consideration, it comes to me. I dare to believe that I have the solution. I say, "Have you eaten anything since you drank coffee with whipped cream at the Café Slavia in Prague."

It's difficult to resist shining my Indiglo on her to gauge a reaction, but I manage. My faith in Lucy ebbs as the minutes tick by. She must have heard me.

Then, every second of 141 minutes after my statement, she responds, "What?"

I say, "I asked if you're hungry."

"No, you did not ask if I am hungry."

"I'm fairly certain that I did." My feigned nonchalance fairly wriggles through my vocal chords. "Or some such."

"No. You said that the last time I ate was at a café in Prague. You even knew it was the Café Slavia."

"Vaclav Havel's headquarters. Fascinating man. Smoked a lot."

"How could you possibly know that?"

"He's holding a cigarette in every photo. The assumption seems warranted."

She rises from the ashes.

Of course, it's too dark to see, but the sound of her standing, the nearness of her voice, and the smell, she's quite ripe, draws the image in my mind.

"You bastard!"

"Lucy, please, be quiet. What's the matter? You are hungry, aren't—"

"I'll be quiet when I'm dead." She steps closer and I can smell her breath. "How dare you? You fucking spied on me. You bastard. You 1% motherfucker."

It's too dark for her to see my smile.

17. Volodya

2011-Nov-16 3:11am Hotel Astra Sarajevo

Volodya feels strange configuring Simon's timeweave. In all these years he's never taken a peak. He wonders if Simon ever looked at his. They promised that they'd never calculate each other's timeweaves. Other than the sense of doom it would cause, knowing your friend's weave would change the way you behave toward them and that would alter that weave in a way that can't be predicted. But now he needs it.

Exhaustion overcomes him and he awakens furious: furiously hungry and furious at fate, but has no recollection of removing his clothes or going to bed. He starts to swing his legs out of bed, but the center of his back has stiffened to immobility. Bruises on his ribs, arms, legs, and head conspire to push him back. Lying down imposes the realization that his left shoulder has been separated.

Winter rotates his head within the protective cone of plastic to face him. "You do not worry, small dog. I will bring him home to you." The words bring the fury back to his spine. This time, he forces his back to obey. He rises from the bed and strides to the small desk.

Fiona has left a note. She'll return with food and coffee. The concept of food distracts Volodya but the sight of fully calculated timeweaves bring him focus and discipline.

The timeweave of history has resolved. The pivot point is behind them now and humanity's future is destined for a hundred year dark age; history's pendulum seems to have swung back to the uncomfortable stability of war and famine. He glances at the few low probability twigs that point to happier times, but just long enough to see that their cumulative likelihood is less than 5%. He hits the link from which the stable line emerges. It's the video that depicts Frankie Woodley shooting at Lucy Montgomery and ends with: "What the 1% does when the 99% doesn't behave."

Volodya's pessimism is not born of negativity. Expecting the worst ought to mean a life of pleasant surprises.

Hoping to find the pony that must live beneath the manure heap of reality, he skips the video and brings up Simon's timeline. The first link shows surveillance video of him on the street outside the Museum that was once Moritz Schiller's delicatessen. He's in that daze he suffers, pacing to and fro, watching his delusions as Winter's empty leash drags along behind. Then an out-of-focus image, identifiable only by his suit, walking near the river. There's a gap of 35 minutes to the next links, all of which occur within a few minutes of each other. They point to surveillance cameras in Sarajevo's old town tourist district. The first shows Simon and Lucy inside a women's clothing shop with Lucy pointing out a window and Simon appearing confused. The two of them look battered, bruised, and torn.

Volodya works through the rest of the links methodically. The mix of relief and foreboding—they survived the assassination attempt but are still within Rader's range—fails to accelerate his process: assemble the data first, ponder the repercussions second. The last image, time-stamped yesterday afternoon, about the time his plane landed in Sarajevo, shows Lucy and Simon running out of Old Town with Klaus close behind. From there, Simon's timeweave shows the spray of a pivot point. Volodya grimaces at the notion that their technology successfully identified the obvious: in most lives being chased by terrorists would qualify as a pivot point.

He confirms that Lucy's timeline ends at the same point and then turns to the joint timeweave of Rader's gang.

Fiona walks in carrying a bag that smells of food and coffee.

She's wielding a new cane; a plain piece of dark hardwood with a simple handle. She leans it against the desk, says, "It's temporary, until we get mine back from Rader," and pulls two large cups of coffee from the bag. The steam draws Volodya's interest. She sets out a wide array of *burek* pastries and *cevapi* skinless sausage.

She asks if he's learned anything. He grunts and says, "Very little." He can't remember the last time he ate with such enthusiasm. The pleasure draws pangs of guilt that it's not shared with Simon.

Finally, he wipes his hands on a napkin. "You did not retrieve Simon's satchel?"

"It wasn't there."

"Simon was in the crash."

"How could he have been?"

"See this photo? His suit is torn, his leg has road rash."

"You think Lucy let him ride with her?"

"Satchel left behind, torn clothes, injuries. Nothing makes sense except that he was in crash."

"The only images of what happened are in the video."

"Hopelessly edited video—but you are correct. Where there is edited video then somewhere also there must be unedited video."

"Well, you know where to look."

"But this green motorcycle? Must have been Rader's crew? The German, perhaps? Filming from behind?"

"I suppose."

"Maybe Simon rode green motorcycle?"

Fiona and Volodya look at each other for a second and then laugh.

Volodya gets back to work. "Simon's computing devices either are inoperable or out of network range. Hmmm."

"Is there a problem?"

"A problem?" He looks up. "Of course there's a problem."

"I mean, if Rader gets Simon's equipment, can he do anything with it?"

Volodya smiles. "If Rader extracts disk from laptop he should come under the illusion that it will help him."

"Everything's encrypted though, isn't it?"

He smiles. "Oh, much better than encrypted."

"What else have you figured out?"

Volodya rises from the chair. "Sit here, I show you."

Fiona sits and Volodya takes a deep breath. He walks her through Simon's timeline.

"You waited this long to tell me that Lucy is alive?" She punches him in the shoulder.

Volodya bites down and funnels the expression of pain into a reply: "Many hours have passed with no sign of her. Rader may have killed her already."

"No he hasn't."

"Why do you say this? You drive me crazy how your hopes drive your beliefs!"

"Is Rader's timeline up to date?"

"Those of his crew. Rader's personal timeline ever lacks resolution."

"Where were they last seen?"

Volodya leans over, manipulates the mouse and clicks. "This is latest image. You see Officer Davis driving white van with Alina in seat?" He clicks another link. "Here is Klaus and Adriaan in tourist district where Simon's timeline concluded."

Fiona: "Rader's still looking for them—they're still out there."

"Aaaackkuugggh," Volodya's frustration works its way down his throat. "My blood sugar, it is low, I …"

Fiona takes his hand and pulls him toward her. "Volodya, it's okay. You don't have to be perfect."

He pulls his hand away and immediately wishes he hadn't. He wants to share her hope, but deep inside, he lives with the underlying assumption that the fates are waiting for him to let his guard down. He says, "One thing is certain: when Rader finds them, he will kill them both."

"Then we have to find them first."

"Or disable Rader's gang before they find them."

"Let's do both."

"Both? But we have no resources to do either! How can you think for instant that. Acklegrump! I cannot do this with—but you have just one leg, even dog is broken!"

"Oh cut it out. Volodya, it's wonderful news! Simon and Lucy are out there waiting for us to find them."

"They wait for Rader, too."

2011-Nov-16 2:54am Old Orthodox Church

Lucy's vociferous response to my knowledge of her last meal, excuse me, previous meal, threatens to rouse the attention of the clergy upstairs. She sets all of her misinformation before me, lays every possible conspiracy at my feet; my responses range from, "partial truth" to "utterly inconsistent with the facts" to "had you been in our position you might have taken the same actions that Fiona, Volodya, Winter, and I took."

Even the most passionate people find it difficult to maintain a full rage for more than several minutes. After 37 minutes, Lucy realizes that it's a one-way debate. When she ceases her monologue, I throw proverbial kerosene onto her emotional embers: "Do you understand that you have become Guenther Rader's tool?"

Literally sitting at the edge of my shelf-seat, I wait for the flames to engulf me, but instead of furthering her conflagration, the comment all but distinguishes her flames. I wait for a comment, but she's silent. Continuing to wait in this hungry, dark exhaustion, my head lolls into a state of semi-consciousness.

I jerk awake. A rhythmic sound captures my attention. It sounds like a tiny barge working its way through a somewhat tinier canal. No, it's Lucy snoring.

I climb down from the shelf. Her breath emerges in puffs of icy green mist in my Indiglo. Her cheek feels frozen, her fingers like frozen mud, and where her thigh is exposed between shreds of denim, it feels like a banana peel just removed from liquid nitrogen—so cold it nearly burns. Or maybe that's the progression of frostbite on my fingers.

I lie next to her with what remains of my coat covering her shoulder and neck with my face in her ash-crusted hair. Our shared warmth forms a quilt of near-comfort around us.

I wake an indeterminate number of hours later. The uncertainty in the duration of our slumber makes me uncomfortable and I can't resist the desire to perform absurd arithmetic involving powers of 60.

Lucy squirms away from me and stretches.

I rise and try to dust myself off. It is now 7:56am.

"Uncle Simon?"

"Yes, dear?"

"What happened? Why does everyone hate me?"

I say, "Life is metastable."

She makes a whimpering sound. At least it sounds like whimpering at first. But then she says, "You crack me up."

"Sorry?"

"Most people would say, 'everyone doesn't hate you' or 'don't be silly' and you say 'life is metastable.'"

"You're hardly in equilibrium."

"You don't make any sense—maybe that's why I believed them. I feel like such an idiot, I almost—" She stops and I can sense her shaking her head. She adds, "I can't believe what I almost did."

"Rader manipulated you."

"Why do you keep calling him that?"

"Rader is his name. Gus Reser is Guenther Rader. I've known him a long time. He's a bad man."

"He tried to kill me."

"He tried to martyr you."

"I thought Stepan liked me. And Klaus and Adriaan and … everyone."

We're quiet again, though I can nearly hear the circuits firing across her mind. When the silence grows too long and thick, I say, "They presented a body of evidence to you."

I climb up to the shelf and she comes with me. We sit side-by-side with our legs dangling. My glo illuminates her profile.

"Was it true?"

"What?"

"That you and Fiona and Volodya helped those corporate assholes make money by ruining people's lives?"

I sense her wrath rising. My desire for her to care tempts me to kindle this fire but my need for peace pushes me to explain.

She says, "I just can't believe that you would do anything that could hurt my mother. Did you? Maybe by accident?"

"No. Of course not."

"But Julian Assange showed me documents with the TLA logo."

"No," I say, "Rader showed you those documents. The documents from Wikileaks did not indict us. The documents—"

"How do you know what I did and didn't see?"

"Well, Lucy." I pause and try to think of a diplomatic way of admitting our lack of respect for her privacy. "You see, well, ummm. We were watching."

"So you did spy on me."

"It's not really spying. It's sort of like monitoring—no, not monitoring, either—we um. Yes, we spied on Rader."

"And me."

"You happened to be there."

"Why?"

I take a deep breath and try to think of a way out of this but every avenue involves deception. "We sincerely respect your privacy, but sometimes in the course of human history, we need to assemble data so that we can prevent catastrophes."

"What are you talking about?"

"The services that Volodya, Fiona, and I perform require a

great deal of data and to access those data, we take on a wide variety of clients."

"Was it true?"

"Had you double-checked the sources of the documents Rader showed you, you'd have confirmed enough to redouble your mistaken belief that I had somehow betrayed our family. But no, of course not. No matter who pays us, Volodya, Fiona, and I do our best to help everyone. It's sort of like Star Trek: 'the needs of the many outweigh the needs of the few.'"

"*Our* family?"

"You and your mother are my family."

"No. Simon, Volodya, Fiona, and Winter are your family. You should be my family, but my mother is stupid."

"Shut up! Gwinnie is a brilliant woman who has never done anything but what she believed was best."

"Whatever," Lucy says. "What happens next?"

"We stay here until we either have to leave or it is safe to go or they catch us. We can make good use of this time. In the last few weeks Volodya, Fiona, and I have performed extensive analyses of your role in history."

"My what?"

"Don't discount yourself. You have a role in history."

"What do you mean?"

"Lucy, you have built a following." Then I remind her of who she is and what brought her to Occupy in the first place. We talk about her ambitions and I tell her about the work that Volodya, Fiona, and I perform. She asks the sensitive questions about whether we have the prerogative to use people's information. I admit that it's a question we avoid entertaining. She won't let go of it, of course, but all I can say is that we mean well. Then she laughs. She laughs so hard that she has to cover her mouth to keep from drawing the attention of people in the courtyard above.

I sense release in her laughter, as though her core is reassembling itself.

When she stops laughing, I say, "Lucy, if you ran for office, people would vote for you."

"What office?"

"You are already an icon and you've been honest with the people who follow you. You're in a unique position, I think you should go with it."

She laughs again but this time with irony. "I don't think I'll be very popular when people realize that I tried to kill someone."

"Volodya and I can fix that," I say. "We can scrub the web."

"A cover-up? Already? I guess I am a politician." She laughs again, but I can't join her.

"Volodya's in trouble," I say.

"What?"

"After he tried to prevent you from coming here, Rader kidnapped him." I describe how we lost contact and then my eyes start to well up. "I'm very worried about my friend Volodya and my dog Winter and my friend Fiona."

She listens to all my worries and then says, "Fiona knows you, Uncle Simon. She'll find Winter. It will be okay."

"What about Volodya? You don't know what Guenther Rader is capable of!"

"Yes I do. He taught me how to use a gun. He tried to kill me. I know exactly what Gus Reser is capable of." She sighs and says, "It's so weird. Do you know what I almost did?"

"You almost made a mistake."

I can hear her shudder. I put my arm around her shoulders and press her against my chest. "Lucy, you didn't make that mistake, after all. It's okay. You're okay."

We sit next to each other on the cleared shelf listening to people above us and traffic on the street.

She says, "Nice riding, by the way."

"I thought so." Then I share my affection for the exhilaration of motorcycling. "Perhaps I will become a bicyclist."

"You mean 'biker.'"

"Of course."

We're quiet another two minutes and then Lucy whispers, "I don't get it. Why would Gus shoot me?"

"Do you know about your mother's relationship with Guenther Rader?"

"My mother?" She sits up and bumps into me. I hadn't realized she'd lain down. "What are you talking about?"

"Guenther Rader nearly ruined your mother thirty-four years ago."

"Ruined?"

Starting with the day I met Gwinnie, I tell her the whole story of our summer in The Grove. She lies back down, now resting her head on my shoulder. Lucy begins to snore.

I lean back among the old bones and sleep overtakes me, too.

Hours later I awake, though it seems more like I'm still asleep, just shifting from one dream to another until I bump my head on the shelf above.

"Harum?" Lucy says, her head is still on my thigh, though that particular thigh is now wholly numb. "Oh, arrgh, my entire body is in pain."

I quiz her on her condition and then I sniff around her wounds. "When did you last bathe?"

"I don't know, in Amsterdam, I guess. Seems like a long time ago."

"Smells like a long time ago," I mumble, but she elbows me and I can hear her smile. "But it doesn't smell like infection." I reach over and touch her forehead. No fever, either. "We need to wash. There must be a faucet up in the courtyard, but it will freeze if we wait too long. Though, if we don't wait long enough, we'll be seen." I contemplate for a few seconds.

Lucy says, "It's gonna freeze us, too."

"Hmm? Yes it won't be comfortable," I say. "We need to find a surveillance camera; preferably several of them."

"So we can avoid them?"

"No, so that we can stare into them long enough for my face recognition software to identify us and alert Fiona that we're okay."

"But they'll see us. The cops and the priests or whoever guards this place. They'll catch us."

"Yes, it's a fascinating exposure-optimization problem."

2011-Nov-16 9:13am Hotel Astra Sarajevo

Volodya hunches over the small hotel room desk. Frustrated by the tiny laptop screen, he toggles between eleven windows, each taking a different approach to the problems, potential solutions, and, what seems most important right now, monitoring Rader's gang.

"We have to get to them first!" Fiona says for precisely the seventh time.

Volodya toggles to the window from which he attempts to hack into Rader's system. He mumbles, "Why this will work now when it has not worked for all these weeks, I cannot say. Trknlible."

She says, "We should be out there searching for them!"

"Yes, one-legged woman, injured man, and dog in absurd collar—making target of ourselves will not help Simon."

"We should go to the police."

He switches to another window. "Here's something. You would hit your Trotsky."

"What am I looking at?"

"A map showing locations where Lucy and Simon have not been seen."

"Sorry?"

"Colors on this map indicate areas of surveillance cameras that have *not* seen Lucy or Simon."

"It's all blue."

"No camera has seen them in eighteen hours." He taps enter

and the map lights up a swath of yellow, red, and purple near the accident, into Old Town, and along several streets. "These are regions where images consistent with Simon or Lucy being seen in the one hour from assassination attempt."

"So, you're saying that we can search everywhere that's not blue?"

"Better to encourage Rader to search in areas that are blue."

"And we do nothing?!"

"I am doing something."

"I have to go look for them."

Volodya taps a function key. The map turns blue but for an orange ellipse near City Hall. "You will die fastest if you approach Italian. She likes to shoot things."

"You know where they are?"

"I have confidence in where they are not."

"Why do you speak in negatives?"

"Statistical accuracy is not a vice."

Fiona stands on one leg and reaches up, stretching. She takes her cane and paces in the space between the two beds. "I hate this bloody cane."

Volodya dives into source code in another window.

Minutes tick by. Fiona paces, Volodya hacks, Winter sleeps.

Then Volodya chuckles, not mirth-filled laughter, the chuckle of a hunter whose trap has sprung.

Fiona: "What have you done?"

He rubs his left shoulder. "Will be a minute or two."

"And then?"

"And then, I will have access—band-limited, of course, but access to Rader's entire system."

"What? You said that was hopeless."

"This approach never occurred to me."

"Just tell me what you did." She completes a circuit from one end of the bed and back. "Don't make me whack you with my cane."

"Fiona, please."

"Tell me what you've done. Just tell me. I need hope."

"Set down your weapon and sit with me, you will want to watch and perhaps you can help."

"Halle-fucking-luiah, let me do *something*."

"Set your laptop next to mine, we will work together."

She does as he says. Volodya finds her acquiescence altogether satisfying.

"Right then," Fiona says, "what am I looking at?"

"Be patient."

She lets loose a breath that indicates a total lack of patience.

He pats her knee. "Rader retrieved Simon's satchel. The PC was destroyed but the hard disk within the PC survived. Of course, he opened it and—"

"But it's encrypted."

"You should let me speak."

"Okay, speak."

"Is extraordinarily unlikely that Rader can extract useful data from the disk, but the instant he connected it to a power source and another computer, the disk launched a cavalry of Trojan horses. Once they have loaded, I will be able to see everything they do—well, not everything. If I take too much of their bandwidth, they'll detect us and remove disk."

"Won't they detect your Trojan horses?"

"We load far more false Trojan horses than real ones. They will analyze the disk and identify hundreds of viruses. But one will go unnoticed because it is written with old-school memory management. You see, Fiona, hackers who learned to code on machines with gigabytes of RAM have no concept of what can be done with a dozen kilobytes."

"We'll see."

"And now you are pessimist?"

"You sound cocky."

"Watch." He types for a few seconds and then lines of text

slowly appear in an old-school DOS window. "I think they will not notice data leaking at this rate."

"It's taking forever—what is it?"

He types again and more lines of text appear.

"It's a directory?"

"On Rader's disk, yes, I believe these are the unedited video files."

"So we can see what happened to Simon?"

"It will take hours to copy them."

"What good does it do, then?"

He switches to another window. "As we acquire data, I believe we can provide some data of our own."

"I like the sound of that."

He types commands into another window. He appreciates her anxiety, no, he revels in her anxiety. "Look at the map on your laptop. You see how different colors move about? The Orange is Alina Romano, the red is Klaus Schmidt; those two are quite happy pulling triggers. The others, except Rader, of course, prefer less hardware-oriented weapons. White is location of van, presumably driven by Officer Davis and carrying Guenther Rader. Stepan Petrov is marked in green. If someone will find Simon, I'd prefer it be Petrov.

"I believe we are engaging the Dutch computer scientist right now, Adriaan Buijs. He must be working in van or hotel room, some sort of base." He clicks into another window and types. "No, they have no hotel or base." He types some more. "Perhaps we can trap them. Their lack of sleep will play to our advantage. I will plant images into the surveillance videos they monitor. None too clear—is awkward work to port still images into video." He goes to yet another window and performs a calculation.

"What are you doing now? And can I do something? Anything?"

"Monitor the map, any flurry of activity will mean Simon and Lucy are found." He finishes the calculation. "I can embed three images of Lucy or Simon and maintain less than five percent chance of being detected. Maybe."

He clicks the mouse with a flourish and leans back. The two of them watch Fiona's monitor.

She says, "The van's moving. Alina and Klauss are moving too. They've found them!"

"No they are on a duck chase."

"A what?"

"They chase their own tail."

"You mean a wild goose chase?"

"That is one try. We can do two more. Maybe three if we must."

"And that's it? That's all we can do?"

"We'll think of other things. Tactics must be deployed with consideration. You are maybe too passionate for this."

"God, I hate you."

Volodya puts his hand back on her knee. "Do you?"

"No, of course not." She turns to him. "Well, figuratively."

He leaves his hand on her knee but resumes working. She turns back to the map and says, "You drive me crazy, but I love our mock-rivalry. In some twisted way that speaks poorly of both of our egos, I can't imagine life without you."

The confession makes Volodya uncomfortable. He takes his hand back.

"When we have received unedited video from which they composed 'What the 1% does when the 99% doesn't behave'—in thirteen hours, we will know more."

Fiona watches the map evolve and tracks areas Rader's team searches. Volodya launches more software and makes more calculations and then takes Winter for a walk.

Stretching his sore muscles feels good. He knows that he'll need them. He returns with lunch, the *Cevapi* he's fallen in love with, *burek* meat pies, and *kadaif* pastries.

Fiona taps the desk. "You're preparing for hibernation?" She glares at him. Every indication of her discontent provides greater motivation for him to be careful, calculated, and cool.

Night falls without any evidence of Simon's whereabouts. Fiona says, "Volodya?"

"Kakiye?"

"Why does the timeweave for human history still predict a 100 year dark age?"

"Impact of edited video."

"Isn't it smart enough to know that Lucy is still alive? If she is, then wouldn't that alone reverse the video's effect?"

Volodya says, "Hmmm. There could be a problem we don't yet see."

2011-Nov-16 10:37pm Old Orthodox Church

The rate that my teeth chatter indicates that the temperature in our dusty refuge flirts with the freezing point.

"Come on," I say and Lucy jogs up the stairs.

We push open the door. She crawls out, looks around, and motions for me to follow.

An icy breeze blows through the tears in my pants, shivering my very timbers.

Lucy asks, "What time do orthodox priests go to bed?"

"Wouldn't piety demand an early-to-bed early-to-rise philosophy?"

She points to lit windows on the second floor of the building beneath which we've spent these two days. A car passes beyond the outer wall, its headlights casting sparse shadows around the courtyard. Lucy steps onto the lawn. I grab her shoulder and whisper, "Wait." The moon is high in the southern sky, a waning gibbous just two days past full, and with our pupils wide open the area is well lit, except in the shadows.

The two of us step along the border garden, one step at a time, watching and listening. In each step, I fear that a motion-triggered spotlight will capture us. I step up on a thick vine and look over the wall at the street.

The sound of a squeaking faucet indicates that Lucy has accomplished one of our goals. I scamper across the lawn to another border garden and help Lucy clean her wounds. The water is freezing but tastes delicious. The light upstairs goes out and Lucy shuts off the water, but I can hear water running through the pipes. The caretaker, bishop, or whoever lives here, is no doubt brushing his teeth or some equivalent. I turn the water back on and we finish washing.

We're clean but colder. We sneak our way back to the wall and the two of us step up on the vine and peer into the street. This sneaking starts to feel foolish and, just as I'm ready to climb over the wall and walk back to the hotel, Lucy grabs my arm. She points at an approaching car. But it's not a car, it's a van, Rader's van.

We cross the courtyard and sneak into the back alley. The lack of surveillance cameras and motion-activated security lights nearly causes me to worry for the security of The Old Orthodox Church. The shade of an arbor conceals an opening in the rear wall that leads to a parking lot and, from there, what seems to be a park or maybe the backyard of a wealthy citizen. Most of the trees have dropped their leaves, leaving skeletal shadows that make everything feel colder. We come up on a small side street and work our way uphill to another street. Half a block along we come to an impressive structure, not a mosque but some sort of Islamic school or administrative building. A long flight of stairs leads to the entrance where I'm certain there must be surveillance cameras.

We walk along the block looking for more accessible cameras but don't find any. "Can never find a surveillance camera when you need one. Wait here, it's quite likely that we'll have to run away. Do you remember how to get back to The Old Orthodox Church?"

"Yes."

"Then wait for me because I've forgotten."

With that, I run up the stairs. Motion-activated lights illuminate me and a spot light goes on below a swivel-mounted camera. I look into the camera and hold steady. After a few seconds, when I'm certain it's acquired an identifiable image, I turn to go back down the stairs, but the door opens and a swarthy fellow wearing a small white cap says something in Bosnian.

Since he sounds steady of temper, I put on my biggest, most American smile and say, "Hi! Is this Starbucks?"

He looks confused. I pretend to look up and around and then add, "Venti half-caf skinny caramel Macchiato with four sugars?" He looks more confused. I say, "My mistake, good evening." He closes the door with an amused but suspicious look. I trot down the stairs, taking advantage of their slope to make a hasty exit without appearing to run. When I reach the street, the door opens again and two men call out.

Lucy and I run back the way we came, duck into the wooded area behind the church. I pull her behind a tree and whisper, "I don't think anyone's following us."

She says, out loud, "Why don't we just go to the cops or something?"

I fear that she's lost her mind. "Turn ourselves in?"

She nods.

"Because I stole a motorcycle. I'm a felon. And you're a murderer!"

"I'm not a murderer."

"Of course not, but the police will believe what Frankie Woodley has told them. And I am indeed a felon." I fear that I make this statement with pride rather than embarrassment.

We cross the parking lot and walk into the courtyard. Staying in the shadows, we walk the perimeter of the church. It seems to double as a museum and, yes, the entrance to the museum has a camera hidden in the eves but no lights.

As we stand in the courtyard, gazing up at the dark museum

entrance and the useless surveillance camera, several cars pass in the street beyond the wall. Their headlights dance through the shadows, one stops in the street with flashing red and blue lights.

As Lucy and I run back to our hideaway, lights on the second floor Deacon's house go on, and as we shut the door behind us, the courtyard lights come up.

2011-Nov-17 7:32am Hotel Astra Sarajevo

Fiona wakes to give Winter his medicine, first the antibiotic, then the painkiller, and finally the tranquilizer.

"No," Volodya says, "don't give him tranquilizer."

"Why?"

"I have feeling about this I can't explain. A feeling. Maybe we need him alert, maybe he can help us."

"What?" Fiona says. "You reckon we'll need Winter to sniff out Simon?"

"Hold off. If he needs tranquilizer we'll give it to him, if not, he'll be prepared."

Now she realizes that Volodya hasn't slept. He's still sitting at the little desk working. "What have you learned?"

"They have split up, the Russian, the German, the Dutchman, the Italian, each of them patrol different ends of the streets where Simon was last seen." He brings up a map of several blocks of Sarajevo centered at City Hall where the attack took place. "Their van drives about these streets all night. I planted last image—had no effect."

"At least they haven't found him."

"He appeared at an Islamic Law School last night, right here." He points to a map, roughly in the center of Rader's patrols.

"What? He's all right?"

"The police were called and are also still patrolling these streets."

"So you saw him?"

"As did Rader."

Volodya leans over and taps Fiona's tablet. It shows an eight second, low resolution clip of Simon staring up without moving, his coat shredded at the shoulder, one sleeve gone, the other stained. He chats with someone in white robes whose back is to the camera and then runs down the stairs. Fiona says, "What's he doing?"

"Maximizing probability that our facial recognition spiders may identify him. Our servers found this video early this morning and so did Rader's."

"What should we do?"

"We wait for Simon to signal us and then we move."

"Rader outnumbers us and they can move faster. We don't have a chance, do we?"

"We are not without cards to play."

"Like what?"

"I haven't thought of them yet."

"Yes, I really do hate you."

Fiona believes that the key to problem solving is phrasing the problem. She contemplates each player and their roles, but the reality grows thicker: Rader is better positioned then they are. "What have you been doing all night?"

Volodya says, "I accomplished quite a bit. Destroyed some evidence, tidied up the databases of a few security organizations—salvaged a good deal of Lucy's reputation, exposed some of Frankie' crimes, just enough to reboot his career, nothing that could ruin him."

He brings up a window on the new laptop. "The local police still use paper records, but at least now their electronic records contradict the paper and their images of the accident only exist in print. Provided we can extract her, they have nothing to associate Lucy with the crime. They will trace Lucy's motorcycle to Rader's Amsterdam address. Simon left a clear, incriminating photograph, but we can disguise him and since they haven't IDed him, he can still travel on his passport."

"You expect that Rader registered that bike?"

"I did it for him."

"You sound almost optimistic."

"You are doing worry part for me." He turns and smiles at her. "I have some good news, too. I have calculated timeweave that should result if we find Lucy before Rader."

"Show it to me."

Volodya hits a key and brings up the timeweave for human history. What had been a geyser of timeline-twigs has become a contained if unwieldy stream.

"We did it? It's all apples?"

"If and only if we get Lucy before Rader does."

Fiona attaches Winter's leash. "I have to take him out or he'll pee in here."

"Please return with coffee."

"We will be near Old Town and city hall. If you find them, just send me a map."

"Fiona, they will see you."

"And I will see them."

* * *

Volodya stretches his back, hamstrings, hips, and neck, but never takes his eyes away from the monitors.

A flurry of computing activity from the white van distracts him from monitoring the positions of Rader's gang. Stepan has initiated a series of searches. Treading as lightly as he can, Volodya pulls half a megabyte from the search results: it's an image of himself along with text messages informing Rader that he killed Braun and escaped.

Volodya hesitates. It's a big risk, but curiosity creates an insatiable appetite. He commandeers Rader's smart phone and activates the microphone.

Now he's pulling megabytes.

Volodya hears Rader's voice: "He is injured. He is old. He is nothing. If he gets in the way we kill him. Easy."

Stepan speaks to Rader: "We're losing bandwidth."

Volodya assaults the keys of his PC, installing a small foothold of software on Rader's phone, and then stops, giving back the stolen bandwidth.

But it doesn't matter because Rader and his gang have been distracted by a new image: A woman with a cane walking a beagle wearing a protective Victorian collar on the street outside the Islamic Law School where Simon was spotted six hours ago.

2011-Nov-17 7:32am Old Orthodox Church

Lucy's wounds are taking longer to scab than mine and I'm an old man with bruises on top of bruises. Waking on hard dirt, my lower back gives at first. Then it assembles enough strength for me to sit up. My left thigh is swollen to the point that my knee won't bend. When I manage to work myself to a sitting position, my head butts the ceiling.

Lucy sits against the wall staring at her hands, a position I associate with people concentrating on smart phones.

Recalling that this space was utterly dark yesterday, I whisper, "What is the source of light?"

"I think we broke the door last night, the light's coming through a crack."

I instruct her to keep watch from that crack. "We need to get our images on the surveillance camera mounted over the museum entrance."

"Wouldn't it be safer to walk out in a crowd or something?"

"Not with torn clothes and exposed injuries. No, Fiona will find us." I say this with far greater confidence than I feel. If our spiders are identified as viral software, she won't be able to find us. I shudder at the thought and then shudder again.

"Uncle Simon, what's wrong?"

"I was just thinking about Volodya."

It's not light enough to see her face, but I can hear the intake of breath.

"Lucy, don't blame yourself. We can only go forward, maybe sometimes sideways, but generally forward."

With that, we work ourselves in position to peek through the crack in the door. My legs and back cramp up, so we take turns. Then, as nine o'clock approaches, a few people assemble in the courtyard. I risk opening the door far enough to lean out and confirm that a queue is forming at the museum entrance. My suit is a wreck, not just torn and bloody, but covered in dust. Lucy's pants are torn, exposing her still oozing wounds; her leather jacket retained its integrity but has opened seams and, on one side, exposed plastic reinforcements on the shoulder and forearm.

Still, she looks less conspicuous than I do.

The museum opens just after nine and the courtyard empties. Lucy steps out of our ancient prison and walks to the entrance. I can tell when she finds the surveillance camera because she looks up as though posing and then pantomimes the location of our little enclave as though Fiona is the only person who will see this video.

18. Winter

2011-Nov-17 9:47am Sarajevo

Volodya catches the image of Lucy before Rader.

He sends a map to Fiona and speaks into her earbug, "I found them. Rader has spotted you. Wait until I give instruction, else you will lead Rader to Simon and Lucy."

Fiona: "I'll circle around."

Volodya: "Yes, good. But go opposite direction, counter-clockwise to old church. You're walking right toward Klaus Schmidt."

Fiona: "How long?"

Volodya: "I will distract them."

He clicks into another window and launches more code. "They will soon see that same image of Lucy from many locations."

Fiona: "I see the white van. Volodya, I can't run."

Volodya: "Fuck. They know I've compromised them." Volodya then alters several files in Rader's system, leaving a clear path back to the TLA computing fleet.

Fiona say, "I'm almost at the church."

"Walk right past it, don't stop, don't pause, don't even look at it."

"The van stopped behind me."

"I see that. I have to do something stupid or you will die."

"Well, isn't that a delightful irony?"

Volodya types commands in each window and then closes them until just one remains: the map with locations of Rader's gang.

"Shit," Fiona says. "Someone stepped out of the van. He's running toward me."

"Ignore him. He'll turn onto a street before he gets to you. Unless I have failed."

Ten seconds pass.

"Fiona? You will appreciate what I have done a great deal."

"I certainly hope to."

Volodya listens to the rhythm of Fiona and Winter walking.

Fiona asks, "How much longer."

"How fast can you move?"

"That's a stupid question. What have you done?"

"You are now six blocks from Simon. They are somewhere near the Old Orthodox Church."

"In the church?"

"Perhaps. The image of Lucy came from their surveillance system—it is all we have. I scrubbed the image so even if a security guard saw her, they won't be able to retrieve it." He hesitates another second. "There is a courtyard and a museum. Take Winter and sit at a bench in that courtyard. If you contact Simon, wait for me as long as you can."

"What about Rader's thugs? What about the police?"

"The police don't know you and Rader's thugs are, umm, they are somewhere else."

Volodya stands, shuts off the laptop and slides it under the bed. He leaves the door propped slightly open as he leaves.

2011-Nov-17 10:12am Sarajevo

Guenther Rader has always taken pride in his ability to withstand discomfort—sleeping on bricks, enduring untreated bullet wounds, and now a broken knee cap, ligament, and bone—but that doesn't mean he can move.

He and Davis sit in the van, parked up the street from the scene of the motorcycle crash. How the dim-witted Simon Wentworth has managed to interfere with his plans eludes him. He is intent that it will never happen again. His youngest protégé, the computer scientist from Moscow, has infiltrated TLA's computing system. Once in, he isolated Lucy Montgomery's position. They have complete control and now they will finish germinating the seeds of this revolution.

Rader directs Klaus by encrypted cell phone from the van and Klaus organizes the operation from the street. The locations of his council are indicated by virtue of their cell phone GPS feeds on a monitor that displays a map of the area.

Alina, Adriaan, Stepan, and Klaus will soon converge on Lucy's location at the Hotel Astra. Stepan even determined her room number.

He calls Klaus: "Move in. Now!"

Rather than Klaus's German, the response comes in Russian: "So nice of you to call, Guenther, we should chat."

"*Was?*"

The van door opens. In a single fluid motion, Volodya grabs Rader, one hand on his throat and the other on the barrel of the AK47 that had been in his lap. Rader flails in midair and then crashes into the curb bad knee first, destroying whatever was left of its integrity. Were it not for that knee, Rader would have continued rolling, come up with the AK47 and demolished Volodya. Instead, Volodya grabs the rifle.

* * *

With Rader sprawled on the street, Volodya points the AK47 back at the van and says, "Officer Davis, you're free to go."

Davis looks up the barrel at Volodya.

"Go home," Volodya says, "I cleaned your record. Go home. Start over. You fix your life, be good cop, good father—and could you please hand me that cane?"

Davis pushes Fiona's cane out the open door and Volodya catches it by the duck head handle.

Volodya turns and raises his boot above Rader's destroyed knee and shifts his weight to impose the greatest possible impact. He looks down.

Rader pulls a sidearm from an inner holster and points it at

Volodya.

"If you shoot me," Volodya says, "I will fall on your knee."

They stare at each other. The AK47 still pointed at the van.

Officer Davis drives away.

Volodya's first thought is to drop the cane, rotate the rifle, and shoot. But then he recalls that Fiona's cane is also a weapon. He pulls what he thinks is the trigger of the stiletto blade.

Three hundred milliliters of single malt scotch spill onto Rader's knee.

As the scotch penetrates Rader's bandage, a look of agony consumes his face.

Volodya kicks the pistol out of his hand.

Rader rolls slowly over and reaches for the curb. He tries to pull himself away. The torn ligaments stretch. His face contorts in a grimace and he says, in Russian, "A bullet, please, a bullet."

Volodya rotates, adding momentum to his weight. He can taste the joy of imposing unbearable pain on this man, of stomping out a virus in the human struggle for justice and peace, but as he uncoils and starts the leap that will end with his boot separating Rader's leg and thigh, that taste turns bitter.

Anticipating the blow, Rader screams. The blow doesn't come.

Volodya steps across Rader, picks up the handgun and puts it in his waistband. He pulls the magazine from the rifle. He looks down at Rader who appears a decade older than his 66 years; a sorry, defeated, old man. Volodya says, in German, "You belong in a rest home."

He wipes the rifle with his coat, throws it into the gutter, and walks away.

A block from The Old Orthodox Church, he turns and says, in English, "I hope you find peace."

2011-Nov-17 10:15am Old Orthodox Church

In the darkness, it's easy to picture the layout of the church above. If this modest structure employs actual guards, Lucy and I could be in trouble, but with just the one camera and no motion-sensitive spotlights, it's difficult to imagine a sophisticated security system. A receptionist probably monitors the camera.

The ceiling is too low and the ground too uneven, but I am compelled to pace.

Lucy whispers, "Uncle Simon, you're making it dusty."

"What if the camera's not even networked?"

"Then we'll find another one." She coughs.

"Try to be quiet." I pivot and liberate another tiny dust storm. "Can we stand another day here?"

"I'm thirsty."

"And hungry, and cold, and … Okay, let's just settle down."

"Uncle Simon, I'm settled. It's okay. You can tell me stories about the Bohemian Club. You can tell me why my mother won't marry you, I've always wondered. She goes from one boyfriend to the next, all a bunch of losers, and you're always there for her but she can't see—"

"Stop that nonsense. Gwinnie loves me and the gentlemen she dates misrepresent themselves to her. Her mistakes are born of her innocence and trust in humanity, her generosity, her—"

"Her stupidity."

"Have I told you about how she met your father? It was all my fault, I could've saved her from that heartbreak, you should've been my daughter—"

"I don't think it works that way."

"Shhh," I say, unsure of what caught my attention.

The two of us go silent. The dust slowly settles, except for one mote that floats down the short stairwell. Then another.

An odd, sort of pulsing rush of wind, several intakes for each outflow, generates an ever-greater flux of motes like some sort of dust-mote Morse code.

Lucy huddles behind me. We work ourselves around the corner and peer up at the door.

I whisper the Morse code characters to Lucy: "C, E, B, T—

wait, that one's not a Morse Code symbol. Maybe it's—"

"Shhh."

I shush.

The duration of the intake grows longer and the outflow comes in shorter, sharper bursts. I try to conceive of other dust mote coding schemes. Then a whine, the sort of sound you might expect from a tortured prisoner is added to the air intake/outflow. I ponder how a third symbol could affect the messaging system. No answers come to mind so I reinterpret the sounds. Some sort of pumping system? That whine reoccurs. It could be ancient hinges straining against corrosion.

Someone has found us! I motion for Lucy to hide. I whisper, "Way back behind the bones."

Having studied those hinges, I can nearly picture the rust dropping from them, but the door doesn't open. I reach down and find the femur that Lucy used to prop the door shut. I heft it like a cudgel but wonder: if you hit someone with a leg bone, does it qualify more as clubbing or kicking? It would be less ambiguous if a foot were still attached, I suppose …

I stand straight up. My head collides with the ceiling. I know that sound!

"My dog! It's my doggy!"

2011-Nov-17 10:21am Old Orthodox Church

I can hear Fiona sigh. She whispers, "Right, we've almost sorted your escape. Can you do a few more minutes down there?"

Lucy and I grumble about cold, dust, thirst, hunger, bruises, cleanliness, and boredom, but Fiona sounds busy with something else.

"Sit. Heel. Damn it, stay!" Then, "Oh bloody hell."

Winter's muzzle pokes in the door. It's open wide enough for him to get in, but something's holding him back. The door opens all the way and, just as Lucy and I move to vacate our dungeon, Winter works his way through wearing a huge blue Victorian collar.

Fiona whispers, "Take care of his stitches."

"Stitches?"

"Yes along his right flank. He saved your life, you know."

Winter makes his way down the stairs in a dust tornado and then bathes me in kisses.

He's still giving me the treatment, wagging, whining, licking, when Volodya says, "Quickly, stay between Fiona and me."

The five of us rush through the courtyard and into a waiting taxi.

Lucy sits between Fiona and me. Winter's on my lap and Volodya's in the front seat.

I can't see beyond Winter's Victorian collar and his tail is thumping the seat in front of me. I massage tiny lump remaining from that injury. Volodya turns around and with Winter's tail brushing his chin, he says, "You are more hungry or more tired?"

Lucy beats me to the obvious: "Hungry."

"Excellent choice in this country of wonderful food." He asks the driver to take us to restaurant Zeljo. It's a short ride. Volodya hands the driver another piece of paper currency and adds, "You never saw us, right?"

The driver does a double take at the note and says, "Yes, *ja, ano!*"

We step out and Volodya says, "I gave him a hundred *Marka* note."

"How much is that?"

"I have no idea, but now I wonder if maybe it is too much."

The servers are happy to have Winter in their mostly empty restaurant as they have just begun to serve lunch. With Winter under the table, Lucy and I sit across from Fiona and fawn over a menu written in a language neither of us knows. Rather than sit, Volodya stands and speaks to the server.

"Do you have *cevapi* and *burek* ?" Volodya asks, but the server doesn't understand. "Maybe I mispronounce the word." Then he describes sausages and pastries. The waiter writes on his pad with the enthusiasm of a craftsman whose work is appreciated.

I ask for toast.

Volodya looks at his phone and says, "I have business to attend. You needn't rush but I will need you in less than an hour for an, umm, appointment."

Fiona flips her cane into position and rises from the table. "I'm coming with you."

Volodya starts at her. She raises an eyebrow and he leaves his thoughts unspoken; wisely, I might add, given Fiona's look of determination. I try to recall the number of times that the two of them have agreed on a course of action without debate, but the waiter delivers cups of dark, sweet coffee and I lose interest.

Volodya hands Lucy a cell phone and a wad of cash. "The taxi will be outside. When I call, please come as soon as possible to the Hotel Astra. Should I not call, please continue to the US Embassy and ask for help getting home."

Distracted by the excitement of liberation, my affectionate pooch, an excellent cup of coffee, and pride that Volodya trusts Lucy above me for responsible tasks, the looming nature of this statement escapes me until four minutes after his departure.

Our mouths are both full when we make eye contact. I say, "They may need our help."

Lucy assembles the *cevapi* into a napkin and sets some money on the table. We both ram two more *cevapi* into our mouths. The server brings a platter of *burek* pastries to the table. We watch him set it down. I grab three of them and Lucy grabs two. The server accepts the cash and provides directions to the Hotel Astra.

2011-Nov-17 10:49am Hotel Astra Sarajevo

"Volodya, I'm not a liability. Put me in position and tell me what to do."

He looks Fiona up and down.

"Mate, I'm well armed."

"You do not know what we might be walking into." He walks faster and she matches him stride for stride. He stops a block from the Hotel Astra and shows her an app running on his phone. The display shows a map of the Hotel and immediate surroundings with four blinking icons. "Klaus Schmidt stands in front of hotel, Alina Romano in the rear, Adriaan Buijs in the lobby, and Stepan Petrov is in our room."

She smiles at him and he catches himself accepting her unspoken praise. "I thought it best we have chance to debrief them."

She says, "I know what you're doing."

"I am so obvious?"

"You're a good man, Volodya."

The image of Karl Braun's corpse floats into his consciousness and he shakes his head. He enters a series of commands in the app. Fiona looks over his shoulder. They wait for three of the icons to move.

The two of them rush through the lobby, enter a corridor and stop. Volodya looks at his phone. "All of them are in the room now." They jog into the lobby. He puts a hand on her shoulder. "Follow as fast as you can." Before she can respond, he adds, "Better to have you back me up than we both walk into trap."

Rounding a corner, he sees that the door to their room is wedged open, as he left it. He double checks the app, wondering if his hack has been hacked. He pulls Rader's pistol out of his waistband, checks the magazine, releases the safety, and prepares to walk into an ambush.

Closer to the door, he hears them arguing. He steps forward and opens the door with the gun leveled. "No one moves."

Klaus, who stands closest to the door, reaches into his coat. Stepan and Adriaan are both seated at the desk where they've, no doubt, been hacking the PC which Volodya primed for just that purpose. Alina rises from between the two beds.

Volodya steps down on the arch of Klaus's foot and grabs the man's wrist while aiming the pistol and his attention at Alina. He twists Klaus's wrist until he drops a weapon. He releases the wrist, and jerks his forearm up into Klaus's chin. The tall shaggy blonde man falls backwards. Volodya steps forward. Alina raises the Uzi.

Volodya apologizes: "*Es tut mir leid*, Klaus. I'm sure you understand." Then, to Alina, "I brought you here so that we could talk, that's all. You're free to go after you hear what I have to say."

Fiona steps through the door behind him.

He says, "I will put my weapon down and trust that you will keep whatever you're carrying to yourself. Ahh, Alina? Yes. Perhaps we could disarm simultaneously? You have a, ummm, propensity for pulling triggers."

Alina looks at Volodya, then at Stepan who says, "Guns have never helped you."

She scowls. "You won't shoot me. Coward."

"You think I am coward?" He offers her an upside-down smile and tosses the gun onto the bed next to her.

Fiona gasps.

Alina looks shocked.

"You are young, talented, intelligent, and have many choices available to you but first you have to recognize your mistakes and repair what you have, umm, broken."

Stepan says, "We never meant to hurt Lucy."

"I want to kill her," Alina says. "Killing Lucy is the key to all the world's problems."

"Kill her?" Stepan says.

* * *

When Lucy, Winter, and I get to the hotel. We tip toe to the door, which is slightly askew. Unfortunately, the words "I want to kill her" kindle Lucy's ire.

She rushes to the door. "Kill me? Why?"

The room is quite crowded and I can barely see over Lucy and between Volodya and Fiona.

Alina orients the Uzi in Lucy's direction.

I pull Lucy to the side, drawing her behind Volodya.

Adriaan steps in front of Alina. Towering over her, he says, "ENOUGH."

Alina points the Uzi at Adriaan.

He grabs it by the barrel, swings it into the air and prepares to throw it to the ground in disgust.

"No, no," Volodya says. "Don't do that."

Adriaan recovers his action and gently sets the weapon on the table next to Volodya's laptop.

Alina reaches for the pistol Volodya tossed on the bed next to her. Adriaan grabs her arm.

"Why? Why did you want me to die? I just don't understand. I was giving everything to the movement. Everything, and you wanted to kill me?"

Stepan says, "Gus told us that you had gone ahead to meet other organizers. We thought we were going to record the plutocrat's meeting and post it for the world to see. Please, Lucy, we would never—"

Adriaan points a finger at Klaus. "You knew what Gus was doing all along?"

Klaus nods as though accepting a lump of sugar in his coffee.

Lucy stares at Stepan. Her disappointment seems to infect him. I say, "Stepan, you'll be okay, it's just part of growing up."

Alina says, "What have you done to Gus?"

Volodya says, "I let him go."

Fiona gasps. "You what?"

"He seemed so pathetic," Volodya says. "And I've learned that revenge is, well, it is not for me. Maybe I am soft in old age."

Alina says, "We haven't broken any laws."

Laughing, Fiona leans over and picks up the pistol and sets it next to the Uzi. She then sits beside Alina and says, "I don't know why he's willing to let you go, but if you don't accept responsibility for your actions, I won't be so kind. You see, I'm quite fond of the taste of revenge."

Alina glares at her. Fiona grabs her chin. Alina reaches into a pocket. Fiona gets there first and pulls out another gun. Fiona tightens her grasp on Alina's chin.

"You're a coward. No spine, no courage, no values," Lucy says. "You don't have the courage to face the world unarmed. You're sick."

As Alina squirms, dots of blood pool at the points where Fiona's fingernails connect to her cheeks.

Volodya puts his hand on my shoulder, drawing Winter and I into the room. He closes the door behind us and then tightens his lips in a way that is meant to convey a message to me. I'm not sure what it is so I look at Fiona and she widens her eyes and nods toward the laptop.

"Ahh," I say, "Lucy, it's okay. Just watch, we're quite good at this part."

Volodya clears his throat and says, "Please relax. I'll not punish you. But you will listen." He looks at each of them and then at Lucy. His chin tightens, then loosens and tightens again. "Please, Adriaan. Sit down. Fiona?"

Fiona lets go of Alina and moves to the chair at the small desk.

"Hmmrefreshski," Volodya says. "Let us start over."

Adriaan sits between Alina and Stepan. Klaus leans against the wall in the corner. Lucy and I stand just inside the door. Winter hops onto the bed and sniffs Alina. I'm taken by the impression that he wears the Victorian collar like some sort of regal robe.

"*Grazi.*," Volodya says. "We have not met, but we know each other." Then he holds out his hand and says, "Stepan Petrov, I am Volodya Kazimer, these are my friends, Simon Wentworth, Fiona Black, and you already know Lucy. It is my pleasure."

Stepan wavers. Volodya reaches down, takes the man's hand, looks in his eyes, and repeats, "It is my pleasure." He duplicates the process with Adriaan and Klaus. Alina pulls her hand away from him and he says, "We have earned each others respect, show it." He steps back to the foot of the bed nearest the door. "If you leave now, you will have to hide from police. Whether it is right or just is irrelevant, you know it is true. You will run until you are caught and that will solve nothing. Or. Or you can take an opportunity, create your own opportunity."

Volodya turns to Fiona and says, "Maybe you can book rooms for Simon and Lucy? They need bandages, comfortable beds, room service, and baths. I want to talk to these ambitious youths about employment prospect." Fiona guides Lucy out the door, but I stay behind with Winter. I know where this is going and want to see how it works out.

Volodya resumes, "Klaus, you might reconsider your goals. Alina, your passion can be virtue for you and all you care about, but it won't help you or anyone or anything as long as you hurt people. Adriaan, Stepan, you are very very good, though you should learn the virtues of memory management …"

19. The Intoxicating Page

2012-Feb-4 The Intoxicating Page

Fiona hands me a glass of Scotch, sets a saucer of beer on the floor for Winter, and gives Volodya a snifter of plum brandy that smells like kerosene. She settles at the table between Volodya and me with a dirty martini.

I savor the taste of the ten-year-old Macallan. I suppose the twelve, fifteen, 18, and 24-year-old varieties are better, but like flying first class, they make me uncomfortable.

I say, "Have you assigned anything to our new employees?"

"Not yet," Volodya says. "I determined what drew them to Rader—usual things, injustice, politics, and sense of hopelessness. Rader offered opportunity to change the world. And so did I." He sips the brandy. "We also discussed the utility of weapons in political conflict."

Me: "You recorded that interrogation?"

Volodya: "And applied emotion-recognition software."

Fiona: "For whatever that's worth."

Volodya: "I was pleased with their shame and humiliation."

Me: "They seem like a fine group."

Fiona: "You encouraged them to pursue their interests?"

Volodya: "Yes, I used the word 'obligated.'"

Fiona: "Obligated to pursue their political goals?"

Volodya: "Yes, and obligated not to hurt anyone for the crime of disagreement."

Me: "They're intelligent people."

Volodya: "Adriaan and Stepan will enjoy San Francisco, find satisfaction, perhaps riches in Silicon Valley."

Fiona: "You're converting them to capitalists?"

Volodya: "It is beauty of America that they convert themselves."

Fiona: "Only those who strike it rich."

Volodya: "Alina has taken a job at Oracle, I fear that she is again in wrong crowd."

Fiona: "What happened to Guenther Rader and Klaus Schmidt?"

Me: "Rader faded away, as he always does, but with one less knee."

Volodya: "And Klaus Schmidt is in New Zealand where he seems to be employed by Kim Dotcom."

She laughs and her martini sloshes in the glass. She turns to me and asks, "How is Lucy?"

I look past Fiona at a table where Penelope, Rob, and Bill work on a pattern recognition project. "She and Frankie have become quite close."

Volodya: "Poor man."

Fiona: "Lucky bastard."

Me: "They have a friendship based on disagreement and mutual disrespect."

Fiona: "More, tell me more."

Me: "They recognize that they can help each other. I convinced Frankie that he needs to understand Lucy's concerns or he'll be blind to justice and I convinced Lucy that she needs Frankie's backing to accomplish her goals."

Volodya grins. "She is going into business?"

Me: "No, Lucy has a vision. She has been accepted into the Columbia Law School. After law school she wants to be a police officer for several years and then become a judge. Eventually, she hopes to be appointed a Supreme Court Justice."

Fiona: "A cop?"

Me: "Apparently Officer Justin made quite an impression on her. She wants to understand the challenge of justice at every level." I add, "I'm taking her to The Grove this summer."

Fiona: "What's she going to do with those right wing power brokers?"

Me: "Argue, I suspect. She studied a great deal of political history when she was with Rader. She wants to understand the lure of power and the motivations of her rivals."

Volodya: "Ohforcorruptignoble."

Fiona: "Stop that. Lucy is special. She won't be seduced by power."

Me: "Her timeweave indicates just 3% chance she'll alter her course—she has always been stubborn."

We sit together, letting our thoughts ferment.

Fiona: "And Frankie?"

Me: "The Woodley-Carlyle Directors fired him and appointed a new CEO. Of course, they're covering up his illegal investments and corporatry ambitions. He still has capital and an 86% percent likelihood of business success."

Fiona: "You steal a steak, you go to jail. You configure global economic ruin, you start a new business."

Me: "Lucy and Frankie are safe and Gwinnie is upset with me for no reason that I can conceive."

Fiona: "All is as it should be."

Me: "It does feel rather like a band-aid solution."

Volodya: "Band-aid on broken jugular."

Fiona: "I'd rather be in this reality on this timeline than any of the alternatives."

Volodya: "That, I will drink to."

We raise our glasses, tink them together and drink. Winter slurps some of his IPA and sneezes.

Wait!

You don't have to leave The Intoxicating Page.
Instead, start reading the next
Time Weavers story.

TOO RICH
TO DIE

By Ransom Stephens

[ ] By clicking this box you agree to our terms and conditions.

1. The pivot

"Give me a hundred, you techie bastard!" A woman in rags reaches out to a twenty-something man with perfectly parted hair.

His eyes lock on the woman as though she poses a mortal threat.

My beagle companion, Winter, stretches his leash toward the woman. With his ears perked and tail wagging, he seems to have taken her side in the conflict. As a techie myself, though not a bastard to the best of my knowledge, I empathize with the young man, but the woman—wrapped in a filthy jacket, her skin grimy and dark hair hanging like twine—merits far more compassion than the man dressed techie-chic with his immaculate white hoodie and jeans creased the way that my suit pants ought to be.

"How's your app, Scratsh?" The woman sneers. "Have you made your fuck you money yet?"

The man tries to leap aside, but she grabs him by the hood and whines, "Come on, Eben, give me five dollars. Help me out."

With her arm outstretched, she exposes a tattoo of excellent quality: A planet on her right shoulder with two arrows emerging from opposite sides of its equator curving down her arm and colliding on her bicep with a starburst at the point where they meet.

The man twists under her arm. She loses her grip and falls. He leaps away, adjusts his glasses, straightens his hoodie, and rushes across Market Street.

The woman moans, her moan becomes a sob and she cries out: "Fuck you." She folds into herself, sinking into a puddle on the sidewalk, and her voice grows softer with each word: "Fuck you, you tool, just FU."

My stroll along Market Street is not purely for physical fitness or to greet the Summer Solstice, though it is a splendid cool day wrapped in the formality of San Francisco's trademark fog. Nineteen days ago my colleagues and I predicted that a pivot point of historical significance would occur right here and now.

I put my hand to my ear to check the status of my earbug—still installed and functioning—and say, "Was that it?"

My dear friend and colleague, Fiona Black, who you will soon meet if you haven't already, is connected by our earbug tech. "Right," she says, "we're now in the rapids of the river of time." She speaks with a delightful vowel-amplifying Australian accent.

Then I hear my friend Volodya Kazimir's sharp Russian accent through my earbug: "Mm. I confirm that a pivot point has occurred. It is a problem." His accent makes everything he says sound like a debate point. He uses the word "problem" often and runs the two syllables together like "prubl'm."

Fiona, Volodya, and I, not to mention Winter, are in almost constant contact either in person or through technology. We are in the business of calculating the probabilities of different possible futures. People say things like "the possibilities are infinite," and it's true, but of course the probabilities are finite. The probable futures combine to form an inter-dependent weave. We project these timeweaves from the trillions of events recorded on networked computing devices, including surveillance systems, private networks, telephone data, text messages, photos, social networking posts, et cetera—the grand record of whats and whos—that lead us to when and where pivot points will occur. The weave usually forms a cable of timelines that follows a somewhat stable path from the past into the future, but immediately following a pivot point, the cable unravels into widely different possible destinies—what Fiona refers to as the rapids of time.

Winter tugs his leash from my wrist and rushes to the poor

woman. Her pants wick moisture from the puddle and tears run down her face. Winter dismisses all etiquette and muscles his way onto her lap. Her lips attempt a smile as Winter kisses away her tears. Winter is a friendly little fellow, but I've never seen him lavish affection so boisterously on a stranger.

I walk over and take his leash. "Terribly sorry, ma'am, he's normally more reserved."

She looks at me, then Winter, then back at me. I lean down and offer a hand. She grips my arm and pulls herself up. Winter delivers a final kiss as she rises. Her lips finally manage a smile but it disappears when she looks across the street at the techie. "I hate that bastard."

I offer my hanky and she takes it. I say, "Is there anything I can do?"

She starts to shake her head but stops and says, "Twenty bucks?"

I take my wallet from my coat pocket. "I only have seven dollars and 32 cents."

She takes it.

The two of us watch the accosted techie on the other side of Market Street. He's bent over as though he has osteoporosis, but straightens when he has to jump out of the way of a young woman riding a skateboard who yells, "Out of my way, Glasshole!" He continues down New Montgomery Street. With his bent-over posture, he looks like he's monitoring the sidewalk to avoid stepping on cracks.

A wisp of fog passes between the woman and me. I turn away because—oh no—I feel it coming on. It starts with overwhelming vertigo, that feeling you get when you stand on a bridge, hoping that you won't jump or fall. You have no intention of jumping and don't expect to fall, but it sure is a long way down. That niggling possibility can gnaw at your gut until you feel dizzy and what started as an absurd fear emerges as possible, and then probable, and then you're falling.

The vertigo builds and I see flashes of green streaks in the fog. I pull my suit jacket tight against the chill, but it's not the cold that makes me shiver, it's something internal, something I don't understand, perhaps a talent, maybe an illness, certainly a curse.

A seam forms. The seams resemble the green edges of sheets of glass, like windows separating inside from outside, one world from another. The vertigo draws me to the boundary and I fall.

The hustle and bustle of Market Street shifts in focus. An executive waits in line for a cable car. As the tinted seam passes through him, his fine pin-striped suit shifts from contemporary elegant to depression-era destitute. The line for the cable car evolves into a soup line and what remains of his executive stature floats away on a foggy gust. His black fedora fades to gray and droops over his eyes, his skin weathers, his lips turn down, and his calloused hands reach for a bowl. I don't know if the world has spun off of its axis, but I have surely spun off of mine. I lean through the different seams and each timeline induces sensations from trepidation to contentment, dread to hope, and anger to calm. Cars dial back their makes and models from hybrids to V8s to fins to horseless and then to horse-drawn carriages. The earth seems to quake as it must have when the big one hit in 1906, but these people of the past don't notice. A panel van tugged by horses and labeled "Bank of Italy" shifts out of focus under a cascade of green-tinted fog and emerges as a bright red Bank of America automatic teller machine.

I struggle under a 25 pound weight that wriggles on my chest and licks my face from chin to forehead: Winter, my service dog, performing his service. As I rise to a sitting position, he squirms away and sits facing me with his white chest out and brown ears folded at attention. I look around, hoping that I haven't distressed anyone. Seven other people recline on the pavement of this block of Market Street, each a case of misfortune. Among them, my episode is not worth noticing, though the distraught woman seems to be monitoring me.

I check my earbug and say, “How long was I gone?”

Fiona replies with her Aussie candor, “Simon, dear Simon—these episodes are growing more frequent!”

I say, “No, they aren’t” and wish I believed it.

“Less than 15 seconds,” Volodya says. “And you lie, my friend, you lie.”

“Reality must be growing less stable,” Fiona says. “You had episodes less than once a year when I first met you.”

“I didn’t.” I lie a second time.

Volodya growls like a suspicious bloodhound. Volodya’s growl indicates three things: first, his disagreement with Fiona’s belief that it is reality that has grown less stable rather than my psyche; second, his impatience with my lie; and third, the unique ability he has to convey several bullet points with what barely qualifies as a syllable. “Please, they are not ‘episodes,’” He says. “Simon, you experience delusions.”

“Delusions, my fine ass.” Fiona’s voice ramps up. “Delusions don’t give 100% accurate insights into how the future emerges from the past.”

I still haven’t found a journal article that describes my curse. An incompetent psychiatrist once diagnosed me as schizophrenic. He even had the gall to ask if I experienced parallel universes—an absurd question, given that the defining quality of all things parallel is their lack of intersection and it is specifically the intersections of different realities that I experience. I’ve since discounted the entire field of psychiatry.

2. The Post

Eben glances back at the woman who just accosted him and shudders. He watches a man in a rumpled gray suit help her up.

A girl on a skateboard zips in front of him. He adjusts his eyewear and rushes past the understated awnings of the Palace Hotel and turns onto Mission Street. He steps ahead of three women into a crisp stainless steel office tower, enters the elevator, and presses the button for the seventh floor. From behind him, one of the women asks him to hold the door. He has no time for such nonsense and ignores her.

The elevator rises too slowly for his taste. He uses the time to polish the ScratshCo logo. The elevator doors open and a tall, thin, impeccably dressed man named Yao Wo greets him with a wide, toothy smile: "Good morning, sir! Your call with the Punjab office has been delayed so you'll have extra time to review accounts—I know how you love mulling through a nice profit-loss statement. Absolutely kick ass way to begin summer, sir, though I do regret that—"

"Seriously?" Eben steps past Wo and strides between cubicles on the way to his office. Eben's company is a reflection of his own finely-tuned efficiency. With only 42 employees, ScratshCo's revenue is seven times that of the world's largest bank but with 1/7000 the payroll.

"Sir, I regret that—"

"I regret you."

"I do what I can, sir." Wo rushes ahead of Eben, carefully threading his way between cubicles to avoid encroaching on Eben's path. He barely makes it to Eben's office in time to open the door and offer him a tablet computer. Eben stops at the door to clear his sinuses; he bobs his head and swallows three times, each with a high-pitched whine. Eben takes the tablet and examines the list of his morning appointments. The day prior to a business trip is always extra busy.

Something doesn't feel right in his office. It's not just the lights, which everyone on the seventh floor knows must be set as dim as possible to reduce costs. He looks up and sees a man and a woman rise from plastic chairs opposite his desk.

The woman says, "Are you Eben?"

To Wo, Eben says, "Who are these people?"

"Yes sir, I regret that—"

"How did they get in here?"

"As I was saying, sir, I fear that—"

"Fears and regrets, whatever. Get them out of here."

The woman taps the chair with her knuckles—the sort of absent-minded nervous twitch that annoys Eben—and says, "Would it be more convenient for us to speak to Allison?"

Eben says, "Allison is dead." He settles into the high-backed leather chair and sets the tablet on his desk. "You're not on my schedule. Run along."

The man clears his throat.

Eben takes off his Glass and sets them in their charging dock. Rubbing his eyes, he says, "Time is money. My money. You have something to say? Get it out."

"Eben." The man coughs up his name but can't seem to get any further.

"Mr. Scratsh," the woman says, "we are from the Human Trafficking and Slave Liberation Fund collecting donations from San Francisco's generous tech executives. Every $50 we collect liberates a slave—"

"Are you slaves?"

"Well, no, but—"

"Then you have no problem. Buh bye."

The man looks befuddled, which nearly gives Eben cause to smile.

The woman says, "Every thousand dollars you contribute can stop the abduction and sale of twenty children." She leans forward as she speaks and her chair scuffs the floor. "Think of the burdens you can lift from thousands of people. With just a bit of compassion you can—"

Eben shakes his head at the scraping sound. "They can earn their freedom in weeks or months or however long, I don't care."

"If only it worked that way," the man says. "No, these people are ensnared in debt. Their captors charge more for room and board than they are capable of earning in the salt fields, sweatshops, and, well, as you can imagine, far worse."

"If I buy a slave's freedom, when will he or she pay me back and at what interest rate?"

"My gosh." The woman shakes her head as though trying to dislodge the concept. "Pay you back?"

"Gosh? Gosh isn't even a word."

Her mouth opens, but she contributes no sound to the conversation.

"Yes, pay me back. Don't you think they want genuine liberty—the real thing—instead of some handed out version?"

She steps forward and puts her fists on the opposite edge of Eben's desk, pushing up to increase her height. "Fifty dollars is nothing to you, but to them it's a life!"

Eben reaches down and presses the lever at his chair's base. The hydraulic action slowly elevates him. When he is eye-to-eye with the woman, he says, "You don't get to judge the value of $50 to me."

"What? You're one of the richest men in the world! You make more than $50 every minute."

"Not in these minutes, I haven't. Buh bye."

Still trembling, the woman says, "All of the major high tech executives South of Market are contributing. We just met with Mark Zuckerberg and he pledged over half a million. Jack Dorsey pledged a hundred thousand, surely I can mark you down for—"

"Null. Mark me down for the whole null set." Eben lowers the chair back to desk-level. "Let laborers labor. Let them pay their debts. Let them earn their freedom just as I have, or at least give them the dignity of dying trying." He turns to his computer and the tasks required before the business trip. He opens the profit-loss database, and commences analysis of the revenue streams from the CurrentSea app, ScratshCo's original and still primary product. He forces himself to focus on his cherished database and watches it update the way that a parent watches a child on a swing.

The next time he looks up, his office is empty.

He turns to the list of scheduled software updates and discovers a bug in the latest release. He sends email to the hacking circle to find and fix it. Then he realizes that it wasn't a bug at all, it was a feature that he had requested. It's the beggars, he realizes. They've put him off his game; the charity beggars and that panhandler on Market Street. He's not sure whether he's more annoyed that she recognized him or that she had the nerve to touch him.

He checks the calendar and is reminded that the first leg of the trip is a frivolous party in a forest—oh how he hates it when the unimportant becomes urgent. Leaning forward, he tries to pull all the details into the big picture. Above software releases, P & L databases, and networking, he pictures himself walking into a magnificent 14th century Paris boardroom to give the most important pitch of his life. On that day, in just three weeks, he'll win the greatest victory and experience the greatest glory of his life. And then, Eben tells himself, no one will impose on his time. He'll wash his hands of the beggars, losers, and quitters forever.

At 11:15, Wo sets a fresh cup of coffee on the saucer at the corner of the desk, but instead of leaving, Wo lingers.

Eben looks up slowly, intentionally.

"Sir?" Wo says.

For the most part, Wo speaks the same English as any other

third generation Californian, but now he speaks with a slight Chinese accent. The 'r' in sir comes out with no ring at all, not quite the clichéd sound of an 'l', but enough to trip Eben's suspicions.

"What do you need?" Eben asks, but he inflects in such a way as to discourage Wo from attempting to impose.

"Will there be anything else, sir?"

"You're clocking out early the day before we travel?"

"It's my son, sir."

Eben looks back at him but doesn't say anything.

"It's cool, sir," Wo says. "I assembled the itinerary and everything is ready to roll."

Eben lets several seconds pass before saying, "Another trip to the hospital?"

"Yes, sir. You approved my request." He leans over and taps an icon on the display of Eben's calendar that displays a virtual seal of approval.

"I suppose you'll want to use my car?"

"You did approve it, sir. And taking Muni can be dangerous for a child with—"

"So I won't be able to rely on you until you're bankrupted by these treatments?" He turns back to his computer, applies a series of commands and then turns the monitor toward Wo. "My car's GPS automatically updates this form." He turns the monitor back. "Will you charge these hours to your flex-time or do you prefer your pay docked?"

"I'm sorry sir, I've spent both weeks of this years' flex-time."

"Be here at end of business."

"Thank you, sir."

Eben leans back and watches Wo scurry away. A mirth-free chuckle dribbles through his vocal chords. Wo's title is Executive Administrative Assistant, though his role at ScratshCo is closer to Chief Operating Officer. Yao Wo would be the most difficult employee to replace, but rather than pay him accordingly, Eben keeps him unsettled and unaware of his negotiating position.

Another hour passes. Eben settles into exchange rate analysis. The feeling brought on by the beggar fades behind the keyboard clattering and hushed discussions in the cubicles beyond his office door—the rhythm of corporate efficiency.

His landline interrupts the calm of analysis. The caller-ID shows that it's his older sister, Sally. He grumbles at the realization that Wo isn't present to deflect the call.

He lifts the handset and says, "Yes."

"Eben?"

"I said, yes."

"Happy Birthday, Husker!"

"You know I hate that nickname."

"The big three-oh!"

"You're still capable of arithmetic."

"Seriously, Eben, how are you doing?"

"Too busy to chat, thank you."

"How's the weather up there?" Sally lives in Santa Barbara near one of Eben's properties.

"Foggy and cold, just the way I like it."

"There's a beach in Cabo with clear skies, hot sun, and gorgeous waves. Break away for a weekend and come with us. If you don't feel like celebrating your birthday then we'll celebrate summer like we did when we were kids. Come on, Husker!"

"I have responsibilities."

"Eben," Sally's voice turns serious, "you're too young to be such a curmudgeon."

"You can only get to my beach by boat."

"What?"

"The law says that the beach at my central coast vacation home is public property, but I won't be there to open the gate, so if you want to use my beach, you'll have to travel by sea like anyone else."

"You think I'm only inviting you—"

"Because you want to have your party on my beach."

"Oh Husker, what's happened to you?"

"I've made some money. Kinda successful. And please, I've outgrown that nickname."

"You haven't outgrown it, you've just forgotten who you are." She sighs. "Everyone would love to see you. Evan is fourteen already, can you believe it? You won't even recognize him—but he still talks about you. He's started programming and he's such a formal kid, thoughtful and patient just like his Uncle Husker. Okay, Uncle Eben."

Eben tries to focus on exchange rates.

"How are you, Eben? Is there anyone in your life?"

Eben remains silent.

"Husker, I'm not giving up on you—even though you're an old man of thirty now. I'm going to invite you every summer and hope that someday you'll accept, but if you don't, well, it's your life."

Eben stares at the phone as Sally disconnects. His knuckles are white and he realizes that his shoulders are tense. When did everyone on earth decide that he owed them something? He's sick of it and this time he's not going to just sit by and let the quitters, moochers, and low-lifes sap his energy. No, this time, he'll tell the world what he really thinks of them.

He opens a social networking web site. He gets an extra twinge of ire at his 5000 "friends;" just another 5000 people who want a favor. He starts typing :

> "Market Street is disgusting. The heart of this rich city is teeming with drug abusers, failures, and the criminally insane—losers of every stripe, human trash. They act like they belong here, like they have a right to our streets. It's unacceptable. In truly great cities, the lowlifes keep to themselves; they sell trinkets, they beg quietly and with well earned shame, and they realize the privilege of spending time in the sophisticated parts of the city. We can

practice compassion and preach about liberty, equality, and fraternity, but the degenerates and the working class should know their place and stay in it. Look, if they offered a penny's worth of value, I'd welcome them. But as it is, they're a liability. As productive citizens, we should install them where they belong and keep them there."

3. The Intoxicating Page

The bell on the door tinkles as Winter pulls me into The Intoxicating Page, Fiona's bookstore-saloon-café which also serves as our US business center, research lab, and software development hub.

It's toasty warm inside. I rub my hands together and inhale the scents of dried ink on paper and dried beer on concrete under the pervading aroma of fresh brewed coffee, sourdough bagels, and blueberry scones. Fiona pairs beverages with literature. The deeper you wander into the store, the more concentrated the alcohol-literature experience. The recessed spot lighting provides perfect illumination for reading, the requisite dimness of a bar, and the diffuse lighting of a café, and it's complemented by acoustic guitar instrumentals. I liberate Winter from his leash. He shakes from nose to tail and then trots through the juice box and Dr. Seuss section to the bar that occupies the store's center. It's an oval-shaped counter of polished walnut centered about a Greek-temple looking column that bears much of the weight of this three story building. Fiona tends the bar from within the oval.

She calls out, "Simon, we're short on time."

Fiona and I met in college, two years after she lost her leg. In the interim, she has determined myriad ways to compensate. She furnished The Intoxicating Page so that she could navigate through the store without using her prostheses—difficult technology when the leg is lost at the hip—or her ridiculously clichéd duck-handle cane. Her short, dark brown hair is parted on the side and shows the first hints of gray. Her blue eyes twinkle with her every thought and her cute little nose contradicts her rather strong jaw line. A tattoo adorns her chest, a crescent moon that dangles from her clavicle and has a witch mounted on its tip dangling high heels into at her spare cleavage, but it is her smile that captures your attention as you enter The Intoxicating Page. Today, her smile is tempered by tension and doubt, which is not at all her default.

Winter hops onto a barstool.

Fiona maneuvers over. "Bloody hell," she says, "I can never get him his biscuit before the drooling starts." Winter accepts his treat and shuffles off to the loveseat in the romance and pink champagne nook for his late-morning nap. Fiona runs a cloth over two small dots of drool, emerges from the bar, and guides me to my other cohort.

Volodya, whose name rhymes with melodious, makes a guttural sound of discontent in a Russian accent. He sits at a table with laptop and tablet computers in what Fiona refers to as the high-brow literature and single malt scotch ghetto. I met Volodya in 1983 at a conference in Sarajevo. He represented Moscow State and I represented the University of California. We argued at length but built a friendship on our shared passion for the capital-T truths of physics. To continue our arguments, we had to hack into the telecommunications infrastructures of the Soviet Union and the United States: our first collaboration.

Fiona pulls me past tables populated by people with their noses in books, laptops, or cell phones. Her remarkable gait betrays the challenge of flourishing with just the one leg but in no way diminishes her ability to deliver me to Volodya. He is a tall, sharp, athletic man with a straight-sloped nose, thin lips, and gray eyes that cut a path straight to your soul. We are both in the early stages of our second half-century, though his taut cable-like arms, firm triangle-shaped physique, and ability to sprint all-out for every second of fifteen minutes gives him the physical prowess of a twenty-year-old. My physique represents men of our age far more accurately.

Volodya wears tight fitting but flexible clothes; I prefer flannel suits that have visited the dry cleaners enough times to have developed the texture of your favorite blanket. I'm neither a tall nor a short man and, having grown up next to a river, I seem to have acquired its characteristics: my skin is a sort of pale gray like river rocks and my hair and eyes are the color of the muddy river bottom. Winter, on the other hand, is a striking creature with a coat composed of contrasting patches of black, orange, brown, and nearly fluorescent white; the very definition of beagleness.

I sit in the chair next to Volodya, take my laptop from my satchel, and say, "How much time do we have?"

"Timing resolution is weeks, not months; could be days, hours, or maybe is already too late," Volodya says, without looking away from his monitor. "It is a problem."

"Until what?"

"Onset of hundred year dark age. Hundred years if we're lucky, unlucky, maybe a thousand."

"A dark age?" Fiona says. "A bit cliché, even for you."

"Since a beggar asked Eben Scratsh for five dollars, every strand of the unraveling timeweave leads to different type of dark age." He examines the timeweave graphic on his monitor. "Dark ages have happened over course of human history and will happen again. Why not now? The hegemony of the United States is in question with no one to step in. Europe on edge of disintegration, the Middle East in turmoil…"

Fiona leans over me. She smells spicy, like sandalwood. "Simon, what did you see?"

I say, "It was very mild. I'm fine," but she rolls her eyes so I describe the mishmash of visions—the transformation of an executive into a pauper, the cable car queue turning into a soup line, and the evolution of the Bank of Italy into a Bank of America ATM.

Volodya says, "You don't believe prediction derived from data, but you believe Simon's delusions?"

"Is it consistent with the timeweave?" Fiona asks.

"Much easier to predict the past than the future."

"You know what I mean." She perches on the table next to him.

His eyes rise from his laptop to her tattoo and when they reach her eyes he says, "History doesn't repeat."

"But if it did…"

"Simon's delusions are not specific, not predictive."

Where most people see their lives as a single image in time, during my episodes I perceive a collage of overlapping, interrelated, entangled shadows and intersections of possible timelines. As if that weren't disconcerting enough, I can shift from one reality to another and when I do, I bring you and the rest of the world with me. While I hold this as a visceral truth, the way that you're aware of night and day without giving it a thought, I have never assembled enough evidence to convince Volodya.

Fiona says, "Eben Scratsh used to work for us. Do you remember him?"

Me: "No."

Volodya: "Yes, of course."

Me: "No you don't—you saw it in his timeline."

Volodya taps his monitor. "Okay. It is true. I have his timeline."

Fiona: "He worked on the Watergate app."

Me: "The one that follows the money?"

Fiona: "Right."

Our timeweave prediction engine consists of a huge library of programs that runs on a fleet of computer servers in our lab in Vienna. Volodya and I design our software but contract freelance programmers to write much of it. Since our work is quite sensitive, not just because of its dubious legality, but because the power of our predictions could easily be used for personal profit at the expense of humanity's attempts in the general direction of civilization, we lead our contractors to believe that they are producing components for smartphone apps. Most of our employees leverage their experience into employment in the tech sector. Eben started his career here at The Intoxicating Page coding for us. We call our company TLA, which stands for Time Line Associates in Vienna where Volodya files our taxes and Three Letter Acronym here in San Francisco where Fiona files them.

"And, as you might expect in this epoch of history," Volodya says, "this dark age begins with a Facebook post." He orients his monitor so that the three of us can read the post.

Fiona is the first to speak. "It's horrible—he calls homeless people human trash." Her voice rises in both pitch and volume: "Privilege of spending time in the sophisticated parts of the city? Install them where they belong?"

Me: "How could 1093 people 'Like' this?"

Fiona: "He pisses off half the world and validates the other half."

Volodya scrolls through the comments, an unfolding debate on the value of desperate, downtrodden, and disaffected human beings.

I say, "The polarization of sympathy and antipathy fertilize suspicion and misunderstanding. Revolution is the inevitable result and even the most idealistic revolutions cause immense suffering."

Volodya: "Bolsheviks could not have been more idealistic."

Me: "Or the French."

Fiona: "Something has gone off. The Eben who worked for us would never say this. We need to find out what happened to him."

Volodya: "You're siding with someone who disparages the weak and poor?"

Fiona: "No historical pivot occurs in a vacuum."

Me: "Look at this comment from one of our other protégés."

Volodya: "Owen Lockett?"

I read Owen's comment out loud: "We're not like this guy! Techies are good, caring people. We like figuring out puzzles and sometimes we get carried away, but we're not greedy assholes like

Eben Scratsh."

Fiona: "We did well by Owen."

Volodya: "He made fuck you money with video game."

Me: "How does one 'fuck you' with money?"

Volodya: "FU money is level of savings people target for early retirement."

Fiona: "He comes in now and then." She motions to the science fiction and absinthe section. "He's working on a game that uses gadgets like Google Glass to augment reality."

Me: "Eben wears Glass."

Volodya: "He does?"

Me: "Yes. Rims with no lenses, just a microprocessor that projects images onto one eye, web access, video, messaging, maps."

Volodya: "Ability to see through Eben's Glass could provide key perspective on this pivot point."

Fiona: "You haven't hacked Google Glass yet?"

Me: "Haven't needed to. No one uses it."

Volodya: "No one but Eben, our only clue to this pivot point."

Fiona: "I'll ask Owen to stop by, maybe he'll help. But right now, we need to identify the woman."

Volodya: "Homeless woman? A pawn."

"Right. The poor woman couldn't possibly be as important to history as the rich man," Fiona says. "It's the lack of prejudice with which Volodya approaches data that has made us so successful."

Volodya shrugs and I nod. Volodya and I have worked together for so long that his shrug and my nod divvy up the tasks at hand. I prepare timeline calculations as he initiates facial recognition software. We launch the code and it crawls through the feeds of hundreds of surveillance cameras on and around Market Street, mostly private security cameras monitoring building entrances, ATMs, and when necessary, smartphone cameras.

Fiona sits at the table with us and Winter hops on her lap. She scratches behind his ears.

"There we are leaving the Ferry building."

"And there's Eben," Fiona says, "Rotten posture, bent over like an old man."

Me: "Sill, it's a purposeful stride."

Fiona: "Nose to the grindstone."

Volodya: "Now woman approaches." The feed shows her reaching for Eben. Volodya pauses the feed with a clear view of her face and says, "Face recognition should return identity in a few seconds."

Fiona: "That's Allison!"

Three seconds later, the name Allison Anatolia appears on the screen with her social security number, birth date, and blank fields that would normally be filled with her current address, phone number, and login usernames.

Me: "She's 29? She looks much older."

Fiona: "She worked for us. Eben must have recognized her. The shock of seeing a former colleague in that state—he must have lost it and gone online to vent his guilt. A right tosser."

Me: "She wrote excellent code—she even commented it."

Fiona: "I wonder what happened."

Volodya pushes back his chair and stands. "It is one question we will ask her."

Switching windows, I configure a search. The servers in our Vienna lab hack into surveillance cameras at ever larger circles centered on that point of Market Street.

Volodya steps to the coat rack near the noir fiction and cheap bourbon bookcase. He puts on his jacket and sets his earbug so that we're in constant contact.

When he's halfway to the door, I say, "She's at the corner of Geary and Polk."

Acknowledgments

Please indulge me as I express my appreciation for the help and support of a few people. I got terrific feedback on early drafts from the authors: Barry Willdorf, James Warner, Pauline Homsi, and Ian Tuttle. My agent, Laurie McLean, recognized early on what I'm trying to do and started helping me do it long before I became her client. And, of course, I'd like to thank Karen, Professor Buckley, and Dear Abby because nothing happens without the support of your mate and your dogs.

Note to you

Thank you for reading *The 99% Solution.* Please don't blame me for the acts, politics, or senses of humor of my characters. If I had better control of them, none of this would have happened. I built Simon Wentworth from a fantasized version of a friend who won't recognize himself in the character; he's so Simon! I have no idea where I got Fiona. I cast Volodya from a man I met at a physics conference in St. Petersburg; he had the constitution of rhino and there was "a problem" every morning. Lucy sometimes reminds me of my daughter, Heather: a small woman with a commanding presence. Frankie, well, everyone knows a Frankie, don't they?

Reading a novel is telepathy. Since you've spent hours in my head, please share your thoughts with me:

Ransom@ RansomStephens.com.

There's also a bunch of stuff at www. RansomStephens.com like descriptions of my other books, science articles I've written, notes on the craft, and so on. If it's ever relevant (and I hope it will be): beer not wine, tea not coffee, rock not jazz. See you at the bar.

With gratitude and affection, I hope you're having fun!

Ransom

Petaluma, California, March 2018

About Ransom

Ransom Stephens, Ph.D., is the author of the novels *The Sensory Deception*, a story of environmentalism, virtual reality, and idealism gone wrong, and *The God Patent*, a perspective-altering novel of science and religion. He also wrote the popular science book *The Left Brain Speaks The Right Brain Laughs: a look at the neuroscience of innovation & creativity in art, science, & life.*

After 15 years in particle physics research, including several as a physics professor, Ransom gave up a tenured gig to become the Director of Advanced Technology at a wireless web startup. In addition to writing novels, he's now a silicon valley consultant who writes about and teaches engineers the physics they need to design your gadgets. Ransom is also a cussing, beer-swilling Raider fan. He lives in Petaluma, California, where he's working on *Too Rich to Die*, the next Time Weavers novel.

CPSIA information can be obtained
at www.ICGtesting.com
Printed in the USA
LVHW09s1117020918
588931LV00001B/37/P

9 781937 791759